J. A. JANCE is the *New York Times* best-selling author of the J. P. Beaumont series, the Joanna Brady series, the Ali Reynolds series, and three standalone thrillers. Born in South Dakota and brought up in Bris-bee, Arizona, she lives with her husband in Seattle, Washington, and Tucson, Arizona.

www.jajance.com

QUEEN OF THE NIGHT

J.A. JANCE

HARPER

Harper
An imprint of HarperCollins*Publishers*
77–85 Fulham Palace Road,
Hammersmith, London W6 8JB

www.harpercollins.co.uk

This paperback edition 2011
· 1

First published in the USA by
William Morrow an imprint of HarperCollins*Publishers* 2010

A catalogue record for this book is available from the British Library

ISBN: 978-0-00-738431-0

Printed and bound in Great Britain by Clays Ltd, St Ives plc

Mixed Sources

Product group from well-managed
forests and other controlled sources
www.fsc.org Cert no. SW-COC-001806
© 1996 Forest Stewardship Council

FSC is a non-profit international organization established to promote the responsible management of the world's forests. Products carrying the FSC label are independently certified to assure consumers that they come from forests that are managed to meet the social, economic and ecological needs of present and future generations.

Find out more about HarperCollins and the environment at
www.harpercollins.co.uk/green

Prologue

*T*HEY SAY IT *happened long ago that a young woman of the Tohono O'odham, the Desert People, fell in love with a Yaqui warrior, a Hiakim, and went to live with him and his people, far to the South. Every evening, her mother, Old White-Haired Woman, would go outside by herself and listen. After a while her daughter's spirit would speak to her from her new home far away. One day Old White-Haired Woman heard nothing, so she went to find her husband.*

"Our daughter is ill," Old White-Haired Woman told him. "I must go to her."

"But the Hiakim live far from here," he said, "and you are a bent old woman. How will you get there?"

"I will ask I'itoi, the Spirit of Goodness, to help me."

Elder Brother heard the woman's plea. He sent Coyote, Ban, to guide Old White-Haired Woman's steps on her long journey, and he sent the Ali Chu Chum O'odham, the Little People—the animals and birds—to help her along the way. When she was thirsty, Ban led her to water. When she was hungry, the Birds, U'u Whig, brought her seeds and beans to eat.

After weeks of traveling, Old White-Haired Woman finally reached the land of the Hiakim. There she learned that her daughter was sick and dying.

"Please take my son home to our people," Old White-Haired Woman's daughter begged. "If you don't, his father's people will turn him into a warrior."

You must understand, nawoj, my friend, that from the time the Tohono O'odham emerged from the center of the earth, they have always been a peace-loving people. So one night, when the Hiakim were busy feasting, Old White-Haired Woman loaded the baby into her burden basket and set off for the North. When the Yaqui learned she was gone, they sent a band of warriors after her to bring the baby back.

Old White-Haired Woman walked and walked. She was almost back to the land of the Desert People when the Yaqui warriors spotted her. I'itoi saw she was not going to complete her journey, so he called a flock of shashani, black birds, who flew into the eyes of the Yaqui and blinded them. While the warriors were busy fighting shashani, I'itoi took Old White-Haired Woman into a wash and hid her.

By then the old grandmother was very tired and lame from all her walking and carrying.

"You stay here," Elder Brother told her. "I will carry the baby back to your people, but while you sit here resting, you will be changed. Because of your bravery, your feet will become roots. Your tired old body will turn into branches. Each year, for one night only, you will become the most beautiful plant on the earth, a flower the Milgahn, the whites, call the night-blooming cereus, the Queen of the Night."

And it happened just that way. Old White-Haired Woman

turned into a plant the Indians call ho'ok-wah'o, *which means Witch's Tongs. But on that one night in early summer when a beautiful scent fills the desert air, the Tohono O'odham know that they are breathing in* kok'oi 'uw, *Ghost Scent, and they remember a brave old woman who saved her grandson and brought him home.*

Each year after that, on the night the flowers bloomed, the Tohono O'odham would gather around while Brought Back Child told the story of his brave grandmother, Old White-Haired Woman, and that, nawoj, *my friend, is the same story I have just told you.*

San Diego, California
Saturday, March 21, 1959, Midnight
58° Fahrenheit

Long after everyone else had left the beach and returned to the hotel, and long after the bonfire died down to coals, Ursula Brinker sat there in the sand and marveled over what had happened. What she had allowed to happen.

When June Lennox had invited Sully to come along to San Diego for spring break, she had known the moment she said yes that she was saying yes to more than just a fun trip from Tempe, Arizona, to California. The insistent tug had been there all along, for as long as Sully could remember. From the time she was in kindergarten, she had been interested in girls, not boys, and that hadn't changed. Not later in grade school when the other girls started drooling over boys, and not later in high school, either.

But she had kept the secret. For one thing, she knew how much her parents would disapprove if Sully ever admitted to them or to anyone else what she had long suspected—that she was a lesbian. She didn't go around advertising it or wearing mannish clothing. People said she was "cute," and she was—cute and smart and talented. She didn't know exactly what would happen to her if people figured out who she really was, but it probably wouldn't be good. She did a good job of keeping up appearances, so no one guessed that the girl who had been valedictorian of her class and who had been voted most likely to succeed was actually queer "as a three-dollar bill." That was what some of the boys said about people like that—people like her. And she was afraid that by talking about it, what she was feeling right now would be snatched away from her, like a mirage melting into the desert.

She had kept the secret until now. Until today. With June. And she was afraid, if she left the beach and went back to the hotel room with everyone else and spoke about it, if she gave that newfound happiness a name, it might disappear forever as well.

The beach was deserted. When she heard the sand-muffled footsteps behind her, she thought it might be June. But it wasn't.

"Hello," she said. "When did you get here?"

He didn't answer that question. "What you did was wrong," he said. "Did you think you could keep it a secret? Did you think I wouldn't find out?"

"It just happened," she said. "We didn't mean to hurt you."

"But you did," he said. "More than you know."

He fell on her then. Had anyone been walking past on the beach, they wouldn't have paid much attention. Just another young couple carried away with necking; people who hadn't gotten themselves a room, and probably should have.

But in the early hours of that morning, what was happening there by the dwindling fire wasn't an act of love. It was something else altogether. When the rough embrace finally ended, the man stood up and walked away. He walked into the water and sluiced away the blood.

As for Sully Brinker? She did not walk away. The brainy cheerleader, the girl who had it all—money, brains, and looks—the girl once voted most likely to succeed would not succeed at anything because she was lying dead in the sand—dead at age twenty-one—and her parents' lives would never be the same.

Los Angeles, California
Saturday, October 28, 1978, 11:20 P.M.
63° Fahrenheit

As the quarrel escalated, four-year-old Danny Pardee cowered in his bed. He covered his head with his pillow and tried not to listen, but the pillow didn't help. He could still hear the voices raging back and forth: his father's voice and his mother's. Turning on the TV set might have helped, but if his father came into the bedroom and found the set on when it wasn't supposed to be, Danny knew what would happen. First the belt would come off and, after that, the beating.

Danny knew how much that belt hurt, so he lay there and willed himself not to listen. He tried to fill his head with the words to one of the songs he had learned at preschool: "You put your right foot in; you put your right foot out. You put your right foot in, and you shake it all about. You do the hokey-pokey and you turn yourself around. That's what it's all about."

He was about to go on to the second verse when he heard something that sounded like a firecracker—or four firecrackers in a row, even though it wasn't the Fourth of July.

Blam. Blam. Blam. Blam.

After that there was nothing. No other sound. Not his mother's voice and not his father's, either. An eerie silence settled over the house. First it filled Danny's ears and then his heart.

Finally the bedroom door creaked open. Danny knew his father was standing in the doorway, staring down at him, so he kept both eyes shut—shut but not too tightly shut. That would give it away. He didn't move. He barely breathed. At last, after the door finally clicked closed, he opened his eyes and let out his breath.

He listened to the silence, welcoming it. The room wasn't completely dark. Streetlights in the parking lot made the room a hazy gray, and there was a sliver of light under the doorway. Soon that went away. Knowing that his father had probably left to go to a bar and drink some more, Danny was able to relax. As the tension left

his body, he fell into a deep sleep, slumbering so peacefully that he never heard the sirens of the arriving cop
cars or of the useless ambulance that arrived far too late.
Danny had no idea that the gunshot victim, his mother,
was dead long before the ambulance got there.

Much later, at least it seemed much later to him, someone—a stranger in a uniform—gently shook him awake.
The cop wrapped the tangled sheet around Danny and
lifted him from the bed.

"Come on, little guy," he said huskily. "Let's get you
out of here."

Thousand Oaks, California
Monday, June 1, 2009, 11:45 P.M.
60° Fahrenheit

It was late, well after eleven, as Jonathan sat in the study
of his soon-to-be-former McMansion and stared at his
so-called wall of honor. The plaques and citations he saw
there—his Manager of the Year award, along with all the
others that acknowledged his years of exemplary service,
were relics from another time and place—from another
life. They were the currency and language of some other
existence, where the rules as he had once known them
no longer applied.

What had happened on Wall Street had trickled down
to Main Street. As a result, his banking career was over.
His job was gone. His house would be gone soon, and so
would his family. He wasn't supposed to know about the

boyfriend Esther had waiting in the wings, but he did. He also knew what she was really waiting for—the money from his 401(k). She wanted that, too, and she wanted it now.

Esther came in then—barged in, really—without knocking. The fact that he might want a little privacy was as foreign a concept as the paltry career trophies still hanging on his walls. She stood there staring at him, hands on her hips.

"You changed the password on the account," she said accusingly.

"The account I changed the password on isn't a joint account," he told her mildly. "It's mine."

"We're still married," she pointed out. "What's yours is mine."

And, of course, that was the way it had always been. He worked. She stayed home and saw to it that they lived beyond their means, which had been considerable when he'd still had a good job. The problem was he no longer had that job, but she was still living the same way. As far as she was concerned, nothing had changed. For him everything had changed. Esther had gone right on spending money like it was water, but now the well had finally run dry. There was no job and no way to get a job. Banks didn't like having bankers with overdue bills and credit scores in the basement.

"I signed the form when you asked me to so we could both get the money," she said. "I want my fair share."

He knew there was nothing about this that was fair. It was the same stunt his mother had pulled on his father, making him cough up money that she had never earned. Well, maybe the scenario wasn't exactly the same. As far as he knew, his mother hadn't screwed around on his father, but Jonathan had vowed it wouldn't happen to him—would never happen to him. Yet here it was happening—and then some.

"It may be in an individual account, but that money is a joint asset," Esther declared. "You don't get to have it all."

She was screaming at him now. He could hear her and so could anyone else in the neighborhood. He was glad they lived at the end of the cul-de-sac—with previously foreclosed houses on either side. It was a neighborhood where living beyond your means went with the territory.

"By the time my lawyer finishes wiping the floor with you, you'll be lucky to be living in a homeless shelter," she added. "As for seeing the kids? Forget about it. That's not going to happen. I'll see to it."

With that, she spun around as if to leave. Then, changing her mind, she grabbed the closest thing she could reach, which turned out to be the wooden plaque with the bronze Manager of the Year faceplate, and heaved it at him. The sharp corner of the wood caught him full in the forehead—well, part of his very tall comb-over forehead—and it hurt like hell. It bled like hell.

As blood leaked into his eye and ran down his cheek, all the things he had stifled through the years came to a head. He had reached the end of his rope, the point beyond which he had nothing left to lose.

Opening the top drawer of his desk, he removed the

gun—a gun he had purchased with every intention of turning it on himself. Then, rising to his feet, he hurried out of the room, intent on using it on someone else.

His whole body sizzled in a fit of unreasoning hatred. If that had been all there was to it, any defense attorney worthy of the name could have gotten him off on a plea of temporary insanity, because in that moment he was insane—legally insane. He knew nothing about the difference between right and wrong. All he knew was that he had taken all he could take. More than he could take.

The difficulty is that this was only the start of Jonathan Southard's problems. Everything that happened after that was entirely premeditated.

1

*P*IMA COUNTY HOMICIDE detective Brian Fellows loved Saturdays, even hot summer Saturdays. Kath, Brian's wife, usually worked Saturday shifts at her Border Patrol desk job, which meant Brian had the whole day to spend with his girls, six-year-old twins Annie and Amy. They usually started with breakfast, either sharing a plate-sized sticky sweet roll at Gus Balon's on Twenty-second Street, or downing eye-watering plates of chorizo and eggs at Wag's on Grant.

After that, they went home to clean house. Brian's mother had been a much-divorced scatterbrain even before she became an invalid. Brian had learned from an early age that if he wanted a clean house, he'd be the one doing it. It hadn't killed him, either. He'd turned into a self-sufficient kind of guy and, according to Kath, an excellent catch for a husband.

Brian wanted the same thing for his daughters—for them to be self-sufficient. It didn't take long on Saturdays to whip their central-area bungalow into shape. In the process, while settling the occasional squabble, being a bit of a tough taskmaster, and hearing about what was going on with the girls, Brian made sure he was a real presence in his daughters' lives—a real father.

That was something that had been missing in Brian's childhood—at least as far as his biological father was concerned. His "sperm donor," as Brian thought of the man who had been MIA in his life from before he was born. He wouldn't have had any idea about what fathers were supposed to be or do if it hadn't been for Brandon Walker, his mother's first husband and the father of Tommy and Quentin, Brian's older half brothers.

After Brian's mother's first divorce, Brandon Walker, then a Pima County homicide detective, had come to the house each weekend and dutifully collected his own sons to take them on noncustodial outings. One of Brian's first memories was of being left alone on the front steps while Quentin and Tommy went racing off to jump in their father's car to go somewhere fun—to a movie or the Pima County Fair, or maybe even the Tucson Rodeo—while Brian, bored and lonely, had to fend for himself.

Then one day a miracle happened. After Quentin and Tommy were already in the car, Brandon had gotten back out. He came up the walk and asked Brian if he would like to go along. Brian was beyond excited. Quentin and Tommy had been appalled and had done everything in their power to make Brian miserable, but they did that anyway—even before Brandon had taken pity on him.

From then on, that's how it was. Whenever Brandon had taken his own boys somewhere, he had taken Brian as well. The man had become a superhero in Brian's eyes. He had grown up wanting to be just like him, and it was due in no small measure to Brandon Walker's early kindness that Brian Fellows was the man he was today—a doting father and an experienced cop. And it was why, on Saturday afternoons, after the house was clean, that he never failed to take his girls somewhere to do something fun—to the Randolph Park Zoo or the Arizona Sonora Desert Museum. Today, as hot as it was, they had already settled on going to a movie at Park Mall.

Brian was on call. Only if someone decided to kill someone tonight would he have to go in to work. Otherwise he would have had his special day with his girls—well, all but one of his girls. That was what made life worth living.

Tucson, Arizona
Saturday, June 6, 2009, 11:00 A.M.
90° Fahrenheit

Brandon Walker knew he was running away. He had the excuse of running to something, but he understood that he was really escaping from something else, something he didn't want to face. He would face it eventually because he had to, but not yet. He wasn't ready.

Not that going to see G. T. Farrell was light duty by any means. Stopping by to see someone who was on his way to hospice care wasn't Brandon's idea of fun. Sue, Geet's wife, had called with the bad news. Her husband's lung cancer had been held at bay for far longer than anyone had thought possible, but now it was back. And winning.

"He's got a set of files that he had me bring out of storage," Sue had said in her phone call. "He made me promise that I'd see to it that you got them—you and nobody else."

Brandon didn't have to ask which file because he already knew. Every homicide cop has a case like that, the one that haunts him and won't let him go, the one where the bad guy got away with murder. For Geet Farrell that case had always been the 1959 murder of Ursula Brinker, a twenty-one-year-old coed who had died while on a spring-break trip to San Diego.

Geet had been a newbie ASU campus cop at the time of her death. Even though the crime had occurred in California, it had rocked the entire university community. Geet had been involved in interviewing Ursula's friends and relations, including her grieving parents. The case had stayed with him, haunting him the whole time he'd worked as a homicide detective for the Pinal County Sheriff's Department, and through his years of retirement as well. Now that Geet knew it was curtains for him, he wanted to hand Ursula's unsolved case off to someone else and let his problem be Brandon's problem.

Fair enough, Brandon thought. *If I'm dealing with Geet Farrell's difficulties, I won't have to face up to my own.*

Geet was a good five years older than Brandon. They had met for the first time as fellow cops decades earlier. In 1975, Brandon Walker had been working Homicide for the Pima County Sheriff's Department, and G. T. Farrell had been his Homicide counterpart in neighboring Pinal. Between them they had helped bring down a serial killer named Andrew Philip Carlisle. Partially due to their efforts, Carlisle had been sentenced to life in prison. He had lived out his remaining years in the state prison in Florence, Arizona, where he had finally died.

Brandon Walker had also received a lifelong sentence as a result of that case, only his had been much different. One of Carlisle's intended victims, the fiercely independent Diana Ladd, had gone against type and consented to become Brandon Walker's wife. They had been married now for thirty-plus years.

It was hard for Brandon to imagine what his life would have been like if Andrew Carlisle had succeeded in murdering Diana. How would he have survived for all those years if he hadn't been married to that amazing woman? How would he have existed without Diana and all the complications she had brought into his life, including her son, Davy, and their adopted Tohono O'odham daughter, Lani?

Much later, long after both detectives had been turned out to pasture by their respective law enforcement agencies, Geet by retiring and Brandon by losing a bid for reelection, Geet had been instrumental in the creation of an independent cold case investigative entity called TLC, The Last Chance, an organization founded and funded by Hedda Brinker, Ursula Brinker's still grieving mother. In an act of seeming charity, Geet had seen to it that his old buddy, former Pima County sheriff Brandon Walker, be invited to sign on with TLC.

That ego-salving invitation, delivered in person by a smooth-talking attorney named Ralph Ames, had come at a time when, as Brandon liked to put it, he had been lower than a snake's vest pocket. He had accepted Ames's offer without a moment of hesitation. In the intervening years, Brandon had worked hand in hand with other retired law enforcement and forensic folks who volunteered their skills and expertise to make TLC live up to its case-closing promises. For Brandon, the ability to do that—to continue making a contribution even in retirement—had saved his sanity, if not his life.

All of which meant Brandon owed everything to Geet Farrell. That was why he was making this pilgrimage to Casa Grande late in the morning on what promised to be a scorcher of a Saturday in early June. Of course heat was relative. By July and early August, the hot days of June would seem downright cool in comparison.

Weather aside, Brandon understood that this was going to be a deathbed visit, but he didn't mind. He hoped that by doing whatever he could to help out, he might be able to even the score with Geet Farrell just a little. After all, this was a debt of gratitude, one Brandon Walker was honor-bound to repay.

Tucson, Arizona
Saturday, June 6, 2009, 1:10 P.M.
94° Fahrenheit

Diana Ladd Walker sat in her backyard gazebo next to a bubbling fountain typing into her laptop. It was shady there, but it was still hot and dry. Soon she'd either have to go into the pool for a dip, or else she'd have to retreat to the air-conditioned comfort of the house.

"So how are things working out for you?" Andrew Carlisle asked.

Rendered speechless, Diana stared at the vision that had suddenly materialized over the top of her computer.

Shirtless and hatless, Carlisle sat in full early-afternoon sunlight with his scarred face and sightless eyes staring up into a blazing blue sky. If he hadn't been blind already, staring at the sun would have made him so.

Examining every aspect of her unwelcome visitor, Diana might have been viewing a close-up shot of someone on Brandon's new high-def flat-screen TV set. Every detail was astonishingly vivid—from the sparse strands of white hair that sprinkled his sunken chest to the grizzled unshaved beard that dotted his gaunt cheeks and the scarred and rippled skin of his forehead and nose.

I did that, Diana thought, gasping involuntarily at the sight of those horrifying scars. *I'm responsible for doing that to a living, breathing human being, back when he was alive.*

Which Andrew Carlisle was not. The man sitting across the table from Diana was most definitely not alive. She knew that for certain. He had been alive when he had come to her house years earlier, intent on rape and murder. Before it was over, he had left Diana with his own special trademark—a fierce bite mark that even now still scarred her breast. But Carlisle had underestimated her back then. He hadn't expected Diana to fight back or to leave him permanently disfigured in the process. All of that had happened long ago—before he had gone to prison for the second time and before he died there. Back in those days there had been no swimming pool or fountain or gazebo in Diana's walled backyard, and she most certainly hadn't been working on a laptop.

"We are not having this conversation," she said to him now.

"Come on, Diana," he urged. "For old times' sake. Let bygones be bygones. Tell me, how's the writing going? What are you working on now?"

She was dealing with some backed-up business correspondence, but she wasn't going to tell him that.

"What I'm working on is none of your business," she responded.

"Of course it's my business," Carlisle insisted. "I'm always interested when one of my students goes on to achieve remarkable success in the publishing world."

"I was not your student," Diana told him flatly. "My first husband was your student, remember? I never was. Go away and leave me alone."

"Give me a break, Diana. I'm still annoyed that *Shadow of Death* won a Pulitzer. You never would have won that award without me. I was the guy who came up with the idea, and the whole book was all about me. You should have given me more credit."

"You didn't deserve more credit," she said. "You didn't write it. I did."

"Oh, well. No matter," he said with a sigh. "After all, fame is fleeting. I thought you'd be glad to see me. Mitch may drop by a little later, too. And Gary. You'd like to see him again, too, wouldn't you? Although, come to think of it, maybe not. That self-inflicted bullet left a hell of a hole in his head. Not so much in the front as in the back. Exit-wound damage and all that. I'm sure you know how those work."

Living or dead, Diana had no desire to see her dead first husband, Garrison Walther Ladd III, nor did she want to see Mitch Johnson, the surrogate killer Carlisle had sent to attack her family in his stead when Carlisle himself could no longer pose a direct threat.

"Shut up," she said.

Tires crunched on the gravel driveway. Damsel, Diana's aging nine-year-old mutt, pricked her ears and raised her head at the sound. She had come to Diana and Brandon as a rollicking pound puppy some eight years earlier when her antics had earned her the title of Damn Dog. Now she was a well-behaved grizzled old dog with a nearly white muzzle and a game hip. She stood up and steadied herself for a moment. Then, with an arthritic limp, she hurried over to the side gate, barking in welcome.

"My daughter's coming," Diana said. "Go away."

"Lani is coming here?" Carlisle sounded delighted. "The lovely Lani? Do tell. Wonderful. Maybe she'll show me her scar."

"What scar?"

"Oh, I forgot. You don't know about that."

"What scar?" Diana insisted.

"Ask her about it if you don't believe me. I understand Mitch left her a little something to remember him by. Let's just say it's a token of my esteem."

Lani had been sixteen when Mitch Johnson, Andrew Carlisle's minion, had kidnapped Diana's daughter.

"What?" Diana asked. "What did he do to her?"

"Why don't you ask her yourself?"

Determinedly, Diana turned her attention back to her laptop. She thought Carlisle would disappear when she did that, but he didn't. He stayed right there with his face turned in her direction. Since he was blind now, he could no longer stare at her, but the same expression was on his face—the same disparaging smirk he had aimed at her once before, long ago in a courthouse hallway.

"You're not welcome here," she told him. "Go away."

Highway 86, West of Tucson, Arizona
Saturday, June 6, 2009, 12:00 P.M.
93° Fahrenheit

Eight-year-old Gabriel Ortiz sat up straight in Dr. Lani Walker's car and seemed to be studying the scenery as it whizzed by outside the windows of the speeding Passat. This was the first time Lani could remember his being tall enough to ride in the front seat. He evidently liked it.

"Where are we going again, Lani *Dahd*?" he asked.

Dahd was Tohono O'odham for godmother, and that

was Lani Walker's role in Gabe's young life. She had been there to deliver him in the back of her adoptive mother's prized Invicta convertible eight years earlier, and she had been there for him ever since, spending as much time with him as possible whenever she was home on breaks—first from medical school and later from her hospital residency in Denver.

She was doing her best to be Gabe's mentor and to give him the benefit of everything she had learned from the mentors in her life, her own godparents, namely Gabe's great-aunt, Rita Antone, and his grandfather, Fat Crack Ortiz. Of course, those people in turn had learned what they knew from the old people in their own lives, from a blind medicine man called Looks at Nothing, and from Rita's grandmother, Oks Amachuda, Understanding Woman.

"We're going to stop by the house to pick up my mother," Lani answered. "Then we're going to a place called Tohono Chul."

Gabe frowned. "Desert corner?" he asked.

Lani smiled at his correct translation. She was glad he was learning some of his native language, and not just from her, either.

"Not a corner, really," she corrected. "It's a botanical garden, devoted to preserving the desert's native plants."

"You mean like a zoo but for plants?" Gabe asked.

Lani nodded. "Exactly. There's a party there tonight. My mother and I are invited, and I thought you should go, too. After all, you're eight—that's old enough."

"What kind of party?" Gabriel asked. "You mean like a birthday party with candles?"

"More like a feast than a birthday party, but with no dancing," Lani explained.

Gabe shook his head. A feast with no dancing clearly made no sense to him.

"There may be candles," Lani added, "but they won't be on a cake. People will be carrying candles around with them so they'll be able to see in the dark."

"Why not use flashlights?" he asked.

Lani smiled to herself. Gabe was nothing if not practical. From his perspective, flashlights made more sense than candles. Gabe wanted light, not atmosphere.

"Candles make for a better mood," she said.

Lani waited while Gabe internalized her response.

After eight years, Lani was accustomed to answering the boy's questions, and she did so patiently enough. That was a godmother's job. As for Gabe's parents? His father, Leo, was too busy running the family auto repair business, and his mother, Delia Cachora Ortiz, was too busy being the tribal chairman to take time out to provide thoughtful answers to Gabe's perpetually complicated questions.

Besides, truth be known, Gabe's city-raised mother probably didn't know most of those answers herself anyway, at least not the traditional ones—the old ones—Gabe was searching for, the ones he wanted to understand. Delia could probably do a credible job of reciting the meteorological reasons for hot summer days like today when the horizon was dotted with fast-moving whirlwinds, but she didn't know the vivid stories of Windman and Cloud-man, who were the mysterious Tohono

O'odham movers and shakers, the entities who stood behind those dancing whirlwinds. Little Gabe Ortiz was always searching for the wisdom and the teachings of the old ways, and those were the ones Lani Walker provided.

"Will there be other Indians there?" Gabe asked now.

"Probably not."

"Only Anglos and us?"

"Yes."

"But why?"

That was by far Gabe's favorite question—the one for all seasons and all reasons. "But why does the ocotillo turn green when it rains? But why do rattlesnakes shed their skin? But why does I'itoi live on Ioligam? But why does it thunder when it rains? But why did my grandfather have to die before I was born? But why? But why? But why?"

Although Gabe's parents were often too preoccupied to answer the curious little boy's constant questions, Lani never was. He reminded her of Elephant's Child in that old Rudyard Kipling story, where the baby elephant was forever asking questions of everyone within hearing distance. Gabe, too, was full of "satiable curiosity," just as Lani had been when she was a child. She, far more than either of Gabe's parents, understood how and why those questions needed to be answered, just as Nana *Dahd* and Fat Crack Ortiz had patiently answered those same questions for her.

"Because Tohono Chul is in Tucson," Lani said firmly. "Not that many Indians live in Tucson these days."

"Rita used to live in Tucson," Gabe responded wistfully. "Now she lives with us. Not with us really. She lives next door."

For a moment Lani thought he was referring to that other Rita, to Lani's Rita, to Rita Antone, Nana *Dahd,* the wrinkled old Indian woman who had been god-mother to Lani in the same way Lani was godmother to Gabe. Eventually she realized Gabe was referring to his thirteen-year-old cousin Rita Gomez. That Rita, some-times called Baby Rita, had been named after her great-aunt, Rita Antone, who was Gabe's great-aunt as well.

There was silence in the car for the next several min-utes as Lani considered how the threads of the Ortiz family had frayed, drawn apart, and then seamlessly re-paired themselves.

Charlotte Ortiz Gomez, Gabe's auntie and Baby Rita's mother, had been estranged from Gabe's grandparents, Fat Crack and Wanda Ortiz, for a number of years. During that time Charlotte had lived in Tucson with her jerk of a husband and her daughter. When Fat Crack died, Char-lotte had adamantly refused to come to the reservation, not even for her own father's funeral.

A year or so later, however, when Charlotte's marriage had ended in divorce, she had come crawling back to the reservation, begging forgiveness. She and Baby Rita had moved into her widowed mother's mobile home in the Ortiz family compound behind the gas station, where Charlotte had looked after her mother until Wanda's death two years ago.

"Well?" Gabe prompted. "If there won't be any Indi-ans there, why do we have to go?"

"Because the Milgahn who are coming tonight want to hear the legend of Old White-Haired Woman," Lani answered. "Tonight is the one night a year when the night-blooming cereus blossom all over the desert. They have a lot of those plants at Tohono Chul and a lot of people will come to see them. I promised the lady who organizes the party that I would come there to tell the story of Old White-Haired Woman."

Gabe's jaw dropped. "But you can't," he objected.

It was Lani's turn to ask. "Can't what?"

"You can't tell that story," Gabe replied. "It's an I'itoi story," he added earnestly, "a winter-telling tale. The snakes and lizards are already out. If you tell that story now and one of them hears you, they could hurt you."

Lani had once asked Gabe's grandfather, Fat Crack Ortiz, about that very same thing. The old medicine man had been invited to come to a party just like this one for the same reason—to deliver the story at Tohono Chul in honor of that year's blooms.

"When they asked me to come, I wondered about that," he said. "So I took the invitation they sent me, I rolled some sacred tobacco, some *wiw*, and I performed a *wustana*. By blowing the sacred smoke over the invitation, I knew what I should do."

"And what was that?" Lani had asked.

"Some of the people have forgotten all about Old White-Haired Woman," Fat Crack had told her. "Yes, the I'itoi stories are supposed to be winter-telling tales, but on this one night, I'itoi himself doesn't object to having that story told."

"The snakes and lizards won't hurt me," Lani told Gabe now. "I'itoi doesn't mind if the story is told on the night the flowers bloom. It's a good story. People need to remember."

Tucson, Arizona
Saturday, June 6, 2009, 1:00 P.M.
93° Fahrenheit

"Your hair looks great," Nicole said, looking up at Abigail Tennant over the bubbling pedicure bath. "Is this a special occasion?"

Abby nodded. "Our anniversary," she said. "Jack and I met five years ago today. He's the best thing that ever happened to me."

"Where's he taking you?"

"I have no idea," she said. "It's a surprise."

"Someplace good, I hope?" Nicole asked.

"It better be," Abby answered with a smile. "This will be the first night-blooming cereus party I've missed in fifteen years."

When the manicure/pedicure appointment ended, Abby took her time leaving Hush. Not wanting to chip her polish, she waited an extra twenty minutes before making her way out to the parking lot. When she arrived two hours earlier, she had lucked out and found a bit of shade under a mesquite tree. She unlocked the old Mark VIII with its push-button door code and found the temperature inside was hot, but not nearly as hot as it would have been without the shade augmented by the fold-up reflecting sunscreen she had placed on the inside of the windshield.

The car had been beautiful and sporty when she bought it new fifteen years earlier and days before she set off for her new life in Arizona. She had lived through a brutal divorce in Ohio. After thirty years of marriage, Hank Southard had seen fit to trade Abby in on a much younger model, a woman named DeeAnn who was barely half his age and extremely pregnant by the time Hank and Abby's divorce was finalized. Two days later Hank had trotted off to Nevada where he had made an honest woman of his mistress by way of a quickie Las Vegas wedding.

Abby had never been able to understand how her son, Jonathan, could have come to the completely illogical conclusion that the divorce was all Abby's fault; that she had, through some action of her own, been the cause of Hank's betrayal. Because Jonathan was an adult by then, it hadn't been a question of custody but a question of loyalty, and Jonathan had stuck with his philandering father.

"Sounds like he was just following the money" was the uncompromising way Jack had explained it to Abby some time later. "Kids are like that. They know which side their bread is buttered on. Hank's pockets probably looked a lot deeper to Jonathan than yours did. Maybe he'll wise up someday."

So far that hadn't happened, but that ego-damaging time was far enough in the past that it no longer hurt

Abby quite so much. When she thought about it now, it seemed like someone else's ancient history.

For one thing, Abby was an entirely different person than she had been then. After being a stay-at-home mom and a dutiful corporate wife for all those years, she had been devastated by the divorce. It had been that much worse when her former husband, his new wife, and their new baby had settled down in a Columbus neighborhood not far from where she and Hank had lived for much of their married lives. In fact their love nest was close enough to Abby's home that they had occasionally run into people who had been friends of Hank's and Abby's back before the divorce. Those supposedly good friends had never failed to mention to Abby that they had run into Hank and DeeAnn buying groceries at Kroger's or flats of annuals at Lowe's.

It wasn't long before Abby found herself stressing that every time she left the house for any reason, she might come around a corner in the grocery store and stumble into them.

She finally decided she had two choices. She could become a recluse and never leave the house again or she could make a change—a drastic change. It took a while, but eventually that's what Abby did—she bailed. She had heard about Tucson, had read about Tucson. She had come here on a wing and a prayer with few friends and fewer preconceived notions, determined to start over. And she had.

Jack's comment about following the money notwithstanding, Abby was fairly well fixed. Thanks to the efforts of an amazingly tough and capable divorce attorney, she'd come away from the marriage in reasonably good financial shape. Abby had invested years of her life supporting Hank's career, and she deserved every penny of whatever settlement came her way. When it was time for Abby to leave town, the divorce settlement had made it possible for her to put Hank and DeeAnn and her previous life in her rearview mirror. Taking a page from Hank's playbook, Abby decided it would be a brand-new rearview mirror.

Without consulting anyone, she had driven her stodgy old silver Town Car over to the nearest Lincoln dealer, where she had traded it in on the metallic-green Lincoln Mark VIII. She hadn't agonized over the deal. She hadn't spent hours in painful negotiations with first the salesman and later the sales manager the way Hank always used to do, making a war out of trying to work the dealership down to the very lowest price. Abby had spotted the make, model, and color she wanted parked on the showroom floor. She had asked the salesman to bring it out so she could test-drive it, and she had driven away with it signed, sealed, and delivered less than two hours later.

Fifteen years after that purchase, the Mark VIII's metallic-green paint was starting to deteriorate in Tucson's unrelenting sun—even though the vehicle spent most days and nights safely stowed in a garage and out of direct sunlight. Much to her satisfaction, however, the vehicle still ran perfectly . . . well, almost perfectly. It had less than 25,000 miles on the odometer. It was one of those cars about which one could truly say, "one-owner vehicle—driven to church and museums." Because that's mostly where she drove it—to church, to the grocery stores, and to Tohono Chul, a Tucson botanical garden where Abby was a faithful volunteer.

As for Hank? Unfortunately for him, Danielle, the headstrong daughter he had fathered with his new wife, apparently took after her mother, and not necessarily in a good way. She was gorgeous but dumb as a stump. Halfway through high school, her GPA was so low that acceptance at even a third-rate college was questionable. Hank had always been brainy. So had his only son, Jonathan. Hank had zero patience with people who weren't as smart as he was. Abby understood better than anyone that having to deal with an intellectually deficient offspring would be driving the man nuts.

Abby still had friends in Columbus, the same ones who, in the old days, had been only too happy to carry tales to her about what Hank and DeeAnn were up to. Now the tables were turned, and those same friends were still happy to carry tales.

It was through them that Abby had heard that her son, Jonathan, Esther (the wife Abby had never met), and the two grandkids she had never seen were living somewhere in the L.A. area, where he worked for a bank. It was also through those same friends that Abby had learned about Danielle Southard's dismal academic record, which had resulted in her being dropped from the varsity cheerleading squad. There had also been a huge brouhaha when Danielle and several other girls were picked up for shoplifting during what was supposedly a chaperoned sleepover.

Abby had eagerly gobbled up the morsels of news about JonJon, as she still thought of her son. As for Danielle's unfortunate missteps? Abby tended to gloat a bit about those. She couldn't help it.

Hank's getting his just deserts, Abby thought. *He's stuck dealing with a dim-bulb angst-driven teenager with issues. All I have to worry about is having my Mark VIII repainted. Such a deal. Seems fair to me.*

2

Tucson, Arizona
Saturday, June 6, 2009, 6:00 A.M.
69° Fahrenheit

*A*S JONATHAN SOUTHARD sat in the car, watching and waiting, he was amazed at how cold it had been overnight out here in what was supposed to be the desert, and also at how much his arm hurt. It was feverish and throbbing. That was worrisome.

At the time, it hadn't seemed like that big a deal. Only a little bite, not a big one. That worthless damn dog had never liked him. As far as he was concerned, the feeling was mutual. Major was Esther's dog—the kids' dog. It seemed to him that the beagle was beyond dim, but as stupid as the dog had always seemed, that night Major had somehow read his mind and known what was going to happen. How could that be? It seemed weird.

Esther wouldn't have had a clue that he had come into the room behind her if the dog hadn't warned her, springing at him from the back of the couch, growling and with his teeth bared. The ferocity of the unexpected attack had forced Jonathan to dodge away and take a step backward. Major had nailed his wrist before he got quite out of reach, drawing blood and knocking the gun from his hand.

When Esther turned around, she didn't see the weapon. All she saw was her husband. "No!" she yelled at Major. "Come here!"

The dog listened to her and paused for a moment—a moment that allowed Jonathan to retrieve the gun. Naturally he had shot Major first. Then he shot Esther. Once he could hear again, once his ears stopped reverberating, he stood there with the gun still in his bleeding hand and listened, afraid the kids would wake up and come running to see what had happened.

In all honesty, that was the first time he even thought of the kids. What about them? He could call the cops and turn himself in, but what would happen to Timmy and Suzy then? He seemed to remember setting up a guardianship thing so that if something happened to Esther and him together, the kids would go first to Esther's sister, Corrine. But what would their lives be like if their mother was dead and their father was in prison for killing her? That might even be worse than growing up as Abby Southard's no-good, worthless son.

He had decided the next step in that instant. If Timmy and Suzy died in their sleep, he could spare them all that suffering—the suffering of living. And that's what he did—he shot them while they slept, one bullet each. That way they would never have to wonder if their parents loved them. Then he closed their bedroom doors and left them there. As long as the doors were shut—as long as he didn't venture back into the living room where Esther lay sprawled on the couch, he didn't have to remember that they were dead. As far as Jonathan was concerned, they were just sleeping.

He went into the bathroom then and collected the whole set of medication bottles Esther kept there. Antidepressants, sleep aids; whatever bottles he could find that said "Do Not Use with Alcohol." You name it; Esther had it. He took them down to his study along with a bottle of single-malt Scotch.

He poured a full glass, but sat there thinking before he swallowed that first pill. He remembered seeing a movie called *The Bucket List,* the one about making sure you did all the things you wanted to do before you died.

He decided right then and there that he would go out with a bang, not the way he had left the bank, slinking out after everyone else had left for the night, carrying the personal possessions from his office in a single disgraceful cardboard box.

Hoping to prove his mother's dire predictions wrong, he had spent his adult life doing what he was supposed to do all this time, twenty-four/seven. Now he was going to do some of the things he wasn't supposed to do. He closed the open pill bottles. Then he showered and dressed, packed a suitcase with a week's worth of clothes, and tossed the collection of pill bottles into the mix. The last thing he did before he walked out the door was set the thermostat down to 65 degrees. Who cared if he ran up the electricity bill? He wouldn't be the one paying it.

Now, five days later and over five hundred miles away, he sat waiting on a residential street in Tucson, Arizona. He'd been doing that for hours now, shifting periodically in the seat, trying to find a comfortable place to rest his throbbing arm. Then, just when he thought he'd maybe go back to the Circle K and pick up some coffee and take a leak, the garage door on the house he was watching slid open.

As the Lexus backed out into the driveway, Jonathan recognized the guy at the wheel as the man he assumed to be Jack Tennant, Abby's husband. Jonathan never referred to her as Mother. He refused to give her that much credit. While he watched, Jack loaded a golf pull-cart and a bag of clubs into the car. That was interesting. If Jack was going to go play golf, Jonathan wanted to know where he was going, how long he'd be gone, and when he'd be back. That's what these recon trips were all about—getting the lay of the land.

When Jack headed down the street, Jonathan followed. It was as easy as that.

Tucson, Arizona
Saturday, June 6, 2009, 12:00 P.M.
93° Fahrenheit

The dream came while Daniel James Pardee was sleeping. In it he was back in Iraq, riding in the Humvee with Bozo, the dog no one else would take, sitting between him and the driver. As in real life, the driver was none too happy when Bozo, panting and grinning that weird doggy grin of his, had scrambled his hundred-plus pounds of dusty German shepherd into the cab along with Dan.

"Oh, jeez!" the driver muttered. "Not him again. That stinking dog's so stupid he'd rather chase birds than bad guys."

That was the reason the dog, formerly known as King and now jeeringly referred to as Bozo the Clown, had been passed along to the newest guy in the unit, Corporal Dan Pardee. "Three's the charm," the CO in Mosul had told Dan. "Either Bozo wakes up and gets serious about his job, or he's out of here."

Dan understood at once that, in military parlance, "out of here" didn't mean some nice doggy retirement program somewhere. It meant termination. Period. Bozo's career with the U.S. Army would be over and so would he.

"Yeah, Justin," Dan told Corporal Justin Clifford, the driver. "You don't smell so good yourself, so leave Bozo the hell alone. Let's get moving."

In the dream Dan knew Justin's name. In real life he hadn't known his name until after "the incident" and until after the wounded driver had been shipped out of theater, first to Germany and then to Walter Reed, suffering from second- and third-degree burns over fifty percent of his body. Both in the dream and in real life, however, the Humvee ground into gear and moved to the head of the supply convoy.

The whole thing went to hell about forty-five minutes later when the world exploded just outside the driver's window. Blinded by smoke and deafened by the concussion, Dan and Bozo had scrambled out through the door on the Humvee's relatively undamaged passenger side. When Dan's hearing returned, the only sound he heard were the agonized screams coming from Corporal Clifford, who was still trapped inside the burning vehicle. Dan was turning back to reach for Clifford and try to pull him out when he saw the insurgent.

It was ironic that that was the word news broadcasters always used to refer to the bad guys—insurgents. Dan often wondered what people back home in the U.S. thought that word meant. They probably figured a group of "insurgents" would be made up of hardened old soldiers, believers in the old ways, who would rather die than vote in a free election.

Not true. This one, the guy materializing like a ghost out of the smoke and dust with an AK-47 in his hands, wasn't old at all. He was a kid—eleven or twelve at most. Whoever had planted the bomb had left this little shit behind, armed to the teeth and lying in wait hoping to ambush anyone who managed to stagger out of the burning wreckage.

Both in real life and in the dream, things slowed down at that point. Corporal Daniel Pardee was faced with two impossible choices. Should he reach inside and try to rescue poor Justin Clifford, or should he leave the other man to die and reach for his M16?

Before he had a chance to do either one, Bozo decided for them both. He slammed into the gun-toting kid from one side, blindsiding him and hitting him with more than a hundred pounds of biting, snapping fury. The kid was knocked to the ground, screeching, while the gun, now useless, went spinning away out of reach.

The whole thing took only a moment. With the kid and his gun out of the equation, Dan turned his full attention back on Clifford. With almost superhuman strength he had managed to haul the injured driver to relative safety. By then, other troops from the convoy were hurrying forward to offer assistance. It took three of them to haul Bozo off the kid and keep the dog from killing him.

When Dan finally got back to the dog, both in the dream and in real life, he was sitting there, panting and grinning that stupid grin of his, except by then the dog's happy grin didn't seem nearly so stupid. Dan had stumbled over to him and gratefully buried his face and hands in Bozo's dusty, smoky fur. It was only when the hand came away bloodied that Dan realized the dog—his dog—had been cut by shrapnel from the explosion, by flying bits of burning metal and shattered glass. Later on Dan figured out that he'd been cut and burned, too. Both of them had been treated for relatively minor injuries, but Dan knew full well that if it hadn't been for Bozo—

that wonderfully zany Bozo—Justin Clifford would have died that day in Mosul.

At that moment, as if on cue, Dan's dream ended the same way the firefight had ended—with Bozo. The dog scrambled up onto the bed, whining and licking Dan's face.

"Go away," Dan ordered. "Leave me alone."

From the moment the bomb went off, Bozo was transformed. When it came time to go on patrol, he was dead serious. He paid attention. He obeyed orders. And he seemed to develop almost a sixth sense about the possibility of danger. Twice he had alerted Dan in time for the two of them to dive for cover before bombs exploded rather than after. And if Bozo said someplace was a no-go, Dan paid attention and didn't go there.

But right now, the dog and the man weren't working. They were in bed. Bozo immediately understood that his master didn't mean it, that his order to go away was one that could be disobeyed. As a consequence, he paid no attention and didn't let up.

The recurring dream came to Dan night after night, or, as now when he was working the night shift, day after day. The nightmare always left him shaken and anxious and drenched in sweat. He wondered if maybe he had cried out in his sleep and that was what caused Bozo to come running.

Dan tried unsuccessfully to dodge away from Bozo by pulling the sweat-soaked covers over his head and turning the other way, but Bozo was relentless. Thumping his tail happily, the dog scrambled to Dan's other side and burrowed under the covers to join him. After all, it was time for breakfast. According to Bozo's time calculations, Dan needed to drag his lazy butt out of bed and get moving.

"All right, all right," Dan grumbled, giving the dog a fond whack on his empty-sounding head. "I'm up. Are you happy?"

In truth the dog was happy, slobbery grin and all.

Tucson, Arizona
Saturday, June 6, 2009, 1:15 P.M.
93° Fahrenheit

Abby turned the key in the ignition and listened as the powerful V-8 engine roared to life. There was maybe the tiniest squeal, as though a fan belt might be slipping a bit, but the motor settled into a steady hum and the air-conditioning came on full blast—blazingly hot at first, but then cooling. While Abby waited a few moments for the steering wheel to be cool enough to touch, she picked up her cell.

Still careful with her newly applied polish, she hit the green send button twice and called Tohono Chul for the first time that afternoon but for the seventh time that day. She wasn't surprised when she was put on hold. Abby, of all people, understood what Shirley Folgum was up against. Trying to ride herd on that evening's party was a complicated proposition.

In Tohono Chul's annual calendar, the celebration of

the night-blooming cereus was an enormous undertaking. On that night alone, as many as two thousand people would show up at the park for the festivities, arriving well after dark and not leaving until early the next morning. All of that would have been complicated enough, if it could have been handled in the established way.

Most big recurring nonprofit-style events come with certain unvarying logistics. Worker bees needed to be organized. Invitations have to be issued. Potential attendees need to be given "Save the date" information. Contracts for entertainment and catering need to be arranged. All of those things held true for the night-blooming cereus party. The big difference—and the big complication—came with the reality that no one ever knew exactly when the party would take place. Not until the very last minute.

Despite years of patient analysis and study by any number of very talented botanists, despite countless computer models examining weather data—daytime temperatures, nighttime temperatures, dew points, barometric pressures, and all points in between—no one had yet been able to crack the code as to when exactly the Queen of the Night would deign to make her annual appearance. Scientific study suggested it would happen sometime between the end of May and the middle of July. As a result of this uncertainty, all preparations had to be ironed out well in advance and then put in abeyance but ready for immediate last-minute execution.

It turned out that was how Abby Tennant herself had stumbled into the event for the first time—at the last minute.

Toward the end of her first June in Tucson, Abby had been dreadfully homesick for her friends and relations back home in Ohio. For one thing, the appalling June heat was nothing short of debilitating. She had almost decided to give up and go back home when a new neighbor, Mildred Harrison, had called.

"There's going to be a special party at Tohono Chul tomorrow night," Mildred had said. "Would you like to come along as my guest?"

Abby's new town house in what was billed as an "active adult community" on Tucson's far northwest side was just down the street from the botanical garden. She had driven past the rock wall entrance numerous times, but she hadn't ever considered stopping in. Somehow she had never guessed that one of the world's ten best botanical gardens would be right there, hiding out in the middle of Tucson.

What interesting plants could possibly grow in the desert? Abby had wondered in all her midwestern arrogance. From what she personally had observed, there seemed to be precious few plants of any kind in this desolate outpost of civilization where, even in May, the heat had been more than Abby could tolerate.

"I suppose they're holding it at night because it's too hot to have a garden party during the day," Abby had groused sarcastically.

Mildred had laughed aloud at that. "It's a party in honor of the night-blooming cereus," she explained. "It's the flower on the deer-horn cactus. We call it the Queen of the Night. Tohono Chul has more than eighty plants that are set to bloom this year, and they all blossom at the same time. They open up around sunset and are gone by sunrise the next morning. Someone called just now to let me know that the bloom will be tomorrow night. Are you coming or not?"

Mildred sometimes reminded Abby of her older sister, Stephanie, who was at times a bit overbearing and more than a little outspoken. On this occasion, Abby had dutifully slipped into full little-sister mode.

"I suppose," she had agreed reluctantly.

The next day she had tried her best to back out of the engagement, but Mildred wouldn't hear of it. Around nine o'clock that evening, Abby had ridden over to Tohono Chul's parking lot in Mildred's aging Pontiac. Arriving in low spirits and with even lower expectations, Abby was surprised to find the parking lot jammed with cars and parking attendants. Along with hordes of other enthusiastic attendees, Abby and Mildred had walked into the park following footpaths that were lit with candles in small paper bags.

"They're called luminarias," Mildred explained. "They're traditional Mexican."

Abby was astonished when she saw the throngs of people who were there that night. She kept wondering what all the fuss was about—but only until she saw a night-blooming cereus in the flesh. Once she caught sight of that first lush white blossom, Abby Tennant fell in love.

She couldn't fathom how such a magnificent white flower could burst forth from what appeared to be a skimpy stick of thorny cactus. She was astonished to find that many of the gorgeous blossoms were as big across as one of Abby's eight-inch pie plates. They reminded her of her next-door neighbor's prizewinning dahlias back home in Ohio, but these weren't dahlias, and the heady perfume that drifted away from each flower on the hot summer air was subtle but elegantly sweet, reminiscent of orange blossoms, but not quite the same.

Abby was dumbstruck. "They're so beautiful!" she had exclaimed.

"Aren't they," Mildred said, nodding in agreement. "And now you know why it's called the Queen of the Night. By the time the sun comes up tomorrow, the blossoms will be gone."

Abby Tennant's first encounter with the night-blooming cereus marked the real beginning of her new life, although her name was still Abby Southard back then. She had been so enchanted by seeing the flowers that she had insisted on taking Mildred to lunch at the Tohono Chul Tea Room the very next week. In the confines of the small cool rooms of what had once been a ranch house, Abby began to see the things about Tucson that she had been missing before—the friendliness of the people, Mildred included, for one thing, and the many subtle beauties of the desert for another.

Abby had taken out her own membership at Tohono Chul only a week or so later. Walking the park's many manicured paths, she gradually acclimated herself to the heat of her new home. She learned to mark the changing seasons by something other than changing leaves. In spring she saw the profusion of yellow flowers on the prickly pear and the fuchsia-colored blossoms of the barrel cactus. In early summer she came to love the bright yellow blooms standing out against the green branches of the springtime paloverde and the dusky pinks and lavenders on the brooding ironwood. She loved watching the birds, especially the brightly colored hummingbirds that hovered around the equally brightly colored flowers.

Somehow, in the process of exploring this desert oasis, Abby Tennant found peace and came to terms with her new home and her new life. By the time of the first snowfall in Columbus that first year, she was no longer homesick. When Christmas rolled around and her friends were complaining about the weather, Abby took herself back to the park and volunteered her services.

At first she knew so little that all she could do was work as a stocker and a cashier in the museum shop. Later, once she was better adjusted to the climate, she went through docent training so she could lead tours and speak knowledgeably about the native plants of her newly adopted home. Because of her enduring fascination with the night-blooming cereus, it was a natural progression of her volunteerism that she went from leading daytime tours to working on the annual Queen of the Night party.

Initially she served on the Queen of the Night Committee, but when the complexity of the event outstripped the committee's groupthink capability, Abby had finally given up and taken charge. When she came on board, there had been a complicated phone-tree system for notifying workers and guests of the impending bloom. Under her direction, phone trees had given way to a more streamlined form of e-mail notices. But after five years of running the show, it was time to pass the reins to someone else, and Shirley Folgum was her handpicked successor.

"So how are things?" Abby asked when Shirley finally came on the line. "Did you hear back from the band?"

"I was talking to the manager when you called. They'll be here for a sound check no later than five. I told them to come in by way of the loading dock."

"And the caterer?"

"She's having trouble locating servers."

"Don't worry. She'll find them. This party is a big deal for her, and we pay her a bundle of money during the summer when there's not much else going on. She'll come through. She always does.

"What about the storyteller?" Abby asked.

Abby had come to love the enduring Tohono O'odham legend about the wise old grandmother whose bravery had given rise to the Queen of the Night. Including that story in the annual festivities was one of the ways Abby had put her own distinctive stamp on the party. She insisted that each year some guest of honor would come to the event and recount the story that had struck a chord in her heart. It seemed to Abby that in saving her grandson, Wise Old Grandmother had saved Abby Tennant as well.

"That's handled," Shirley reported. "Dr. Walker and her mother are planning to have lunch in the Tea Room this afternoon before the party starts. Unfortunately, she's due back at work in the ER at the hospital in Sells by midnight. That means the last scheduled storytelling event can't be any later than nine."

"Good," Abby said. "Earlier is better than later."

"Are you going to stop by for a last-minute checklist?" Shirley asked.

"No," Abby said with a laugh. "I don't think that's necessary. It sounds as though you have everything under control."

Tucson, Arizona
Saturday, June 6, 2009, 1:30 P.M.
93° Fahrenheit

Lani *Dahd* used her key to unlock the front door of her parents' house. She stepped inside, with Gabe following close on her heel. He had been here before and was always astonished by the place.

For one thing, the house, built of river rock, was bigger than any of the houses he knew on the reservation. Although the people who lived here were Milgahn, Anglos, the place was full of a rich profusion of baskets—Tohono O'odham baskets. There were yucca and bear-grass baskets on every available surface—on walls and tables and the mantelpiece. Gabe had been told that many of them had been made by his great-aunt Rita.

"How did your parents get so many baskets?" Gabe had asked. "Are they rich?"

Lani *Dahd* thought about that for a moment before she answered. By reservation standards, the Anglo couple who had adopted her when she was little more than a toddler were rich beyond measure.

"Yes," she said finally. "I suppose they are."

"But why?" Gabe asked.

"Because my mother writes books," Lani answered.

"What about your father?"

"He was a police officer."

"Why are they so old?" Gabe asked.

Lani's father was almost seventy. Her mother was in her mid-sixties. In the Anglo world that wasn't so very old, but on the reservation, where people were often cut down by alcoholism and diabetes in their forties and fifties, that seemed like a very advanced age.

"They just are," she said.

"Why do they have different names?" Gabe asked. "Mr. Walker and Mrs. Ladd. Aren't they married?"

"Yes, they're married," Lani explained, "but my mother was already writing books by then. It made sense for her to keep her own name instead of changing it to someone else's."

This time Gabe was without questions as he followed Lani through the house. While she stopped off in a bathroom, Gabe walked on alone to the sliding door that he knew led to the patio.

Damsel, the household dog, stood outside the sliding door. Gabe opened the door and leaned down to pet the dog. Looking away from Damsel, he saw Mrs. Ladd—an older Milgahn woman with pale skin and silvery hair—sitting in the shade of a little shelter on the far side of the pool. A very ugly blind man was sitting there with her.

Once again the dog demanded Gabe's attention. When he turned away from Damsel, Lani was stepping through the slider and coming outside. By then the man had disappeared. Gabe hadn't heard him leave. He glanced around the backyard, looking for him. It seemed curious that he could have left so silently, but the man was no-where to be seen. He was simply gone.

"Mom," Lani said, frowning when she noticed her mother's bathrobe and bare feet. "Why aren't you dressed?"

"I am dressed," Diana said. "What's wrong with a robe?"

"But I thought you were going into town with us—to Tohono Chul. The three of us have a reservation for lunch at the Tea Room, and then tonight there's the night-blooming cereus party."

"I can't," Diana said. "I'm busy."

Lani had lived with her adoptive mother's career as a reality all her life. From an early age she had understood how deadlines worked. When there was something to do with writing that had to be completed by a certain time, her mother was simply unavailable.

"What?" Lani asked. "An emergency copyediting job? How come the deadlines always come from the publisher and never the other way around?"

"Not copyediting," Diana said. "Something else."

"Look," Lani said. "It's Saturday afternoon. You've al-ready worked all morning. Let it go. I talked to Dad. He's on his way to Casa Grande to see a friend of his. Take a break. Come with us right now. It'll be fun. The blossoms start opening around eight. I'll have you back home no later than ten-thirty. You can work all day tomorrow if you need to."

Diana thought about that for a moment. Finally, making up her mind, she picked up her computer. "All right," she said. "I'll go get dressed."

She stood up and walked into the house, closing the door behind her.

"Who was that man?" Gabe asked.

"What man?"

"The man who was talking to your mother."

"I didn't see any man," Lani said.

"He was right there," Gabe said, "and then he was gone."

Lani glanced around the yard. Like Gabe, she saw no one. "Maybe he went out through the gate."

Gabe shook his head.

"What did he look like? Was he young or old?"

"Old," Gabe said. "The skin on his face was all lumpy."

"Like wrinkled?"

"No. Bumpy. Like a popover when you cook it."

In other tribes, popovers are called fry bread. Flattened pieces of dough are dropped into hot grease. As the dough cooks, the outside surface fills with air and puffs up.

Despite the hot air around her, Lani Walker felt a chill. She knew of only one man whose face had puffed up like a popover when it was covered with hot grease thrown by her mother, but that had happened long before Lani was born. Lani knew about it not only because her brother, who had been there at the time, had told her the story. Lani also knew because she'd seen the photographs in her mother's book, which had also mentioned that Andrew Philip Carlisle had been dead for years.

"He's not here now," Lani said. "You must have been mistaken. Come on," she added. *"Oi g hihm."*

Directly translated, that expression means "Let us walk." In the vernacular of the reservation, it means: "Let's get in the pickup and go."

Gabe evidently understood that this was one time when he'd be better off not asking any questions. Without a word of objection and with the dog at his side, he came into the house behind Lani, took a seat on the couch in a room filled with beautiful Tohono O'odham baskets, and waited patiently until it was time to leave.

Tucson, Arizona
Saturday, June 6, 2009, 1:00 P.M.
93° Fahrenheit

While the coffeepot burbled and burped, Dan dished up Bozo's food—dry dog food along with a dollop of canned food for flavor. Dan couldn't help but notice that the tinned dog food—beef with gravy—smelled more appetizing than some of the MREs he had encountered during his tour of duty in Iraq.

Our tour of duty, Dan corrected himself mentally as he placed the dish of food in front of the salivating dog. He still remembered his first one-sided conversation with the dog no one had wanted.

"Look," he had said while Bozo listened to his voice with rapt, prick-eared attention. "Let's get one thing straight. When we work, we work; when we play, we play, but you've got to know the difference."

"Hey," one of the guys had said, pointing and laughing. "Looks like Chief here is turning into one of those dog whisperers. Is it possible old Bozo actually understands Apache?"

From the time he was four, Dan had been raised by his grandparents on the San Carlos Reservation in Arizona, where Dan had been ridiculed for being half Anglo and half Apache. Back then he had coped with his tormentors by playing class clown, so maybe Bozo had a point. And maybe that's one of the reasons Dan and Bozo had bonded. Daniel Pardee was in Iraq wearing his country's uniform and doing his country's job, but he was sick and tired of the constant jokes about his Apache background. Maybe Bozo was tired of the jokes, too.

"I was just telling him that some of the people around here are jerks," Dan replied. "I told him he needs to know who his friends are."

By the time Dan's deployment neared its end, he had pretty much resigned himself to leaving Bozo behind. By then Bozo's reputation was such that the other guys were clamoring to take him on. That was when Ruthie's "Dear John" letter arrived. He and Ruthie Longoria had been childhood sweethearts and had dated exclusively all through high school. The idea that they would marry eventually had been a foregone conclusion, but the ending had been all too typical. Somehow Dan had known what was up before he even opened the envelope. For one thing, she had sent it via snail mail rather than over the Net.

"We're too young to make this kind of commitment," she had told him. "We both need to see other people, but we can still be friends." Yada yada yada.

Sure, like that's going to happen! It was long after Dan had come back home that he finally learned the truth. Ruthie had already found a new man before she ever cut Dan loose.

Still, at the time he read the letter, he was pissed as hell—more angry than sad—but he was also grateful. He understood that he had dodged a bullet as real as any of the live ammunition on the ground in Iraq. If that was the kind of woman Ruthie Longoria was, he was better off knowing about it before the wedding rather than after—a wedding and honeymoon he'd been dutifully saving money for the whole time he had been in the service.

With that monetary obligation off the table, however, Dan decided to cut his losses. If he couldn't keep his woman, he would sure as hell keep his dog. So Dan took the money he had set aside to pay for a wedding and paid Bozo's way home instead. It took all the money he'd had and more besides. His maternal grandfather had helped, and so had Justin Clifford's family. Finally all the effort paid off. After months of paperwork and red tape and after being locked in quarantine for weeks, Bozo came home—home to Arizona; home to San Carlos; home to being a half-Apache dog.

With the wedding in mind, Dan had lined up a post-military job with a rent-a-cop security outfit in Phoenix, but that was because Ruthie loved Phoenix and wanted to live there instead of on the reservation, and that's exactly where she and her new boyfriend—now husband—had gone to live.

Dan did not love Phoenix—at all. Instead of taking that security job, he went back to the reservation, stayed with Gramps, as he called Micah Duarte, his widowed grandfather, the man who had raised him. Sitting in the quiet of Gramps's small but tidy house, Dan had tried to figure out what he wanted to do with the rest of his life. At age twenty-nine it had seemed that he was too old to go back to college, even though his veteran status would have made that affordable. After the excitement of Iraq, Dan was bored, and so was Bozo. And even though Gramps never said a word, Dan worried that he and his dog were wearing out their welcome.

Then one day two years earlier, when they were eating breakfast at the kitchen table, Gramps put a newspaper in front of him.

"Here," he said, pointing. "Read this. It sounds like something you'd be good at."

That article, in the *Arizona Sun*, told about a special group of Indian trackers, the Shadow Wolves, who worked homeland security on the Tohono O'odham Nation west of Tucson by patrolling the seventy miles of rugged reservation land that lay next to the Mexican border. Members of the elite force came from any number of tribes and were required to be at least one quarter Indian. Dan qualified on that score, with a quarter to the good since he was half Indian and half Anglo. Shadow Wolves needed to be expert trackers, and Dan qualified there, too.

His taciturn grandfather, who had spent all his adult life working on a dairy farm outside of Safford, may not have been long on language skills, but he had taught his grandson how to ride, hunt, and shoot, occasionally doing all three at once.

Micah Duarte counted among his ancestors one of the Apache scouts who had trailed Geronimo into Mexico and had helped negotiate the agreement that had brought him back to the States. In other words, being a tracker was in Daniel's blood, but Micah Duarte had translated bloodlines into firsthand experience by teaching his grandson everything he knew.

Together Dan and Gramps had hunted deer and javelina, usually with bow and arrow rather than with firearms. Hunting with a bow and arrow required being close to your quarry, and getting that close meant you had to be smart. You had to be able to read the animals' tracks and know exactly what was going on with them and with their neighbors.

Once, when Dan was in his late teens, he and Gramps had been deer hunting in southeastern Arizona. Toward the end of the day they had spotted a jaguar and followed the big cat back to its lair, not to kill it—just to see it. At the time, Dan had been astonished to learn that jaguars still existed in the States.

"Not many Apaches have done that," Micah had told

Dan later that evening as the two of them sat by their campfire. "I'm not a medicine man, but I think perhaps it is a sign."

The comment wasn't said in a boastful way, but the quiet dignity of the statement had somehow infected the impressionable teenager who had cut his teeth watching *Star Wars* movies and who knew far more about Luke Skywalker and Darth Vader than he did about Apache warriors like Geronimo and Victorio or even about his own forebears. That experience more than any other had prompted him to enlist in the army after graduating from high school.

Now, after Iraq, the more Dan read about the Shadow Wolves, the more they intrigued him, especially since they were a part of ICE and the Border Patrol, so his previous work experience in the military would be a point in his favor.

That was the start of it. Dan had applied for the Shadow Wolves, where he had been accepted into the training program and where he had aced every test. The job paid well enough that, even though he was unmarried, he was able to use his VA benefits to buy his first house. It was still a sparsely furnished home on Tucson's west side, but it came with a spacious fenced backyard where Bozo had the run of the place. Best of all, unlike so much rental property, it didn't come with a lot of rules, including the dreaded NO PETS ALLOWED prohibition.

Yes, this was a place both Dan and Bozo could call home.

Once on board with the Shadow Wolves, Dan found

it easy to prove his worth. He loved the work and he was good at it. As the weeks passed, however, with Dan going off to work and with Bozo staying home, he could see that the dog was growing more and more depressed. Bozo understood work. He knew that Dan was working and he wasn't, and the dog didn't like being left behind. Bozo demonstrated the extent of his separation anxiety by chewing up any number of expensive items—shoes, boots, holsters, and drywall—anything that was within easy reach.

Dan knew the dog well enough to understand the problem. He had two choices—either lock the dog in a pen outside and leave him there all day long or else put the dog to work, too. Talking Bozo's way into Shadow Wolves hadn't been easy.

"In case you haven't noticed, Wolves don't need K-9 units," Captain Meecham told him. "Period. Besides, as near as I can tell, Bozo is definitely not an Indian."

Meecham's bloodlines and face said Kiowa even if his name did not.

"Let me show you what he can do," Dan had offered. "Wouldn't it make sense if we knew in advance if a vehicle was carrying illegal drugs as opposed to just illegal aliens? Get yourself a bag of grass from the evidence room and hide it in one of the cars outside in the parking lot. Let's see how long it takes Bozo to find it."

Dan had taught Bozo that little trick at their newly purchased, once foreclosed, home in Tucson. As a target, he had salted his own car with a small amount of grass he had taken off one of his neighbors' junior-high-school-aged kids who was standing on a nearby street corner selling it to his classmates. Dan didn't arrest the kid because what went on inside the Tucson city limits was outside Dan's jurisdiction, but he knew he had scared the hell out of that pint-size dealer.

It took Bozo less than five minutes to transform Aaron Meecham into a believer. Once turned loose in the parking lot, Bozo had trotted purposefully up and down the aisles before stopping and vaulting into the back of Aaron's immense Toyota Tundra and barking wildly at the stainless-steel tool chest where Aaron had hidden the weed.

"Okay, okay," he said. "I'm impressed. I suppose we can try it for a while, unofficially, that is."

Aaron had gone back inside then. As Dan walked Bozo through the parking lot and back to his vintage Camaro, the dog alerted two more times—at other vehicles, at co-workers' cars.

"They're working here and using weed themselves?" Dan asked the dog. "It's a good thing Captain Meecham didn't hang around long enough to see that. If he had, there'd be hell to pay."

Now, a year after that test run, Bozo rode shotgun in the front seat of Dan's green-and-white Border Patrol SUV every time Dan went out on patrol. He loved it. So did Dan. Because of the rough terrain and the possibility of high-speed chases, Dan had found a dog harness that allowed him to fasten Bozo's seat belt and keep him secure.

The dog was almost eight years old now. He had started

limping a little again. The vet said that he had developed a bit of arthritis in his left rear leg, the one that had been damaged by the IED, and that maybe it was verging on time for Bozo to retire, but Dan didn't want to think about that, not yet.

At the moment the two of them worked four ten-hour shifts a week. They went on duty at 8:00 P.M. and were off again at 6:00 A.M.

Dan was glad to have Bozo's company through the long boring hours of patrolling and to have him there as backup during the occasional confrontation. Even the fiercest thug tended to give it up when faced with Bozo's snarling countenance. And if one of them ever fought back and harmed the dog? Dan wasn't sure what he'd do, but he didn't think it would be inside the regulations.

While Bozo finished eating, Dan took his coffee, settled down in his one good chair, and turned on the TV. Punching the clicker, he paused briefly at CNN to pick up the headlines, and then moved over to his DVR to watch ESPN's coverage of last night's Padres game.

And that was how Dan Pardee spent a lazy Saturday afternoon, drinking coffee and watching the Great American Pastime with his faithful companion at his side.

Life didn't get any better than that.

3

Casa Grande, Arizona
Saturday, June 6, 2009, 1:00 P.M.
96° Fahrenheit

*S*UE AND GEET Farrell had lived in the same three-bedroom ranch-style home in one of Casa Grande's older sections for as long as Brandon had known them. As he drove down the broad flat avenue that June afternoon, Brandon could tell that the neighborhood had seen better days. The street was lined with dead and dying palm trees. It took water to keep palm trees alive, and these days people were cutting back on water bills.

In front of Geet's house four wilting palms still clung stubbornly to life, but the yard around them was a weedy, parched wasteland. Not xeriscaped—just dead. As for the house itself? The composition roof appeared to be close to the end of its lifetime, and the whole place could have used a coat of paint except for the peeling trim around the windows, which needed scraping and several coats. A wheelchair-accessible van with handicapped plates sat forlornly in the driveway as silent testimony to the losing battle being waged inside the house. Brandon parked next to it.

At the front door a sign over the doorbell button asked visitors to abstain from ringing it and to come around to the kitchen door so as not to disturb the patient. When Sue answered Brandon's light knock, he was shocked by how worn and tired she looked. She was dressed in nothing but an oversize T-shirt and a pair of cutoffs. With her hair lank and loose and with her face devoid of makeup, she looked like hell. Geet may have been the one who was dying, but Sue Farrell was also paying a terrible price.

"How're you doing?" he asked, giving her a hug.

"Not all that well," she admitted.

"Why?" he asked. "What's going on?"

She shrugged and shook her head. "It's tough. Everybody leads you to think that hospice is this really great thing, that once you accept it, life just smooths out and everything is peachy keen. What a load of crap! The hospice people are here a couple of times a week, and I'm grateful for that, but when Geet was in the hospital, he had round-the-clock nursing. Here at home, it's up to me twenty-four/seven. People offer to help out from time to time, but it's mostly my problem."

"Is there anything I can do to help today?" Brandon asked.

Sue thought about that for a moment. "He's asleep right now. I gave him some pain meds a little while ago. If you could sit here with him long enough for me to go to the grocery store and to pick up some prescriptions from Walgreens . . ."

Brandon's heart ached for her. Sue Farrell needed to run away, too. Looking at her haggard face, he caught a glimpse of his own possible future.

"Of course," he said. "Not a problem. Take your time. Do whatever you need to do. In fact, if you want to kick up your heels and go visit a friend or see a movie, that'll be fine, too. I'll be happy to look after Geet for you. It's the least I can do."

Sue's eyes filled with tears. "Are you sure?"

"I'm sure," he said. "Where is he?"

"In the living room," Sue said. "We moved most of the furniture out and set it up as a hospital room. I hope it's not too warm for you. He's so cold that we keep the thermostat set at eighty-five."

"That's not a problem, either," Brandon replied. "Now that I've given up jackets and neckties in favor of Hawaiian shirts, the heat doesn't bother me."

Sue led Brandon into the small living room, where the blinds were down. The only light in the room came from the bright colors of a flat-screen television set over the fireplace where, in sound-muted silence, Speedvision was showing practice runs for Sunday's NASCAR race.

Most of the room was taken up with sickroom equipment—a hospital bed, a walker, a wheelchair, an oxygen tank, a side table covered with medication, a power lifter to help get Geet in and out of bed, and a rolling portable potty. Everything there was designed to make the patient's life livable, while at the same time stripping him of the last bit of dignity.

Other than the television set, the only piece of living room furniture that remained was a long cloth-covered sofa. Apologizing for the mess, Sue hastily stripped a sheet and pillow from that and carried them away to another room. No wonder she looked tired. Exhausted. That couch was probably where she was sleeping, or not sleeping, during her unending shift at Geet's bedside.

After Sue left the room, Brandon took a seat on the newly cleared couch. Geet was snoring quietly. He seemed to be sleeping peacefully. Sue appeared to be the one who needed some rest.

G. T. Farrell had always been a big man, a hearty man. Now he was a shadow of that former self. The hands that lay on top of his covers looked bony and frail. His hair had gone sparse and stark-white. The gray pallor of his sagging skin told Brandon that the man wouldn't last long. For Sue's sake, Brandon found himself hoping the battle wouldn't last much longer.

Brandon remembered too well his own recovery from bypass surgery several years earlier. He had hated it. He had hated being weak and needy, and he had hated the trouble he had put Diana through. No doubt Geet felt the same way, and Diana would, too, if it came to that.

When it comes to that, Brandon thought.

When Sue emerged from the bedroom, she had changed into a turquoise-colored pair of shorts with a matching shirt. She had pulled her hair back into a po-nytail and had dabbed on some makeup. She wasn't one hundred percent, but she was decidedly better than she had been when she first answered the door. She was also carrying a banker's box.

"This is the case Geet wants to turn over to you," she said, setting the box down next to him on the couch. "While you're just sitting here you might want to go through it."

"Sure," Brandon said easily, but he didn't mean it.

This was Geet Farrell's case to pass along, not his wife's. Brandon Walker had no intention of opening the box and looking inside it until Geet himself had given the go-ahead. The poor man might be dying, but Geet deserved that much respect, that much self-determination.

Sue gathered her purse and car keys and then stood uncertainly by her husband's bed, as if reluctant to leave.

"Give me your cell number," Brandon said gently. "I'll call if anything happens, but you need a break."

Sue nodded gratefully and gave him the number. She also gave him some instructions about Geet's pain meds. Then she rushed out the back door before she had a chance to change her mind.

In the silence her departure left behind, Brandon sat there watching the silent race cars speed around and around an oval track, but he didn't really pay attention. He was far too preoccupied with real life—his own real life.

For months now there had been little warning signals that things weren't quite right. Brandon's history with his father should have set the alarm bells ringing, but denial is an interesting thing. He hadn't discussed his concerns with Diana. By mutual agreement, it was off the table. He also hadn't mentioned it to the kids, Davy and Lani. But now the jig was up, and Brandon would have to deal with it and discuss it.

Earlier that week, he'd come back to the house from a meeting and found Diana in despair.

"What's the matter?" he asked.

"I just talked to Pam," Diana said. "They hate the book."

Pam Fender was Diana's longtime agent.

"Who hates the book?" Brandon asked. "And what book are we talking about?"

"Everyone hates the book," Diana said bleakly. "*Do Not Go Softly,* the manuscript I just turned in. Cameron hates it and so does Edward. They're turning it down."

Cameron Crowell was Diana's longtime editor in New York. Edward Renthal was her publisher and Cameron's boss.

"They can't turn it down," Brandon objected. "They bought it. They paid for it."

"They paid an advance on delivery and acceptance," Diana corrected. "If they don't accept the book, they may want their money back."

Brandon had been thunderstruck. "How could that be?" he had asked. "And why?"

"They say it's not up to my usual standard."

Over the years, Brandon and Diana had developed a system that called for Brandon to read the manuscripts only when they were finished. That way, Diana had a pair of fresh eyes looking for typos in the material before sending it off to her agent and to her editor. Brandon had read *Do Not Go Softly*. He hadn't liked it much, but he figured that was just one man's opinion.

"Can't you fix it, rewrite it or something? What does Pam say about all this?"

"She's asking them to hire someone else to do the rewrite."

"You mean like a ghostwriter?"

"That way they'll still be able to use my name on the book, and we'll be able to keep part of the advance. She's hoping to get them to take the remaining advance from upcoming royalty checks."

Shadow of Death, the book Diana had written about her experience with a serial killer named Andrew Carlisle, had won her her first Pulitzer. Considered a classic now, right up there with *In Cold Blood*, the book was still in print and still earning royalties.

"How do you feel about that?" he had asked.

Diana shrugged. "It means I'm over," she said. "Washed up. Finished. I'm going to go down to Pima College and sign up for a pottery class."

Brandon got it. He and Diana had lived their married lives in a world that was half Anglo and half Indian. Rita Antone, Diana's housekeeper and nanny, had brought the Tohono O'odham people, traditions, and belief systems into their home right along with her beautifully crafted baskets. Some of those beliefs had to do with aging. Among the Desert People there came a time when old women were only good for making pots or baskets, and weaving baskets had never been Diana's long suit.

For the past several days, while Brandon had been grappling with the financial fallout from all this, Diana had gone into Tucson and signed up for a pottery-making class at Pima Community College.

The idea that she would simply turn her back on the problem had jolted him. It wasn't like her just to give up like that. That was a wake-up call for him, that things had progressed further than he'd been willing to admit.

Financially they'd be fine. Their house was fully paid for. Thank God, their kids were both through school. Yes, the economic downturn had hurt them, but much of the money they had set aside over the years was still there. Pam was still hoping to find an acceptable ghostwriter who might allow them to finagle the deal to keep a portion of the advance and of the royalties. That idea, however, was contingent on Diana's being willing to go out on the road to promote the book as though it were her own.

At first hearing that idea had sounded like a good deal, but Brandon wondered if it would work. By the time the pub date rolled around, would Diana be in any condition to deal with the rigors of a national tour or go out and do signings and interviews? Especially interviews.

Geet's eyes blinked open. He looked around in dismay for a moment, then focused on Brandon.

"Hey there," he said. "I must have dozed off. How long have you been here?"

"Not long," Brandon replied. "Just a couple of minutes."

In actual fact, it had been over an hour. One silent set of auto-racing laps had morphed into another, but Brandon had been too preoccupied to pay any attention to the muted announcer's narrative, which scrolled across the bottom of the screen.

"Where's Sue?" Geet's voice was whispery and hoarse, as though he needed to clear his throat but couldn't. His breath came in short, tortured gasps.

"She went out to run some errands."

"Good. She hardly ever gets out these days," Geet said. "This is real hard on her."

It's hard on you, too, Brandon thought. "Can I get you anything?" he asked. "Water? A soda?"

Geet shook his head. "Did Sue give you the box?"

Brandon patted it. "It's right here." He made as if to take the cover off, but Geet stopped him.

"Don't look at the contents now," Geet said. "You can do that later." He spoke in short sentences, as though anything longer was too much effort. "Right now we need to talk."

He punched a button that raised the head of the bed. Then he opened a drawer in the bedside table and took out a stack of envelopes. From the looks of them, most appeared to be greeting card envelopes. One was not. That was the one Geet handed to Brandon. There was no return address in the upper left-hand corner.

"I've been working Ursula Brinker's murder all my adult life," he said. "She was a kid when she got murdered. I had just signed on to my first law enforcement job. I was a campus cop at ASU. Ursula died in California—on a beach in San Diego during spring break. ASU was a real community in those days—a smaller community. She was a cute girl—an outstanding student—and everybody took it hard."

Brandon nodded. He knew it was true. He also knew much of this history, but he let Geet tell the story his own way.

"When Ursula's mother won that huge Mega Millions jackpot of lottery money and wanted to start The Last Chance, she came looking for me. Hedda Brinker wanted to help others, but bottom line, she wanted to help herself."

Geet paused for a spasm of coughing. Brandon waited until it passed. Geet took a sip of water before he continued.

"So I've been working Ursula's murder all along," he said.

"Any leads?" Brandon asked.

"When it came to 'alternate lifestyles' in 1959, you could just as well have been from another planet."

"What are you saying?" Brandon asked. "That Ursula was a lesbian?"

"I don't know that for sure. I've heard hints about it here and there, but nothing definitive. I've spoken to all the girls who went to San Diego on that spring-break trip, all but one, her best friend, June Lennox. Holmes is her married name. I've known where she lived for a long time, but she would never agree to speak to me before this."

That caused another spasm of coughing.

Brandon understood the issue. As a TLC operative without being a sworn police officer, Geet would have had no way of compelling a reluctant witness to cooperate.

"And you couldn't force the issue," Brandon said.

Geet nodded. "The letter came two months ago, just as I was going in for another round of surgery."

"You want me to read it?"

"Please."

The note on a single sheet of paper was brief:

Dear Mr. Farrell,

    It's time we talked. Please give me a call so we can arrange to meet.

Sincerely,
June Lennox Holmes

The 520 prefix on the phone number listed below her name meant that it was located somewhere in southern Arizona—or that it was a cell phone that had been purchased in southern Arizona.

"Did you talk to her?" Brandon asked as he folded the note and returned it to the envelope.

Geet shook his head. "I've been too sick," he said. "I thought that eventually I'd bounce back and be well enough to follow up myself. At least I hoped I would be, but that's not going to happen. This time there doesn't seem to be any bounce, and I need some answers, Brandon. I couldn't find them for Hedda, but maybe you can find them for me."

Opening the top of the brimming evidence box, Brandon put the envelope inside, then closed it again.

"So you'll do it?" Geet asked.

"I'll do my best," Brandon said.

"Don't take too long," Geet cautioned. "I don't have much time, but don't say anything about that to Sue. She doesn't know how bad it is."

Yes, she does, Brandon thought. *She knows, and so do you. Maybe it's time the two of you talked about it.*

Tucson, Arizona
Saturday, June 6, 2009, 2:00 P.M.
93° Fahrenheit

"Who was your company?" Lani *Dahd* asked her mother, as they left the house in Gates Pass and headed into Tucson. Mrs. Ladd was in the passenger seat, while Gabe had moved to the back and was listening to the conversation.

"What company?" Mrs. Ladd returned.

"I don't know," Lani said. "Gabe told me there was a man sitting and talking to you when we got to the house."

Frowning, Mrs. Ladd turned and looked questioningly at Gabe. Her eyes were a startling shade of blue, like the color of the blue jays that sometimes strutted around the yard. Her skin was surprisingly pale. Her silvery hair had been pulled back with a turquoise-studded comb.

"No one was there," Mrs. Ladd said after a long moment, turning back to Lani. "Just me. Gabe must have been mistaken."

Gabe was shocked. He wasn't mistaken. He had seen the man with his own eyes, and he was telling the truth. Lani *Dahd* and his parents always said it was important to tell the truth, no matter what. And he did. So why was it okay for Mrs. Ladd to lie and say that the man wasn't there when he had been?

Now that Gabe thought about that man again, the one who wasn't there, he realized one more thing about him. The man sitting across from Mrs. Ladd at her patio table was blind. He had to be. He had been sitting there staring up into the sky, looking directly at the sun. He couldn't have done that if he hadn't been blind already.

Gabe started to voice his objection and to insist once again that the man really had been there, but then Mrs. Ladd suddenly changed the subject.

"I'm going to sell the car," she announced.

"The Invicta?" Lani asked.

Invicta? What was that? Gabe knew the makes and models of lots of cars because they came through his father's auto-repair shop every day, but he had never heard of a car by that name. Maybe it was some brand-new car that people on the reservation didn't have yet. They mostly liked pickups. Invicta didn't sound like a pickup.

"But you love that car," Lani objected. "Why on earth would you sell it?"

"Do you want it?" Mrs. Ladd asked.

"No," Lani said. "On my salary, I could never afford to keep it in gas. Maybe Davy would like it."

Gabe knew that Davy was Lani's older brother. Gabe also knew that Davy and his wife were getting a divorce.

"I don't think so," Mrs. Ladd said. "He's already got two cars as it is."

"You still haven't said why you're getting rid of it," Lani insisted.

"I need the space in the garage," Mrs. Ladd said. "I want to turn that part of it into a studio. Do you know where I can get a pottery wheel?"

"A studio?" Lani repeated. "And a pottery wheel? Why would you want one of those?"

"Why do you think?" Mrs. Ladd said impatiently. "To make pots."

Gabe knew lots of old women who made pots. Well, maybe not lots, but several. That's what the Tohono O'odham said women were supposed to do when they got too old to do anything else—they were supposed to make pots. It seemed to him that Mrs. Ladd, with her white hair and pale skin, was already that old. As a result, Gabe didn't find the possibility of her making pots nearly as odd as her daughter did.

"Are you kidding?" Lani asked. "You've never done that before. Ever. Why would you start making pots now?"

"Yes, I did make pots once," Mrs. Ladd replied. "Back in Joseph. There were lots of artists there. Some of them even came to the high school and taught classes."

Gabe had no idea where Joseph was. It sounded far away. Maybe it was up by Phoenix.

"Does Dad know about this?" Lani asked with a frown.

"Yes," Mrs. Ladd said. "I told him."

As the two women in the front seat fell silent, Gabe

found himself drifting. He wondered if it was hard for Lani to be an Indian with Milgahn parents. It seemed to him that it made sense to have two parents that were the same kind—from the same tribe.

As they headed north on Silverbell toward Ina, the steady movement of the car and the accompanying silence got to be too much for him. Gabe's eyes fell shut, his chin dropped to his chest, and he fell asleep.

In his dream the man was there again, just as he had been earlier, sitting beside Mrs. Ladd's bright blue swimming pool. Only this time, something was different. Gabe wasn't alone on the patio. Lani *Dahd* was there with him.

And then the man spoke. "Why, I'll be," he said, turning his empty eyes away from the sun and toward the spot on the patio where Gabe and Lani stood side by side. "If it isn't Lani! Come over here and have a seat. I was hoping you'd drop by."

Sells, Tohono O'odham Nation, Arizona
Saturday, June 6, 2009, 5:00 P.M.
94° Fahrenheit

Delphina Escalante Enos stood in line at Bashas' while Rosemary Sixkiller ran the cartload of groceries through the register. Delphina's four-year-old daughter, Angelina, sat in the child seat of the cart clutching an open box of animal crackers. She munched them carefully, always biting off the heads first.

"You sure look happy," Rosemary observed.

Rosemary and Delphina had been school classmates, first at Indian Oasis Elementary and later at Baboquivari High School. Rosemary had graduated. Delphina had not. Pregnant at age fifteen, she had dropped out of school to have the baby. Then, when Angie was only two months old, Joaquin Enos, the baby's father, had run off to take up with someone else. For the better part of three years, Delphina and the baby had stayed on with Delphina's parents in Nolic, but her father was ill now—with diabetes—and having a busy baby underfoot was too hard on everyone.

Realizing she had to do better for her child, Delphina had earned her GED and had managed to get a job doing filing for the tribe. It was at work where she had met Donald Rios, a man who hailed from Komelik Village and who was also on the tribal council. His family had land and cattle.

By reservation standards, the Rios family was well-to-do. Their family compound consisted of four mobile homes set around a central courtyard—a concrete central courtyard. They also had their own well—one that was deep enough to work even in the dead of summer. That was unusual, too. Most of the time a well would belong to an entire village rather than to a single family. But it wasn't just Donald's comfortable circumstances that made him so appealing to Delphina.

Donald was everything that Joaquin Enos had never been. Donald was kind and caring. He had a job that he went to every day. He was responsible, and he loved Delphina and her baby to distraction. He never came to see

Delphina without bringing something for Angie—a toy or a book or a packet of stickers.

He was someone Delphina was comfortable with. That made far more sense to her than the fact that his family might have money. All his relatives—parents, brothers, and sisters—were reputable, churchgoing people—Presbyterians. As far as Delphina's own family was concerned, there were plenty of skeletons in those closets—people who had done bad and who were no longer mentioned at family gatherings.

But the other thing the Rios family had going for them was a strong connection to the old ways. Maybe it was just because they lived so close to I'itoi's home on Babo-quivari that they held to many of the old traditions. Delphina loved hearing Donald talk about his beloved old grandmother and how she had told him stories—the traditional I'itoi stories—when he was a little kid. Delphina liked to think that some time when it wasn't summer, he would tell those same stories to Angie, so she would know them, too.

Right then, though, standing in the checkout line in Bashas', Delphina beamed at Rosemary's comment. The clerk's assessment was true. Delphina Escalante Enos was happy—really happy—for the first time in her whole life.

"Donald is taking us to the dance at Vamori tonight," she admitted shyly, ducking her head as she spoke. "Both of us," she added, nodding in Angie's direction. "He was hinting around that there's something he wants to show us before we go to the dance."

"It's a full moon," Rosemary said. "Maybe he'll give you a ring."

Delphina nodded, but she didn't say anything aloud. An engagement ring was just what she wanted.

When Donald had stopped by her office on Friday afternoon, he had been teasing Delphina, trying to make her blush. He had told the other girls in the office, the ones Delphina worked with, that he had something special he wanted to show her on their way to the dance. After he left the office the girls had been talking, and they all seemed to think the same thing. Since Donald and Delphina had been going out for a couple of months, it made sense that it would be time for him to give her a ring.

"He's a nice guy," Rosemary said. "He comes in here a lot to buy food from the deli. I don't think he's a very good cook."

"I can cook," Delphina declared. "If we got married, he could buy the groceries and I would cook."

"Sounds like a good deal to me," Rosemary said.

They were quiet for a few moments while Rosemary packed Delphina's groceries into her cloth bags and then loaded them back into the shopping cart. By then Angelina was done with her box of animal crackers and wanted another one.

"No," Delphina said, shushing her whiny four-year-old. Then she turned back to Rosemary. "Are you coming to the dance, too?" Delphina asked when that job was finished.

The feast and dance at Vamori were always good ones, the best ones of the summer, people said, with plenty of food at the feast house and with a band playing chicken-scratch music from sunset to sunrise.

"I guess," Rosemary said. "At nine. After I get off work, if I'm not too tired."

Delphina took her groceries out to the parking lot and loaded them into the back of a battered old Dodge Ram pickup. Then she strapped Angie into her booster seat.

The truck wasn't much, but she was grateful to have it. Before Leo Ortiz, over at the gas station, sold it to her, she and Angie had been forced to walk back and forth to work and to the grocery store from their decrepit mobile home on the road to Big Fields. Walking there wasn't bad in the morning when it was cool, but after a long day at work, coming home in the afternoon heat had been hard, especially when Delphina had groceries to carry or when Angie was too tired to walk. Sometimes other people would give them rides, but most of the time they walked.

The pickup truck was something else Donald had done for Delphina. He was the one who made that happen. He and Leo Ortiz, the man who ran the garage in Sells, were good friends. Someone's old truck had broken down and been towed into Leo's garage. When Leo gave the owner the bad news about how much a new engine would cost, the guy had walked away—without bothering to pay for the towing.

Pickups were always in demand on the reservation, so Leo had gone ahead and put a new engine in the vehicle. He was getting ready to sell it when Donald asked if he would sell it to Delphina—on time. All she had to pay was one hundred dollars a month, and that's what she was doing. In another year, the truck would be all hers.

In the meantime, because she hadn't been able to buy insurance, she drove it only on the reservation, not in town.

By the time Delphina and Angie got home, the place was like an oven. She turned on the swamp cooler while she put away the groceries, then went into the bedroom—the coolest room in the house. Without having to be told, Angie had gone there to take a nap. After a moment's thought, Delphina joined her.

That's what you do the day before an all-night dance, Delphina thought as she drifted off. *You sleep in the afternoon so you don't get too tired.*

Much later, when Delphina woke up, she remembered the wonderful dream that had come to her while she was sleeping. In it, she and Donald were very old people who had been married for a long, long time. They were old but content.

And on that June afternoon, the thought of that made Delphina Escalante very happy. It seemed to her that with Donald Rios in her life, her future looked bright. Things were finally changing for the better.

Tucson, Arizona
Saturday, June 6, 2009, 4:00 P.M.
93° Fahrenheit

Jack Tennant counted his lucky stars that Abby had zero interest in golf. She wasn't interested in playing, didn't care where he played or with whom, and she never asked

questions about his rounds. Oh, he volunteered information on occasion, but only bits and pieces here and there.
Today he'd had plenty to do during his very busy morning, none of which involved golf, but he had a properly
filled out scorecard ready and waiting.

"I broke a hundred today," he told Abby proudly when
she came in from her trip to the beauty shop that day.
Abby insisted on calling the place she went a spa. It
seemed like a beauty shop to Jack. As far as he could
tell, the difference between the two meant that a spa was
more expensive.

"Did you?" she asked. "In all this heat?"

"Yup." He grinned, tossing the phony scorecard in her
direction. "Today Ralph, Wally, and Roy didn't stand
a chance. I took all three of them to the cleaners. But
you're right. It was hot as blue blazes out there. By the
time I got home I needed a shower in the worst way."

Ralph, Wally, and Roy were Jack's usual golf part-
ners. It was easy for him to beat them since they didn't
exist anywhere except as names on bogus scorecards he
had gathered from various public courses around town.
He called them his Phantom Foursome. As far as Abby
knew, he played golf with them at least three rounds a
week, usually with very early tee times.

Those faux golf games came in handy on days like
today, when Jack had needed several hours that were entirely his own. If you figured on two hours coming and
going, four and a half hours to play, on a slow day, and
another hour or so for lunch or a beer afterward, that's
how much time it took to be part of a foursome, which
Jack was not.

Oh, he liked golf well enough, but he wasn't into groups, not anymore. He'd cultivated a couple of good golf buddies once upon a time, long ago, but one of them had died of melanoma and another had put a bullet through his head. These days when Jack played golf, he tended to show up at various public courses without a reservation. He'd go out as a single attached with some other group. He played well enough to hold his head up, but he resisted being invited to play again. He preferred playing on his own, except for occasional times when he needed his imaginary pals to provide suitable cover. The fact that Abby never showed any interest in meeting them made it that much better.

He was about to ask how party preparations were going when Abby's cell phone rang. "It's Shirley again," Abby told him, glancing at the telephone readout. "She has a terrible case of opening-night jitters."

"She'll do fine," Jack said reassuringly.

"That's what I told her."

While Abby spoke to Shirley, Jack turned his phone back on. On golf mornings—even pretend golf mornings—he always turned his own phone off completely. On golf courses, Jack couldn't tolerate playing with guys who held up everybody else by gabbing on their cell phones. "Just leave me a message, if you need to," he had told Abby. "I'll turn the phone back on once we finish our round and call you back as soon as I can."

"Everything under control, I hope?" he asked when Abby ended the call.

She nodded. "I think so. At least I hope so. They're just used to having me around to run the show."

"And you will be again," Jack said, giving her a quick kiss in passing. "But today's our anniversary, and we're going to celebrate in style. Right now, though, I'm going outside to have a smoke. I won't ask if you'd care to join me," he added with a grin. "I know better."

"Oh, Jack," she said, wagging a finger at him in mock disapproval. "You really should give up that nasty habit."

"Why?" he returned with a sly grin. "I have no intention of living forever. Do you?"

"Well, no," she said.

"See there?" he asked. "I'm determined to enjoy the time I'm here, and I really like cigars."

"All right, then," she said resignedly. "Go smoke 'em if you've got 'em. Would you like me to mix up a batch of Bloody Marys while you're gone?"

"Please," he said. "I'd like that a lot."

Outside, in the shaded ramada Abby referred to as his "smoking room," Jack Tennant sat on a chaise longue and thought about the rest of the day. It had taken him months of time and plenty of effort to put his plan in place. Now it was.

Two days ago, when he told Abby that he had scheduled an event that would preempt her being able to attend the annual party at Tohono Chul, he had worried that there might be a major blowback from her. That certainly would have been the case with his first wife, the departed and not much lamented Irene. If he had presented her with a last-minute change of plans that would have disrupted something on Irene's calendar, all hell would have broken loose.

With Abby, however, that hadn't happened. That was one of the things Jack appreciated about this second-time-around marriage. Abby was flexible where Irene was not. And she actually liked surprises. Irene had hated them. Once Abby learned there was a conflict, she had simply brought Shirley to the plate as her party-supervising pinch hitter. No fuss, no muss.

Blowing a cloud of smoke in the air, Jack gave himself a silent pat on the back. He felt slightly guilty that Abby had gone to the trouble and expense of having her hair and nails done. In fact, she had hinted that Fleming's would do very nicely for dinner, but the truth was, where Jack was planning on taking her, no one was likely to notice her hair and nails—no one at all.

Yes, he thought. *This is going to blow her socks right off.*

4

Tucson, Arizona
Saturday, June 6, 2009, 4:00 P.M.
93° Fahrenheit

*J*ONATHAN HAD FOLLOWED Jack Tennant all day
long. Early that morning, thinking his mother's husband was on his way to a golf date, he had been surprised when, rather than stopping off at a nearby golf
course, the man had headed out of town. Jonathan was
new to Tucson. As the city limits fell behind them, he assumed they were heading for some upscale resort. When
they crossed into the reservation, he was even more
convinced. There was probably a casino somewhere up
ahead—a casino with a golf course.

Jonathan was careful to stay well back of Tennant's
vehicle. For as long as he and Esther had owned the min-

ivan, he had despised the silver color, but today, driving through the waves of heat on the blacktop, he knew that the vehicle was almost invisible from any distance away. It got hairy when they entered a small community named Sells. Worried that his target might turn off or stop, Jonathan closed the gap for a while, but once Tennant turned onto a secondary road heading south from Sells, it was possible to increase the distance again.

When Tennant went bouncing off onto a narrow dirt track, Jonathan drove a little farther before he, too, pulled over and stopped. Unsure where the dirt track would lead and worried about getting stuck, he simply waited. Fifteen minutes later, a cloud of dust told him Tennant was once again on the move. He came out of the brush and turned north. The fact that the Lexus had come and gone with no apparent difficulty made it seem likely that Jonathan would be able to do the same.

And he did, following Jack Tennant's tracks off into the desert where a small turnaround had been carved out of the brush. Stepping out into the blazing heat, Jonathan followed a series of footprints that beat a faint path into the brush. To his amazement, the trail was lined with a series of unlit luminarias. The pathway led to a small clearing where a table and two chairs had been set up as if in wait for some kind of dining experience. An unlit candelabrum sat in the center of the table, and place settings for two, including napkins, silverware, and glasses, had been carefully laid out on either side of the table.

Jonathan found this both fascinating and puzzling. He would have stayed longer to explore, but he wanted to get back on the road and follow Jack Tennant wherever else he might be going. Back in the moving Caravan, he disregarded the OPEN RANGE signs and roared down the road at speeds well over eighty miles per hour. Before he reached Sells, Tennant's Lexus was once again in clear view.

It took over an hour to make it back to Tucson. Jack stopped off at what appeared to be an upscale shopping center and did some grocery shopping before he returned to the house. By then Jonathan's arm was on fire. On the way back to the Tennants' town home, Jonathan spotted an Urgent Care facility.

Better one of those than an ER, he thought.

Once he saw Jack Tennant pull into the garage and park next to his wife's aging green Lincoln, Jonathan went back to Urgent Care to have someone look at his arm.

They did more than look. With a doc in a box supervising the procedure, a physician's assistant and a nurse lanced the wound, cleaned it, and then put the arm in a sling. They also gave Jonathan a prescription for a course of antibiotics. He gave the Urgent Care folks Jack Tennant's name and a phony social security number. When he went to the closest Walgreens to have the prescription filled, he wasn't at all surprised to find that they had Jack Tennant's name on file in their pharmacy.

"Do you want to leave this on express pay?" the clerk asked.

"Sure," Jonathan said. Sitting waiting for the prescription to be filled, it pleased him to think that his mother's husband's Medicare account would be billed for Jonathan's medications. He also doubted anyone would catch on to the switch for a very long time, if ever.

With his prescription in hand, Jonathan headed back to his observation post. On the way, though, he stopped at Sonic and stocked up on fast food. He didn't know how long he'd have to wait before he found out what was going on, but if Jack and Abby Tennant were planning on an intimate dinner date out in the desert, Jonathan was determined that there would be at least one uninvited guest in attendance.

Tucson, Arizona
Saturday, June 6, 2009, 4:30 P.M.
92° Fahrenheit

When Jack finished smoking his cigar, he went back inside the house. In the family room he found a tray loaded with drinks laid out on the counter in the wet bar. On it were glasses, a pitcher of premixed Bloody Marys, a bucket of ice, a bottle of Tabasco sauce, and a plate of celery sticks for stirring, as well as a dish of salted peanuts. The peanuts were for Jack. He loved them. The Tabasco sauce allowed them to season each drink to taste. Abby liked her Bloody Marys spicy enough that sweat would pop out on her forehead as she drank them. Jack preferred a somewhat milder recipe.

Jack found Abby sitting on the couch with her newly polished toes tucked up under her. She appeared to be lost in contemplation. He paused long enough to pour his own drink before joining her on the couch.

"A penny for your thoughts," he said, touching her glass with his.

She smiled at him. "Just remembering," she said. "Thinking about what my life was like five years ago."

"You remember that day, too?" he asked.

She nodded. "Every detail," she said. "I woke up that morning up to my eyelids in party problems. It was the first time I was completely in charge of the bloom party, and I was totally focused on that. For a change I was so busy doing other things that I was finally able to forget how much I hated being divorced. I believe it was the first time that ever happened."

"And you never saw this coming?" he asked, smiling at her. "You never saw us coming?"

"Never," she answered. "If I'd had an inkling of how much my life would change that day, I would have been more petrified about that than I was about the party. I might have been too nervous to get out of bed."

"I don't think so," Jack said, shaking his head. "You can't convince me you were scared of anything. The moment I saw you, I was smitten. I remember telling myself, *'Wow! There's one put-together lady. She's ten feet tall and bulletproof.'* "

Widowed for more than a year, Jack Tennant had stopped off in Tucson to visit his brother and sister-in-law as one of the last stops at the end of a year-long solitary road trip, one he told people he had taken in order to find himself.

Five years earlier, he and Irene had been on the brink of divorce when Irene's doctor had delivered the bad news—a diagnosis of ovarian cancer. Their health plan from his years in the insurance world was a good one, but it was tied to his retirement. Had they divorced, Irene's situation wouldn't have been covered.

Because of that, they had stuck it out. Or rather he had stuck it out until the bitter end. And it had been bitter. Irene had told him time and again during that time that if it hadn't been for the insurance coverage, she would have left him in a heartbeat. Having that thrown in his face while he'd been trying to be a good guy had hurt, and the hurt had been worse every time he heard it.

Once Irene was gone, he had sold the house in California—against everyone's advice about not making any kind of major decisions too soon after the death of his spouse. In the end it turned out Jack was right and everyone else was wrong. He had unloaded their property in Pasadena for a tidy bundle long before the economic downturn gutted the California real estate market. Then he put the money in the bank, bought himself a brand-new Lexus, and hit the road.

For the better part of the next year he was a vagabond, setting off on a grand-circle tour, visiting places on a whim and as weather permitted, crisscrossing the country and visiting all the interesting and quirky places Irene had never wanted to visit. She was especially opposed to anything resembling a tourist trap, as she called them.

In the course of his travels Jack had put 25,000 miles

on his no longer new Lexus. He had motored to Yosemite in California, Ashland and Crater Lake in Oregon, Mount St. Helens and the rain forests of western Washington, Yellowstone in Wyoming, Glacier in Montana, Zion in Utah, the Black Hills of South Dakota, the pristine lakeshore of upper Michigan, Niagara Falls, Independence Hall in Philadelphia, and the battlefield at Gettysburg; Washington, D.C.; Charleston, South Carolina; Branson, Missouri; the Alamo in Texas; as well as Albuquerque, Roswell, and Carlsbad Caverns in New Mexico.

He had called Zack from Albuquerque, just to say hello. He hadn't planned on stopping by to see him, but Zack had shamed him into it.

"If you're on your way back to California, we're right on the way."

That wasn't exactly true since Albuquerque was a lot farther north, but Jack had allowed himself to be persuaded mostly because he wasn't eager to get back to California. His kids still lived there, but Jack no longer did.

The fateful phone call had taken place toward the end of June. At the time Jack had known nothing about Zack's and Ruth's involvement with Tohono Chul. As docents they would have lots to do the night of the bloom party, but they didn't mention the possibility of a party on the phone when he gave them his ETA. In hindsight he now understood why that was—they hadn't known exactly when the party would take place because no one knew exactly when the night-blooming cereus would do its thing.

He had driven up to their house at nearly five o'clock

on a very hot June afternoon. Zack and Ruth had ushered him and his suitcases into the house. Then, after a little bit of small talk and giving him half an hour to shower and change clothes, they had loaded him into the car to go to the park to, of all things, a flower show.

At least that's how Jack understood it. Jack Tennant had learned several things about himself during his months of solo traveling. Irene had always loved flowers—all kinds of flowers—but Jack didn't much care for them. His low opinion about them hadn't improved, not after visiting the Rose Festival in Portland, Oregon, nor after seeing the autumn leaves in New England and the cherry blossoms in Washington, D.C. So although Jack had no interest in flowers and wasn't particularly excited about the one they were raving about, he behaved as a polite guest should and went along for the ride.

Once inside Tohono Chul, Zack had raced off to make sure the luminarias that lined the park's dirt paths that night stayed lit. Ruth had a job to do, too, in the gift shop, so she handed Jack a glass of punch and introduced him to Abby Southard. Then his sister-in-law had taken off, leaving Jack and Abby chatting.

Not long after that, a rotund old Indian man dressed in boots, jeans, and a splashy black cowboy shirt took to the microphone. For the next half hour he regaled the people in the audience with a story—a Native American legend—about the supposed origin of the flower in question. Since Jack had yet to see a night-blooming cereus with his own eyes, he supposed this was a lot of fuss over nothing.

As this grown-up version of story time ended, one of the volunteers had hurried up to notify Abby Southard that they were about to run out of punch and ice. She had no more than dispatched someone to the nearest grocery store to handle that crisis when a frantic guest had appeared with the disturbing announcement that a rattlesnake seemed to have taken up residence close by one of the blooms.

On the way to the park, Zack had explained that Tohono Chul was devoted to preserving native desert flora. It was only natural, then, that the park would preserve some of the local fauna as well. Without turning a hair, Abby explained to Jack that rattlesnakes were as likely to show up at the Queen of the Night party as people were. Then she used a handheld walkie-talkie to summon a man with a snake-stick to take charge of the offending reptile and move it to a somewhat less traveled part of the park.

Jack had been intrigued. He had never met a woman who could handle both a punch crisis and a rattle-snake crisis at the same time. Irene had been petrified of snakes—and lizards and spiders and bees and wasps. By comparison Abby had seemed downright fearless, and good-humored besides.

"So you have to wrangle both the punch bowl and the rattlesnakes?" he had asked.

"Yup," she said with a grin. "That's me all over."

Fascinated, Jack had spent most of the rest of the evening hanging out with her, and it was with Abby Southard at his side that he had seen his first-ever night-blooming cereus. Truth be told, he wasn't that impressed—with the flower, that is. Oh, he managed a polite ooh and aah over the size of it and over the smell—which didn't do that much for him, either, but he could see that Abby was enchanted with the night-blooming cereus, and he was enchanted with her.

He made like the old woman in the Indian legend and put down roots right away. After only two nights in Zack and Ruth's guest room, he had taken himself off to one of those corporate long-term-stay hotels, the kind that come furnished with everything from sheets and pillows (bad ones) to pots, pans, and dishes.

Zack thought paying rent was a bad idea. He said that if Jack was going to stay around Tucson, he ought to find himself a real condo to buy, maybe one on a golf course. But Jack had no interest in going on a real estate hunt. He had set his sights on some other prey, and Abigail Southard was it. Because she came with a perfectly nice home of her own, he saw no need to fork over money to buy another. He figured two would be able to live as cheaply as one, especially if they had more money in the bank.

Jack Tennant and Abby Southard had met on the twenty-sixth of June and had married on the twenty-sixth of July. Everyone had told them it was stupid to jump into matrimony that way. Zack and Ruth had both disapproved, and so had Abby's older sister, Stephanie.

"What's the big rush?" Zack had asked. "I mean, at your age, it's not as if you knocked her up or something."

Emmy and Lonnie, Jack's own forty-something kids, hadn't much liked the arrangement, either. They had both been invited to the justice of the peace ceremony, and both had declined. Jack suspected that Abby's son, Jonathan, would have taken much the same position, but he had been estranged from his mother for years—in fact, he hadn't spoken to her in over a decade. The good news there was that Jack and Abby hadn't had to deal with Jonathan's disapproval along with everyone else's.

All the naysayers were still nay-saying, waiting for the "hurried" marriage to end in disaster. In the process Zack and Ruth Tennant had pretty much removed themselves from Jack and Abby's circle of friends. They had even gone so far as to sever their connections with Tohono Chul, including resigning their docent positions. Abby had worried about that, but their departure hadn't fazed Jack.

"So much for what the relatives think," he had told her with a grin. "If they can't take a joke, screw 'em. The only thing that matters is what you and I think. By the time we met, both of us were old enough to understand we don't have all the time in the world. Let's make hay while the sun shines."

And they had done so. On the fifth anniversary of their meeting and one month short of their fifth wedding anniversary, the two of them were as happy as they had ever been. They were better matched, too—better matched than Jack had been with Irene, once he retired, and than Abby had ever been with Hank.

Irene hadn't been that bad initially, he reminded himself. When Jack had been a young hotshot executive, working his way up, she had been a powerhouse. She had been a good mother to his two now grown children. When the kids were little and Jack was putting in the long hours at work, Irene had been the parent who had done most of the child rearing. By the time the kids were out of the house, however, and once Jack retired, he and Irene had discovered that they had nothing in common. Not only had they fallen out of love, they had fallen out of like as well.

For Abby and Jack Tennant, love really was lovelier the second time around. When they were out in public and holding hands, people sometimes said they were cute. That didn't bother Jack, either. He still felt like a damned newlywed, and he didn't care who knew it.

Then there was the matter of quiet. The two of them had been sitting there for some time, sipping their drinks in companionable silence while watching several hummingbirds buzzing around the colorful feeder Abby had hung in the mesquite tree outside their front door. It seemed to Jack that Irene had never had a quiet, introspective moment in her life. There were the times when she had given him the silent treatment—sometimes for days on end—but that was always the calm before the storm when some big blowup was brewing. It wasn't a comfortable silence so much as an ominous one.

During the time Jack had been alone and in the years since he and Abby had been together, Jack had come to relish times like these when simply being in the same room together was enough.

"What time is our reservation?" Abby asked, emerging from her own reverie and breaking into Jack's.

"We should probably leave around six," he said. "It'll take an hour to get there."

"What should I wear?"

In fact, Jack had already handled that issue. Abby had a jumpsuit that she'd had made to use for outdoor workday events at Tohono Chul. Jack had smuggled that, along with Abby's pair of hiking boots, into the trunk, along with the packed hamper and cooler. Hiking or work clothes would be far better suited for what he had in mind than some dress-up outfit that would snag on the first bit of mesquite that got in Abby's way, but telling her that would give the game away. Jack was determined to keep the secret until the very last minute.

"As long as you wear the blindfold," he said, "you can wear anything you want."

Abby had one of those beauty-mask things for sleeping, one that would fit over her ears without messing up her hair. He had told her in advance that the blindfold was essential.

"I thought you were kidding about that."

"Nope," he said. "Not kidding."

Abby gave him a kiss and then stood up. "All right," she said. "I think I'll go have a little lie-down. A nap would be good for what ails me."

"Mind if I join you?" Jack asked.

"You're welcome, as long as you're there to sleep. No funny business."

"Of course," he said, but he had his fingers crossed when he said it.

As he followed Abby back to the bedroom, he suspected she knew that all along.

Casa Grande, Arizona
Saturday, June 6, 2009, 4:00 P.M.
96° Fahrenheit

Geet was asleep again and Brandon was dozing on the sofa when Sue Farrell came back home. She looked like a new woman. Instead of going to see a movie, she had stopped off for a haircut. She looked altogether better.

"How are things?" she asked anxiously. "I was gone longer than I planned."

"Once he woke up, we talked for the better part of an hour," Brandon told her. "After that he went back to sleep."

She nodded. "An hour of conversation is about as much as he's good for. Did he ask for more pain meds?"

"No," Brandon said. "He said they make him too groggy."

"Being groggy is better than being in pain," Sue said.

Of course that was a matter of opinion. For right now, Brandon Walker was willing to take Geet Farrell's word for it over Sue's.

Brandon lugged the Ursula Brinker evidence box out of the house and loaded it into the back of his Honda CRV. It was a relief to get out of the sickroom—to walk away from the hopelessness and heartbreak that was everywhere in Geet and Sue Farrell's home. He started the engine. As he waited for the air-conditioning to cool things off enough so he could touch the steering wheel, Brandon thought about checking in with Diana, but then he remembered she wasn't home. Lani had called last night to invite her mother along to Tohono Chul for lunch, after which they would hang around the park for the major evening do, held each year in honor of the night-blooming cereus.

Brandon had two reasons to be happy about that. Number one: It meant that Diana would be out of the house and doing something fun for a change. Number two: He, Brandon, didn't have to go along. He'd had tea on occasion at Tohono Chul's Tea Room, and it wasn't his kind of place. As for the party? That wasn't his kind of thing, either. The people there would see to it that Diana was treated as a visiting dignitary, and that was fine, but there were times when Brandon could take only so much of being Mr. Diana Ladd.

Thinking about the Tea Room, however, reminded Brandon that he hadn't eaten since breakfast. It was now almost four o'clock in the afternoon—a very long way past his usual late-morning lunchtime. Once he left Geet and Sue's neighborhood, he found himself on one of Casa Grande's larger multi-lane streets. He drove past the first Burger King he saw without even slowing down, choosing instead to pull in at a Mexican food joint called Mi Casa Ricardo.

It was the kind of place Brandon Walker liked—family-owned and unpretentious. He ordered iced tea, a cheese crisp, and carne asada fajitas. He knew he was ordering too much food, but he counted on having some leftovers to take home to Damsel, who firmly believed that restaurant doggie bags had been invented solely for her benefit.

His cell phone rang as he took the first bite of cheese crisp. "How was it?" Ralph Ames asked.

Brandon knew Ralph wasn't referring to the cheese

crisp. Brandon had called Ralph in Seattle as soon as he had received Sue Farrell's phone call summoning him to Casa Grande.

"Pretty rough," he said.

"How long do you think he has?" Ames asked.

"Not long," Brandon answered. "He's put up a hell of a fight, but we're down to short strokes. I'd say a couple of weeks at the most. Maybe only days."

"I had been planning to come down to Arizona the end of next week," Ralph said. "I'll see if I can move that up some. I'd like to see him before it's too late."

"He gave me the Brinker file," Brandon said.

"Good," Ralph said. "I expected that he would. You're the logical successor on that one. Weeks ago Geet mentioned that he had a new lead. I know he was hoping he'd be able follow up on it himself, but of course—"

"Right," Brandon said. "The clock wound down before he had a chance. I told him I'd look into it right away. There's nothing I'd like better than to tell Geet in person that we finally have some answers."

"Amen," Ralph Ames said. "I know that would mean more to him than anything else you could possibly do."

"I'll do my best," Brandon said.

Tucson, Arizona
Saturday, June 6, 2009, 5:00 P.M.
92° Fahrenheit

Even though it was more than an hour early, by five o'clock Bozo was parked in front of the door that led to the garage. When it came time for Dan to leave, the dog wasn't taking any chances on his being forgotten, and he wasn't.

When Dan saw K-9 units on *Cops,* the dogs always rode in the backseat. Not in Dan Pardee's world. The dog that had saved his life was front and center. Well, front and rider's side. As they headed out to the reservation, Bozo rode with his head hanging out the window. It was a lot hotter to ride with the window open, but Dan was happy to do it. Bozo deserved that and more.

First they stopped by Motor Pool and filled up with gas. Then they headed out onto the reservation. Just east of Sells the highway climbed over a low pass. Each time he drove down the far side and saw the high school campus and the town of Sells spread out in front of him, Dan was always surprised by how alien he felt. When he had signed on with the Shadow Wolves he had imagined that being an Indian working on a reservation would make things simple—that this was a place where he would finally fit in. And that was true—he did fit in with his unit, with the Shadow Wolves themselves, but he didn't fit in on this particular reservation any more than he had fit on the San Carlos.

On the San Carlos the difficulty had stemmed from

the fact that Dan was only half Apache. On the Tohono O'odham, it was because he was any Apache at all. His last name didn't give it away. After all, Pardee was his father's name, an Anglo name. But in almost no time at all, the people who lived there had figured out that Dan's mother had been Apache. Just his manner of speech gave him away. Among the Tohono O'odham being Apache was not okay—definitely not okay.

In the old days, the various Apache tribes—and there were several—had lived by their wits, raiding other tribes of what they had grown and gathered. It was no accident that in the vocabularies of any number of the Southwest Nations the word for "enemy" and the word for "Apache" were one and the same.

In an effort to fit in and to know something about his surroundings, Dan had bought himself a worn paperback copy of an English/Papago dictionary. The faded red-covered volume was seriously outdated because the Tohono O'odham had stopped referring to themselves as Papagos several decades earlier.

It was in perusing the dictionary and trying to teach himself some of the necessary place names that Dan had learned that as far as the Tohono O'odham were concerned, the all-encompassing Apache/enemy word was *ohb*.

Once the reservation gossip mill managed to spread the information that the new Shadow Wolf, the one with the dog—*gogs*—was *ohb*, Dan got the message. Bozo, the *gogs*, was okay. As for the human with him? Not so much.

They arrived in Sells in the broiling late-afternoon

heat. Dan parked his green-and-white Ford Expedition in the shade of a mesquite tree at the far end of the parking lot in the town's only shopping center.

Dan had no qualms about rolling down the windows and leaving Bozo alone inside the vehicle while he went into the grocery store. Bozo had an unerring understanding of who constituted a threat and who did not. Little kids who came by the Expedition to say hello to Bozo or give him a pat on the nose ran the very real risk of being kissed on the ear or slobbered on. If a bad guy happened to venture too close to the vehicle, however, he might well lose a hand or a finger.

Inside the store, Dan gathered a few items including two ham sandwiches—one for him and one for Bozo—a couple of bags of chips, two Cokes, and several bottles of water. Those would give him enough calories and help keep him alert through the long nighttime hours—hopefully long empty hours—before his shift ended at six the next morning.

Even though the line at Rosemary Sixkiller's register was longer than the other ones, Dan went through hers anyway. Of all the clerks in the store, she was the only one who was consistently nice to him.

"There's a dance at Vamori tonight," she told him as she rang up his items. She gave the ham sandwiches a disapproving shake of the head as she put them in the bag. "You know you could go to the feast house there instead of eating these. They're probably old."

Dan had checked the sell-by date on the package, and Rosemary was correct. The sandwiches were right at the end of their sell-by date. He also knew she was teasing him about the dance. That was one of the reasons he always stopped at her register. To Dan Pardee's ear, "Sixkiller" didn't sound like a Tohono O'odham name. He suspected that Rosemary, like Dan, wasn't one hundred percent T.O., or maybe even any percent. He appreciated the fact that she didn't seem scared of him and that she joked around with him a little, even though they both knew why he wouldn't be showing his Apache face at a Tohono O'odham feast house anytime soon.

"Can't," he said. "I'm working."

Which was more or less the truth. Other Shadow Wolves did stop by feast houses now and then. Chatting with the locals gave the officers a chance to learn about what was going on in any given neighborhood— what people might have seen that was out of the ordinary, including the presence of any unfamiliar vehicles coming or going. Because the Tohono O'odham's ancestral lands had been cut in two by the U.S./Mexican border, those strange vehicles often belonged to smugglers of various stripes and were, as a consequence, of interest to Homeland Security. Dan knew better than to try using the feast-house chitchat routine. He was the ultimate outsider here. What he found out about activities in his sector he had to find out the hard way—by personal observation.

Leaving the store with his small bag of groceries, Dan found two little girls standing outside the Expedition feeding bits of popcorn to a very appreciative Bozo.

When Dan walked up to the vehicle, however, the two girls ducked their heads and sidled away without speaking to him or even acknowledging his presence.

Yup, he told himself. *Daniel Pardee, the ultimate outsider.*

"Okay," he said aloud to Bozo. "Let's go to work."

Bozo looked at him, thumped his tail happily, and grinned his goofy canine grin.

With that they headed out of town, driving south toward the village of Topawa and then, beyond that, along the west side of the Baboquivari Mountains. Baboquivari itself, Waw Giwulk, or Constricted Rock, was an amazing rock monolith that towered over the surrounding flat desert landscape.

Driving through the pass just east of Sells always left Dan with the sense that he was a foreigner, but when he drove past Waw Giwulk, Baboquivari, his apartness seemed to melt away. That odd sensation puzzled him. He had no idea why that would be. He understood that Baboquivari was the legendary home of I'itoi, the Tohono O'odham's Elder Brother. As such, it seemed to him that the mountain should have rejected Dan Pardee in the same way the people did.

Strange as it seemed even to him, he always had the weird idea that I'itoi was somehow welcoming him home. The same feeling washed over him that Saturday afternoon. How was it possible that he seemed to belong here in this wild stretch of untamed Sonora Desert in a way he belonged nowhere else?

Finally, however, he came to his senses. "What was I thinking?" he asked his partner, Bozo. "I must be making it up. I'itoi would never throw out the welcome mat for someone like me, not for an *ohb*."

Bozo loved the sound of Dan's voice. He thumped his tail happily. It wasn't a very satisfying response, but under the circumstances it was the best Dan could hope for.

"Sounds like you're of the same opinion," he said, giving Bozo's head a fond pat. "For some reason we both belong here."

5

*W*HEN BRANDON RETURNED to the house in Gates Pass, he pulled into the garage and parked his CRV next to Diana's hulking Tampico red Buick In-victa convertible. She had told him just that morning that she intended to sell it—that she wanted him to take it up to Barrett Jackson, the collector car auction place in Scottsdale, to see what he could get for it.

The idea that she was even thinking about unloading her treasured car had come as a real shock to him. The old Buick convertible had been little more than a wreck when Diana had won it at a charity auction, and she had paid good money for Leo Ortiz to bring the vehicle back from the dead. Now it was a real collector's item, all spit and polish and complete with custom-made red and white imitation leather seats that were unashamed copies of the factory originals.

If she went through with that idea, Brandon doubted Diana would get as much as she expected from selling her pride and joy, but still, why do it? Even with their book-contract difficulties, it wasn't as if they needed the money. They didn't.

When Brandon stepped inside the back door, Damsel greeted him ecstatically. Despite years of lobbying on Brandon's part, Diana continued to regard pet doors as magnets for other unwanted critters. Damsel had been left inside for so long that she went racing outside without even noticing the doggie bag containing Brandon's leftover fajitas. Once she was back inside and downing her treat, Brandon lugged Geet Farrell's box into his study and set it on his desk.

Once upon a time the room had been a treasure trove of mementos from Brandon's law enforcement days. There had been photos of him meeting various dignitaries, including one of him shaking hands with President Nixon. Nixon may have left office in disgrace, but Brandon still had a soft spot in his heart for the man who had campaigned for office as a "law and order" candidate.

And maybe part of Brandon's fondness for Nixon came from his own understanding of disgrace, because a similar fate had befallen Sheriff Brandon Walker. Richard Nixon had been brought low by that pesky group of "plumbers." Brandon's downfall had come about due to his two ne'er-do-well sons, Tommy and Quentin, who had never given their father anything but heartbreak.

And the truth was, Quentin had been more at fault than Tommy ever was. Tommy hadn't lived long enough to grow into anything worse than an overgrown juvenile delinquent. When he disappeared, Brandon and Diana had assumed he had simply run away. Instead, he had died years earlier while on a grave-robbing expedition out on the reservation. His parents might never have learned the truth about their son's disappearance if it hadn't been for Mitch Johnson's attack on Lani, which had led to the discovery of Tommy's skeletal remains.

Quentin, on the other hand, had lived long enough to become a genuine criminal. His involvement in a prison-based protection racket had been an important component in Brandon's losing his bid for reelection to the office of sheriff. And later on, when Quint was paroled from prison for the second time, things had gotten worse instead of better.

While imprisoned in Florence, Quentin had come under the spell of not one but two crazed killers, both of them sworn enemies of Brandon Walker and Diana Ladd. Diana had helped her friend, Rita Antone, see to it that a former English professor named Andrew Philip Carlisle had gone to prison for the murder of Rita's granddaughter, Gina. Brandon had done the same thing for a remorseless killer named Mitch Johnson, who liked to go out into the desert and use illegal immigrants for target practice.

Incarcerated together in the Arizona State Prison at

Florence, Carlisle and Johnson had hatched a complicated program of revenge against Brandon and Diana. Quentin, most likely without realizing what their real motives were, had somehow been drawn into their vortex. The last time Quentin set foot in his father's house, he had come there with the newly paroled Mitch Johnson, who was operating as Andrew Carlisle's proxy. Functioning in a drug-addled stupor, Quentin had vandalized his father's office, smashing his keepsakes and a lifetime's worth of mementos. Quentin had done all that without realizing that he and his adopted sister, Lani, were the real targets in Mitch Johnson's scheme.

In the pitched battle that followed, Lani had managed to save herself, and she had tried to save Quentin as well, but he had been badly injured. Over the next several years, Quentin's physical condition had deteriorated, step by step, into a situation where he had become hooked on prescription medications and had died as a result of an accidental overdose.

Long before that, though, when Brandon and Diana were still dealing with the immediate crisis, Diana had offered to have the broken plaques and photos repaired and reframed. But Brandon had refused. He was done with all that. Repairing the damage would have hurt more than letting all that stuff go. Instead, Diana had done a makeover, one that included new paint and a new desk and, eventually, more of Diana's burgeoning collection of baskets.

And that was fine with Brandon, even though collecting baskets was Diana's passion, not his. He could look at them impassively and not be reminded of what he continued to regard as his greatest failure in life—his sons.

That was one of the reasons the month of June bothered him so much these days—because of Father's Day. He had done all right with his stepson, Davy, and with Lani, his adopted daughter. And then there was Brian Fellows, Tommy and Quentin's half brother, who had worshipped Brandon from afar, sopping up the fatherly crumbs Quentin and Tommy had disdained, and who was now one of the Pima County Sheriff's Department's senior detectives in his own right.

Taking Lani and Davy and Brian into consideration, maybe Brandon Walker wasn't a complete failure in the fatherhood department—just where his own biological offspring were concerned.

Even so, remembering Tommy and Quentin was something that hurt him every day—every single day of the year—Father's Day or not.

Finally, in order to banish the old insecurities, Brandon sat down at the desk and opened the banker's box. Before he made any effort to contact the woman who had written to Geet, he needed to familiarize himself with as much of the case as possible.

Plucking a pair of reading glasses out of the top desk drawer, he reached into the box, pulled out the first document he found there, and began to read.

Sells, Tohono O'odham Nation, Arizona
Saturday, June 6, 2009, 8:00 P.M.
79° Fahrenheit

As Dan drove along the highway south of Sells, he examined the occupants of every vehicle he met and every one he passed. Most of the southbound cars were fully occupied with Indians and were headed for the dance. Among the ones coming north, Dan saw nothing out of line. He recognized the vehicles as belonging to people from nearby villages. They were headed into Sells to shop or into Tucson for the same reason.

South of Topawa, the Anglo name of a village called Gogs Mek, or Burnt Dog, the narrow paved road gave way to rough gravel. Here and there, the tan rocky dirt along the roadway was punctuated by *ho'ithkam*—ironwood trees, *kukui u'us*—mesquite trees, and low-lying *shegoi*, greasewood or creosote bushes.

Dan practiced his self-imposed vocabulary lessons as he drove, not because he thought speaking the language would win him acceptance on the reservation but because he wanted to prove to himself that he could do it.

When Micah Duarte had brought him home to San Carlos, Dan had resisted all of his grandfather's efforts to teach him Apache. Now Dan studied Tohono O'odham on his own. It was a means of seeking forgiveness, not from Gramps. Micah Duarte had never expected or demanded such a thing. No, Dan Pardee was seeking forgiveness for himself from himself. That was a lot more difficult to come by.

He passed the tiny village of Komelik, which, roughly translated, means Low Flat Place. Compared to the mountains jutting up out of the desert to the left of the road, this was low and flat and mostly deserted. After that, every time a set of tire tracks veered off the road and out into the desert, Dan stopped the Expedition, got out of the vehicle and examined the story left behind in the dust and dirt. Months of patient study had allowed him to put many of the resulting tire tracks together with the people who drove individual vehicles.

The track with the half-bald front tire belonged to a vehicle that had been permanently knocked out of alignment when the driver, an old man named James Juan, had struck a cow on the open-range part of the highway near Quijotoa, a bastardization of Giwho Tho'ag, or Burden Basket Mountain. Dan spotted the tracks of a pickup hauling a livestock trailer. That, no doubt, belonged to Thomas Rios, who along with his son successfully ran several head of cattle on a well-managed family plot of land near Komelik.

The tires on the small sedan probably belonged to the Anglo man Dan had seen hanging around on several occasions lately—mostly when he was working day shift. The guy drove a white Lexus—not exactly reservation-style wheels—but he was always alone, always drove the speed limit, and never failed to pass along a friendly wave. One of the other Shadow Wolves had talked to the guy. He was evidently some kind of naturalist doing research in the desert with Thomas Rios's full knowledge and approval.

Today the Anglo man had driven off into the desert and then had come back out again, but so had another vehicle, one whose tracks Dan didn't recognize. That one, too, had turned off the road and then come back. So it might be worthwhile to check into that later, but right now he wanted to head on south.

After the Gadsden Purchase divided the Tohono O'odham's ancestral lands, the Desert People had pretty much ignored the international border, crossing back and forth at will, especially at a place on the reservation known as The Gate. All that had changed in the aftermath of 9-11. As border security tightened in other places, immigration and smuggling activities had multiplied on the reservation, bringing with it far more official scrutiny from Homeland Security, most especially from the Border Patrol.

Now, as Dan Pardee did every other time he was on night shift, he drove to The Gate first. Then, during the course of the night and the remainder of his shift, he would work his way back north.

Sells, Tohono O'odham Nation, Arizona
Saturday, June 6, 2009, 7:30 P.M.
79° Fahrenheit

Donald Rios had told Delphina that he'd come by the house in Sells at seven to pick them up and go to the dance. By six, Delphina was showered and dressed. By six-thirty, she had bathed Angie, dressed her, and carefully braided her daughter's straight black hair. Then Delphina sat back to worry while Angie settled in to watch *Dora the Explorer* on the TV set in the living room.

Maybe he won't come, Delphina worried as she sat at the kitchen window and stared out at the empty yard. *Maybe he'll stand us up.*

That belief, of course, was a holdover from her days with Joaquin Enos, who had never been a man of his word. With Joaquin, even the smallest promise was made to be broken. He had been handsome enough to appeal to a fifteen-year-old and had thought nothing of knocking her up, but he hadn't wanted to have anything to do with her or Angie once the baby was born.

So now all of Delphina's old insecurities kicked in: What if Donald didn't come after all? She had already told Angie that they were going to the dance. Would they have to go alone? Was there enough gas in the pickup to make it all the way to Vamori and back? When the clock turned over seven o'clock and Donald still wasn't there, Delphina plunged into a fit of disappointment. He wasn't coming. All men were just alike, and Donald Rios was as bad as the rest of them.

Then, at a quarter to eight, almost an hour after he was supposed to be there and after Delphina had already given Donald Rios up for lost, he drove into her yard. She had the porch light on and she could see that his Chevy Blazer was shiny and freshly washed. With all the dust in the air, people on the reservation considered the act of washing a car either as an exercise in futility or as a deliberate rain dance.

When he knocked, Angie abandoned her pal Dora and went racing to the door to let him in. Donald Rios was a large man. Standing on the shaky wooden step outside Delphina's door, he looked more than a little silly in his dress-up boots and shirt, holding a child's pink-and-yellow pinwheel in one hand and a wilted handful of grocery-store flowers in the other.

"Sorry I'm so late," he said with an apologetic smile, handing the pinwheel to Angie and the flowers to Delphina. Angie took her present and raced back to the TV set with barely a thank-you while Delphina opened the door and ushered him inside.

"Indian time?" she asked, accepting the proffered flowers. She didn't have a proper vase, so she put the flowers in a water glass and set them on the kitchen counter.

Donald laughed sheepishly. "I had to do something for my mother," he said. "If it had been real Indian time I would have been a lot later. Are you ready to go?"

Delphina nodded.

"*Oi g hihm*," Donald called to Angie. "Let's go."

He didn't need to say so twice. Pinwheel in hand, Angie came on the run, ready to do just that—clamber into his Blazer and go.

Tucson, Arizona
Saturday, June 6, 2009, 6:00 P.M.
81° Fahrenheit

Jack Tennant was relieved when Abby emerged from the bedroom wearing a turquoise-colored pantsuit and a pair of sandals. He wouldn't have objected if she'd turned up in a dress and heels, but he knew the slacks would make for an easier wardrobe change when it came time to slip on the jumpsuit. Abby still had a fair amount of midwestern modesty about her. Stripping down and getting naked or nearly naked in the middle of nowhere wouldn't come easily.

That wasn't to say it wouldn't ever happen. With women you never could tell. Jack had the air mattress along just in case his powers of persuasion outstripped Abby's objections. After their sweet afternoon nap interlude, what they did later on that evening to celebrate their anniversary was no longer such a pressing issue, at least not as far as Jack was concerned.

When they got in the car, Jack insisted that Abby put on the blindfold, and she was a good sport about it. Hoping to keep their destination secret for as long as possible, he headed west on I-10 toward Marana rather than going south through town. In Marana he turned off on Sandario Road. That was as much as Abby could take.

"I can't stand this anymore," she said, whipping off the blindfold. "Where in the world are you taking me?"

The jig was up.

"To the reservation," he said. "Out beyond Sells."

"But there aren't any restaurants—" She stopped abruptly because she got it. "You found one, didn't you," she said accusingly, but beaming as she spoke. "You found a night-blooming cereus out in the desert somewhere. That's where we're going!"

Jack nodded, because Abby was right, up to a point. After months of using his phantom foursome to cover his activities, after asking and gaining permission to explore various people's lands both on the reservation and off it, Jack hadn't found just "a night-blooming cereus." He believed he had found what might be the granddaddy of them all!

The deer-horn cacti on display at Tohono Chul sometimes had as many as seven or eight blooms on them. This one, an old giant that had wound its way up into an ironwood tree, had at least a hundred buds on it. Jack had been afraid something would go wrong. Maybe the plants growing in the wild would be on a different schedule from the ones in captivity, as it were. So he had come out and checked on the buds on his plant and then had made secret visits to Tohono Chul to make sure the buds there seemed to be progressing along the same schedule. And they had. They were.

He was sure that tonight when the flowers bloomed in the garden, the ones in the desert would be blooming as well. There, hundreds of people would be in attendance. Here, there would be only Jack and Abby and maybe Thomas Rios's son, Donald, who was about to become engaged himself. When Thomas had told him about that and asked if Jack would mind if Donald and Delphina stopped by for a little while to see the flowers, Jack hadn't had the heart to object. After all, this was Thomas Rios's land to begin with.

"Absolutely," he had said heartily. "The more the merrier."

And he had meant it, too. He had made sure there was enough food for everyone and extra dishes and silverware just in case. He worried a little about the wine. He knew you weren't supposed to have liquor on the reservation, so he might wait to pour that until after Donald and his girlfriend left to go to a dance. There would be a full moon tonight. There would be plenty of time for him and Abby to savor the flowers, the night, and the claret.

Abby reached over and gently lifted Jack's hand off the steering wheel. She held the back of it to her lips, kissed it, and then returned it to the steering wheel.

"Thank you," she said. "You really are a remarkable man."

Jack smiled at her. "Words to warm a man's heart," he said.

"But how did you manage to pull this off? Did someone find it for you?"

"Don't expect me to tell you all my secrets," he said. "I may want to surprise you again sometime."

Smiling, she leaned back in the seat and closed her eyes. The nap they had both missed this afternoon was starting to catch up with her. Truth be told, it was catching up with Jack as well, but he hummed a few bars of their special song, *"Solamente Una Vez,"* to keep himself awake.

Everyone else knew the song as something schmaltzy

about the Thousand Guitars, but a young dark-eyed singer with a local mariachi band had translated it for them that night after they had stood before the justice of the peace: "Only once in a lifetime does the light of love fall across your garden path."

And tonight the garden is the desert, Jack Tennant thought. *And the light of love will be a full moon.*

So while Abby slept, Jack drove. She snored a little, but he was far too much of a gentleman to tell her that.

It's one of our little secrets, he thought to himself. He was incredibly grateful that, at their supposedly advanced ages, there was still enough room in their lives to have secrets. And fun. For a moment, and it was only a moment, Jack felt a fleeting bit of wistfulness for poor Irene, because she hadn't lived long enough to find that out. Even if she had lived long enough, he suspected Irene never would have figured out the fun part.

That was another place where Abby had Irene beaten six ways to Sunday.

Tucson, Arizona
Saturday, June 6, 2009, 6:00 P.M.
81° Fahrenheit

Jonathan was working his way through his second takeout burger when Jack Tennant backed his Lexus out of the garage. Then, with him holding the passenger door open, a woman came out through the garage and let him take her hand as she got into the car.

Just seeing her made Jonathan's heart leap to his throat. The last time he had spoken to his mother in person had been the afternoon he graduated from Wheaton. Both his parents had been there. It was the last time Jonathan had seen them together. He had known even then that his father had a side dish, but with a nag for a wife, who could blame him?

He had been standing there having his picture taken with Esther when his mother came up to him, smiling. "I'm so proud of you," she had said. "I thought this day would never come."

Of course you didn't, Jonathan had told himself. *Because you always thought I was dumb.*

"Do your homework. Study harder. Don't hang out with those loser friends of yours. Listen to decent music instead of that punk rock. Don't drink. Don't do this. Don't do that." When he was little, Jonathan had thought he had the best mother in the world. By junior high, that had changed. By high school they were in an undeclared war. By college the hot war became a cold one.

"Well, it did," he had said to her then. "No thanks to you."

With that, Jonathan had walked away from his mother and stayed away. Permanently, until now. It turned out that absence hadn't made the heart grow fonder. If anything, his opinion of her had deteriorated. Over the years, she became the root cause of everything that went wrong with his life.

When Jonathan's marriage began to come apart at the seams, it was because Esther was just like his mother.

Jonathan's father had told him that Abby was a spend-thrift, and Jonathan believed it. His mother had spent Hank's money; Esther had spent Jonathan's. And every criticism Esther had leveled at him seemed to be an echo of his mother's words and voice. He knew that his father was living a hellish existence with his relatively new wife and dipshit daughter, Jonathan's half sister.

But here was Abby living a seemingly carefree existence with this new husband. She had made a couple of halfhearted e-mail attempts at reconciliation over the years, but Jonathan hadn't been interested. He didn't need a mother in his life any more than he needed a wife. One was gone and the other would be soon.

As he pulled into traffic a few vehicles behind the Lexus, it struck him that he had felt precious little remorse about what he had done so far. No, make that no remorse. He was relieved. Isn't that what they always said during trials, that the killer showed no remorse? He wouldn't, either.

In the hours after the murders in Thousand Oaks and before he drove away from the house just prior to sunrise, he had used Esther's phone to buy himself some time. He had sent out a series of text messages to people in her address book—even to the boyfriend he wasn't supposed to know about—letting them know that she and Jonathan were taking the kids to Yosemite for a couple of days. Once the bodies were found in Thousand Oaks, once it made the news, maybe he'd feel something, but by then he expected to be somewhere south of the border, sipping margaritas and living off the funds he had already transferred to an account in the Cayman Islands. That was the thing about continuing education. In teaching bankers how to counter illegal money transfers, the instructors had inadvertently taught them how to *do* it as well.

So the money that he didn't have with him would be there waiting for him wherever he ended up. In the meantime, he knew that he had spared his own children the pain of knowing that one or the other of their parents had rejected them. He knew that feeling all too well. Yes, he had turned away from Abby, but only after she had already abandoned him.

He had taken care of Esther. Tonight he would even the score for his mother's betrayal as well. Once he had fixed that, he would be able to move on into his new life, whatever and wherever that might be. His old life was over. Jonathan Southard had finally gotten a little of his own power back—power both his mother and his wife had leached out of him.

Once again he was careful to stay in the background. He expected they'd be going back to the reservation, so he was a little surprised when they set off in an entirely different direction. Eventually Jack turned off the freeway, first onto Cortaro Road and finally onto Sandario. When that happened, Jonathan knew he had been right all along about where they were headed. He could afford to relax. He would get there when he got there.

Jack and Abby Tennant could start their little party without him, but he was the one who would finish it.

South of Sells, Arizona
Saturday, June 6, 2009, 8:10 P.M.
78° Fahrenheit

Dan was glad to be driving south toward the border. Coming from Tucson, he had been driving into the setting sun. This was much better.

This would be his second full summer with the Shadow Wolves. Brainwashed by what's on television, most people probably expected that every shift had at least one high-speed chase and maybe a running gun battle or two. That had been Dan's preconceived notion as well, but Aaron Meecham had disabused him of that notion at his first official Shadow Wolves briefing.

"Okay, guys," Aaron had said. "Meet Dan Pardee, a San Carlos Apache who comes to us via Iraq and the U.S. Army." There were a dozen uniformed men assembled in the briefing room that morning. Most of them nodded in welcome and three gave Dan a discreet thumbs-up. In other words, several guys there had the same kind of military credentials Dan did. That meant that, in a tight spot, whoever had his back would be someone he could count on.

The guy sitting directly in front of Dan, a Paiute from Nevada named Russell Muñoz, turned back to Dan. "Welcome to the most dangerous cop job on the planet," he said. "Got my passenger window shot out just last night, thanks to some jerk-face *federale* from across the border who decided to use my SUV for target practice. And all we get to carry around with us is a lightweight piece-of-crap Beretta."

Dan had to agree with that. Packing a new government-issue Beretta 96D didn't inspire a whole lot of confidence on Dan's part. If he was going to be involved in a shooting war, he would have preferred the comforting presence of his old M16.

"And you did not return fire, correct, Mr. Muñoz?" Meecham asked.

"I did not," Muñoz replied grudgingly. "If you ask me, it's about time somebody rescinded that standing order. If those bastards shoot at us, we should be able to shoot back. Why do we have to do this job with both hands tied behind our backs?"

"That order stands, Muñoz, and don't you forget it," Meecham told him. "I don't want you creating an international incident with that little Beretta of yours. If you were to return fire, all hell would break loose around here, and the full wrath of the gods of DC would rain down on all our heads."

Meecham paused and looked around the room. "Let's see a show of hands. How many of you think guns are the biggest problem you have when you're out on patrol?"

Russell's hand shot in the air. No one else's did.

"Since its inception, this unit has had only one fatality, Mr. Pardee," Meecham explained, speaking directly to Dan. "Mitchell Davis was a Rosebud Sioux, and he was wearing his Kevlar vest when he died. If he'd taken a bullet to the chest, he probably would have been fine. He had stopped a group of illegals. What killed him was the one-pound rock one of them picked up and used to bash in his skull.

"Guns are expensive," Meecham continued. "Ammunition is expensive. Rocks are free, and they're everywhere. Fortunately for us, most of the *federales* aren't well trained, and they can't hit the broad side of a barn. That window they shot out last night was pure luck—good luck for them and bad luck for you, Mr. Muñoz. What makes you think it was a *federale*?"

"I saw it," Muñoz grumbled. "I heard it."

"Was it dark when this happened?"

"Yes, it was dark," Muñoz replied. "Of course it was dark. I'm working nights now, remember?" Russell Muñoz was beginning to sound aggrieved, as though he thought Meecham was picking on him.

"Exactly," Meecham said with a smile. "And after that flash, you were blind as a bat for a couple of seconds. If someone had rushed you right then, you wouldn't have seen them coming. Rocks don't have a flash, but they don't make any noise, either. They're the ultimate stealth weapon—silent and deadly. In other words, Mr. Pardee, watch out for rocks and for people throwing them."

Dan nodded. "Got it," he said.

The meeting had broken up shortly after that. As soon as Meecham left the room, Russell Muñoz turned back to Dan. "Beretta, my aching ass," he said. "One of these nights I'm going to bring my AK-47 along for the ride and give those dickheads a taste of their own medicine."

"With your dashboard camera recording the whole thing for posterity." That was from Kevin Ramon. He hailed from San Xavier District near Tucson and was the only full-blooded Tohono O'odham member of the unit.

He was also one of the guys who had given Dan the old thumbs-up.

"Already thought of that," Russell told them. "I'm fixing up a Kleenex box that I'll be able to drop over the camera as needed. What Meecham can't see and doesn't know won't hurt him."

Kevin raised a disparaging eyebrow. "If you say so," he said.

With that, Russell Muñoz had stormed from the room. Dan had been taken aback by the whole exchange. You could maybe disagree with your superior officers, but doing so in public was out of bounds.

"I'll bet he doesn't even own an AK-47," Kevin said. "And if he ever tried to fire one, he'd probably shoot himself in the foot."

This was probably not the best time for Dan to mention to one of his fellow Shadow Wolves that he himself really did have such a weapon.

It was the same AK-47 that he and Bozo had earned that day in Iraq. While Dan and his dog were taken away to be stitched up and bandaged, some of the other guys in the convoy had taken charge of the kid's dropped weapon. They had carefully dismantled it and sent it home, one piece at a time, with directions inside to each of their loved ones that they should forward all pieces on to Micah Duarte in Fort Thomas, Arizona.

By the time Dan's deployment ended and he was back home, he had been amazed to discover that his grandfather Micah had reassembled the weapon from all those separate pieces. The gun was back together—cleaned, ready and waiting, and it was stored under lock and key at Dan's house in Tucson.

"That's not to say we never have shoot-outs," Kevin continued. "The mules who drive drugs for the cartels are usually armed to the teeth. They shoot first and ask questions later, but if that happens, don't look to Russell to help you out. The *federales* may not be the best shots, but neither is Russell. Just wait'll you see him on the target range," Kevin added. "He's pathetic."

"But I thought we were supposed to be the best of the best," Dan argued. "Best shots, best trackers."

Kevin shook his head. "All that and ex-military, too, but as far as I know, the only uniform Russell ever wore was for Cub Scouts."

"How'd he get in, then?" Dan asked.

"Pull," Kevin returned. "His father's a big mucky-muck in the BIA. He pulled a few strings, and here we are stuck with Russell. Take my word for it, one of these days he's going to screw up bad enough that someone's gonna get killed. As for Meecham's rock lecture? Don't take it personally. Meecham made it sound like it was meant for you, but it wasn't. He was mostly talking to Muñoz."

Several months later, after Dan had talked Bozo's way into the unit, he had his own up-close and personal experience with one of those "stealth" rocks. Dan now sported a jagged scar on his left cheek where he had been nailed. Kevin said it gave him "character," but Dan knew the damage would have been far worse if it hadn't been for Bozo. The dog had barked a warning, letting Dan know someone was there. Dan had ducked for cover just in time. The rock had grazed him, but had it not been for Bozo's timely intervention, Dan Pardee might have died on the spot, or he could have lived the rest of his life with only one eye rather than two.

Each night Dan wasn't paired with Russell Muñoz, he counted himself lucky. Russell's academy-acquired skills didn't measure up to the real ones Dan, Kevin, and the others had picked up in military firefights. In crisis situations, when split-second decisions were called for and when someone's life was hanging in the balance, Dan didn't think Russell would be able to hold up his end. The Paiute was all bluff and bluster and precious little action, and no one had yet to see any sign of Russell's legendary AK-47.

Bozo, on the other hand, was just the opposite. The dog didn't spend any time bragging about what he would or wouldn't do, or agonizing about it, either. He simply did it. When the guy hiding on the cliff above him was getting ready to heave that potentially lethal rock in Dan's direction, Bozo didn't stand around discussing the relative merits of an AK-47 over your run-of-the-mill Beretta. Nope, the dog simply stepped up and did what needed to be done.

When they were on patrol, Bozo always rode shotgun in Dan Pardee's front seat. Why wouldn't he? The dog was his partner. He had earned the right to sit there.

Komelik, Tohono O'odham Nation, Arizona
Saturday, June 6, 2009, 7:46 P.M.
78° Fahrenheit

Jack had barely finished parking the car before Abby was out of it and ready to don the overalls and hiking boots he had brought along for her. "Where is it?" she asked. "Can I go look now?"

"Nope. First things first."

Carrying the cooler in one hand and the hamper in the other, he led her over to the waiting picnic table. The candles he had placed on the table earlier, long white tapers, hadn't fared well in the afternoon heat. They tilted at odd angles, but Jack could see that the fact that the little clearing had been suitably dressed for this evening's event was making a big impression on his wife.

"This is beautiful," she said. "You really went all out, didn't you?"

"Wait until you see the best part," he said, setting down the hamper and the cooler.

"How far is it?" she asked.

"Not that far. We'll light the luminarias as we go."

And they did, walking side by side and lighting the candles along the path as well as the cluster Jack had placed around the base of the ancient ironwood tree. Sticks of hardy deer-horn cactus wound around the trunk and encircled the tree's lower branches. Slender stalks holding the massive blooms protruded from the cactus. A few of the white blossoms were beginning to open. In the deepening twilight, some of the flowers seemed to spring straight from the tree bark itself.

"It's glorious!" Abby exclaimed, clapping her hands. "Can you smell them?"

Jack nodded. Even he couldn't help but notice the flowery aroma, a perfume that was like a cross between plumeria and orange blossom, sweetening the hot desert air.

"How many blossoms?" she asked.

"I counted over a hundred on this one plant."

"That's amazing," Abby said. "I never knew the night-blooming cereus could grow this big. How in the world did you find it?"

"It took time," Jack admitted with a grin. "Let's just say I didn't play nearly as much golf this spring as you thought I did."

Abby poked him in the ribs. "You rascal," she said.

"Happy anniversary," he said. He reached down and turned on a battery-powered camping lantern. "This will give us a little more light when we come back in the dark. Now what say we go back and have our picnic? By the time we finish with that, I'm guessing our very own Queen of the Night will be in full bloom."

6

South of Sells, Arizona
Saturday, June 6, 2009, 10:00 P.M.
71° Fahrenheit

*C*ONSIDERING THE FACT that it was a full moon, Dan's sector seemed surprisingly quiet that night. With the summer rains still weeks away, daytime temperatures were nonetheless intense, especially for people out walking through the Sonora Desert's barren wasteland. With no concrete or blacktop to hold the heat, once the sun went down, temperatures plummeted, sometimes as much as thirty degrees. That was when the walkers often set off on their long and treacherous marches north. They tended to walk at night when it was cool and hole up during the heat of the day.

According to the memos sent down by the folks in

Homeland Security, supposedly this was all about the war on terror, but in the year and a half Dan had been a Shadow Wolf, he had apprehended zero terrorists and literally hundreds of nonterrorists. The illegals spilled across the border day after day and night after night in a never-ending flood. They came to do backbreaking work in the fields or in the construction industry; in slaughter-houses and in restaurants.

The vast majority of them came with the burning desire to come to the United States and make something of themselves; to grab some small part of the American dream. As for the smugglers? By and large they were in it for themselves alone. They spared no thought and even less sympathy for the lives of the people they put in jeopardy.

Sometimes the illegal immigrants had paid money to be crammed into speeding Suburbans or rental trucks that crashed during high-speed chases and spilled dead and dying people in every direction. Sometimes illegals were taken to overcrowded houses and held as prisoners until their relatives could raise enough additional money to free them. But most of the illegals Dan encountered were the poorest of the poor—the ones who walked, making their way across the border and through the broiling desert, walking on bleeding feet and often dying of thirst in the process.

Several times Dan had come across the bodies of people who had fallen victim to heat and thirst and had been left behind to perish in the desert. Of those, Dan now recalled the three young women he had found dead.

All had been in their late teens or early twenties. There was no sign of homicidal violence. All had died of natural causes—if sunstroke and dehydration could be considered natural. One of them had appeared to be five or six months pregnant at the time of her death.

Looking at her, waiting for the medical examiner's van to find its way there, Dan had been outraged. "What the hell were you thinking?" he had demanded of the lifeless corpse. "What made you think that whatever you'd find here for you and your baby girl was better than what you had at home?"

That case had gotten to him—and still did. He wished he'd found her soon enough to save her and maybe even the unborn child. He still wondered about them from time to time. Where did they come from? Did the baby's father have even the smallest inkling of what had happened to them? Was he already here in the States somewhere, waiting for them to show up and wondering what had happened to them? Or was he back home in Mexico? Maybe he was a creep and she had run away from home trying to escape from him.

As far as Dan knew, the lifeless victim had never been identified. She had been buried in an unmarked grave in the pauper's corner of a Tucson cemetery. Dan had asked to be notified about the burial, and he was. He went to it wearing his full dress uniform. It seemed to him that he owed the poor young woman that much.

There was only one other person in attendance—a woman dressed entirely in black. Catching sight of her, Dan hoped she might be a relative. That hope lasted only until the end of the brief service. As Dan walked away from the grave site, the woman fell into step beside him.

"What the hell are you doing here?" she had demanded.

She was a middle-aged Anglo woman who shook her fist in Dan's face as she spoke. Fortunately for her, Dan hadn't brought Bozo along to the cemetery with him.

"I'm the one who found her," he said. "I came to pay my respects."

"Respects, my ass," she retorted. "You guys are the ones out there killing these poor people."

Dan had simply turned and walked away. Later he had read about an organization of women who made it a point to have a visible presence at the funeral of every illegal who died attempting to cross the border, and not just the ones who died on the reservation, either. They called themselves the WWC—Women Who Care.

The Shadow Wolves had another name for them. They called them witches.

Komelik, Tohono O'odham Nation, Arizona
Saturday, June 6, 2009, 10:15 P.M.
69° Fahrenheit

On his way back from The Gate, Dan stopped on the shoulder periodically and scanned the surrounding desert with his night-vision goggles. The temperature had plummeted. When he was outside the truck he was glad to slip on a windbreaker. There was plenty of southbound vehicular traffic heading to the dance at Vamori, but not much northbound. For a change, there was no sign of walkers or of overloaded SUVs, either.

On the far side of Baboquivari, the full moon was turning the sky a lighter shade of gray, but it would take time for the moon itself to gain enough altitude to be visible over the crest of the hulking mountain barrier.

At Vamori, Dan turned into the parking lot and made his way through the collection of parked cars in search of any vehicles that didn't fit in with the pickups and aging minivans that were the preferred mode of reservation transportation. Driving with the window open, he smelled the wood smoke from the cooking fires outside the feast house. A generator roared somewhere in the background, providing electricity to light the dusty dance floor and to power the speakers for the thumping chicken-scratch band.

On his side of the car, Bozo whined. "Smells good, doesn't it," Dan told him. "We'll stop at the next wide spot in the road and have that sandwich."

That opportunity came a few miles later as they neared Komelik. The turnoff where he had noticed activity earlier seemed to have had several visiting vehicles since he had stopped to look at the tracks on his way south.

That seemed as good a reason and place to stop as any. Leaving Bozo in the vehicle, Dan squatted in the road and examined the new tracks that overlaid the old ones. He could pick out another pair of sedan tracks along with another vehicle, probably an SUV. It was possible that the vehicles might belong to illegal traffickers of some kind, but with the dance going on only a few miles away, it could mean something as harmless as someone stopping off to have a few beers without drawing the attention of the Tohono O'odham Nation's Law and Order.

"Come on," he said to Bozo as he opened the door and unfastened the dog's harness. "We'll eat later. Let's go have a look."

Just then the moon finally crested the mountain, and the desert lit up in a wash of silvery light. Distant strains of music from the dance, mostly a faint drumbeat, traveled on the still night air. Other than that, the night was quiet. Eerily quiet.

Dan could smell something—a flowerlike perfume, although he couldn't imagine what kind of flower would be blooming way out here in the middle of nowhere. The two things taken together—the strange scent on the air and the silence—struck Dan as odd. Bozo, too, seemed uneasy. He growled softly and the hackles rose on his neck. Attuned to his dog's every mood, Dan reacted accordingly as the hair on the back of Dan's neck rose as well.

"What is it, boy?" he asked. In answer, the dog whined again.

"Let's go see."

Keeping hold of Bozo's leash, Dan moved forward. A quarter of a mile into the desert, Dan caught sight of a vehicle, a Chevrolet Blazer with Arizona plates. It sat parked just behind a small white sedan. That meant that the people in the two vehicles were here together. It also meant that if something bad was going on, Dan could be outnumbered two to one or more, although really, Bozo's presence evened those odds.

Despite the pair of vehicles and the probable number of people, there was no sign of laughter or conversation in the vast moonlit wilderness, and no sign of movement, either. That was another oddity. If people were sitting around drinking beer, there would be talking and laughter and, most likely, cigarette smoke as well.

Dan approached the Blazer warily. The back passenger door was open. Glancing inside, Dan caught sight of a child's booster seat of some kind and a child's plastic pinwheel. On the floor were a pair of tiny tennis shoes, but there was no sign of a child.

"There's a little kid out here somewhere, Boze," Dan said reassuringly to the dog. "So it's probably okay."

But Bozo didn't act like it was okay. The dog was still on high alert, which meant Dan needed to be on alert as well.

In front of the sedan, Dan caught sight of the first real sign of trouble. Two women's purses lay open and empty in the ground, with a collection of stuff—lipsticks, papers, photos, ID cards, and credit cards—scattered all around. He also spotted two men's wallets.

There were two purses and two wallets. That told Dan that he had stumbled on a robbery—a robbery with at least four victims. Was it still in progress? He touched the hood of the sedan. It was still warm, as in daylight warm, but the engine had been off long enough to cool down. That meant that the vehicle had been parked here for some time.

Far more wary now, Dan drew his weapon but kept a tight hold on Bozo's leash. "Quiet," he whispered to the dog. "Heel."

Leaving the debris field and the Blazer behind, dog and man stepped forward again. Ahead of them in the desert he saw a glow that wasn't moonlight and wasn't firelight, either. It was possible he was seeing lights from another vehicle—the bad guy's vehicle—but the light was more diffuse than headlight beams would have been. No, the glow came from some other source, and it wasn't all in one spot. Parts of it seemed to flicker a little while another part was steady, but there was still no sound at all, nothing but an unnerving silence.

Dan knew that whatever had happened was bad. His first move should have been to turn around, return to his Expedition, call in his position, and radio for help. But he also knew that help of any kind was miles away. If there were people here who were being held against their will, he, Dan Pardee, was their only hope. Waiting for backup could take too long.

Walking silently, Dan and Bozo rounded a thick clump of mesquite. Beyond that they caught sight of some of the light source. On either side of a rough path and set about eight feet apart were glowing luminarias. They had been lit for some time. The small candles in the sand-filled paper bags were beginning to sputter and go out. Some of them had already done so.

Dan knew that luminarias were used mostly in celebrations, so this event, whatever it was, had started out as a party of some kind, a party that had gone terribly wrong. Beside him, Bozo strained at his leash. The dog's ears were pricked forward, his body tense.

Dan knew that perps were often more scared of facing dogs than they were of facing weapons. For one thing, bullets could go astray. Dogs, on the other hand, hardly ever missed their target.

Right now, the only thing Dan and Bozo had going for them was the element of surprise. It was possible that the bad guy was long gone. It was equally possible that he had relieved his victims of some booze in addition to their purses and wallets and was now passed out somewhere nearby. There were plenty of stupid bad guys out there—ones who got drunk or high before they bothered getting away.

Dan had utmost faith in Bozo's innate sense of what constituted danger and what did not. His response to threats was immediate and unrelenting, complete with biting jaws and snapping teeth, but he posed no peril to people who were harmless. That was part of what made Bozo so valuable. Some dogs can sniff out tumors or sense oncoming seizures. In Iraq, Bozo had demonstrated an uncanny ability to sense danger—to perceive and unmask a potential suicide bomber hiding inside a woman's burka.

He was doing the same thing now. Kneeling down, Dan released the catch on Bozo's collar.

"Show me," he whispered.

Most police dogs are trained to charge forward, barking a warning as they go. Not Bozo. He sprang forward, silent and lethal, and went racing down the candlelit path with

Dan behind him in hot pursuit. Unlike the dog's lightning paws, Dan's feet made an ungodly noise, enough that he might well waken whomever was sleeping.

So much for surprise, he thought.

Bozo disappeared over a small rise. Before Dan could clear it, he heard a bloodcurdling scream—a child's scream. Dan topped the rise in time to see movement. A small flash of white raced away from him into the desert, still screaming.

The child, Dan thought. *The child from the car seat. A terrified child.*

"Down," he shouted at Bozo. "Leave it!"

The dog dropped to his belly as though he'd been shot. Most of the nearby luminarias had gone out. Dan paused long enough to extract his flashlight from a belt loop. As soon as he turned it on, he saw the first body. A woman, an Indian woman from the looks of her, lay facedown on the path several feet ahead of him. Hurrying to her side, he knelt and felt for a pulse. There wasn't one. He could see a small wound in the middle of her back, but under her he could see the pool of blood from an exit wound that had soaked into the dirt. She hadn't died immediately, but he knew she had bled out shortly after being shot.

Silence had descended once more. Wherever the terrified child had gone, he or she was quiet now, quiet and hiding. No wonder. Anyone who had witnessed this horror had reason to be petrified, but before Dan went searching for the frightened child, he needed to assess what he was up against.

"Right here," Dan whispered to Bozo. Once again, man and dog moved forward as one.

Ten feet down the path they came across the next body. This one, an Indian male who looked to be in his early thirties, lay on his back. He'd been shot twice—once in the chest and once in the head. He, too, was dead.

"So the woman was running away and she was shot in the back," Dan said, explaining what he was seeing to himself as well as to the uncomprehending dog. "This guy here probably was trying to fend off the bad guy."

The man had been dead for some time—long enough for most of the visible blood to dry. Dan knew that meant there was a good chance that the perpetrator had taken off, but maybe not. Perhaps that was only wishful thinking on his part. Just to be on the safe side, he didn't holster his weapon. The last of the luminarias burned out, but a steady light still glowed in the distance.

The path rounded a looming clump of mesquite. There Dan found something that made no sense. The remains of a cloth-covered dining table and two chairs lay on the ground surrounded by a scatter of broken glassware, dishes, and silverware. Two still forms lay on either side of the fallen table, forms Dan suspected were also bodies.

Closer examination proved that to be true. These two, presumably Anglos, appeared to be an older couple somewhere in their sixties or maybe seventies. It looked as though the two of them had been seated at the table when they were attacked. The woman lay next to one of the chairs, as though she had been taken by surprise. It appeared to Dan that the man had sprung forward to fend off the attacker and had been shot full in the face.

Dan squatted on his haunches and looked around. These two victims, like the other two, had been dead for some time, even though the coppery smell of blood still lingered in the air, along with that same pervasive scent of flowers.

Bodies and flowers, Dan thought. *Like a funeral.*

"So where's the kid?" Dan muttered to Bozo.

Standing up, he looked around, shining the flashlight in every direction. There was no sign of the child, but whoever it was had fled in the direction of the still-glowing light, the steady one, which was now just beyond another low rise.

"Hello," he called. "I'm a police officer. Border Patrol. Where are you? Let me help you."

There was no reply, but that was hardly surprising. If the kid had been here earlier and had seen all these people being shot, no wonder he had run away when he caught sight of someone else carrying a drawn weapon.

"Come on," he said to Bozo. "We'll look for the kid in a little while. Right now we need to call this in."

Together they jogged back to the Expedition, where Dan radioed into Dispatch, letting them know what he'd found and giving the location of the crime scene as well as the condition of the four homicide victims.

Seconds later, Paul Jacobs, the night-watch supervisor, came on the line. "Drug deal gone bad?"

"Unlikely," Dan answered. "Maybe a straight-out robbery."

"Could it be we've got members of rival cartels duking it out?" Jacobs suggested.

"No," Dan said. "I don't think so. I don't know that many elderly Anglo drug dealers. Besides, there's no sign of a weapon on any of the victims, and no sign of the shooter as well."

"Should I set up roadblocks?"

"I doubt it," Dan said. "It's probably too late for those to do any good. The killer's back in Tucson by now or else in Mexico."

"You told Dispatch the victims are both Anglo and Indian?"

"Yes," Dan said. "Two of each."

"Dispatch is contacting both Law and Order and Pima County?"

"That's right. There's a dance at Vamori tonight. Law and Order probably has a presence at that."

"Is it possible these four people left the dance and came to that location to do some partying?"

"They weren't together," Dan said. "There were only two chairs."

"Chairs?" Jacobs objected. "I thought you said this was out in the middle of the desert."

"It is. It looks to me like the Anglo couple was having a picnic—at a table with a white cloth and good dishes. I'd say the Indians just happened by. I recognize both vehicles. The Lexus I've seen poking around here off and on when I was working day shift. As for the Blazer? I'm pretty sure it belongs to an Indian who lives somewhere around here. I think his father runs cattle in the area."

"You called in the vehicle information?"

"Yes," Dan said. "Records has it."

Bozo whined again, looking off into the desert. Dan's heart beat hard and fast in his chest. Maybe he was wrong and the killer was still lurking out there some-where in the dark.

Bozo made as if to head off into the brush. Dan called him back.

"Wait a minute," he said. "Come here."

"Who are you talking to?" Jacobs wanted to know. "I thought you said there was no one else at the scene."

"It's my dog," Dan said into the radio. "I've gotta go."

He slammed the microphone down. "Bozo," he or-dered. "Right here!"

If the killer was still out there, Dan had the ultimate secret weapon—Bozo. If this turned out to be nothing more than a game of hide-and-seek with a petrified little kid, Dan Pardee could trust Bozo to handle that as well.

Remembering the tiny pair of tennis shoes he had seen on the floorboard of the Blazer, Dan hurried over to the vehicle, collected one of the shoes, and held it out to the dog long enough for Bozo to get the scent.

"Find it," he ordered.

For the second time that evening, Dan released Bozo's leash and the dog galloped away from him while his master, Beretta in hand, raced after him.

This time, Bozo ran on a trajectory that took them straight from the cars toward the steadily glowing light. Unable to keep pace with the dog, Dan reached the source of the light—a battery-powered lantern sitting under a towering ironwood—just as a barefoot child, a little girl, darted out from beneath the tree, screaming.

"Ban," she sobbed, racing toward Dan with her arms outstretched. *"Ban! Ban! Ban!* Don't let him eat me!"

Dan managed to reholster his Beretta as the girl threw her body against his knees. He reached down and swung her up to his hip, where she clung to him like a burr.

Dan knew enough Tohono O'odham to realize that she had mistaken Bozo for a coyote.

"Sit," Dan said to Bozo. To the girl, he added, "Not *ban*. This is a dog. *Gogs*. His name is Bozo. He won't hurt you."

For this one child at least, Dan Pardee wasn't *ohb*. He was her savior. She wrapped her arms around his neck and continued to sob, her tears soaking his shirt. There was blood on her arms and on her legs and feet. No doubt she had cut herself running barefoot through the rocks and brush. She was quaking, whether from fear or cold, he couldn't tell.

Dan was still standing under the tree holding her when, out of the corner of his eye, he saw a hint of movement in the tree above them. He started to reach for his pistol again, but then, looking more closely, he realized that what he had seen was the light from the lantern reflecting off a flower—an immense white flower. An even closer inspection revealed that there were actually dozens of the huge white blooms glowing luminously along the ironwood tree's sturdy trunk and winding their way up into the branches.

The girl stopped crying abruptly, but her breath still came in hiccups. She was shivering. "That's a dog?" she asked, pointing at Bozo. "Are you sure?"

"Yes, I'm sure he's a dog," Dan told her reassuringly. He slipped off his windbreaker and wrapped it around her.

"What's his name again?"

"Bozo."

"That's a funny name," she said.

"He's a funny dog," Dan said. "Would you like to pet him?"

He started to kneel down next to Bozo, but the little girl wasn't totally convinced. Shrinking against him, she resumed her death grip around his neck.

"What about you?" he asked. "Do you have a name?"

She nodded and gave him a tiny shy smile. "Angie."

"Where's your mommy, Angie?" he asked.

Still trembling, she took a long shuddery breath. Her eyes were enormous. "Over there," she said, pointing. "She's sleeping. She won't wake up."

"Did you see what happened?"

Angie shook her head. "I was sleeping. When I woke up, the car wasn't moving. Donald wasn't there. Mommy was gone, too, but I saw a man, a Milgahn man, walking away from the car. He was carrying a gun."

Dan took a deep breath. The investigation into what had happened here had just taken a gigantic step forward. This massacre in the desert had a witness—an eye-witness.

"This man with the gun," Dan said, "did you know him? Is he someone you had seen before?"

The little girl shook her head somberly.

"No."

"Weren't you scared?"

Angie nodded. "A little," she said. "Mommy always says when Bad People come around, you should be very still so they don't notice you. That's what I did. I was quiet, and pretty soon he went away. After a while, I went looking for my mommy. She's sleeping. So is Donald, and those other people, too."

"Do you know the other people?"

"I just know Donald," she said.

"And what were you doing here?"

She shrugged. "We were on our way to the dance, but Donald said there was something he wanted to show us first. He said it was a big surprise and that we'd really like it, but that when we got there we'd have to get out of the car and walk."

Dan nodded. So the victims had come expecting a surprise. Instead they had unexpectedly driven into an ambush by an armed gunman. With that in mind, it surprised Dan to realize that Angie had been more scared of coyotes than she had been of someone carrying a gun.

"My name is Dan," he told her now. "Like I said before, this big guy here is my dog."

"Can I pet him?" Angie asked. Now that she'd been properly introduced to Bozo, she was evidently ready to be friends.

"Sure." Dan had been holding Angie. The night air was chilly, but Bozo was panting. Dan set the child down next to the dog. Bozo stood still as a statue while the tiny girl wrapped her arms around his neck and buried her bleeding face in the soft fur of his shoulder.

"Bozo and I are here to help you," Dan said. "Are you hungry?"

Angie nodded.

"Thirsty?"

"Yes."

"My truck is back over there," he said. "I have some sandwiches, some chips, and some sodas in a cooler. Would you like one of those?"

"I'm not supposed to drink Cokes," she said, frowning, "but sometimes I do. Will you wake my mommy?"

"I'll try," he said. It was a lie, but it was the best he could do under the circumstances. "First let me get you back to my truck. Since you're barefoot, I'll carry you."

Without a word, she let go of Bozo's neck and held out her arms to him. He lifted her up and carried her back the way they had come rather than back past the two vehicles and the four bloodied victims. As they walked, Angie's face rested in the crook of his neck. He was glad she didn't look up at his face right then because she would have seen he was crying, too.

He had been in a scene similar to this one once before; only back then, Dan Pardee had been the child, and someone else—some other uniformed police officer— had been carrying a no-longer-innocent child away from a room filled with unimaginable carnage.

Tucson, Arizona
Saturday, June 6, 2009, 10:30 P.M.
73° Fahrenheit

As they drove back to the house in Gates Pass, Gabe fell asleep in the backseat. Lani was grateful for the break from his never-ending questions. It let her concentrate on worrying about her mother.

For much of the day, Diana had been strangely silent, and Lani didn't know what to make of her mother's odd behavior.

Lani had been back home for only a few months now, and she was living in the hospital housing compound out at Sells rather than at home with her parents in her old room. Since returning to the Tucson area, Lani had noticed that her parents had changed while she'd been away in Denver doing her residency. She supposed that part of the changes had to do with their getting older, but then so had she. She wasn't the same person she had been when she graduated from high school or even when she had gotten her premed degree from the University of North Dakota. Since she had changed, it made no sense that she should expect her parents to remain the same.

"You should get married," Diana said now.

"Married?" Lani repeated, nearly driving off the narrow road in surprise.

That was the last thing she expected her mother to say. Lani had been focused on her career—on becoming the best possible physician she could learn to be and on bringing those skills back to her own people, where native-born doctors were in short supply and where doctors who were Tohono O'odham were completely nonexistent. But the question itself shocked Lani. She was still mulling a possible answer when her mother continued.

"Yes, married," Diana said. "I want to live long enough to have another grandchild."

She and Brandon Walker already had one grandson. Davy and Candace's son Tyler was nine now. As far as Lani was concerned, he was a spoiled brat and obnoxious besides. He hadn't had the benefit of being raised by Nana *Dahd*, and it showed. There was something to be said for the old traditions in which the aunts and uncles supplied the discipline, but Candace had made it clear to all concerned that help with her son in that regard would not be welcome.

"We barely see Tyler as it is," Diana said. "And the minute the divorce is final, no matter what the custody agreement says, what's-her-name is going to take him back to Chicago to her parents, and we won't get to see him at all."

What's-her-name? Lani wondered, repeating her mother's phrase. *Davy and Candace have been married for more than ten years, and Mom can't remember her name? What's going on?*

That's what she thought, but it wasn't what she said aloud. "Davy is an attorney," Lani replied. "He's not going to let that happen."

"The problem with Davy is that he's a nice guy," her mother corrected. "His wife's been walking all over him for years. That's not going to change, so you should get married."

Lani couldn't see how one thing automatically led to the other, but she decided that it was better to treat the whole discussion as a joke rather than be distressed by what she couldn't help but regard as an invasion of her privacy.

"I'll think about it," Lani said, laughing. "But don't hold your breath. I don't see many prospects for matrimony walking into my life any time soon."

She hoped that was enough to put the discussion to bed. Unfortunately, the next topic of conversation was even worse.

"What did Mitch Johnson do to you?" Diana asked.

"Mitch Johnson?" Lani repeated. "Why bring him up after all these years?"

"Tell me," Diana urged. "He must have done something to you. What?"

"You know what he did to me," Lani answered. "He kidnapped me and tried to kill me."

That was the obvious part. Drugging her, kidnapping her, and torturing her when Lani was sixteen years old had been yet another move in Andrew Carlisle's and Mitch Johnson's ongoing war with Diana Ladd and Brandon Walker. The ultimate goal had been to rob them of everything they held most dear—their children. Mitch had planned to kill both Lani and Brandon's son Quentin.

In this conversation, Lani knew exactly what Diana really wanted to know. It was one of Lani's darkest secrets. Fat Crack had known about it, but as far as she knew, he was the only one.

Mitch Johnson had burned her. He had heated up kitchen tongs and then he had clamped the red-hot metal on the tender flesh of her breast. She understood that, in performing that particularly barbarous act, Mitch had been functioning as Andrew Carlisle's instrument and doing his master's bidding. The scar he had left on Lani's body mimicked the mark Andrew Carlisle's teeth had left on her mother during his attack on Diana years before Lani was born. At least two of Carlisle's other victims had been defiled in the same fashion.

As a child Lani had seen the scar on her mother's body, and she hadn't questioned it. In fact, when Lani was five, in an attempt to be more like her mom, she had gone so far as to use her mother's concealer to draw a similar pale circle on her own body.

Nana *Dahd* had been a constant presence in Lani's young life, and that was the only time she remembered Rita Antone being angry. She had ordered Lani to scrub the offending makeup from her body and never to talk about it, lest someone do the same thing to her.

Years later, when it had happened, when Mitch had burned her in just that way, Lani had been ashamed because she believed she had brought it on herself—that she had somehow attracted this terrible thing and caused it to come to her.

After that, Mitch had taken Lani and a still-drugged Quentin to a limestone cavern under Ioligam, I'itoi's sacred mountain, which the Anglos call Kitt Peak. Deep in the cavern, Lani had managed to outwit her would-be killer by turning the darkness to her advantage. In a desperate game of hide-and-seek, she had managed to stay tantalizingly out of reach and had fooled him into chasing her into a darkened passageway where he had plunged to his death.

The Tohono O'odham are a peace-loving people who

kill only to feed themselves or in self-defense. When a warrior kills an enemy in battle, tradition dictates that he undergo *e lihmhun*, a sixteen-day-long purification ceremony that includes both fasting and solitude.

For that whole time, Lani had stayed on the mountain by herself, with Fat Crack Ortiz, tribal chairman and medicine man, as her only companion. Each day he would bring her that day's single meal of salt-free food. It was to Fat Crack, and only to him, that Lani had confided the full extent of her injuries.

Fat Crack had been a reluctant joiner of the medicine-man circle. Before being tapped to assume that mantle by an old blind medicine man named Looks at Nothing, Fat Crack Ortiz had been blithely living his life as a practicing Christian Scientist. Although he still believed in the tenets of Mary Baker Eddy, he had not inflicted his own beliefs on Lani. Instead, Fat Crack had driven into Tucson, stopped at the nearest Walgreens, and purchased salves and ointments to soothe the burns on her breast.

By the time the sixteen days were up, the wound had healed enough that Lani hadn't bothered to mention it to either of her parents. She had spent the rest of her high school and college years assiduously avoiding naked showers in PE or dormitories. Her roommates in North Dakota had teased her about being a prude, but the scar, faded now with the help of a scar reducer, was Lani's secret. Fat Crack had been dead for years. She had told no one else, but now her mother was asking her about it. Why?

They pulled into the driveway outside Brandon and

Diana's home. A motion-activated floodlight came on, illuminating the whole area. Moments later, the porch light came on as well. Lani's father opened the door.

The silence between mother and daughter had gone on far longer than it should have.

"Well?" Diana insisted.

"Mitch Johnson tried to kill me and he failed," Lani said. "End of story."

Except Lani knew that wasn't the end of the story at all. Something else was going on here. She wished she could sit down with her father and talk to him about it. Between them they might be able to figure out what was happening with Lani's mother, but that wasn't possible, not tonight.

Brandon walked over to the passenger side of the Passat, opened the door, and helped his wife out of the vehicle.

"It's about time you brought her home," he said, smiling across the now-empty seat in Lani's direction. "I was about to come looking for you or send out a posse."

Lani was grateful for his teasing. It gave her exactly what she needed just then—a change of subject.

In the backseat, Gabe's eyes opened and he sat up straight. "Where are we?" he asked.

"Dropping my mother off," Lani answered.

"I'm going to sit up front then," he said.

Lani waited until he had clambered into the front seat and buckled himself in.

"*Oi g hihm,*" he said, smiling at her. "Let's go."

"By all means," Lani said, grateful to escape. "Let's."

7

Highway 86, West of Tucson, Arizona
Saturday, June 6, 2009, 11:00 P.M.
73° Fahrenheit

*L*ANI DROVE TOWARD Sells with the full moon rising behind the fast-moving Passat. Once she entered the open-range part of the highway, she slowed down in order to keep an eye out for wandering livestock that might be crossing the road in the moon-bright semidarkness. As she passed the turnoff for Little Tucson, she saw flashing lights in her rearview mirror. She pulled over and let the police vehicle speed past.

She recognized the Pima County logo painted on the side of the vehicle. That probably meant that there was a wrecked car somewhere out here in the night. She didn't doubt that she'd know the details soon enough when ambulances brought the dead and dying into her ER at the hospital in Sells.

Back on the road, Lani kept going over her mother's strange question. She also continued thinking about what Gabe had told her much earlier in the day about an old man with strangely puckered skin sitting by her parents' swimming pool, a man whose presence Diana had absolutely denied. Now Lani wondered if Gabe had been right and if Andrew Carlisle had, against all odds, made an unwelcome ghostly appearance in the house at Gates Pass.

Lani more than anyone understood that Gabe Ortiz was a spooky kid. He often seemed to know things he wasn't supposed to know, but that wasn't surprising, because Lani still did that occasionally, too.

Fat Crack Ortiz had suffered from diabetes, an ailment so common on the reservation that it was sometimes referred to as the Papago Plague. He had refused all treatment for the disease, both medicinal and traditional, and eventually the disease had killed him.

The feast held at Ban Thak, Coyote Sitting, the night of his funeral was one of the biggest ones in recent memory. The women in Fat Crack's life—his widow, Wanda, their daughters-in-law, Christen and Delia, along with the women from the village—had worked long into the night. Lani Walker and Diana Ladd had been there, too. Later, after cleaning up and as they were getting ready to leave, Delia's water had broken. When it became apparent that there was no time to get the mother to a hospital in time for the delivery of her baby, Lani had stepped in to assist. Thus Gabe Ortiz had been born on the Tampico red leatherette of Diana Ladd's prized Invicta convertible.

Holding the newborn child in those first few moments of life, looking down at a wrinkled new face that resembled a wrinkled old face, Lani had also understood that Gabe would be more than just his grandfather's namesake. He would be a medicine man, a *siwani,* like the others who had gone before him—like Fat Crack, Looks at Nothing, Understanding Woman, and Lani Walker herself.

That knowledge about Gabe's real destiny, like the scar on her own breast, was another of Lani Walker's treasured secrets. It was why she spent so much time with the boy—why she made such a concerted effort to teach him fully all the things he needed to know.

On this night, though, she needed to tell him something else, and in telling it she couched the tale in the old traditional language. Part of it was one of the old legends, the story of Rattlesnake Skull village and the people who haunted that bad place. That portion of the story had been handed down in legend from that time in the far distant past when I'itoi, Elder Brother, first emerged from the center of the earth. But part of it was much newer than the rest. It was Lani's own story, and she wanted Gabe to hear that as well.

After all, if he was going to be a medicine man in the twenty-first century, Gabe would need to know both.

They say it happened long ago that some Bad People, PaDaj O'odham, people who followed the Spirit of Evil, lived in a vil-

lage called Ko'oi Koshwa, Rattlesnake Skull. One day maraud-ing Apaches, the ohb, *came to Rattlesnake Skull. They killed all the people there except for one young girl who went to live with them.*

Later the Tohono O'odham learned that this girl loved one of the Apache warriors. They believed that she had betrayed her people to impress him, and it was because of her that the people of Rattlesnake Skull village died.

This made the Tohono O'odham very angry, so they asked I'itoi to help them find Oks Gagdathag, Betraying Woman. I'itoi, the Spirit of Goodness, led them to the place where she was hiding. They brought her back to the land of the Tohono O'odham and shut her in one of I'itoi's sacred caves on Ioligam, the mountain the Milgahn, the whites, call Kitt Peak. There were many ways in and out of the cave. Betraying Woman could have escaped, but she knew that she deserved to be punished, so she stayed there alone until she died.

After that no one went back to live in Rattlesnake Skull be-cause everyone knew it was a Bad Place. One day two Milgahn, white men, were wandering in the desert. They came upon Rat-tlesnake Skull. While they were there, the men were infected by the spirits of the Bad People. After that, even though they were not ohb, *they were* s-ohbsgam, *Apache-like, and they went around killing people and doing bad things. One of the people they killed was a Tohono O'odham girl named Gina.*

There were two of these s-ohbsgam. *The first one liked being bad. The other one, a man with a wife and a baby, knew he had done wrong, and he killed himself. The first one would have gotten away, but the wife of his dead friend talked to the judge and so the Apache-like Man went to prison.*

After he got out, he started killing people again. One of the people he wanted to kill was the woman who had helped put him in prison, and he came looking for her. When he found her all alone, he thought he had won, but the woman had a friend, an old Indian woman who knew how to sing for power. She sang a powerful song, a war chant. Even though the other woman was Milgahn, the old woman's song gave her enough courage to fight back. When the man came too close she burned his face with hot fat, and from then on the Bad Man was blind, and he is blind to this day, even though he's dead.

That, nawoj, *my friend, is the story of the Woman Who Fought the* S-Ohbsgam.

Highway 86, West of Tucson, Arizona
Saturday, June 6, 2009, 11:30 P.M.
73° Fahrenheit

The story ended. For a long time after that, Lani and Gabe were silent. She didn't want to say anything more, but she wondered how much of all that the child understood. He understood it all.

"Is that the man I saw this morning by your mother's swimming pool?" he asked. "The one who was sitting there talking to your mother—the one you couldn't see."

"Yes," Lani said quietly. "I think so."

"But why?" Gabe asked. "If he's dead, why would he come back?"

"I don't know," Lani said. "That's what we have to find out."

Tucson, Arizona
Saturday, June 6, 2009, 11:00 P.M.
73° Fahrenheit

Pima County Detective Brian Fellows hung up the phone and returned to the bedroom. When he switched on the light in the closet, his wife, Kath, groaned and pulled a pillow over her face.

"What time is it?" she grumbled.

"Eleven. Go back to sleep."

"What's going on?"

"A quadruple homicide out on the reservation."

"Great," she said. "Why is it, when it comes to homicides on the reservation, you're always William Forsythe's favorite go-to guy?"

"You know why as well as I do," Brian answered.

In terms of political correctness, Sheriff William Forsythe was only one very small step beyond the outdated notion that "the only good Indian is a dead Indian." The Tohono O'odham Nation took up a large segment of Pima County's landmass, but since whatever crime happened there often had to do with Indians or illegal aliens, Sheriff Forsythe was usually only too happy to relegate it to the low end of the priority scale. Sending Brian to work those remote cases was Forsythe's way of continuing to punish Fellows for his long and close association with Forsythe's immediate predecessor, Brandon Walker.

No doubt Sheriff Forsythe thought sending Brian to the reservation would tick Detective Fellows off, but like Br'er Rabbit, Brian didn't mind being thrown into the reservation briar patch. As for Sheriff Forsythe? The guy was a jerk. Brian hoped that someday Forsythe would no longer be an issue. Either the people of Pima County would come to their senses and elect someone else, or Brian would put in his twenty years and then be gone. At this point there was no way to tell which would come first.

Kath sat up in bed and propped the pillow behind her. "Who's going with you?" she asked.

"Just me," he said.

"For a homicide with four victims?" she asked. "What is it, some kind of drug war?"

"Maybe," Brian said, pulling on his shoes. "Dispatch said the victims are two Indians and two Anglos. It was called in by one of your Shadow Wolves guys. Pardee, I think the name is."

When Kath and Brian met, he had been a lowly deputy with the sheriff's department while she was a full-fledged Border Patrol officer. For a time after their marriage, they had both enjoyed being out in the field in their respective departments, comparing notes and chasing bad guys, but after the birth of their twins, Amy and Annie, things had changed.

With two little girls counting on them, they no longer thought it such a good idea to have both of them putting themselves in harm's way on a daily basis. When a spot had opened up in Personnel, Kath had taken off her Kevlar vest, turned in the keys to her patrol car, and chained herself to a desk and a computer.

"With both Anglo and Indian victims, that'll be a jurisdictional nightmare," Kath mused.

"You've got that right," Brian agreed.

"Where did it happen?"

"South of Topawa," he said. "On the way to Vamori."

"I guess that means you won't be home for Sunday school and church tomorrow."

He leaned down to kiss her good-bye. "Probably," he said.

"All right then," she said. "If you see Dan Pardee and his wonder dog, Bozo, tell them hello."

"Bozo? As in the clown?"

"From what I've heard, Bozo is anything but funny. Dan was out on patrol and a guy tried to bean him with a rock. Bozo took exception and would have torn the guy limb from limb if Dan hadn't stopped him. In other words, no fast moves around Bozo."

"Right," Brian said. "I'll do my damnedest not to piss off the dog."

"Take care," Kath told him.

Nodding, Brian pocketed his wallet, his badge, and keys. On his way down the hall he popped into the girls' room and laid a kiss on each of their foreheads. One of Brian Fellows's rules for living decreed that you had to kiss the people you loved every time you went to work, because one of those times you might not be coming back.

Only after his daughters' kisses had been properly bestowed did Brian Fellows head out of the house. He took off his Husband and Daddy hats and put on the ones marked Murder and Mayhem. That's what you had to do in order to do the job—you compartmentalized.

What was work was work. What was home was home, and never the twain should meet.

Komelik, Tohono O'odham Nation, Arizona
Saturday, June 6, 2009, 10:45 P.M.
67° Fahrenheit

As Dan carried Angie back toward the Expedition, he could feel her body relaxing. Gradually his jacket warmed her, and her trembling ceased. By the time they got to his vehicle she was dead weight in his arms and sound asleep. There was no question about giving her something to eat or drink. Instead he stretched her out in the backseat. For several long minutes after putting her down, he sat next to her just listening to her breathe. He was glad she was sleeping. It was better for everyone concerned, but most especially for Angie herself, if she didn't have to see or remember what came next.

Dan had already called for assistance before he'd gone looking for the girl. He had no idea how much time had passed since then, but so far there was no sign of backup, and there was no way to tell how much longer it would take for other units to respond. Once they did, Dan understood that the crime scene would be disrupted. Unlike Dan and his fellow Shadow Wolves, the other officers would be far more accustomed to dealing with pavement and sidewalks than they were with dirt. He doubted that any of them would be capable of Shadow Wolves–type tracking.

Dan may have been the one who found the victims, but he understood that solving this horrific multiple murder was none of his official business. Still, he wanted to know more—wanted to know who had done these terrible things and why. He could have just sat there and waited, listening to Angie breathe, but he didn't. Slipping Angie's tiny shoes out of his pocket, he put them on the car seat next to her. Then, after ordering Bozo to stay next to the Expedition, Dan walked back to the Blazer.

He skirted around the outside of it, finding in the process that all four windows were rolled down, so it seemed likely that the vehicle's AC wasn't working. Examining the dust just outside the rear passenger door, he saw the set of barefoot tracks Angie had left behind after she had climbed out of the vehicle to go in search of her mother and found her "sleeping." Remembering the child's innocent words made Dan's heart hurt.

He canvassed the scene, trying to suss out who had been the real intended victims of the attack. The several gunshots, he concluded, had been very specific. Druggies and drug smugglers both tended to spray the area with indiscriminate bullets. The gunshots here had been for one purpose only—to kill. They hadn't been to bluff or to scare someone away.

From the way the tracks told the story, Dan could tell that the Anglo couple had been surprised while they were seated at the table. The Indian couple had arrived later, either during or just after the initial attack. It made sense that, since the two Indians were merely collateral damage, the killer hadn't bothered to search the

Blazer thoroughly enough to spot the little girl watching him from the backseat. The Milgahn man with the gun probably believed he was getting away with this. He had no way of knowing that he had left behind an eyewitness.

The only tire tracks Dan saw in the area were from the Lexus and the Blazer. The ones from the Blazer were clearly the most recent ones. The earlier tracks, including Dan's, had been obliterated, but the presence of just those two meant that the killer had approached the scene from some other direction.

Dan walked back out to the road. He had a choice of turning north or south. Since south seemed to be closer to the makeshift grotto with its lantern and flowers, that was the way Dan turned. Fifty yards back down the gravel road, he saw where another vehicle had pulled off and stopped. Someone had exited the vehicle there and walked off into the desert.

Dan was reasonably sure the tire tracks he saw here were much like the ones he had seen earlier in the day, ones that had subsequently been obliterated by the arriving Lexus and Blazer. Whoever had done this had followed the Lexus earlier, so he had a reasonably good idea of where to find his victims. Then, instead of driving up and alerting them to his presence, he had maintained the element of surprise by approaching on foot.

Silent, Dan thought. *Just like a one-pound stone.*

He marked the spot with a crime scene flag that would let the CSIs know to come back here to make tire and footprint casts, although, in Dan's experience, crime scene investigation wasn't likely to be a huge priority on the reservation.

He was walking back to the Expedition when two Law and Order officers showed up—Martin Ramon and Damon Mattias. Dan escorted them around the perimeter of the crime scene, telling them what he knew and what he had surmised and pointing out what he thought might be important in terms of evidence.

In the years the Shadow Wolves had been patrolling the reservation, the unit had gained a measure of respect from the locals. When it came to credibility, it helped that Officer Martin Ramon's older brother, Kevin, was also a member of the Shadow Wolves team.

The two Law and Order patrol officers listened carefully to everything Dan had to say. Both of them jotted copious notes into notebooks. When they approached the second body, Officer Mattias nodded.

"It's Donald Rios, all right," he said. "His family lives around here. We should go tell his father."

The look on Martin Ramon's face made it clear that going to tell some poor unsuspecting man that his son was dead was the last thing he wanted to do.

"I guess we'd better," he said. *"Oi g hihm."*

It was only after they left to go in search of Thomas Rios that Dan Pardee remembered the sleeping child. Since he hadn't mentioned her to them before, he didn't mention her to them now. The fewer people who knew about Angie right then, the better.

Moments after they drove away, headed toward Komelik, an aging Crown Victoria with a full light bar on top arrived at the turnoff. Motioning for the driver to pull over, Dan approached the vehicle.

"Detective Brian Fellows," the driver said, rolling down his window and displaying his badge. "Pima County Homicide." He parked his vehicle on the shoulder of the road and scrambled out of it. "You must be Dan Pardee," he said, offering his hand.

Dan nodded.

"My wife said to tell you hello," the detective added. "Kath Fellows."

"Kath as in Personnel?" Dan asked.

Detective Fellows grinned. "One and the same. Now let's get down to business. I just got off the phone with the M.E.'s office. They'll be here eventually, but they're running into trouble rounding up extra vans. Four victims at one time is more than they can handle. Now show me what we've got."

They set off on Dan's second guided tour of the crime scene. Detective Fellows was packing a small digital camera, and he used it to take photos of everything, including all visible footprints and tire tracks. Dan could tell from the detective's reaction that the sheriff's department wasn't likely to be doing much in-depth crime scene investigating, either. Whatever Fellows found and whatever Dan showed him would probably be crucial.

Detective Fellows took photos of each of the victims. All of them had been stripped of jewelry and watches. And there was no money to be found among the debris from the wallets and purses.

"So maybe it's a straight robbery then," Fellows suggested. "The Indian couple may be married, but I doubt it. The DMV lists Donald Rios as the sole owner of the Blazer."

And Angie called him Donald, not Daddy, Dan thought.

That probably would have been the time for him to tell Detective Fellows about the existence of that eyewitness, but Dan kept his mouth shut. He wasn't ready to relinquish Angie to anyone else, and he knew now that the other officer long ago probably hadn't wanted to let loose of the child he had rescued from another horrific crime scene, either.

While Fellows photographed the last two victims, Dan walked as far as the ironwood tree. By then the last of the luminarias had burned themselves out. Even the light from the battery-powered lantern seemed to be fading. That was bad enough, but when Dan looked inside the tree, he was saddened to see that the huge white flowers, once breathtakingly beautiful, were beginning to shrivel and die as well.

Brian Fellows walked up behind him. "The night-blooming cereus," he explained. "They bloom once a year for one night only, and then they're gone. What about brass? Did you see any?"

Dan shook his head. "Not so far," he replied. "We'll probably have more luck looking for that in daylight."

"Maybe," Fellows said, "but if the guy knew enough to pick up his brass, we might be dealing with a pro."

"From one of the cartels?" Dan asked.

Fellows nodded in agreement. "Could be," he said.

That was Dan's assessment, too. As far as he could see,

the killer's only misstep concerned the child. He had been so caught up in killing the four adults that he had somehow overlooked Angie.

When Dan and Detective Fellows completed their circuit of the crime scene and returned to Dan's Expedition, Bozo was still lying next to it. He raised his head and gave Brian Fellows an appraising look as they passed. The detective evidently measured up, since the dog immediately returned to resting his head on his paws and with apparent unconcern closed his eyes.

"I assume that has to be Bozo, the only non-Indian Shadow Wolf?" Fellows asked.

Dan nodded. "That's right."

"I was warned about him. Kath said I should mind my manners around him."

"Always a good idea," Dan agreed.

Just then, Angie stirred inside the car and made a small whimpering sound. The noise was enough to bring both Bozo and Detective Fellows to full attention.

"Who's that?" the detective asked. "What's that?"

"A little girl," Dan said. "Her name is Angie—Angie with no last name. She was in the Blazer. Somehow the killer missed her. I found her wandering around in the desert, barefoot and scared to death."

"She's not hurt?"

"Not seriously," Dan said. "She's got some cuts and scratches on her face, legs, and feet that probably need to be looked after."

Brian glanced inside the car. "It looks more serious than that," he said.

"You mean the blood on her clothes?" Dan asked.

Brian nodded.

"I think most of that came from another victim. Angie stayed with her mother's body until I showed up."

"How come she's still alive?"

"Because when all hell broke loose, she kept quiet," Dan replied. "That's what her mother said she should do around bad people. She saw the man with the gun. After he left, she went looking for her mother. She thought her mother was sleeping."

"You're saying she saw the guy with the gun?" Brian asked.

Dan nodded. "An Anglo guy with a gun."

"She saw the shooter but not the shooting?"

Dan nodded.

"Do you think she can identify him?"

Dan shrugged. "Beats me," he replied. "She's little. Four . . . maybe five years old."

"Doesn't matter," Brian Fellows said. "If the bad guy *thinks* she can identify him, her life won't be worth a plugged nickel."

That was Dan's assessment as well—that once the killer learned of Angie's existence, the child might well become a target. He also worried that if CPS got involved, the situation could be even worse. "Protective" might be CPS's middle name, but when it came to holding off killers, CPS would be about as useful for Angie as having a "no contact" order is for your run-of-the-mill domestic-violence victim.

The Law and Order patrol car returned, followed by an

aging Ford F-100 pickup truck. Both vehicles parked on the shoulder of the road. An older man, slightly stooped and wearing blue jeans with frayed cuffs around a pair of down-at-the-heels cowboy boots, stepped out of the truck. His passenger, a woman of about the same age, stayed where she was.

With Officers Ramon and Mattias flanking him, the old man limped slowly past the Blazer to the spot where the young Indian man lay on his back. The old man looked down at the victim for a long moment, then nodded.

"It's him," he said stoically. "That's my boy."

Then, without another word and without a hint of a tear, the old man walked back to the pickup. He spoke to the waiting woman in Tohono O'odham. You didn't need to speak the language to understand the anguish and to hear the quiet dignity those words expressed. Then, leaving the woman to her own grief, Thomas Rios returned to the little group of officers, where Officer Ramon made the official introductions. Dan wasn't surprised to see that Thomas Rios was someone he already knew.

"There's a little girl here," Detective Fellows said to Thomas. "Can you tell us who she is?"

"That's probably Angie, Delphina Enos's little girl. Delphina is . . . was . . . Donald's girlfriend. He had bought her a ring. He was going to ask her to marry him."

"And Ms. Enos lived where?"

"In Sells," he said. "But her family lives in Nolic. She was a nice girl."

"To your knowledge did either of these people have any connection to the drug trade?"

Detective Fellows was the one who asked the question. The old Indian examined him with a long piercing look before he replied.

"No," he said finally. "Not at all. Donald was a good boy—a good man. He didn't do drugs. He didn't drink."

"You know that Donald and Delphina aren't the only victims here tonight?" Fellows asked.

Thomas Rios nodded. "Yes. Martin told me. An old Milgahn man and woman, right?" he asked.

"Yes," Fellows said, pointing. "He drove that white Lexus."

"I knew him," Thomas said quietly. "He asked me if I would let him look around my land. He was searching for a deer-horn cactus. I told him about this one." He waved in the direction of the faded lantern and the ironwood tree.

"He wanted to find some to show to his wife," Rios continued. "He told me yesterday that he'd be bringing her here tonight to see the flowers. It was supposed to be a big surprise."

It was a surprise, all right, Dan thought.

After that, they walked around to the front of the old man's pickup. He stood with one boot resting on the bumper and answered the officers' many questions with a soft-spoken style that was equal parts quiet dignity and unyielding endurance. Listening and watching carried Dan back to that other time, that long-ago time, and to another old Indian man.

**Los Angeles, California
October 1978**

The next morning Dan had awakened in a strange household, with people he didn't know. The strangers were kind enough to him. They fed him and gave him clean clothes to wear, but they didn't answer his many questions. Halloween came and went. Dan didn't get to go trick-or-treating. His mother had bought him a Spider-Man costume to wear, but that hadn't come with him the night he had been carried out of the apartment. If anyone ever went back to retrieve it, Dan never saw it.

Dan kept asking where his mother was and when she would come to get him. He noticed that when the woman bothered to answer him at all, she said that she didn't know, but that someone else, someone who wasn't Dan's mother, would come for him soon. His father had told lies all the time. Dan noticed that the woman never looked at him when she said those things, and Dan suspected that she was lying, too.

Dan was only four years old at the time. He wasn't able to put all his feelings into words, but he finally figured it out, even though no one said so in so many words. He finally came to understand that something terrible had happened to his mother. Maybe she was hurt. Maybe she was sick. He tried not to think about the sounds of his parents quarreling on the far side of his bedroom door. He tried not to think about all those noisy firecrackers exploding out in the living room, but as the long lonely days passed one after another, he finally realized those noisy pops he had heard hadn't been from firecrackers, not at all.

Dan had seen his father's gun. Adam Pardee kept it on a high shelf in the closet. He often told Danny that he'd take his belt to him if he ever so much as touched it. Dan knew he could have reached the shelf if he had tried, if he had climbed up on a chair, but he never did. Daniel maybe didn't believe what the nice woman told him about someone coming to get him, but harsh experience had made him believe in Adam Pardee's belt.

Then, one morning—several days later, although in Danny's mind it seemed much longer—the woman had rushed Dan through his cold cereal at breakfast and then had herded him into the bathtub.

"Your grandfather's coming to get you," she announced with a cheerful smile. "Isn't that wonderful!"

It wasn't wonderful for Dan. He didn't know his grandfather, had never met him, didn't know he had one.

"What grandfather?" he asked.

"Why, your mother's father," she replied, sounding surprised. "He's coming all the way from Safford, Arizona, to pick you up and take you home."

Dan knew that wasn't right. Home was here in California with his parents, not in Arizona with some stranger. He didn't even know where Arizona was. It sounded like it was far away.

An hour or so later Dan found himself sitting on the sagging couch in the living room waiting for the doorbell to ring. He was dressed in faded jeans and an equally faded Star Wars T-shirt. The clothing was several sizes

too large for him. The remainder of his meager possessions—a toothbrush, a comb, a small tube of toothpaste,
and a freshly laundered and neatly folded Spider-Man
bedsheet—had been packed into the paper bag that sat
on the couch beside him.

When the doorbell rang, he raced to answer it. As soon
as he flung the door open and saw who was outside, Dan
knew there had to be some mistake.

The wizened, wiry old man standing on the front porch
might have been a cowboy straight out of the Old West.
He came complete with boots, belt, and a pearl-button
Western shirt. That wasn't so bad. The real problem was
that he was an Indian. Dan had seen Indians before—in
the movies and on TV. The man's coal-black straight hair
was slicked down and combed back flat on his head. His
face was both broad and angular. His skin was brown,
much browner than Daniel's. His eyes were almost black.
Dan's were light brown—almost hazel.

"Daniel?" the old man asked.

All Dan could do was stare and nod wordlessly.

The stranger held out his hand, but Dan backed away
from him.

"My name is Micah," the old man said. "Micah Duarte.
Rebecca, your mother, was my daughter. I've come to
take you home."

Was. Dan heard the word and understood at once what
he had just been told, what the smiling woman hadn't
been willing to tell him. This was like in the movie when
Bambi's father comes to Bambi after hunting season and
says, "Your mother can't be with you anymore."

Leaving the stranger on the porch, Dan walked away from the door, climbed back up on the couch, and clutched his paper bag to his chest. He did his best not to cry.

His father hated it when he cried. "Don't be a sissy," Adam Pardee always said. "Only sissies cry." Dan had cried in the movie when Bambi lost his mother, but he didn't cry for his own mother, not then, not with that strange Indian man watching him.

The woman bustled in from the kitchen, smiling and wiping her hands on a towel as she approached the man who still waited outside on the porch. He wasn't smiling. Neither was Dan.

"You must be Mr. Duarte," she said. "Please do come in. I'm Hilda Romero. I see you two have already met." She turned to Dan. "Are you ready to go?"

"I don't want to go," he said, shaking his head. "I want to stay here. I want to live here."

Mrs. Romero smiled again. It seemed to him that she was always smiling, but he didn't believe that, either.

"But Mr. Duarte is family," she said. "Your real family. He's going to take you home with him. He's going to look after you."

"I don't want him to," Dan insisted stubbornly. "I want my mother to look after me."

Micah Duarte said nothing. He gave only the smallest shake of his head, a gesture that meant exactly what Bambi's father had meant. Dan's mother was gone—gone forever. She wasn't coming back for him, but still Dan didn't move. He stayed where he was, on the couch.

"We have to go," Micah Duarte said softly. "Safford is a long way away. My boss would only let me have today off. I drove all night to get here, and I told Maxine we'd be back home tonight."

Dan didn't know who Maxine was and he didn't want to.

"But I don't know you," Dan objected, practically shouting.

Micah Duarte nodded. "I know," he said. "Your mother didn't like being an Indian. She hated it. That's why she ran away and came here. She was very beautiful. She thought she'd be able to be a movie star."

He shrugged as if to underscore the futility of his daughter's empty dream.

Dan, who had never heard anything at all about his mother's people, was thunderstruck. "My mother isn't an Indian," he declared. "She can't be."

"She was," Micah insisted, using that terrible word again, "was" spoken softly and sadly. "She was Apache, and you are, too, Daniel. Come now. We need to go. We can talk along the way."

He held out his hand. Once again Dan shook his head.

For a moment longer Dan sat there, resisting, but the force behind Micah Duarte's command was like a physical presence. Finally, as if his feet had minds of their own, they hopped down from the couch and carried him across the room. He stepped out through the door and onto the porch. Then, almost against his will, Dan reached up and took his grandfather's hand.

Even though Adam Pardee was a stunt man doing pretend tricks for the movies, his hands had always been smooth and soft. That was one of the reasons he always used the belt—on his son and on his wife. He didn't want anything to damage the looks of his hands; he couldn't afford to bark or scrape his knuckles.

Micah Duarte's hands were large and anything but smooth. They were cracked and rough and covered with bumps Dan would later learn were calluses—calluses that came from working long hours with tools and doing hard physical labor. Micah made real stuff happen, and he didn't care how his hands looked or felt.

Together Daniel and Micah walked across the porch, down the steep steps, and along the short walkway. Outside the yard, a very old pickup was parked next to the sidewalk. Micah walked up to the passenger door, opened it, and gestured for Daniel to get inside.

He didn't. He stopped in the middle of the sidewalk. "I want my mother," he said. "Where is she?"

Micah's eyes misted over. He turned away from the boy's question and for a long time said nothing. Instead, he walked as far as the front of the truck and planted one booted foot on the front bumper the same way Thomas Rios was doing right now.

"Your mother is dead," he said at last. He patted the pocket of his shirt. "She sent us a letter. She was afraid your father might do something bad. He was drinking too much and doing other stuff. She wrote to see if Maxine and I would let her come home. We would have, but the letter came too late for us to help her. Since I couldn't come to get her, I came to get you. Understand?"

* * *

Dan hadn't understood all of it right then, not really, but he hadn't cried, either. Not because Micah Duarte might think he was a sissy. It was because Dan knew enough about Indians to know that they didn't cry. Ever.

In view of everything his own grandparents had done for him, Daniel Pardee could only hope, for Angie Enos's sake, that there was someone in her life, someone like Micah and Maxine Duarte, who would step up to the plate, take in a poor motherless child, and lavish her with love and affection.

A silence fell over the small group of men gathered around Thomas Rios's F-100.

"Anything else?" Detective Fellows asked, glancing questioningly at the other officers.

All three shook their heads. Dan had no additional questions to ask primarily because he hadn't been paying attention. He had been far away in another place and time. When he came back on track, Detective Fellows was speaking to Thomas Rios in what sounded to Dan like pitch-perfect Tohono O'odham.

The two Law and Order officers seemed surprised by that. *Nawoj* was the only word Dan was able to pick out from the string of conversation. He knew *nawoj* meant friend or friendly gift. When Detective Fellows finished speaking, Thomas Rios nodded and the two men shared a brief handshake. After that, the old man got back in his pickup and drove away.

"What did you say to him?" Dan asked.

"That I'm sorry for his loss," Brian Fellows answered.

"How'd you learn to speak the language?"

"I learned from some friends here on the reservation," Fellows said with an unassuming shrug, as though it was no big deal. "I had a friend, an Anglo guy named Davy Ladd. He taught me, and so did an Indian lady named Rita Antone and an old medicine man everyone called Fat Crack. The three of them taught me everything I know."

Now I understand, Dan thought. *No wonder he's the detective they assigned to this case.*

8

*G*ABE FELL ASLEEP again soon after Lani finished telling him the story. Even though she believed Gabe hadn't lied when he told her about seeing the image of Andrew Carlisle sitting with her mother, she knew it wasn't true, not in any real physical sense. The man was dead, after all—he had died in prison years earlier. But she also understood that something about his brooding spirit—his dangerous, *ohb*-like presence—was once again intruding into the lives of Diana Ladd and Brandon Walker. Lani also understood why her mother had vehemently denied seeing him. That was clear enough. Adults who were known to speak to people who weren't there were usually thought to be crazy.

On the other hand, children who conducted conversations with imaginary friends were often considered to be bright and creative. Little Gabe Ortiz certainly qualified as bright and creative, but Lani feared there was far more to this than simply an overly active imagination on his part.

Gabe hadn't made up the burned and puckered skin on the ghostly apparition's face. Lani knew about the panful of hot grease her mother had flung at Andrew Carlisle when he had broken into the house in Gates Pass and attacked her. Lani had seen photos of Carlisle's face both before and after their life-and-death encounter. The two photos sat side by side in the photo section of Lani's mother's prizewinning book, *Shadow of Death*. One featured a head shot of a handsome but arrogant young man whose smug expression had spoken volumes about his contempt for others. The second pictured the grotesque features of that same face wrecked by mounds of scar tissue and with a pair of sightless eyes staring out at nothing.

Yes, they were both photos of the same man—the same one Gabe had evidently seen as well, but for Lani the most worrisome part in all of this was something he must have told her mother that had resulted in Diana's pointed question about Mitch Johnson and what he had done to Lani when he had kidnapped her and held her hostage years earlier.

Once Mitch Johnson was dead, Lani had gone to great lengths to keep her mother from knowing all of what had happened during that dreadful time, and especially about the welt of puckered scar tissue his red-hot tongs had seared into the flesh of her breast. Now, though, her mother's question seemed to indicate that she had been given some hints about what had happened that night and about Lani's carefully guarded secret.

Lani was convinced that something else was at work here, something sinister. She felt as though she'd been given a warning of some kind—a glimpse into the future that told her something dangerous was coming. She wished once again that there had been time tonight to sit down and discuss it with her father. Or with Fat Crack. The old medicine man would have known what these evil forebodings meant and how one should deal with them.

The full moon was shining high overhead, and it was close to eleven thirty when Lani and Gabe finally arrived in Sells, sixty miles from Tucson. She drove straight to the hospital housing compound and stumble-walked Gabe into her house and down the hall to her second guest bedroom. Once he was tucked into bed, Lani showered and dressed in a pair of scrubs.

By then it was only a matter of minutes before her shift was due to start at midnight. There was no sense in trying to grab a quick nap. Besides, Lani wasn't sleepy. Her body was still accustomed to the sleep-deprived schedule she had maintained as both an intern and as a resident. Tomorrow, after she got off shift, there would be plenty of time to sleep.

She fixed a cup of instant coffee—plastic coffee, as her father called it—and then sat at her small kitchen table to drink it. She didn't worry about leaving Gabe alone. He spent the night with her often enough. He knew that, if there was a problem—any kind of problem—all he had to do was walk across the parking lot to the hospital to find her.

Lani wished she could take Fat Crack's deerskin pouch, his *huashomi,* out of her medicine basket and put it to good use, but there wasn't enough time for one of the old medicine man's discerning ceremonies. She needed uninterrupted time to smoke the sacred tobacco, the *wiw,* or to examine whatever images might be hidden in Fat Crack's collection of crystals. Those were things that could be done only on Indian time. The hospital ran on Anglo time, with a time clock for punching in and punching out.

Lani had lived in both the Anglo and Indian worlds all her life, and she was accustomed to the accompanying dichotomy. She was also used to being more than one person at one time. That, too, had been part of her lifelong reality.

Before her adoption by Brandon Walker and Diana Ladd, Lani had been known as Clemencia Escalante from the village of Nolic. Her biological mother, a teenager more interested in partying than in raising a child, had left her baby in the care of an aging grandmother. Once the older kids in the village had gone off to school, Clemencia, still a toddler, had wandered into an ant bed and had almost died of multiple ant bites. The superstitious Escalantes had regarded Clemencia as a dangerous object and had refused to take her back. Fat Crack's wife,

Wanda, a social worker, had brought the abandoned baby to the attention of her husband's aunt Rita Antone. It was at Rita's instigation that Brandon Walker and Diana Ladd had adopted her.

Lani knew that people on the reservation who knew the story still sometimes referred to her as Kuadagi Ke'd Al, the Ant-Bit Child. Her adoptive parents had given her the name Lanita Dolores after Kulani O'oks, the Tohono O'odham's greatest medicine woman, the Woman Who Had Been Kissed by the Bees. Nana *Dahd,* her godmother, had called her Mualig Siakam, Forever Spinning, because, like Whirlwind, Lani had loved to dance. And after she had used Bat Strength in her fatal encounter with Mitch Johnson in the cave under Ioligam—after she had been saved by the timely intervention of bat wings in the darkness of I'itoi's cave—Lani often called herself Nanakumal Namkam, Bat Meeter.

But tonight, in the Indian Health Center at Sells, Lani couldn't be anyone else but Lanita Dolores Walker, M.D.

Putting her dirty cup in the dishwasher, she left her housing compound apartment and headed for the ER.

Vamori, Tohono O'odham Nation, Arizona
Sunday, June 7, 2009, 12:00 A.M.
67° Fahrenheit

Tribal chairman Delia Ortiz's feet hurt—like crazy. She had been on them all day long. Even though it was Saturday, she had spent most of the day at work in her office at Sells. Now here she was at the dance at Vamori.

Delia's husband, Leo, loved the dances for good reason. He and his brother, Richard, played in a chicken-scratch band, and the summer dance at Vamori was one of their favorite gigs, but they had grown up on the reservation. Delia had not.

She had spent most of her early years as an "in town" Indian, most notably in Tempe and later on the East Coast. Fat Crack Ortiz, a previous tribal chairman, had wooed her back to the Tohono O'odham reservation from Washington, D.C., by offering her the job of tribal attorney. The fact that Fat Crack later became her father-in-law in addition to being her boss was one of the unintended consequences of her acceptance of that position.

Not long after Fat Crack's death, Delia herself had been elected tribal chairman. In terms of what was going on at the time, an "in town" Indian was exactly what had been and still was required for the job.

The U.S. government has a long ignoble history of cheating Indians and disregarding treaty arrangements. That was still happening. Tribes, including the Tohono O'odham, were still having to file suit against the BIA in order to get monies that were lawfully due them. Now, however, with casino operations changing reservation economics, there was a new wrinkle in Anglo cheating. The casinos belonged to the tribes, but the mostly Anglo operators were slick and accustomed to winning at every game. They were more than prepared to take the tribes to the cleaners the same way they did ordinary gamblers.

Whenever those kinds of issues needed to be handled,

Delia Chavez Cachora Ortiz was up to the task. She brought to the job of tribal chairman qualifications that included a top-flight East Coast education as well as a prestigious cum laude Harvard law degree. Her curriculum vitae was fine when it came to dealing with intractable bureaucrats. There she found she was often able to out-Milgahn the Milgahn.

Not having grown up on the reservation, however, Delia was less prepared for the day-to-day aspects of doing the job at home—for keeping the peace between the various districts on the reservation; for making sure roads got graded and paved in a timely fashion; for settling disputes over someone picking saguaro fruit in someone else's traditional territory.

She had also learned that everything she needed to know to do her job most likely wouldn't show up in official visits to her office, or on the tribal meeting agenda, either. For that kind of in-depth knowledge and insight she needed to be out in public—mingling with the people, learning their concerns, and familiarizing herself with their age-old antipathies and alliances. The only way for her to do that was to go where the people went, and they went to the dances.

That meant Delia Ortiz went to the dances, too, not that she liked them much. She didn't. For one thing there were far too many of them—usually one a week or so. Depending on whether they were summer dances or winter dances, they were either too hot or too cold, and sometimes, like this one at Vamori, the dance was both too hot and too cold in the course of the same night.

They were also dusty and loud and they seemed to go on forever, generally lasting from sundown to sunup. But that's where she had to be, picking up tidbits of gossip while standing in line at the feast house or talking to the old people who, even in the summer, gathered around the fires to keep warm.

Delia's mandatory attendance at the all-night dance at Vamori was one of the reasons she had given Lani permission to take Gabe to Tucson for the Queen of the Night party and then, afterward, to spend the night at Lani's place in the hospital housing compound.

At events like this Delia found it difficult to juggle the dual requirements of being both a mother and an elected official. Gabe was a naturally curious child with a propensity for getting into mischief. It was impossible for Delia to keep an eye on him all the time while someone was trying to tell her about what was going on in Ali Chuk Shon, Little Tucson, or Hikiwoni Chekshani, Jagged Cut District.

Delia was standing by one of the cooking fires and talking to a woman whose husband, a diabetic, was having to undergo dialysis three times a week, when Martin Ramon came looking for her. The serious look on the tribal police officer's face told her something was badly amiss. Delia's first thought was that something terrible had happened to Gabe. Everyone knew Lani Walker had a lead foot and drove that little Passat of hers far too fast.

"What's wrong?" she asked.

"There's been a shooting," Officer Ramon told her. "Four people are dead."

"Where?" she asked. "Here on the reservation?"

Martin nodded. "Over by Komelik," he said.

Waving good-bye to the woman, Delia excused herself and followed him. "Let me tell Leo," she told Officer Ramon. "Then, if you don't mind waiting a few minutes, I'll go there with you."

She made her way across the dusty dance floor, dodging between couples dancing their old-fashioned two-step. When she reached the band, she waited until that song ended.

"What's up?" Leo said, smiling as he asked the question.

"I have to go," she said. "Something's wrong at Komelik."

Without a word, Leo reached for his car keys and offered them to her.

"No," she said. "You and Richard will need the truck to bring home your instruments. When I finish at Komelik, I'll have one of the officers take me home."

She followed Martin Ramon to his patrol car, dreading where she was going and what she was going to see, but incredibly grateful for Leo Ortiz. His automatic reflex of unwavering kindness toward her and toward everyone else was one of the things she treasured about him. And it wasn't an act, either. He wasn't one person in public when he wanted to impress people and someone else at home the way her first husband, Philip Cachora, had been.

At one of his gallery openings or when he had been wooing some well-heeled art fancier, Philip had been smooth as glass, Mr. Charm himself. The rough edges had all turned up at home where he had been a lying creep of a drug user and unfaithful to Delia besides. Leo's life was an open book to her and to everyone else as well.

"Four people?" Delia asked Martin Ramon after she strapped herself into the seat. "Indians?"

"Two are," he answered. "We've got a positive ID on one of them. Thomas Rios from Komelik identified his son Donald. We think the woman is Donald's girlfriend, Delphina Enos."

"That new clerk from Nolic?" Delia asked. "The one with the little girl. Is she all right?"

"The little girl is hurt but not that bad," Martin answered. "Mostly cuts on her feet and on her face. She was found walking barefoot in the desert."

"By herself?"

Martin nodded grimly. "One of the Border Patrol's Shadow Wolves found her—a guy by the name of Dan Pardee. He found the four bodies first and then located the little girl a while later. My understanding is that he's taking her to the hospital in Sells right now so she can be checked out."

"What about the other two victims?"

"They're both Anglos from Tucson. Thomas Rios says he gave the man permission for them to be on his land. They came to look at the deer-horn cactus, the Queen of the Night, which was supposed to bloom tonight."

"What happened?" Delia asked. "Did the Anglos end up having some kind of beef with Thomas Rios's son and the fight ended up in a shoot-out?"

"No," Martin said. "That's not it at all. For one thing, we didn't find any weapons at the scene. That means someone else is the shooter. It looks like cash and jewelry are missing from the victims' wallets and purses, so it may be a simple case of robbery. It could also be some kind of drug deal gone bad, although when we talked to Mr. Rios, he said his son wasn't involved in any of that bad stuff."

"Maybe these poor people stumbled upon someone else's drug deal."

Officer Ramon nodded. "That could be. Four people who were all in the wrong place at the wrong time."

Damn, Delia thought. *Something else to give the Nation a bad name and make tourists run in the other direction.*

Komelik, Tohono O'odham Nation, Arizona
Sunday, June 7, 2009, 12:10 A.M.
67° Fahrenheit

The first contingent of medical examiner vans arrived on the scene shortly after midnight. Fran Daly herself, Pima County's most recent chief medical examiner, stepped out of the passenger side of the first-arriving vehicle.

When the previous M.E. had taken his retirement and left the premises, his longtime assistant, Fran Daly, had finally received a much-deserved promotion. A former rodeo rider, she was an odd woman and tough as nails. Even roused from sleep in the middle of the night and with her curly white hair standing on end like so many unruly cotton balls, she still managed to be all business. She was at ease with herself and others. She was also at ease with the job she had to do. Once on the ground, she looked around, shivered, and then reached back inside the van's front seat to retrieve a windbreaker.

Detective Fellows, the only Pima County investigator on the scene, took Fran in hand and led her around the crime scene, following the same careful pathway Dan Pardee had used.

"We've positively identified one victim," Brian told Fran. "Donald Rios's father came by a little while ago."

"Good," Fran said. "No next-of-kin notification for one of them then. Who are the others?"

"Two of them appear to be an Anglo couple from Tucson, tentatively identified as Jack and Abigail Tennant."

"And the Indian woman?"

"She's believed to be Donald's girlfriend, Delphina Enos. She was currently living in Sells, but she's originally from a village called Nolic. A child we believe to be Delphina's daughter was found wandering barefoot around the crime scene. She's being transported to the hospital at Sells."

"Life-threatening injuries?" Fran asked.

Brian shook his head. "Minor injuries," he replied. "Traumatized by what happened, of course, but she doesn't appear to be physically hurt. Instead of calling for an ambulance, we got the booster seat out of the Blazer and put it in the back of Dan Pardee's Expedition. He's the guy who's taking her to the hospital."

"Who's Dan Pardee, a member of the tribal police?"

"Pardee's Border Patrol, a member of the Shadow Wolves unit," Brian explained. "He's the one who initially located the crime scene. It appears that the assailant or assailants went through the victims' purses and wallets and dumped everything they didn't want out on the ground. Dan looked through what was there and found a couple of ID cards in case he needed some kind of identification in order to have the little girl treated at the hospital in Sells. Cash and jewelry appear to be missing, but everything else was still here."

"You said the Indian woman was from somewhere called Nolic?" Fran asked. "Never heard of it. I'm not sure how I'll manage her next-of-kin notice."

"That probably won't be necessary," Brian said. "One of the guys from Law and Order went to get Delia Ortiz."

"The tribal chairman?" Fran asked.

Brian nodded. "According to Mr. Rios, Delphina worked for the tribe. Ms. Ortiz should be able to give us a positive ID and some idea about her next of kin. I'm reasonably certain Law and Order will take care of notifying her relatives."

"What about the Anglo couple?"

"As I said, I've got their names and a tentative address in Tucson, but that's about all."

"It's a start," Fran said.

Running the beam from a flashlight over the dead woman's body, she shook her head. "The shooter took this woman down with a single shot," Fran said. "If he's that serious about killing people, how come the little kid isn't dead?"

"Good question," Detective Fellows said with a rueful smile. "Maybe they just aren't making crooks the way they used to."

Sells, Tohono O'odham Nation, Arizona
Sunday, June 7, 2009, 12:45 A.M.
70° Fahrenheit

Dan had learned that the Tohono O'odham call June Hashani Bahithag Mashath, or Saguaro-Ripening Month. That's also the month when the Sonoran Desert routinely bakes in an unrelenting dry heat during the day that can turn to a comparatively icy chill at night. That had already happened by the time he turned into the hospital parking lot at Sells. The seventy-degree external temperature reading seemed downright chilly compared to what it had been earlier in the afternoon.

An ambulance with its lights still flashing was parked in the portico outside the emergency room. Dan steered his Expedition into an almost empty parking lot where his oversize vehicle took up most of what was striped off to be two compact spaces. Then, after rolling down the windows and ordering Bozo to stay, Dan unbelted Angie and carried the sleeping child inside the building.

She was still wearing her bloodied clothing. He set her down carefully on a bench next to the wall. He had rescued a toy—a pink-and-yellow pinwheel—from the backseat of the Blazer. After placing that near her hand, Dan stepped forward for what he expected to be a protracted battle with the emergency-room clerk. The woman glanced at Angie's sleeping, bloodstained form and then eyed Dan speculatively, as though she was convinced that Dan was responsible for the little girl's injuries.

"What happened to her?" the clerk wanted to know.

"She was running around out in the desert without any shoes," Dan explained. "She has cuts on her face, feet, and legs."

The clerk shrugged and sighed as if this didn't seem to be something serious enough to merit an emergency-room visit. "All right, then," she said. "I'll need to see proof of enrollment."

Dan slipped both Delphina's and Angie's ID cards out of his shirt pocket and handed them over to the clerk. She studied them carefully for some time. When she finally started typing information into her computer, Dan watched her flying fingers and thought about what else he had found there on the ground, the one item he hadn't shared with the Pima County investigator—a wallet-size photo of Delphina Enos holding Angie.

In the picture a smiling Delphina had beamed proudly down at her baby daughter while Angie, dressed in a lacy white dress, smiled back. It was a peaceful photo, a loving photo.

She's wearing a baptism dress, Dan had thought the moment he saw the photo. After studying it briefly, he had slipped it into his pocket right along with the two ID cards.

The clerk finished typing and cleared her throat. "Who are you?" she asked. "Are you the father?"

Dan shook his head. "No," he said. "I'm just the guy who found her."

"You're not a relative, then?"

"No relation."

The clerk stiffened. "If that's the case, I'm afraid we can't treat her," she said, shaking her head dismissively. "This isn't a life-or-death emergency. She isn't even bleeding anymore. Have her mother bring her in tomorrow morning. A doctor can look at her then."

The woman was only doing her job, but Dan felt an unreasoning rage growing inside him. He recognized his anger for what it was. Eye color wasn't the only thing he had inherited from his biological father. He also had Adam Pardee's hot temper. It was one of the things about his grandson that Micah Duarte had done his best to counter.

Dan's grandfather had taught him when to fight and how to fight and when to back off and walk away. As a teenager, Dan had been astonished to learn that Gramps knew karate. Micah saw to it that his grandson was one of the few black belts on the San Carlos.

Calling on those lessons now, Dan forced himself to take several deep breaths.

"Her mother can't come in tomorrow morning because she's dead," he explained to the clerk, keeping his voice low and steady but forceful. "Somebody murdered her earlier tonight out in the desert. They shot and killed the mother and left this little girl alone in the desert. As an Indian she qualifies for treatment at this facility. I want her checked out. If you can't help me, then let me talk to someone who can."

Dan knew what Adam Pardee would have done about then. He would have slammed both fists on the counter or knocked something off it onto the floor, preferably something breakable. Dan did what Micah Duarte had trained him to do. While the clerk was thinking about what Dan had said, he walked away from her. He went back over to where Angie lay sleeping, sat down on the bench beside her, crossed his arms over his chest, and waited. He didn't look at the clerk, but finally he heard her sigh, get up, and walk away from her desk. She went through a swinging door and disappeared.

Sitting there, Dan could still feel the stiff paper from the photo inside his shirt pocket. He, more than anyone in the world, knew what the future most likely held in store for this unfortunate little girl. Yes, Angie had lost her mother. Since Donald Rios had been Delphina's boyfriend, that most likely meant Angie's father was no longer a presence in her life, either, making her an orphan twice over.

At the tender age of four she would have few conscious memories of her mother, but Dan understood that in terms of physical remembrances she would probably have even less.

By the time pieces of Delphina's life had been taken into evidence; by the time her friends and relations had sorted through the dead woman's belongings and skimmed off what they wanted, Dan knew that there would be precious little of her dead mother left for Angie to cling to—nothing but that one single photo that he had managed to salvage.

And how did Dan Pardee know this? Through bitter experience—because that was the way it had been for him.

Someone probably still had copies of school yearbooks that showed his mother as she had been when she was in high school. And he dimly remembered there being photos of her in their apartment before she died. Those had all been head shots she'd had taken when she was still hoping to find work in Hollywood and going out on interviews and auditions.

He didn't remember the photos in any detail. What he did remember was that his mother had been beautiful back then—with surprisingly narrow features and a winning smile. None of those pictures, however, had survived the police investigation in the bloodied apartment living room. Or, if they had, none of them had come into her son's possession once the investigation was over.

Dan had only two things left from his mother and from that time. One was the faded letter, written on a scrap of notebook paper, that Rebecca Pardee had written to her parents back home in Arizona, asking for their help. It was the same letter Micah Duarte had carried in his shirt pocket the day he had come to L.A. to collect his grandson.

The other was a fragment of a set of Spider-Man sheets Dan's mother had bought for Dan's bed and had given him for his birthday. It was the same top sheet that anonymous cop had wrapped the little boy in when he had plucked the sleeping child out of his bed. The cop had used the sheet to cover the little boy's face so he wouldn't see the awful carnage in the living room and his mother's blood-spattered body.

Maybe the cop had hoped that if Dan didn't see it, he wouldn't have to remember it, either.

Hilda, his foster mother, had washed the sheet, folded it, and put it in Dan's paper bag the morning Micah had come to fetch him. That and the letter were the only two things Dan still possessed that he knew for sure his mother had once touched. He had treasured the sheet and slept with it in his bed night after night until it was little more than a frayed rag. Before he went to Iraq, he had cut a small piece of it out of the hem—the only part that still held together. He had placed that faded scrap of material inside the envelope along with his mother's letter to her parents. Dan then placed the envelope inside his wallet. That treasured envelope had gone with him to war in the Middle East and it had come home from the war. It was here with him now.

Taking the photo from his pocket, he opened his own wallet. He thumbed through the contents until, tucked in among his credit cards, he found the envelope with its now-illegible address. He slipped the photo of Delphina and Angie Enos into the fragile envelope next to the faded letter and that precious scrap of material. Then he returned the envelope to his wallet, closed it, and put it away. He would keep the photo safe. Someday he would give it to Angie. It would be the one meaningful gift Dan Pardee could give the little girl—a photo of her mother smiling down at her.

Sitting there in the waiting room, Dan couldn't help wishing that someone had done the same for him.

Just then the clerk reappeared behind her desk. "Dr. Walker will see you now," she said, gesturing them toward a swinging door. "Right this way."

Sells, Tohono O'odham Nation, Arizona
Sunday, June 7, 2009, 12:00 A.M.
71° Fahrenheit

Lani's first patient that night had been a snakebite victim. Jose Thomas of Big Fields had been out cutting wood two days earlier. He had picked up a dead mesquite branch only to be bitten on the hand by a rattlesnake lurking in the cooler earth underneath the branch.

"Only a little rattlesnake," he mumbled over and over. *"Ali Ko'oi."*

The snake may have been little, but the damage wasn't.

Snakebites were commonplace on the reservation. As a result, the hospital at Sells maintained a constant stock of antivenom. Most of the time, people who had been bitten came to the hospital as soon as possible after the incident. As long as they received antivenom treatment immediately, few of them suffered long-term ill effects.

While still in high school, Lani had worked at the Arizona Sonora Desert Museum both after school and during summer and winter breaks. She knew, for example, that Arizona is home to seventeen different kinds of rattlers, five of which are found in and around the Tucson area.

Their venom came with varying strengths of toxicity, the most poisonous of which was the Mojave. When treating patients, medical professionals needed to know which kind of snake venom they were dealing with. That wasn't always possible, especially when the victims were young children. Then the doctors involved just had to make an educated guess.

The problem with Jose Thomas was that he was an old man who lived alone.

Make that a stubborn old man, Lani thought grimly.

And he hadn't come in to be treated right away. In fact, if it had been left up to him, he wouldn't have come to the hospital at all. He had treated himself by lancing the wound, pouring some tequila on it, and then pouring more of the tequila down his own throat. By the time Jose's grandson had stopped by to see him, Jose was in bed, delirious and barely conscious. He was running a dangerously high fever. The damaged flesh surrounding the bite was beginning to rot and fall away.

Once he was in the ER, Lani's first goal was to bring down the fever by bathing him in ice. Then she ordered him plugged full of liquids and antibiotics. At this point, he had developed secondary infections—including pneumonia—that were more serious than the bite. She treated the bite itself as best she could, but her initial examination told her that it was more than likely that Jose would probably lose the hand. That wouldn't happen until after he was stabilized. Until then, surgery of any kind was out of the question.

As Mr. Thomas was wheeled into the ICU, the ER's admitting clerk, Dena Rojo, came into the cubicle. "We've got a problem out there," she said, nodding toward the door.

"What kind of a problem?"

"A Border Patrol officer with a little girl. She's got some cuts on her face, feet, and legs. I don't think it's serious enough for you to bother, but . . ."

"An illegal?" Lani asked.

Indian Health Services was generally exactly that— for Indians only. Exceptions were made in emergencies, when other patients could be given access to immediate care regardless of race or nationality. Border Patrol officers often found injured and dying immigrants on the reservation. During the summer, dehydration was a killer. So far this year there had already been fifteen immigrant deaths among illegal immigrants attempting to cross the border, and that was with the summer months just now heating up.

That was the basis of Lani's inquiry. Dena shook her head.

"Indian," she said. "Her name is Angelina Enos. We've treated her before. She has a chart."

"What's the problem then?" Lani asked.

"The guy who brought her in is no relation of hers," Dena said. "He just found her out in the desert somewhere and brought her here."

"Where are her parents?" Lani asked.

"Her father's been gone for a long time," Dena replied. "Now someone has murdered her mother."

"Who'll be responsible for her long-term?" Lani asked.

Dena shrugged. "Probably the grandparents. I think they live out at Nolic, but they don't have a phone."

Lani winced at that. She knew the village of Nolic, The Bend. That was where she had come from a long time ago, before she became Lani Walker. The fact that Lani's blood relatives had rejected her was what had given her this other life—and a chance to be here at Sells in her scrubs, ready to help some other unfortunate child.

"Have him bring her in," Lani said.

"You're sure?" Dena asked.

"I'm sure."

Sells, Tohono O'odham Nation, Arizona
Sunday, June 7, 2009, 1:00 A.M.
68° Fahrenheit

Angie woke up as Dan carried her into the ER and set her down on the examining table.

"Where are we?" she asked. "Where's my mommy?"

"We're at the hospital here in Sells so someone can look at the cuts on your legs and feet," Dan explained. "Your mommy's not here right now."

Angie studied his face for a long time. Finally she nodded.

Hoping the clerk had clued the ER staff in on what had happened out by Komelik, he looked to the doctor for help. He did not expect Dr. Walker—Dr. Lanita Dolores Walker, as her name tag said—to be a woman or an

Indian. And he certainly didn't expect her to be beautiful. It turned out she was all three.

She stepped forward and gave Angie a reassuring smile. "This nice man brought you here so we could look at your feet and your legs," she said. "You have quite a few scratches. What happened?"

"I went for a walk in the desert," Angie said in a whisper. "I left my shoes in the car."

Dr. Walker touched Angie's knee. It was scraped and scabby. It was also hot.

"I'll bet you were out in the desert for a long time," she said. "Have you had anything to drink? Are you thirsty?"

"I was going to give her something to drink and something to eat, too," Dan said quickly. "But she fell asleep as soon as I got her back to the car. The way things were going, I didn't want to wake her up."

Nodding, Dr. Walker called for a nurse to bring a bottle of Gatorade. Then she turned back to Angie. "What were you doing out in the desert?"

"I was there with my mommy and Donald."

While Angie sipped her drink, Dr. Walker examined the cuts and scrapes on the little girl's feet and legs, cleaning them and dosing them with antiseptic as she went. When Angie whimpered in pain, Dan stepped forward and took her hand.

"It's okay," he said. "It may hurt a little, but this will make it better."

"I've heard about Mr. Pardee here," Dr. Walker said to Angie. "I understand he usually has a big dog with him."

Angie nodded. "His name is Bozo," she said. "I got to pet him."

"He didn't bite you?" Dr. Walker asked.

Angie shook her head. "I thought he would, but he's really nice."

Dan was taken aback again. He supposed that, in terms of gossip, the reservation was like any other small town. Dr. Walker had probably heard tales about the terrible *ohb* who worked with the Shadow Wolves and who went on patrol in the company of an immense and supposedly incredibly fierce German shepherd.

"Can I use the bathroom?" Angie asked.

"Sure," Dr. Walker said. "I'll have the nurse take you."

The same nurse who had brought the Gatorade lifted Angie down from the examining table, took her hand, and led her away toward a restroom. Watching her walk away from him, Dan felt like his heart was going to break. But, of course, that was what was going to happen here. The door to the examining room wasn't the only one that would swing shut. From now on, strangers would be taking charge of Angie's life and handing her off to whoever was destined to care for her. As Dan had explained to the admitting clerk, he was only the guy who had found her, nothing more.

"That's a good sign," Dr. Walker was saying.

"What?" Dan asked.

"That she needs to use the bathroom. She probably isn't that seriously dehydrated. We won't need to give her IV fluids."

"Oh," he said. "I'm glad of that." He didn't want to see Angie poked with a needle—any kind of needle.

"What kind of a name is Pardee?" Dr. Walker asked. "It doesn't sound Apache to me."

"It's not," Dan answered. "It's a made-up name—my father's made-up name. He was a stuntman in Hollywood. An Anglo-Irish, I believe. A Milgahn," he added.

Dan might have pointed out that Lanita Dolores Walker didn't sound like a Tohono O'odham name, either, but he didn't. Realizing that he had said the word Milgahn aloud, he was embarrassed. When Dr. Walker replied with one of her glorious smiles he decided she was either laughing at him or else she liked it. Dan couldn't tell which.

"How did you learn that word?" she asked.

"I bought a dictionary," he said. "I've been studying."

The doctor's smile disappeared, but she nodded. "All right, then," she said. "Now, getting back to Angie. Has the mother's family been notified?"

Dan shook his head. "The M.E. was just arriving as I left the scene, but I talked to Detective Fellows. He said that officers from Law and Order most likely will handle the next-of-kin notification."

"That's true," Dr. Walker said. "Although Brian Fellows could probably do it, too. He's a good guy. People would accept it from him."

"You know Detective Fellows?" Dan asked.

Dr. Walker nodded. "We go way back. But no matter who does the notification, it's going to take some time. I'd rather Angie weren't there while all of that is going on. Too traumatic."

Me, too, Dan Pardee thought.

"So I'm going to admit her for right now," Dr. Walker continued. "I'm sure her family will show up to collect her first thing in the morning, but if you'd like to sit with her for a while, until she gets settled into her room, I'm sure that would be fine."

"Thank you," Dan said. "I'll be glad to."

Thank you more than you know.

Tucson, Arizona
Saturday, June 6, 2009, 11:00 P.M.
72° Fahrenheit

Once Diana showed up, Brandon let Damsel out for her last walk. When they came back in from that, Diana was sitting in the living room studying the baskets.

"How was it?" he asked.

"How was what?"

"The party?"

"Abby wasn't there," Diana said.

"Abby?"

"Abigail Tennant. She's been doing the night-blooming cereus party for years. She was the one who originally invited Lani to do the storytelling honors tonight. It's not good manners to issue that kind of invitation and then be a no-show yourself."

Brandon shrugged. "Maybe she came down with something," he said.

"It's still rude," Diana insisted. "How was your day?"

Diana had been so distant of late that Brandon was a little surprised by her question. "Geet Farrell's wife called and wanted me to stop by, so I did."

"I remember Geet. How is he?"

"Not so good," Brandon answered. "I'm afraid it won't be long now."

"I knew he had cancer. Are you saying he's dying?"

Brandon nodded. "They're doing hospice care at home," he said.

"Why did he want to see you?"

"He handed over a case file to me—an unsolved homicide from 1959."

"That's a while ago," Diana said, smiling.

"It is," Brandon agreed. "I've spent the afternoon going over what he had, including a lead that came in just before they slapped Geet in the hospital this last time. I called the woman tonight after I got home. She lives down by Sonoita, and she invited me to come see her. I'm driving down there tomorrow morning. Want to come along?"

"Tomorrow?" Diana asked. "If the case is already that old, why the big rush now?"

"Because, as I said, Geet is dying," Brandon said. "This case is one that has deviled him for years. If it turns out to be solvable, I'd like to do that for him before it's too late."

Diana nodded. "I see," she said.

"Would you like to ride along?"

"Could we take the Invicta?" Diana asked. "With the top down?"

Brandon started to object. It was June, after all. It was likely to be hot as blue blazes, but this was the first time in a long time that Diana had shown much interest in anything. Besides, the last he had heard she wanted to unload her pride and joy. It would be fun to take it on one last road trip.

"Sure," he said. "We'll plaster ourselves with sunscreen and wear hats and long-sleeved shirts, but it sounds like fun. Are you coming to bed?"

"You go on ahead," she said. "I'll be there in a while."

Tucson, Arizona
Sunday, June 7, 2009, 1:00 A.M.
70° Fahrenheit

Diana watched as Brandon went down the hall, switching off most of the lights as he went. She liked the fact that he continued to be thrifty—had always been thrifty— even when there had been no need to be.

Once he was gone, she returned to studying the many baskets that decorated the walls of the room, baskets her beloved friend, Nana *Dahd,* had made with her own hands, weaving them out of bear grass and yucca and devil's claw and yucca root with the *owij,* the awl, Rita Antone had inherited from her own basket-weaving grandmother, Understanding Woman.

Diana sat there for a long while, wondering if Andrew Carlisle would make another appearance. She had seen him several times in recent days, always when she was alone; usually when she was outside—by the pool or in the front yard; occasionally in the kitchen, but never here. Never in this room—the room where she and Rita

Antone had sat together when Davy was little, with Nana *Dahd* weaving her baskets and telling her stories, steeping the whole household in Tohono O'odham culture and tradition while Diana tried to see her way clear from being a teacher on the reservation to becoming a writer.

"Nana *Dahd* is still here, isn't she?" Diana Ladd said aloud to an absent Andrew Carlisle. "At least her spirit is. That's what keeps you away."

With that, Diana Ladd got up and followed her husband down the hall to the bedroom. She hadn't been sleeping well for weeks, but tonight, once she crawled into bed next to Brandon, his gentle snoring lulled her to sleep.

It seemed to her that Rita Antone and Brandon Walker were still protecting her from Andrew Philip Carlisle.

9

*D*RIVING BACK TO Tucson, Jonathan could not believe how anything could have gone so completely wrong in such a short time. He had waited around long enough to let his mother and her husband enjoy their last meal. After all, even guys on death row got to have that. Then, just after eight-thirty, he had walked up and found his mother and her husband sitting there enjoying their oddball evening tête-à-tête. He hadn't said anything. He didn't have to.

Startled, she had looked at him as soon as he stepped into the circle of light. There had been a gasp of recognition. Then, smiling, she had stood up and taken two steps toward him, holding out both of her hands in greeting—like she was surprised but glad to see him. Like she was actually welcoming him! How dare she!

"Why, Jonathan," she had said. "However did you find us way out here?" Then she had turned to her husband, to Jack. "No, wait," she said to him. "You did this, didn't you? It's the rest of the surprise!"

Surprise my ass! Jonathan had thought. He had answered that phony smile of hers just the way he had intended to—with a nine-millimeter slug right in the middle of her forehead. The sling on his arm had half concealed the weapon, so she had never seen it coming. She was still smiling that sappy, stupid smile of hers as she went down, knocking over the chair she had been sitting on and taking the cloth-covered table with her as she fell. He saw the glassware and dishes tumble off the table and shatter, but he didn't hear them.

"What the hell . . . ?" Jack had roared.

Jonathan heard that even as the gunshot reverberated in his ears. Bent on fighting back, the old man had erupted out of his seat, but then Jonathan shot him, too. He liked doing it just that way—two shots and two kills, no wasted bullets.

For a time—a few seconds, anyway—he had stood there examining the scene and enjoying the moment. He had done what he had set out to do. He felt no regret, only a sense of accomplishment. He had put the witch down; both witches, as a matter of fact. Two women who had made his life hell on earth. Now they had both paid the price for every unkind word and every slight. They were gone. Done.

He smelled smoke. One of the fallen candles had set fire to the tablecloth. The last thing he needed was for a brush fire to attract attention. Quickly he stomped the fire out before it could spread. But then, to his horror, Jonathan heard the sound of voices, a man and a woman talking and laughing and coming closer.

He realized that while his ears were out of commission from the gunshots, a vehicle must have arrived without him noticing. Whose was it? Who was coming and what were they doing here? Surely no one else had been invited to Jack and Abby's little party. The table had been set for two. There had been only the two chairs.

Jonathan moved to the middle of the luminarias' path and stood there waiting for the new arrivals to round the curve. At last a couple, an Indian man and woman, appeared in front of him. The man was leading the way while the woman followed.

The man stopped, looked questioningly at Jonathan, and frowned. "Who are you?" he asked. "Where's Jack?"

As far as Jonathan was concerned, the two of them had no business being there, but what was he supposed to do, let them go? Let them turn around and walk away? Like that was going to happen!

So he shot them, too, one after the other. He hit the man full-on. The woman turned and tried to run but he shot her in the back. As they went down, just like that, Jonathan was thankful for all the hours and weeks he had spent shooting at the target range. This was the payoff.

He stood for a while after that with his heart pounding. For some reason, shooting the two strangers seemed far worse than shooting his own mother. After all, she deserved it. They did not, but in realizing the enormity of what he had done, a certain level of self-preservation kicked in as well. He needed to do something that would throw the investigation off his trail long enough for him to get over the border and into the interior of Mexico. If he could make it that far and connect up with the money he had sent on ahead, he'd be fine.

He needed to do something that would make this incident look like something other than what it was. When he saw his mother's purse, it came to him. Robbery. That should do the trick.

Jonathan had had the foresight to bring along some latex gloves. Donning a pair, he walked to the bodies one by one. Carrying his weapon in one hand in case anyone else showed up, he collected his mother's purse and the men's wallets. Just for good measure, he took their jewelry and cell phones as well. Jack's simple gold wedding band wasn't impressive, and neither was the small diamond on his mother's finger. Ditto went for the Indian guy's immense turquoise ring and the engagement ring, still in a jeweler's box in his jeans. Taken together, the whole stack didn't amount to much, but he pocketed it all.

When he reached the Indian woman, she wasn't quite dead. "Help me," she moaned. "Please."

Jonathan thought about putting her out of her misery with another bullet to her head, just to end her suffering, but he decided against it. If someone had heard the shots earlier, they might still be listening and trying to decide where they were coming from. He couldn't risk another. Besides, it was a shame to waste a bullet if he didn't have to.

Like his mother, the Indian woman had carried her purse with her when she got out of the car—even in the middle of the desert.

Why do women do that? Jonathan had wondered as he leaned down to pick it up.

He stood in front of Jack Tennant's Lexus and sorted through the purses and wallets. Then, leaving the empty husks of belongings behind, he walked away. He didn't hurry. He didn't need to hurry. They were dead. They weren't going anywhere. With any kind of luck it would be hours or even days before someone found them.

Once in his own vehicle, Jonathan drove back out to the road, where he was relieved to see no oncoming traffic visible in either direction. He had been holding his breath as he approached the highway. Now he let it go. When he breathed back in, even he couldn't ignore the rank stench in the minivan. He had practically lived in it for days, waking and sleeping. The floorboards were covered with the empty wrappers and boxes and cups of the fast food that had sustained him during this long hunting excursion. Now that it was over, however, he needed to find a room, get himself cleaned up, and then make his getaway. He rolled down the window and let in some of the chill night air.

There was still nothing from Thousand Oaks. The story he had spun about taking his family on vacation must have worked. Must still be working.

Once Jonathan managed to get across the border, he figured he'd be home free.

Sells, Tohono O'odham Nation, Arizona
Sunday, June 7, 2009, 1:30 A.M.
67° Fahrenheit

By the time Dan saw Angie again, she had been changed into a hospital gown and settled in a bed. The bedside tray had been stocked with food—cheese and crackers, tapioca pudding, and a dish full of cubes of red Jell-O— the kind Dan had always tried to stick to the ceiling in the school cafeteria. Bozo might have been the current family clown, but he certainly wasn't the only one.

As Dan watched Angie mow her way through the food, he realized that he had skipped his ham sandwich. As a consequence, so had Bozo.

"Is that any good?" he asked.

Angie looked at him, smiled, nodded, and popped another Jell-O cube into her mouth. "Where's my mommy?" she asked.

Dan had lied to her before and let her believe the less hurtful fiction that her mother was still sleeping. It seemed to Dan that someone else should be the one to give Angie Enos the bad news—the definitive, once-and-for-all answer about what had happened to her mother. Dan was a complete stranger—an innocent passerby. It wasn't fair for that difficult job to be left up to him. Where were Angie's grandparents? Shouldn't they be the ones to do this? Or what about some beloved aunt or uncle? Shouldn't someone with more of a claim on Angie and her future perform this difficult task?

But right then, at that precise moment in Angie's hospital room, Daniel Pardee was the only person available.

He didn't answer for several moments. *How can I explain something like that?* he wondered. *What words can I use and how much will she be able to understand?*

Dan had seen the information listed on Angie's tribal enrollment card. Her birthday was in November. That made her four and a half years old. As far as he knew, the movie version of Bambi wasn't shown in theaters anymore, but maybe Delphina had rented the video.

Finally he decided that the best thing to do was to tell the truth. That was how Gramps had always dealt with tough things—by saying straight out whatever was going on rather than by beating around the bush or trying to fudge what needed to be said.

"Angie," Dan said gently, "I'm sorry to have to tell you this. Your mommy is dead."

Angie's enormous eyes welled with tears. "I thought she was asleep."

Dan shook his head. "I know," he said. "But she wasn't."

For a long time, Angie sat there quietly, staring at him through her tears.

"My dog died," she said finally. "He ran out into the road and got run over by a truck. Mommy said that dying meant he wouldn't be back. Does that mean my mommy won't be back?"

"That's correct," Dan said. "She won't be."

"Not ever?"

"Not ever."

"Is she in heaven? Mommy says that when people die, they go to heaven."

"I'm sure that's where she is," Dan said with a conviction he didn't necessarily feel. For his own part, Dan Pardee had stopped believing in heaven and hell a long time ago.

Angie put down her spoon and pushed the food tray away. "I'm not hungry," she said.

Dan carried the tray across the room and put it on a dresser. "Of course you're not."

"Who'll take care of me, then?" Angie asked. "Donald?"

Which meant Dan had to deliver the next blow as well. "Angie, Donald's dead, too. Just like your mommy."

"Who, then?" Angie asked.

Dan shrugged. "Do you have a grandpa and grandma? Maybe they'll look after you."

"Grandpa's sick," Angie said.

"What about your father?" Dan asked. The name Joaquin Enos was also listed on Angie's enrollment card. "You have a father, don't you?"

Angie simply looked at him and didn't reply. That in itself was answer enough. The father had never been a factor in the Angelina Enos equation, and he wouldn't be one now.

"Don't worry about it," Dan said. "I know how hard it is not to worry, but someone will look after you, Angie. Right now, you should probably lie down and try to get some sleep. We'll sort all this out tomorrow morning."

She reached out and grabbed hold of Dan's hand. "Will you stay here with me?"

"I will," he said. "But first I need to go out and feed Bozo and give him some water." Dan also needed to call in and let Dispatch know that no one was out on patrol in his sector right now. Given the obvious police presence at Komelik, it didn't seem likely that a major number of illegal entrants would be attempting to use that route tonight. As far as Dan was concerned, his presence at Angie Enos's bedside was far more pressing.

"You'll come right back?" Angie asked. "You promise?"

"I promise."

Telling the lady at the desk that he was just stepping outside for a moment, he hurried over to his Expedition. There he let Bozo out of the SUV long enough for the dog to relieve himself. Then Dan poured a couple of bottles of water into the metal bowl he kept in the back of the luggage compartment. While Bozo lapped up the water, Dan unwrapped the two sandwiches and gave them to the dog. All he reserved for himself were the bags of chips. Then he called Dispatch.

All that took time. When Dan finally made it back to Angie's room, he expected her to be sleeping. She wasn't, primarily because by then a night nurse was in the room, taking her vitals.

"I knew you'd come back," Angie said.

Dan nodded. "I told my boss that you needed Bozo and me to stay here for right now."

"Bozo is his dog," Angie explained to the nurse.

Unimpressed by this tidbit of information, the nurse rolled her eyes.

When she left the room, Dan eased his long frame into a chair that didn't necessarily fit his body, or any human body for that matter. It looked like a chair, but it was the least comfortable specimen of chairness Dan Pardee had ever had the misfortune of encountering. As soon as he settled into it, however, Angie reached out again, took his hand, and fell fast asleep.

Dan sat in almost that same position for the next three hours. He stirred only when his feet went numb or his hand did. And while he sat there, a file drawer he usually kept closed and safely locked away from conscious thought popped open—the file drawer marked "Adam Pardee."

Safford, Arizona
1979

Even from prison Adam Pardee had refused to sign over his parental rights. As a consequence, Micah and Maxine Duarte had been forced to go to court to gain custody of their grandson. Fortunately Micah's boss, a prosperous Safford area dairy farmer, was able to help them find an Anglo attorney who made it possible for the Indian couple to navigate the Anglo legal jungle.

When it was time to enroll Dan in kindergarten, the guardianship issue had been settled to the satisfaction of the courts, perhaps. In the court of public opinion, and more important at Fort Thomas Elementary School, Dan Pardee's status was still very much in doubt.

Although Micah Duarte soon morphed into Dan's beloved Gramps, his wife, Maxine, was another matter. She was always kind to Dan—kind but distant. Up until her death five years ago, she had always been Grandmother, never the less formal Grandma. Maxine had looked after Dan and cared for him, but she had seemed incapable of allowing herself to unbend in the presence of her dead daughter's child. To Dan's knowledge, his grandparents never discussed Rebecca, or if they did, it certainly wasn't in Dan's presence. Maybe part of Maxine's reticence had to do with the fact that Dan looked so much like his father, although no one had mentioned it at the time. Dan found that out for himself much later while doing Internet searches into his own history.

Even as a child, Dan Pardee had had his father's eyes. As he grew, he developed his father's height and long legs, as well as his rangy good looks. All of that meant that Dan didn't fit in well with the other kids on the San Carlos. He was neither fish nor fowl. He wasn't Apache enough for some or Anglo enough for others.

And his troubled family history often caused difficulties as well. For one thing, school and Sunday school programs often focused on holidays with traditional "family values."

Art projects to make greeting cards to celebrate Mother's Day or Father's Day didn't take into account the feelings of a kid whose father had murdered his mother. There weren't any cards that covered that contingency. When it came time to do a "family history" project for eighth-grade social studies, Dan flunked it fair and square. He wouldn't answer the questions and didn't turn in the paper. His teacher was baffled. Gramps was not.

As an eighth grader, Dan hadn't wanted to know any of that ugly stuff, but while he was sitting in Iraq with time on his hands and computer access, he had made it his business to track down everything the Internet had to offer on Adam and Rebecca Pardee. Surprisingly enough, there was plenty of material available with the click of the mouse.

For one thing, an enterprising true-crime writer named Michaella Reece had written a book called *The Return of the Stuntmen*, which was a book about three different Hollywood stuntmen who had gone off to the slammer for one crime or another, only to be welcomed back to the Hollywood fraternity once they had paid their respective debts to society. By the time Dan knew the book existed it was out of print, but he had ordered a used copy from Amazon.

It turned out that the three men had a lot in common in addition to being stuntmen, including a long history of dishing out domestic abuse. They had all murdered women. One, Adam, murdered his wife; the second, his stepmother; the third, his girlfriend. And they all got slaps on the wrist with sentences in the seven-to-ten-year range with time off for good behavior. And they all went straight back to work once they got out of prison. The book had been published several years earlier, however, and Dan wondered how much work stuntmen were getting these days in the face of competition from computer-generated graphics that tossed images around rather than flesh-and-blood people.

In reading the book Dan saw the head-shot photos of his mother once again. Rebecca Duarte Pardee had been beautiful, even with her long dark hair turned into a froth of seventies-style curls. It galled Dan to realize that his father had served his time and been released from prison for his mother's murder months before Dan graduated from the eighth grade.

Growing up, he often thought about going back to California to confront his father. By the time he was in high school, he had been convinced that, in a physical matchup, his karate training would give him an edge. During his class's senior trip to Disneyland, Dan went so far as to find Adam Pardee's name, address, and phone number in the phone book. He had made tentative arrangements to ditch the group the next day and go do just that, but one of the other kids, Frank Warren, had squealed on him, and it didn't happen. Not then.

But by the time Dan returned home from Iraq, he was ready to see his father. He still had his karate training, but his years in the army had toughened him both mentally and physically far beyond what he'd been as a high school senior.

Because his deployment ended at almost the same time as his second enlistment, he told his grandfather that he'd be staying on in California for a few days with some buddies from L.A. Not that there were any buddies in L.A. He left the airport in a rented red Taurus and drove to the same address he had found ten years earlier, which turned out to be a down-at-the-heels bungalow in a not-so-nice neighborhood in South Pasadena.

It was apparent that in recent years both the neighborhood and the house had fallen on tough times. Knocked-over garbage cans and graffiti-covered fences and walls said that this area was fast becoming a no-man's-land. Squaring his shoulders, Dan stepped out of the car and walked up the cracked and crumbling sidewalk. The wooden steps creaked under his weight.

If the house is that bad, Dan surmised, *then things aren't going that well for Adam, either.*

Dan paused for a moment before he rang the bell, reciting the words he had prepared to say in greeting: "Hello, Adam. I'm Dan, your son. And here's a little something for killing my mother." After which he intended to plant his fist in the older man's face.

Except the person who answered the door wasn't Adam Pardee. A sallow-faced woman cracked open the door and peered out at him. Her lower lip was split. Her right eye was swollen shut. She was holding an ice pack to a bruise on her battered cheek. Clearly Adam was up to his old tricks.

"Yes?" she said. "Who are you? What do you want?"

The sight of her face hit Dan like a blow. If his mother had lived, this might have been her future and his. Yes, Rebecca had asked her parents for help, but would she have been strong enough to walk away? A lot of domestic-violence victims never did. In fact, maybe that was what had provoked that final confrontation—maybe she had told Adam that she was taking Dan and leaving.

But this woman, this sad-faced woman who was standing in the doorway of Adam's house, wasn't responsible for what had happened years in the past. Even if Dan called his father out and beat him to a bloody pulp, Dan knew what would happen eventually. Adam Pardee was a coward and a bully. Once he was able to do so, he would go back to beating the current woman in his life—his wife, girlfriend, whatever. All Dan could do for her was to refuse to be a party to it. In all likelihood she'd be beaten again—that was a given—but it wouldn't be Dan Pardee's fault.

"I was looking for an old buddy of mine," he mumbled quickly, making up the story as he went along. "His name's John—John Grady."

"You're mistaken," she said. "There's no one here by that name."

"Who is it?" an irate male voice shouted from somewhere inside the house. "What do they want?"

Dan recognized the voice and the tone. Both had haunted his dreams for years. "Sorry," he said to the woman as he backed away from the door. "I must have written the address down wrong."

She closed the door and latched it. Hearing the sound of his father's angry voice shouting through another closed door and across the intervening years made Dan's heart hurt, but he understood that what Adam Pardee did or didn't do, now or ever, was no longer Dan's problem. With Micah Duarte's words about knowing when to walk away echoing in his head, Dan returned to his waiting Taurus. He drove back to LAX, where he caught the first available flight back to Phoenix.

His grandfather picked him up at Sky Harbor. "I thought you were staying in L.A. for a couple of days."

"I was," Dan said, "but I changed my mind."

"And the dog?"

"Bozo's still in quarantine. Once he clears that, they'll fly him to Sky Harbor, too."

"Okay then," Micah Duarte said. "Let's go home."

San Diego, California
Saturday, June 6, 2009, 9:02 P.M.
59° Fahrenheit

"Nine-one-one Emergency. What are you reporting?"

The woman on the other end of the line sounded nervous and uncertain. Louise Maynard was accustomed to that. Ten years into doing the job, Louise was used to prying the necessary information out of whomever was calling.

"It's my sister," the woman said shakily.

"Name?" Louise asked.

"My name or my sister's?" the woman asked.

"Both," Louise told her.

"My name is Corrine Lapin," she said. "My sister's name is Esther, Esther Southard. She lives in Thousand Oaks."

The caller couldn't see it, but by then Louise was shaking her head in frustration. "Excuse me, ma'am, but you've called the emergency communications center in San Diego."

"I know," Corrine said. "That's because I'm in San Diego. Yesterday was my birthday, and Esther didn't call.

She always calls on my birthday. I'm probably just being silly, but I'm worried that something is wrong."

As far as Louise was concerned, calling because someone has missed your birthday wasn't exactly like calling 911 to report that your fries at McDonald's were served cold, but it was close.

"This line is for emergency calls only."

"But it is an emergency," Corrine insisted. "I was afraid if I tried calling the Thousand Oaks Police Department that they'd just blow me off."

Louise understood that Corrine might well be right. After all, all 911 operators weren't created equal.

"So what's going on?" Louise asked.

"There's no answer at Esther's house," Corrine said hurriedly. "And I've tried calling her cell, too. At first the calls kept going directly to her voice mail. Now it says that her mailbox is full, and she hasn't called me back."

"Maybe she's just busy," Louise suggested.

The caller immediately rejected that idea. "She sent me a text message on Monday saying that she and her husband were taking the kids and going away for a few days. She said they'd be driving up through Yosemite, but I'm worried something has happened to them. Maybe they're lying in a ditch somewhere. Esther is like superglued to her iPhone. She doesn't go anywhere without it."

Louise had heard lots of wild things in her years as an emergency operator, and she had developed an instinct for what was bogus and what wasn't. This sounded real.

"Give me your sister's address," she said now. "I'll contact Thousand Oaks PD and have them look into it."

"Thank you," Corrine said. "I'm sure everything is fine. Esther will probably be mad at me for pushing panic buttons, but things have been so tough for them lately. Her husband, Jon, lost his job. She was afraid the bank was going to foreclose on their house."

Nodding, Louise typed that information into her computer as well. The story was sounding more and more plausible by the moment.

"Why don't you give me your contact information," she said pleasantly to Corrine. "Just in case the responding officers need to get back in touch with you."

When Corrine hung up a minute or so later, Louise could hear the relief in her voice, but Louise had a bad feeling about that. She suspected that Corrine Lapin's relief wouldn't last very long. Job losses and home foreclosures were up all over California. So were cases of murder and suicide.

With a click of her mouse, Louise passed Corrine's information along to her 911 counterparts in Thousand Oaks. That done, she knew the situation was out of her hands. Unless a case made it into the local media, Louise never knew about what happened later, and that was just as well.

Not knowing all the gory details was what made it possible for her to do her job. Otherwise she would have been paralyzed every time she took a new call.

Yes, Louise Maynard was far better off not knowing about what had happened to Corrine Lapin's sister Esther because she had a hunch that whatever it was, it wouldn't be good.

Sells, Tohono O'odham Nation, Arizona
Sunday, June 7, 2009, 3:10 A.M.
65° Fahrenheit

Dan heard the thump, thump, thump of the approaching helicopter rotors. The familiar racket was enough to rouse him out of a restless sleep. For a moment he was back in Iraq, reaching for his weapons, bracing for action. Then he realized where he was—in a hospital room in Sells, Arizona, with a little orphaned Indian girl named Angie sleeping peacefully in the hospital bed beside his chair.

As the sound of the arriving helicopter jarred him awake, he forced his stiff body upright and sprinted toward the door and down the hall. Bozo was fearless about almost everything but not about helicopters. Suicide bombers didn't scare him. Exploding IEDs didn't bother him, either. His sensitive nose was able to sort out the presence of explosives, so he knew they were there and he was able to warn Dan.

Helicopters, on the other hand, could drop out of the sky toward them with no advance warning. One had done so when they'd been out on patrol. It was brought down by a handheld missile launcher, and it had fallen to earth only a few yards from where Dan and Bozo had been on patrol, killing both crew members on board.

As Dan bounded out the front door of the hospital, he saw the medevac helicopter landing in a far corner of the parking lot. He could also hear Bozo. Confined in the Expedition, the dog was on full alert and barking frantically. As Dan made for his vehicle, he caught sight of a patient being wheeled toward the helicopter.

Dan opened the door and Bozo leaped out, crashing into Dan in the process and almost knocking him over. The dog continued to bark, warning everyone within hearing range of what he perceived as a dire threat.

"It's okay, Bozo," Dan said, catching the dog by his collar, holding him, and calming the terrified animal as best he could. "It's not going to hurt you."

Bozo remained unconvinced. He continued to bark until the helicopter took off once more, disappearing into the moonlit distance.

While a pair of orderlies walked the empty gurney back into the hospital, Dr. Walker came across the lot.

"Bozo, I presume?" she asked. "He sounds pretty fierce."

"That's Bozo sounding scared as opposed to sounding fierce," Dan told her. "He's frightened of helicopters."

"Really?" she asked.

"Really," Dan said.

Dr. Walker didn't ask why Bozo was scared of helicopters, and Dan didn't go into it. He was afraid he was going to get a lecture on all the noise. This was a hospital zone, after all.

"You left him out here in the car?" she asked.

"He's fine," Dan said. "He would have been fine if it hadn't been for the helicopter."

Bozo had quieted now. As Dan went to get the water bowl and a couple more bottles of water, Dr. Walker reached out and patted the dog's head.

"Sorry about that," she said. "The helicopter, I mean. We had a snakebite victim. We managed to get him stabilized enough to have him transported to the Phoenix Indian Medical Center."

Dan Pardee knew all about the Indian Medical Center in Phoenix. It was where his grandmother, Maxine Duarte, had died. While undergoing chemo, she had developed a raging infection and had died of it with so little warning that Micah, at work in Safford, hadn't been able to make it to the hospital in time.

"You're staying the whole night?" Dr. Walker asked.

Dan nodded. "I told Angie about her mother," he said. "I also told her that I'd stay with her until someone comes to pick her up later this morning."

Bozo finished drinking the water, then walked over to one of the back tires to raise his leg.

"You're sleeping on one of those god-awful chairs in Angie's room?" Dr. Walker asked.

Dan nodded. "Not the best," he agreed, "but I've slept in worse places."

"I'll see if I can get them to find a roll-away for that room. What about Bozo?"

"Now that the helicopter is gone and he's had a drink, he'll be fine."

"Why don't you bring him inside?"

Dan was astonished. "Into the hospital?"

"Sure," Dr. Walker said with a grin, her white teeth flashing in the moonlight. "Didn't you tell me Bozo is a certified therapy dog?"

"Dr. Walker," he began, "I said no such thing."

"Just bring his water dish along," she said. "You're welcome to call me Lani."

"And I'm Dan," he said. "Dan Pardee."

Dan Pardee, the ohb.

Tucson, Arizona
Saturday, June 6, 2009, 11:00 P.M.
73° Fahrenheit

Jonathan was careful to pay close attention to the speed limit as he drove into town. His heart skipped a beat when he saw flashing lights west of Three Points, but then he remembered the Border Patrol checkpoint. He drove up to it and stopped briefly before being waved through with no difficulty and no questions asked.

Back in Tucson proper, he made his way to one of the freeway hotels near downtown. Jonathan was from California. It made no sense to him that you'd have all the freeway entrances and exits blocked for miles. Few travelers seemed to have made their way to the nearly deserted businesses close to downtown. When he pulled into the Los Amigos Motel, the parking lot was almost empty, and the bored night clerk was more than happy to take cash for the room as opposed to a credit card.

Jonathan's arm was giving him fits again. Once inside the room, he gulped down another dose of antibiotics and then made his way into the shower. The guy at Urgent Care had told him to keep the bandage dry, so he covered his bandaged arm with a hotel laundry bag and then held his right hand out of the shower as best he could. It felt good to let the hot water sluice over him even though washing his hair and scrubbing his body using only his left hand to grip the tiny bar of soap felt very strange.

Out of the shower, he lay on the bed and used Jack Tennant's phone to call Aero Mexico. They had a flight leaving for Cancún at eleven-thirty the next morning.

"Do you wish to make a reservation?" the reservations clerk wanted to know.

"I'm not sure if I can make this work. I won't know until tomorrow morning. Does it look overbooked?"

"Not at all," the clerk told him. "I'm sure there will still be empty seats tomorrow."

"Good," he told her. "I'll book the reservation when I'm sure I can get away."

Relieved, Jonathan set the phone's alarm clock function to awaken him at eight, then closed his phone and stretched out full length on the bed. After living in the minivan for several days, even a bad bed was a big improvement.

He knew that guilty consciences were supposed to keep you awake, but he didn't feel guilty. He had done what had needed to be done for a very long time. Now he was worn out. Within moments he fell sound asleep and slept like a baby.

Komelik, Tohono O'odham Nation, Arizona
Sunday, June 7, 2009, 1:15 A.M.
65° Fahrenheit

Brian Fellows was sitting in his Crown Victoria and grabbing a drink of water when Delia Ortiz herself appeared on the scene. Brian hadn't seen the woman for years, not since her father-in-law's funeral, but he recognized her as soon as she got out of Martin Ramon's patrol car. Brian also knew that in the intervening years she had become a person of real consequence on the reservation.

"It's good to see you again, Chairman Ortiz," he said, extending his hand.

"Yes," she agreed, "but this isn't good." She waved one hand in the general direction of all the crime scene activity. "I don't like having the drug wars showing up on the reservation. Were the dead people involved in that?"

"Maybe," Brian said. "But then again, maybe not. Mr. Rios claimed his son wasn't involved in anything like that, but we're asking for a warrant to search Donald's place at Komelik just in case. What can you tell me about Delphina Enos?"

"She's from Nolic," Delia said. "She had a baby but the father ran off. She was staying with her parents, but there were some problems there. I helped her get a job in Sells—a job and a place to live."

"I'll need a warrant to search her place, too."

Delia nodded. "Law and Order will get you whatever you need."

"Good," Brian said. "We'll all have to work together on this—the tribe, Pima County, and Border Patrol."

"All right."

"Donald Rios's father gave us a positive ID on his son. Can you do the same for Delphina?"

"Yes."

"Good. That would be a big help."

"I'll do that for you if you'll do a favor for me."

"What's that?"

"Martin told me on the way here that you speak Tohono O'odham. Is that true?"

"Yes."

"I suppose you know that I don't."

Brian recalled something about that—something about Delia growing up far away from the reservation. "A little," he said.

"The people in Nolic are old-fashioned," she said. "I'd like you to go there with me to translate, if necessary. I know my officers could do it, but it might be better . . ."

Brian Fellows got it. Delphina Enos's grieving relatives would be so traumatized by the news they probably wouldn't remember if the information came to them in English or Tohono O'odham or a combination of both. But if officers from Law and Order were on the scene when the notification took place, they'd be more than slightly interested if their fearless leader was anything less than fluent in what should have been her own language.

"Sure," Brian said easily. "I'll be glad to go along and help out."

That was how, two hours later, Detective Brian Fellows found himself sitting in a grim concrete-block house that belonged to Delphina's parents, Louis and Carmen Escalante.

The house had been built some forty years earlier under a briefly and never completely funded program called TWEP, the Tribal Work Experience Project, which had allowed for the building of the bare bones of any number of houses on the reservation. Some had been successfully completed and improved. This one had not. The yard outside was littered with junk, including several moribund vehicles—two rusty pickups and one broken-down Camaro.

Brian fully expected to conduct the next-of-kin notification out in the yard, but Delia's presence resulted in their being invited into the hot interior of the house. They walked up a makeshift wheelchair ramp into a sparsely furnished living room. The place was stifling. A decrepit swamp cooler sat perched in one window, but it wasn't working. At least it wasn't running.

Brian and Delia were directed to a dilapidated couch. Louis, looking thunderous, sat nearby in his wheelchair. Carmen brought a chair in from the kitchen and seated herself on that while Detective Brian Fellows, speaking in Tohono O'odham, explained that their daughter had been killed in a gun battle south of Topawa.

Louis and Carmen took the terrible news with what Brian thought to be remarkable restraint. Louis listened in silence and nodded.

"What about Angie?" Carmen asked softly. "Is she all right?"

"She's in the hospital at Sells," Delia Ortiz said, breaking into the conversation in English. "She's not seriously injured. She's got some cuts and scratches. As I understand it, the hospital is keeping her there mostly for observation. You can go pick her up in the morning."

Carmen nodded in agreement. Her husband was the one who spoke out.

"No!" Louis said forcefully.

Carmen gaped at her husband while Brian, unsure of what was going on, glanced back and forth between them.

"You don't mean that," Carmen said. "Angie's just a baby."

"I told Delphina not to get mixed up with that boy," Louis growled. "She did it anyway. Let Joaquin look after her."

"But he doesn't even know Angie," Carmen objected. "Joaquin's never come around, not once. I heard that he was in jail somewhere."

Louis shrugged. "Let his parents do it, then. Angie can be their problem, not ours."

Without another word, Carmen Escalante rose from where she sat, picked up her chair, and disappeared with it into the kitchen. Brian glanced at Delia Ortiz. What he read in her face was absolute contempt for both these people, the husband and the wife. No wonder the tribal chairman had found Delphina Escalante Enos a job to do and a place to live far away from this vindictive excuse for a father and a spineless mother.

"I'm sorry to have to ask you this kind of thing," Brian said. "If you'd rather I came back later . . ."

"Ask," Louis Escalante growled. "What do you want to know?"

"Was your daughter involved in drugs of any kind?"

"I don't think so," Louis said. "But you should talk to that man of hers. I've heard that about Joaquin Enos. He does all kinds of bad things. His daughter will probably grow up to do the same. Someone else will have to look after her, if they're brave enough."

"What do you mean, brave enough?" Brian asked.

Louis shrugged. "She's alive," he said, as if that was all that mattered. "If everyone else is dead, why is she still alive?"

"Because the killer didn't see her," Brian said.

"Yes," Louis said, "Kok'oi Chehia."

"Ghost Girl?" Brian asked.

Louis seemed startled that Brian understood what he had said. He shrugged and looked away.

When the interview was over, Brian drove Delia back to her home in Sells. He knew that at one time she and Leo had lived in the house Delia had inherited from her aunt Julia in Little Tucson, but sometime in the recent past they had moved back into the Ortiz family compound behind the gas station.

Delia directed him to the proper mobile home. Brian pulled up next to it. Rather than getting right out of the vehicle, Delia sat for some time with her hand resting on the door handle.

"Now you know why I gave Delia a job," she said at last. "She and the baby needed to move out of there."

Brian nodded. "Yes, I can see that," he said. "But I'm surprised that the Escalantes won't take in that poor little girl. She's their granddaughter, for Pete's sake. That doesn't make any sense to me. What happened to her mother isn't her fault."

"No, but that's how the Escalantes work," Delia added. "Louis was talking about how bad Joaquin Enos is, but they're not nice people, either."

Brian knew enough to say nothing more. Instead, he waited for Delia to finish. "Louis is Lani Walker's uncle," she said finally. "Her blood uncle."

Brian Fellows, who knew a lot about Lani Walker's history, was taken aback. "Are you saying this is the same family, the people who wouldn't take Lani back after she was bitten by all the ants?"

Delia nodded. "The same family," she said. "They wouldn't take Lani back because they thought she was dangerous."

"And now they're claiming Ghost Girl is dangerous, too," Brian muttered. "What will happen to her?"

"We'll check to see what the father's family has to say," Delia told him. "If they don't want her, either, then I guess CPS will have to step in and decide what to do with her."

"Angelina Enos is a possible witness to her mother's murder," Brian said after a pause. "The only reason she's alive right now is that the killer doesn't know she exists. If you place that little girl in state custody, you'll leave a bureaucratic trail behind her—a paper trail that can be followed or a computer trail that can be hacked. People who want that kind of information know it's there to be had for a price.

"Whoever killed those four people at Komelik tonight

did so in cold blood and without a moment's hesitation. That means they won't think twice about coming back to take out an eyewitness, either, even a four-year-old eyewitness, and they'll do whatever it takes to find her."

"You think so?" Delia asked.

"Absolutely," Brian said.

Delia thought about that for a while. Finally she sighed. "All right then, Detective Fellows," she said. "I'll see what I can do, and I appreciate your help."

"You're welcome."

"And I hope you catch whoever did this," she said. "The People need you to catch him."

Brian Fellows nodded. "Yes," he said, "I understand."

And he did.

10

San Diego, California
Saturday, June 6, 2009, 10:00 P.M.
58° Fahrenheit

*O*NCE CORRINE LAPIN had placed the 911 call, she
felt as though she had done everything she could
do. She watched TV for a while, but then she went to bed,
leaving her cell phone on the bedside table next to her
just in case someone did call her back. Sometime after
one in the morning, when she was deep in sleep, the
musical ring tone roused her.

"Ms. Lapin, please," an officious woman's voice said.

"This is she," Corrine answered. "Who is this? Are you
calling about my sister?"

There was a momentary pause before the woman replied. "Yes, I am. My name is Detective Mumford," she

said. "Detective Alexandra Mumford with the Thousand Oaks PD. I'm afraid I have some very bad news."

Corrine's heart began to hammer wildly in her chest. "Don't tell me something's happened to them!" she breathed.

"After your 911 call was forwarded to our department, we dispatched a patrol car to do a welfare check," Detective Mumford continued. "No one came to the door, but when officers went around to the side of the house, they were able to see what appeared to be signs of foul play."

"Foul play," Corrine echoed. "Are you saying . . . ?"

"I'm afraid the people we found inside the residence are all deceased, Ms. Lapin." Alex Mumford's voice was sympathetic but firm. "They have been for several days."

"Deceased?" It was only by repeating the words that Corrine was able to make sense of what was being said. "You're telling me they're dead? That can't be true. All of them—all four of them?"

"So far we've located only three victims," Detective Mumford said. "Four if you count the dog. An adult female and two children, a boy and a girl, and a dog."

That was astounding. The people were all dead, and Major, too? He was Esther's beloved beagle. Until Esther had real kids, Major had been like a child to her. She loved that dog to distraction, and he loved her. Naturally Jonathan had despised the dog.

Thinking those thoughts, Corrine started to cry, but then she realized Detective Mumford was still speaking to her, asking a question. ". . . where he might be?"

"Where who might be?" Corrine asked raggedly, pulling herself together.

"Mr. Southard," Detective Mumford said. "Your brother-in-law. It's possible that he's a victim of foul play, too, but . . ."

Corrine stopped crying, her tears transformed into a flood of fury and anger. "He did this, didn't he!" she declared.

She threw off the sheet, scrambled out of bed, and groped for the light switch. She punched the speakerphone button so she could still hear the detective's voice as she began pulling on clothes.

"That no-good son of a bitch did this to them! He killed them all and left them to rot. How did they die?"

"There's evidence of gunshot wounds. A single wound to the head of each of the human victims. The dog was shot twice. He was found next to the adult female. There was blood on his muzzle. My guess is the dog was trying to protect her, and he may even have succeeded in biting the assailant before he was killed. We'll be running tests on him as well, hoping to find DNA evidence that will help identify the assailant."

Corrine's hands shook as she pulled a T-shirt on over her head—a Disneyland T-shirt. She had bought matching shirts for all of them when she and Esther had taken the kids there for spring break. But that was another time and place, forever banished to the past. She was no longer crying. She would not cry. She wouldn't give Jonathan Southard the satisfaction.

"We'll need some information from you," Detective

Mumford said. "And if you can handle it, a positive ID would also be helpful. That's going to be tough, though. As I said, they've been dead for a while. So there's some decomposition."

Corrine threw her purse strap over her shoulder and grabbed the car keys off the counter.

"How long have they been dead?" she said. Her voice cracked as she asked the question.

"The M.E. will have to make a final determination on time of death," the detective said. "I'd say they'd been there for a day or two, maybe even several. The air-conditioning is turned up to the max, so it's hard to tell."

The idea that Esther and Timmy and Suzy had been lying there dead for days was utterly unthinkable! Yes, there had been problems in the marriage. With an arrogant jerk like Jonathan Southard, that was a given. And yes, Esther had talked to Corrine about divorcing him. That was something she and Esther had discussed in the hotel room at Disneyland late at night when the kids were safely asleep. What kind of animal would kill his family instead of giving his wife a divorce?

No, Corrine thought, correcting herself. *Jonathan Southard isn't good enough to be called an animal. That was unfair to Major.*

"I'm on my way," Corrine said. "I'm driving up from San Diego. I don't know how long it will take at this time of night."

"Excuse me, Ms. Lapin, but under the circumstances, are you certain you should make that trip by yourself?" Detective Mumford asked. "It might be a good idea to have someone else come along to do the driving."

"No," Corrine said. "It's the middle of the night. I'm not going to wake up someone else. I'll be fine."

And Corrine Lapin was fine—fine but furious. As she drove, she thought about calling their parents. They were on a Baltic cruise right then. She could probably reach them on a ship-to-shore call, but she couldn't remember how many hours ahead they were. Besides, she didn't want to throw them into turmoil until she knew for sure, until there had been a positive identification. There would be time enough then to call them to deliver the devastating news.

Corrine drove like a bat out of hell in almost zero traffic and with no enforcement. She arrived at Esther's house at five o'clock in the morning to find a collection of police vehicles and medical examiner vans still blocking the street. The porch light was on, and lights shone in every window.

Corrine bounded out of her car and started forward at a run as two attendants wheeled a loaded gurney—a gurney with an adult-size body bag—down the sidewalk toward a waiting van. Half a block from the house a uniformed police officer barred the way.

"I'm sorry, ma'am," he said, holding up his hand. "You can't come any closer. Police business."

"I've got to get through," she said frantically. "That's my sister's house. Call Detective Mumford. She knows I'm coming. I'm here to do the ID."

The cop spoke into a police radio as another attendant carrying a small wrapped bundle emerged from the house. Moments later a woman walked out the front door and strode purposefully across the front yard.

"Ms. Lapin?"

Corrine nodded.

"We should probably wait until the bodies have been taken back to the morgue."

"No. I need to do it now so I can contact my parents. They're on a cruise. I need to know for sure before I try calling them."

Detective Mumford shook her head. "All right. Wait here."

Corrine waited. The detective walked over to the van. The attendants had loaded the gurney into the van and closed the door. After conferring with them for a few moments, Mumford returned.

"All right," she said. "But you need to be prepared. This won't be easy."

"I'll be okay," Corrine insisted.

But she wasn't okay. The gurney was removed from the van. As soon as the attendant zipped open the body bag, a cloud of putrid air exploded into the night. Covering her mouth and nose, Corrine approached the gurney. The face she saw was swollen and rotting, but she knew it was Esther's. There was no doubt about that.

Nodding hopelessly, Corrine turned away and then was desperately sick, heaving into the expanse of front-yard grass Esther had planted and loved so much. While her back was turned, she heard rather than saw the bag be zipped shut. Moments after that, the door to the van closed as well. The engine started.

As the van lumbered down the street, Detective Mumford returned. She placed a comforting hand on Corrine's shoulder. With the other hand she gave the woman a bottle of water.

"Thank you," she said. "I know how difficult that was. We'll need to ID the children, too, but we'll do that later."

Corrine nodded and said nothing.

"The whole house is considered a crime scene, so you can't stay here," the detective continued. "We'll have people here processing the scene for the rest of the night and on into the morning. You should probably get some rest. My niece Kimberly works nights at the Westlake Village Inn. Do you know where that is?"

Corrine nodded numbly.

"Go there," Detective Mumford said. "I called Kim and told her you might be coming. She has a room reserved in your name, and she'll give you a good deal on it. Tomorrow morning, or rather, later on this morning, one of our investigators will come by to interview you and to do the remaining IDs. It may be me or it may be someone else, but right now, you need to take care of yourself."

"I'll have to let my parents know how soon we can plan on scheduling a funeral."

"The timing of all that will be up to the M.E.'s office," Detective Mumford said. "They'll have to perform the autopsies. That takes time. In the meantime we need to concentrate our efforts on locating Mr. Southard. Does he have relatives in the area, someone to whom he could go for assistance?"

Corrine shook her head. "Not that I know of. His parents are divorced and remarried. His mother lives somewhere in Arizona," Corrine said. "From what Esther told me, he hates her guts. I don't think he'd go to her for help even if he was dying."

"And his father?"

"His name is Hank," Corrine said. "Hank Southard. He lives in Ohio somewhere. I met him once, at the wedding, but that's all I know about him."

Detective Mumford was taking notes as Corrine spoke.

"Would you say there was trouble in your sister's marriage?"

"I know there was," Corrine said. "She was planning on leaving him."

There was more Corrine could have said. She knew for a fact that Esther wasn't blameless. She loved to spend money—had always spent money. She had also hinted to Corrine about having a "friend" on the side, but that was no excuse for murder. So rather than going into any of that, Corrine spared her dead sister's reputation and made it all out to be Jonathan's problem and Jonathan's fault.

"Her husband lost his job months ago," Corrine said. "According to Esther, they were about to lose the house. Jonathan had made plans to take money out of his 401(k). She had to sign so he could access it."

"How much money?" Alex Mumford asked.

"I don't know the exact amount. He was a middle manager for Thousand Oaks Federal before it merged with two of the big banks. He worked for them for the better part of fifteen years."

"What about the timing on the payout?" Detective Mumford asked. "Any idea when it was due?"

"Soon, I think," Corrine told her. "But Esther never mentioned to me if it came or not."

"Go get some rest," Detective Mumford advised. "When I know more, I'll be in touch."

Once Corrine was gone, Alex Mumford picked up the phone. Getting a court order to examine bank and telephone records at that hour on a Sunday morning wasn't an easy sell, but she had been a homicide cop long enough that she knew who to call.

At that stage of the investigation, Jonathan Southard most likely should have been named as nothing more than a person of interest. But as far as Detective Mumford was concerned, there was very little doubt.

Southard had slaughtered his entire family. He had killed his wife and his children and even the family dog. It was up to Alex Mumford to make sure that the creep didn't get away with it.

Tucson, Arizona
Sunday, June 7, 2009, 5:00 A.M.
62° Fahrenheit

Jack Tennant's driver's license info with the DMV yielded a brother named Zack Tennant with an address in Catalina Foothills Estates. Brian was there at 5:00 A.M. to give Jack's relatives the bad news about what had happened on the reservation. Hearing about it seemed to hit the brother especially hard. While her husband went to collect address information for Jack's son and daughter, Ruth Tennant gave Brian a hint as to why.

"Zack and Jack had been estranged for a while," she explained. "Jack and Abby had one of those hot and heavy romances. Zack and I didn't approve. In the course of their rush to the altar, some things were said that should have been left unsaid. The rift probably could have been healed, but now it never will be."

When Zack returned to the living room, his eyes were red, but he brought with him contact information for Jack's daughter, Carol, who lived in San Francisco, and his son, Gary, who lived in Chula Vista.

"You'll be in touch with them?" Zack asked. "You'll let them know what's happened?"

"When it comes to something like this, I don't believe in telephones," Brian assured him. "I'll be in touch with the local police departments. They'll have officers go out and speak to them in person."

"Good," Zack said. "When they do, tell the kids to call me. I'll do what I can to handle things on this end."

After leaving the brother's residence, Brian drove to Jack and Abby Tennant's town home in a development called Catalina Vue. On the way he phoned in the next-of-kin information he had gleaned from Zack. He had mentioned that he thought Abby had a grown son somewhere, and Brian was curious why, rather than using her offspring as an emergency contact, Abby had used a woman named Mildred Harrison, who was evidently her next-door neighbor.

Just after 6:00 A.M. that morning, Detective Fellows

stood on Mildred's shaded front porch and rang her doorbell. A bathrobe-clad woman cracked open the front door.

"Who are you?" she demanded over a television set blaring in the background. "Do you have any idea what time it is? What do you want?"

"My name's Brian Fellows, Detective Brian Fellows with the Pima County Sheriff's Department. Are you Mildred Harrison?"

"I am," she said. "What's this about?"

In reply Brian, saying nothing, held up his ID wallet.

"Just a minute," she said. "Let me get my reading glasses."

Before Mildred returned to the door wearing her glasses, she paused long enough to turn down the volume on the television set. Back at the door, she reached for Brian's identification, which she examined in some detail before handing it back.

"All right," she said, unlocking the security chain and opening the door. "It looks legit, but these days a woman living alone can't be too careful. What's this all about?"

"I understand your neighbor, Abby Tennant, listed your name as an emergency contact on her driver's license."

"Has something happened to Abby?" Mildred asked. "Yes, I know she put my name on her license, and she's on mine, but that was back before she got married. The person you'll need to contact now is her husband, Jack."

"I'm sorry to have to tell you this," Brian said. "Abigail Tennant is deceased and so is her husband. We're attempting to notify Mrs. Tennant's next of kin. We also need someone who can give us a positive ID."

Mildred had returned to the door barefoot and carrying a porcelain coffee mug in one hand. That crashed to the floor, splattering coffee and pieces of broken cup in every direction.

"Dead?" she gasped, looking at Brian in horror, all the while backing away from the doorway. "Abby's dead? That's impossible! You can't be serious!"

"I'm afraid I'm very serious, ma'am," Brian said.

Mildred Harrison hadn't invited him into her home, but when she wobbled and looked as if she was in danger of falling, he stepped over the threshold uninvited, took her by the arm, and led her to a nearby sofa.

"This is terrible," she moaned. "I can't believe it! I just can't!"

As she rocked from side to side in a combination of shock and disbelief, Brian made himself useful. Returning to the open doorway, he began collecting pieces of broken mug. Once he had most of those in hand, he walked as far as the kitchen, where he located a trash can under the sink and a roll of paper towels on the counter. He returned to the living room carrying both of those and started mopping up spilled coffee.

"Thank you so much," Mildred said, dabbing at her eyes. "You shouldn't have to clean up my mess."

"It's not a problem, ma'am," he said. "I don't mind doing it at all, but I would appreciate your help."

"Of course," she said. "Whatever you need."

"As I said, we're attempting to do next-of-kin notifications. Does Abby Tennant have any near relations living around here?"

"No. Her son lives in California somewhere—I'm not sure where. His name is Jonathan, Jonathan Southard. I've never met the man, but he must have a screw loose somewhere. He somehow got it into his head that his mother was the cause of his parents' divorce, even though his dad had taken up with another woman long before the divorce was filed. Jonathan blamed everything on Abby and hasn't spoken to her in years. It broke her heart, I can tell you that much."

"What about her ex-husband?"

"His name is Hank, Hank Southard. As far as I know, he still lives in Ohio. But tell me. What happened to them? Was it a car wreck, or what?"

Brian shook his head. "There was a shooting overnight . . ."

"Oh, my!" Mildred exclaimed. "Don't tell me! Is this about those four people out on the reservation? That story was just on the news a few moments ago, but I never would have imagined in my wildest dreams that it was someone I knew."

"Yes," Brian said. "That's where it happened. Out on the reservation."

"Who did it? Drug smugglers? Usually when people around here get killed like that, you can bet it has something to do with the drug trade, although why they'd go after Jack and Abby I can't imagine. Abby barely uses aspirin, and I can't see Jack shooting back. I never heard of him carrying a weapon of any kind. And why drug smugglers would go around doing that kind of thing with a baby in the car! That's more than I can fathom."

"What baby?" Brian asked.

"That's what the reporter on the news said—that four people had been gunned down and that the only survivor of the incident was some poor little girl who had been transported to the hospital in Sells. I believe he said she was something like four years old."

Great, Brian thought grimly.

He had wanted to keep Angelina Enos's presence at the crime scene out of the public eye in order to keep her from being targeted. Obviously he had been overruled by someone higher up the food chain.

"When's the last time you saw Mr. and Mrs. Tennant?" Brian asked.

"I talked to Abby yesterday afternoon," Mildred said. "She had just come back from having her hair and nails done. I thought for sure she'd be coming to the party at the park last night, but she told me that she and Jack had made other plans."

"What party?" Brian asked.

"The Queen of the Night party at Tohono Chul. It only happens once a year. Abby Tennant has been in charge of that event for years. She was supposed to be this year, too, but she backed out at the last minute. She told me she had an unexpected conflict and she was overbooked."

In a homicide investigation, Brian understood that it's important to know everything about the victims, including any last-minute sudden changes of plans.

"Why did she back out?" Brian asked.

"It was their anniversary," Mildred explained. "She

and Jack met at the Queen of the Night party five years ago. According to Abby, Jack had come up with some out-of-this-world 'big surprise' for their celebration and Abby went along with it. Men are like that, you know," she added. "When one of them comes up with some tom-fool idea, it's better not to make a fuss."

"But Jack didn't say anything to you about what he had in mind?"

"No. Not a word. All I know is it was supposed to be a big surprise. I think Abby thought he was taking her out for a nice dinner. I didn't have the heart to tell her I had seen him loading all kinds of stuff in his car—a folding table, chairs, a picnic hamper, and a cooler. You don't need a cooler to take someone out to a nice restaurant for dinner. If my husband had ever pulled a stunt like that, I don't know what I would have done. When a woman goes to the trouble of having her hair and nails done, she doesn't want to be dragged off to somebody's godforsaken picnic."

Brian had a pretty clear idea that an outdoor picnic wasn't all Jack Tennant had had in mind. Before Law and Order arrived, Brian and Dan Pardee had followed the trail of footprints and the luminarias to that humongous night-blooming cereus. It occurred to Brian that Jack Tennant had gone to a lot of trouble to honor his anniversary by creating his very own Queen of the Night party. Brian was sure it had been a spectacular surprise, but that was before it turned into a massacre.

"Other than Jack Tennant loading stuff in the car, did you see anything else out of the ordinary?"

Using the arm of the sofa for support, Mildred Harrison hauled herself upright and then tottered over to a picture window that looked out on the street. In front of the window was an easy chair along with a small table. On it sat a pair of binoculars and a notebook.

She picked up the notebook, opened it, and brought it back to Brian, who had taken a seat on the couch.

"We had some break-ins around here a year or so ago and kids rummaging through mailboxes," she explained. "So we started a neighborhood block watch program. I went out last night to the party at Tohono Chul, but most of the time I'm right here at home, so I volunteered to serve as block captain, and I do keep watch."

Brian looked down at the open notebook, its lines covered in an old-fashioned spidery script. The writing was so shaky that it was almost illegible.

"Check out the last two pages," Mildred advised. "The last entry is for yesterday, and the one before that is for the day before. See it there? I saw the same vehicle two days in a row—a light gray minivan with California plates—and I made a note of it each time."

"Make and model?" Brian asked.

Mildred shook her head. "I have no idea. These days all those minivans look alike to me, but all the same, you can see I took down the plate information, just to be on the safe side. I did that because I hadn't heard that anyone on the street was expecting company, not in the middle of the summer. Sure, out-of-towners come to visit in droves in January, February, and March, but most Californians have better sense than to show up in Tucson in June or July."

"This may or may not be related," Brian said, "but did you happen to get a glimpse of whoever was inside?"

"Both times I saw the vehicle, there was just one person in it—the driver."

"Man or woman?"

"Definitely a man."

"Race?" Brian asked.

"White, I'm sure. He was going bald, so probably middle-aged. He wore glasses—well, sunglasses, anyway."

"Other than the minivan," Brian said, "did you notice anything else out of the ordinary?"

"No," Mildred said. "That's about it. Unleashed dogs wandering around, garbage cans left out on the curb that should have been taken inside, and that sort of thing. Nothing else comes to mind."

Brian stood up, took out a business card, and gave it to her. "If you'll excuse me, I need to get back to that next-of-kin situation, but thank you. You've been most helpful. If you think of anything else, though, don't hesitate to call."

Mildred studied his card. "You probably think I'm just a nosy old lady," she said. "That's what Carl would have said. He was my husband. He's dead now, but he was always after me to mind my own business."

Brian smiled at her. "I'm not sure how old you are," he said, "and I'm not so sure about your being nosy, either, but believe me, in my business there are times when we need all the help we can get."

Brian hurried out to his car. Despite what he'd told Mildred, he doubted anything would come of the license information. Just to be on the safe side, though, he pulled out his cell phone and asked Records to check it out.

Sells, Tohono O'odham Nation, Arizona
Sunday, June 7, 2009, 8:00 A.M.
69° Fahrenheit

Just before Lani got off shift at 8:00 A.M. on Sunday morning, she took a detour past Angie Enos's room, popped in briefly, just long enough to say hello. Now that Angie had been moved out of the ER, another physician was in charge of her case. The little girl was sitting up in bed eating breakfast.

Angie looked up at Lani from her dish of Lucky Charms. "Are you a leopard?" she asked.

"A leopard?" Lani asked, glancing in Dan Pardee's direction for help. He shrugged his own bafflement.

"What makes you think I'm a leopard?" Lani asked.

"Spots," Angie said.

Lani held up her bare arm where dozens of tiny white blemishes dotted her skin. Lani was so accustomed to them that she no longer noticed them.

"Ants," Lani said.

Angie's eyes widened. *"Kuadagi?"* she asked.

Lani nodded. "When I was little—younger than you are—the people who were supposed to be watching me left me alone for too long. I got into an ant bed and the ants bit me," she explained. "There were so many ant bites that I almost died. I had to go to a hospital just like this one."

"My mommy doesn't like me to get near ants," Angie said. "She said they can be bad."

"It's true," Lani said.

She noticed that Angie still referred to her mother in the present tense. The reality of her loss had yet to sink into Angie's little brain.

"You're not giving Mr. Pardee or Bozo any trouble, are you?" Lani asked.

Angie looked at the Shadow Wolf in his now somewhat bedraggled Border Patrol uniform. He looked tired. A dark five o'clock shadow bristled on his cheeks, but Angie gave him a sweet smile. "Even though he's a grown-up, he says I can call him Dan."

"I'd take him at his word then," Lani said. "Come to think of it, maybe I'll call him Dan, too. But I'm going off shift now, so I probably won't see you again."

"Okay," Angie said with a shy wave.

Lani went outside. An irate charge nurse was waiting for her at the end of the hall. "What's a dog doing in that room?" she demanded. "We have no business—"

"It is our business," Lani interrupted. "That poor little girl's mother was murdered last night. The dog is helping take her mind off her troubles, and believe me, that's exactly what she needs."

"When she goes, the dog goes," the nurse declared.

"I'm sure," Lani agreed.

"When will she be released?"

Lani glanced at her watch. She had more than half expected that Angie's family would have arrived overnight to check on her. She was a little surprised that they had yet to put in an appearance, but she was sure they'd be there soon.

"My understanding is that someone is supposed to come pick her up this morning," Lani said. "One of her relatives. Next-of-kin notifications were being done last night."

The charge nurse picked up Angie's chart. "Do we know who'll be picking her up?" she asked.

"My guess would be the grandparents," Lani said. "You'll need to sort that out with her attending. I'm off."

Lani left the hospital then. Weariness was catching up with her. She needed to get Gabe fed and on his way home, and then she planned to go to bed herself. Fortunately she had today and tomorrow off. That would give her a chance to catch up on her sleep. It had been a busy night in the ER. Once Jose Thomas had been shipped off to Phoenix Indian, Lani had treated two maternity cases, one of which had ended with the normal delivery of the infant. The other had required an emergency C-section. By the time Lani got off work, both mothers and both newborns were doing well.

She walked across the parking lot and through the hospital housing compound, where Lani was surprised to see Delia Ortiz's aging Saab parked in front of her house. On dance weekends, when Gabe stayed with Lani, she usually returned him to his parents' place later on in the morning, giving them a chance to catch up on their sleep.

Delia's car was parked in Lani's driveway, but she

wasn't in it. That meant she was probably inside. Lani and Delia knew each other, but they had never been close. The idea that Delia had gone inside Lani's home without an express invitation and without Lani's being there violated some age-old Tohono O'odham traditions where hospitality was a gift to be given rather than something to be expected or demanded.

Lani paused for a moment outside the front door, listening for the sound of the television set. Gabe Ortiz loved Saturday and Sunday morning cartoons, but there was only silence.

Turning her key in the lock, Lani let herself inside. Delia Ortiz was sitting in a rocking chair, dozing. She jerked awake when the door opened.

"Sorry to stop by unexpectedly like this," Delia said. "I hope you don't mind, but I needed to talk to you."

"Where's Gabe?" Lani said, looking around.

"I sent him home."

Whatever this was, it was something Delia didn't want her son to hear. That made Lani uneasy. "Can I get you something?" she asked. "Coffee?"

"No, thanks. No coffee. After this, I need to go home and take a nap."

Lani needed sleep, too. Instead of going to the kitchen, she sat down on the couch and waited, allowing the silence between them to stretch.

"He had a good birthday," Delia said eventually.

Lani nodded. She hadn't been invited to Gabe's eighth birthday party. She had been at work, but there was more to it than that. There was a certain rivalry between these two young women, a kind of sibling rivalry, even though they were not related. Both of them had been put forward by their mutual mentor, Fat Crack Ortiz. He had brought Delia home from Washington and he had seen to it that the Tohono O'odham paid for Lani's medical education. So they were both women of influence on the reservation, but they were not friends. Not birthday-party friends.

"I'm glad," Lani said.

"He loves video games," Delia said.

Lani knew that, too. In many ways, Gabe Ortiz was an ordinary little kid. In other ways, he was extraordinary.

"You gave him to me," Delia said after a pause.

"I wrapped him up in a towel and handed him to you," Lani said with a smile. "You're the one who had to do all the hard work."

"What would have happened to us if you hadn't been there that night to help?"

Lani shrugged. "Probably nothing," she said. "It was a normal delivery. Faster than expected, but normal. You were both healthy. Anyone could have helped you."

"But you're the one who did," Delia said. "I don't think I ever said thank you."

"You made me Gabe's godmother," Lani said. "That's thanks enough."

"Maybe," Delia said.

Lani was puzzled. So far there was nothing about this oblique conversation that couldn't have been said in Gabe's presence, especially if he was engrossed in watching cartoons. But rushing the process wouldn't have been polite, so she sat back and waited.

"Now maybe I can return the favor," Delia said.

Lani blinked at that, but she said nothing.

"Angelina Enos is still in the hospital?" Delia asked.

Lani nodded. "Yes. As soon as her family arrives, she'll be released to them."

"They won't come," Delia said flatly. "Nobody is coming for her. I spoke to her mother's parents last night and to her father's parents earlier this morning. Joaquin Enos is in jail in Phoenix. His parents are already taking care of two other grandchildren. They can't take another."

"What about Delphina's parents?" Lani asked.

"They're from Nolic," Delia said.

Lani blinked again. Nolic was where she was from, where she had been from, years ago before she became *wogsha*, an adopted Indian child, and before she went to live in Tucson with Brandon Walker and Diana Ladd.

"Delphina's parents are Carmen and Louis Escalante," Delia continued. "Delphina was your cousin. Carmen and Louis are your aunt and uncle."

Lani sucked in her breath. "Some of the same people who didn't want me," she said.

"Yes," Delia agreed. "Since you were an ant-bit child, they believed you were a dangerous object. Now they think the same thing about Angie—that she's dangerous. Louis called her Kok'oi Chehia."

"Ghost Girl?" Lani asked.

Delia nodded. "Louis called her that because she wasn't killed when everyone else was. He's also convinced that she'll grow up to be a bad person like her father." Delia shrugged and added, "Maybe she will be bad someday, but maybe she'll grow up to be like her mother. My brother is like my father; I'm like my mother. It can go either way."

"But Angie needs to have a chance," Lani said.

"Yes," Delia said, "that's true, and it's why I'm hoping you'll take her."

Lani's jaw dropped. "Me?" she echoed.

"Yes, you," Delia said determinedly. "You're Angie's cousin, after all. If a blood relative steps in to take her, I believe we can keep CPS from getting involved. Since Angie is an eyewitness in the death of her mother, Detective Fellows thinks it's important to involve the state in the process as little as possible."

For several long moments neither of them spoke.

"I'm too young to be a mother," Lani said at last. "I don't have a husband and I don't know enough."

"Delphina had just turned twenty, and she didn't have a husband, either," Delia pointed out. "All she had was her GED, but she was making her way and doing a good job of raising her daughter. You're what—thirty?"

Lani nodded.

"That makes you plenty old enough to be a mother," Delia continued. "You're also a trained doctor. You'll make a good mother."

"What makes you think so?"

Delia shrugged. "When Fat Crack came to Washington and told me I'd be a good tribal attorney, he didn't ask to see my school transcripts or ask for references. He already knew I was right for the job. You're right for this one."

With that, Delia stood up. "I know this is a shock," she said. "I know you need to think about this before you answer. Take as much time as you need. We both know Angie is safe as long as she stays in the hospital. Call me later. Let me know what you decide. If you're going to take her, I'll handle everything else."

Delia left then. She let herself out while Lani, too stunned to move, sat where she was. What was it her mother had said to her yesterday? It had been something about wanting another grandchild. Lani doubted this was what her mother had in mind.

Sometimes you have to watch out what you ask for, Lani thought. *You may just get it.*

11

Tucson, Arizona
Sunday, June 7, 2009, 6:30 A.M.
71° Fahrenheit

*A*RMED WITH THE licensing information, it didn't take long for Records to come up with Jonathan Southard's silver Dodge Grand Caravan minivan and an address in Thousand Oaks, California. Mildred Harrison had called it gray, but the DMV said silver.

"Can you get me a phone number on that?" Brian asked.

That took a little longer. While Brian waited, he considered his options.

Under most circumstances, he would have called the other jurisdiction and involved them in the process. But for right then, the easiest thing to do was to call the house directly and find out if the guy was at home. If he was, that would mean someone else was driving Southard's car, which, at this point, had not been reported stolen. If he wasn't home or if his wife had no idea where he was, then that would be the time to call for reinforcements.

The Records clerk came back on the line and gave Brian a number in Thousand Oaks. He wondered briefly if it was too early to call, but then he realized this was summer. That meant California and Arizona were on the same time zone. The phone rang four times. Just when Brian was convinced the call was going to go to voice mail, someone—a woman—picked up.

"Hello," Brian said. "Is Jonathan Southard there?"

"Who's calling, please?" the woman asked.

Brian didn't want to go into all that if it wasn't absolutely necessary, but the woman wasn't leaving him a lot of wiggle room.

"Just tell me," Brian said irritably. "Is he there or not?"

"This is Detective Alexandra Mumford with the Thousand Oaks Police Department," she said frostily. "Maybe you'd like to tell me what your business is with Mr. Southard."

Brian was taken aback. "It turns out I'm a detective, too," he said. "Detective Brian Fellows with the Pima County Sheriff's Department in Arizona. I'm investigating a quadruple homicide that occurred in our jurisdiction some time last evening. Four people were gunned down. A vehicle matching the description of Mr. Southard's had been spotted in the vicinity of one of the victims' homes—"

"What victims?" Detective Mumford interjected.

"One of them, Abby Tennant, is apparently Mr. Southard's mother."

"Crap!"

"What does that mean?" Brian asked.

"I've spent most of the night in Mr. Southard's home in Thousand Oaks," Alex Mumford told him. "We had a call from his wife's sister down in San Diego last night. She was concerned that she hadn't heard from her sister, Esther, in several days. A couple of uniforms were dispatched to the Southards' residence to do a welfare check. They're the ones who found the bodies."

"Bodies?" Brian repeated. "What bodies? How many?"

"Three in all. One adult female and two children, a boy and a girl. Oh, and also the family dog. The dead woman's sister drove up from San Diego and gave us a positive identification on the mother."

Brian was stunned. "So we're up to seven victims now? Crap is right! If Southard has murdered his wife and kids and his mother and stepfather, who else is left?"

"That would be his father," Alex told him. "He lives somewhere in Ohio. Let me see what I can find out about that, and I'll call you back. Does this number work for you?"

"Yes."

Detective Mumford was all business. "I'll see about getting a court order to go after Southard's cell phone records. We may be able to get a line on him that way. I'll get back to you."

"Good," Brian said.

When she hung up, Brian didn't bother closing his phone. Instead, he called Kath. "I won't be at church," he said. "The victim count just went up, three in California and four here."

"That's the problem with the cartels," Kath said. "They're mobile."

"This is worse than a cartel," Brian said. "It's personal. It's some asshole who's decided to target his whole family. He's taken out his wife, kids, and mother so far, plus his stepfather and two innocent bystanders. We think he may be on his way to Ohio to take out his father as well unless we can get a line on him first."

Brian heard his wife's sharp intake of breath. "You're right," she said. "That's far worse than cartels. Where are you now?"

"On my way in to the office."

"Be safe then," Kath said. "See you whenever you get here."

Sells, Tohono O'odham Nation, Arizona
Sunday, June 7, 2009, 9:00 A.M.
71° Fahrenheit

For a long time after Delia left, Lani sat there thinking, wondering what was the best thing to do about Angie, the right thing to do.

She knew that even offering to foster the child could well mean long-term heartbreak for both of them. Yes, Delia had said that both sets of grandparents had already indicated that they weren't interested in caring for Angie and that the father was a nonstarter in that regard. But what would happen to Lani and to Angie if they formed a bond only to have some other person, a closer relation than a mere second cousin, come forward to claim the child? What then?

And what if that other person could offer Angie a home where she would have the benefit of both a mother and a father? Lani understood full well that she would be taking on child rearing as a single parent, one who came with odd working hours and a very demanding job. Or what if the father threw a wrench in the works by refusing to sign over his parental rights? Lani knew from dealings with child welfare folks in Denver that they were always predisposed to return children to their natural parents, even when said parents had very little going for them.

But not being able to offer Angie a home with both a mother and a father was no excuse for Lani to refuse to take her in. As far as she could see, even when Delphina was alive, Angie hadn't had the benefit of a father figure in her life. Donald Rios might have been able to offer her that, but Donald Rios was dead.

Lani was tempted to pick up the phone and call her brother or her parents to ask for their opinions and advice, but she didn't. Davy was dealing with his own difficult family issues now. It wasn't fair to involve him. As for asking her parents? Lani glanced at her watch. She had no doubt that her father would be up by now, probably making his Sunday-morning breakfast special of blueberry muffins and a spinach frittata. She knew where his feelings would lie. Lani understood better than anyone that Brandon Walker's supposedly gruff demeanor did little to conceal his notoriously soft heart.

Take Damsel, for example. Lani had been away at school that Thanksgiving morning when someone had abandoned a bedraggled, starving puppy on her parents' doorstep. Diana had found the dog and would have called Animal Control to come get it. Brandon was the one who had lobbied to keep the poor animal. He was also the one who had come up with the name, Damsel. And much as he might grumble about "that damn dog," Lani knew how much he cared about her and how often he slipped her supposedly forbidden treats.

Lani smiled now, thinking about how Brandon had done the same for her, both when she was little and later on as well. When she was going to school and later during her residency, a note from her dad, usually one sent for no particular occasion, could always be counted on to have a stray hundred-dollar bill tucked inside it, along with a written admonition not to spend it all in one place.

Lani knew without asking that her parents would accept Angie as their own. If Lani brought the child into the family, Angie would instantly have two loving grandparents, which was apparently two more than she had at the moment. But the real question to be answered was whether saying yes to Delia's proposition was the right thing to do.

This was a momentous decision and one that shouldn't

be hastily made. On the other hand, if there was any delay, Angie would be released from the hospital into the care and keeping of Child Protective Services. Lani knew that once children were caught up in the bureaucratic nightmare of "the system," they seldom emerged unscathed.

In a contest between what Lani had to offer Angie Enos and what the child welfare system could offer, there was really no question. On that score, Lani was the hands-down winner. As things stood now, she and she alone had a chance to save Angie Enos from that fate, but was that what she was supposed to do?

Looking for an answer and almost without thinking, Lani stood up and walked into her bedroom, where she opened the top drawer of her dresser and removed her medicine basket, the one she had woven during her sixteen-day exile on Ioligam. In the tightly woven basket she kept the treasures Understanding Woman had given her granddaughter, Rita Antone, as well as the ones Rita and Fat Crack had passed along to Lani. From the bottom of the basket Lani retrieved two leather pouches. The soft one held Fat Crack's crystals. The other one, cracked and ancient, had once belonged to Fat Crack's blind mentor Looks at Nothing. Now, as then, it held a properly gathered supply of *wiw*, Indian tobacco.

Taking both pouches with her, Lani returned to the living room. She set the tobacco pouch aside for the moment and opened the other one, letting the four sacred crystals fall into the palm of her hand. She had learned over the years that the crystals, when properly used, could be a tool of discernment.

Fat Crack had taught her that it was always best to look at an image of the object in question rather than at the object itself. In this case the object in question was Angelina Enos. Lani had no photo of the child, nothing that she could use. But since the question had to do with whether Lani should take Angie into her life, maybe a photo of Lani would do.

The lanyard with Lani's hospital ID, complete with a photograph, was right there on the coffee table. She picked it up. One crystal at a time, she viewed the photo through the intervening lens. The distortion from one crystal made it look as though she was laughing while another made her look sad even though the photo itself remained unchanged.

But the very process of focusing on the image with absolute concentration worked its particular magic. Suddenly she could see what Delia had been trying to tell her. Yes, she and Angie were blood kin, but their real connection was far greater than that.

What had happened long ago to the Ant-Bit Child was happening again to this Ghost Child. Rather than being accepted by their blood relations, they were both being shunned by them. And it turned out, they were the same blood relations—the Escalante clan from Nolic. It was almost as though I'itoi himself had laid out the pattern. It was as though the two of them were two sides of the same coin.

"Yes," Lani said aloud to herself. "I can see why Angie and I were meant to be together."

She was still holding the crystals in her hand. She had been awake for the better part of twenty-four hours.

When she stopped concentrating all her focus and energy on the photo, it wasn't surprising that she fell asleep, dozing off for a time while still sitting upright on her worn secondhand couch.

Tucson, Arizona
Sunday, June 7, 2009, 7:00 A.M.
72° Fahrenheit

Always an early riser, Brandon Walker was up by five. By seven he was totally engrossed in his Sunday-morning culinary tradition. The blueberry muffins were just coming out of one oven and his spinach frittata was on its way into the other when Diana came down the hall. She had her hair pulled back in a ponytail. An Arizona Cardinals baseball cap was perched on her head.

"Smells good," she said, sniffing the air and pouring herself a cup of coffee.

"Brandon Walker's Sunday-morning surprise," he answered with a grin, although that was hardly a surprise since those were the same dishes he made pretty much every Sunday morning. "If we're going to go out and tackle the desert, we'll have to keep up our strength. And if we're taking the Invicta, we need to head out before it gets too hot."

Brandon was the cook in the family. Cooking wasn't something that really interested Diana Ladd. If she had to, she could cook well enough to survive, but that was about it. For a long time, Nana *Dahd* had done the cooking for the family. Once she was gone, Brandon had stepped into the breach.

"I see you're dressed for travel," he said as he set glasses and silverware on the breakfast bar in the kitchen.

"Yup, sunscreen and all," she replied.

For a long time now, for weeks, Diana had seemed lost in a kind of despair that Brandon hadn't been able to penetrate. She had always been reserved and quiet, preferring to observe those around her rather than being the life of the party. But this had seemed more serious than that, especially in light of what was going on with her publisher.

Brandon had gone so far as to suggest that perhaps they should see a doctor and look into the possibility of having Diana take antidepressants. That suggestion had met with firm disapproval. This morning, however, the fog seemed to have lifted. Diana's answering smile gave him cause to hope. Maybe he had been pushing panic buttons for no reason.

"I sent June Holmes an e-mail and told her we'd be there around nine-thirty or so. If we go any later than that, we'll roast. Or else we'll have to ride with the top up, which," he added, nodding toward the baseball cap, "probably isn't what you had in mind."

"Yes," she said. "Definitely top down."

"And what about Damsel?" Brandon asked.

Diana shrugged. "She's welcome to come along, as long as she doesn't mind riding in the backseat. When you go in to interview the lady, the two of us will stay with the car or in the car, depending on if you park in the shade."

Diana's good mood held all through breakfast and during the initial part of the drive to Sonoita. Speeding down the freeway with the sun broiling down on them and with the wind roaring in their ears, there wasn't much chance to talk. From time to time, Brandon glanced in the rearview mirror at Damsel, who sat with her nose thrust outside the car and with her long ears flapping in the breeze. Soon after they exited I-10 onto Highway 83, Diana suddenly went somber again. The change in her mood was so abrupt it was as though a bank of clouds had suddenly passed in front of the sun or someone had flipped a switch.

Damn, Brandon thought. *I was hoping it would last all day.*

Highway 83, South of Tucson, Arizona
Sunday, June 7, 2009, 8:30 A.M.
75° Fahrenheit

Diana saw Max Cooper sitting there in the backseat out of the corner of her eye.

Her father—or rather the man she had always thought to be her father—was dressed the way she remembered him dressing back when she was a child and still believed he was her father.

He wore a pair of rough work pants held up by heavy-duty suspenders. Even though it was the dead of summer, he still wore a set of flesh-colored long johns, the kind he had always worn for working in the woods and for overseeing the garbage dump in Joseph, Oregon. His chin was covered with rough stubble, and the anger that had always burned in his eyes when he looked at her was still there, as malevolent as ever.

He's dead, Diana reminded herself. *He isn't here, not really. My mind is playing tricks on me.*

Max Cooper had succumbed to cirrhosis of the liver at least a decade earlier. Diana had no idea what had become of Francine, his second wife, and she didn't care. But here he was with his arms folded belligerently across his chest, glowering at her from the backseat of her Invicta while Damsel, unaware of his threatening presence, continued to stare at the passing scenery.

"It won't work," he said. "You can sell the car if you want, but getting rid of it won't keep you from doing what needs to be done. Why don't you just go with the flow, take the easy way out?"

Ignoring him, Diana stared at the road unspooling ahead of them, at a hot ribbon of pavement winding over parched rolling hills topped with tinder-dry winter grass.

"Diana," Brandon asked. "What's wrong? What's going on?"

"Go away," she said. "Leave me alone."

Of course, she meant those words for Max Cooper. In this case, Brandon was an innocent bystander. Max had appeared there in the backseat of the moving vehicle as if by magic. Diana wanted him to disappear that same way.

"I know what you had in mind," Max said with a snide smile. "Take this thing off the same curve out by Gates Pass, the one where Lani wrecked years ago. No seat belt.

No roll bars. No nothing. You'd be gone just like that. Best for all concerned, don't you think?"

Max snapped his fingers. To Diana's surprise she could hear that finger snap, even over the rushing wind. How did he know she had thought such a thing? And how did he know that was exactly why she wanted to unload her Invicta? So she wouldn't be tempted. If what the future held for her was drifting further and further into some kind of dementia or even Alzheimer's, that was bad enough. Her committing suicide wouldn't help anyone, most especially the people she loved.

She turned to Brandon. "How soon do you think you can get this up to Scottsdale for the auction?"

"Are you sure you want to sell this old boat?" he asked. "You've always loved it, and nobody makes cars like this anymore."

"I'm sure," she insisted. "I'm ready to let it go."

"If it's going to be car-show worthy, then it'll have to be detailed," Brandon said. "Since Leo Ortiz did the original restoration work on it, I could check with him and see if he has time to do it."

Diana nodded, then turned to look at Max Cooper to see what he thought of that.

Naturally he wasn't there. By then the only passenger in the backseat was Damsel—Damsel and nobody else.

It's coming, Diana thought. *I can still remember Brandon's name and mine, but I still can't remember Davy's wife's name. And I'm seeing people who aren't there. At least I don't think they're there, but what if other people can see them, too, like little Gabe Ortiz did the other day? What does that mean? Do they exist, or am I just losing it?*

She looked over at Brandon. He was wearing sunglasses, but she could see the frown behind the green lenses. He wasn't frowning because he was concentrating on driving. He was worried about her. She loved him for that, but she didn't want to be the cause of it.

About the time Andrew Carlisle had gotten out of prison and come looking for Diana, Brandon's father had taken off in Brandon's Pima County patrol car. They'd found him much later, wandering in the desert near Benson. Ultimately he had died of exposure, turning a seemingly harmless joyride into tragedy.

Exposure. That's what the death certificate had said, but that was back in the seventies. People didn't talk about Alzheimer's then the way they did now. That was what had really gotten Toby Walker, and Diana understood it was likely to get her, too. Driving the Invicta off a cliff was tempting—a siren call urging Diana onto the rocks when she knew it would take more courage to stay and face whatever was coming.

In Diana Ladd Walker's heart of hearts, she knew that leaving Brandon too early would hurt him more than staying and facing down the enemy together.

Grateful for Brandon's reassuring presence, she reached over and rested her hand on his thigh. His frown lifted. He turned and smiled at her. Then he squeezed her hand and lifted it to his lips.

And that's why, she thought, deliberately shaking off the evil spell Max's unwanted presence had cast over them. *Because he loves me more right now than Max Cooper ever loved anybody.*

Max Cooper had married a girl who was pregnant with

another man's child. In small-town Joseph, Oregon, he had grudgingly given her illegitimate daughter, Diana, the benefit of his own slender claim on small-town respectability, but that was all he had given her—his name and that was it. As a child, she had faced his constant torment—the beatings and the verbal abuse—with implacable resistance and without even once rewarding him with what he wanted—with tears or whimpers.

She had fought him then and she would fight him now. If Max Cooper was in favor of Diana's committing suicide, then she would be against it—to her very last dying breath.

Sells, Tohono O'odham Nation, Arizona
Sunday, June 7, 2009, 8:00 A.M.
69° Fahrenheit

There was silence for a time after Dr. Walker left Angie's room. Dan could easily imagine someone being hospitalized for a snakebite. That was entirely understandable, but he had a difficult time getting his head around the idea of nearly dying of ant bites. That was far more difficult to fathom. But from the number of blemishes left on the doctor's skin, not just the visible ones but the ones that had to be hidden under her clothing as well, there must have been hundreds of bites. No wonder she had almost died from the poison.

"I got bit by an ant once," Angie told him conversationally. "Will I have a spot, too?"

"Do you have a spot now?" Dan asked.

Angie shook her head.

"Then you probably won't," Dan assured her. "Dr. Walker probably had so many bites that they got infected. That's what caused the scarring."

"I'm scared of ants," Angie said. "Are you?"

"I wasn't before," he said, "but maybe I am now."

Angie pushed away the table with her empty breakfast tray on it. "When can I go home?" she asked.

"I don't know," Dan said. "I'm sure someone will tell us."

"But I won't be going home with my mommy."

"No," Dan said. "Not your mommy."

It hurt him to know that the reality of her situation was finally penetrating. The place she had lived with her murdered mother was most likely now a designated crime scene. It was reasonable to assume that Angie wouldn't ever be going back there, and wherever she did go, her mother would never be there.

Turning her face away from Dan, Angie lay back down on the bed and cried herself to sleep. Once she drifted off, Dan took Bozo and hurried out of the room. He drove to Bashas', where he bought food for Bozo, another set of nearly out-of-date sandwiches for himself, and three children's books for Angie. As far as books were concerned, the pickings were thin. He came away with one about a talking dump truck, one about a princess, and a coloring book about someone named SpongeBob SquarePants, whoever that was. He also bought a big box of crayons.

Angie was awake when he returned. "Where were you?" she demanded.

"I had to get some food for Bozo and for me," he told her.

"Why didn't you eat some of mine?"

"Hospitals don't work that way," he said with a smile. "That food is all for you, but I did find these." He handed her his peace offering.

Time passed slowly. There were stickers on the last several pages of the coloring book, and those were a far bigger hit than the crayons were. Watching Angie apply them with studied concentration, Dan found himself wondering how this little girl's life would turn out. Would there be some loving grandparent to take up the slack, as Micah Duarte had done for him?

"He was a bad man," Angie said eventually.

She was obviously thinking about the Milghan man with the gun. "Yes," Dan agreed. "He was."

Dan's lifestyle had given him very little contact with young children. He had no idea how much she understood of what had happened or how soon she would be able to process it.

"I'm sorry Donald is dead, too," Angie added matter-of-factly. "He was a nice man. I liked him. He gave me this." She held up the pink-and-yellow pinwheel that she had kept hold of waking and sleeping.

Dan nodded. "I'm sorry about Donald, too," he said.

There was another long period of quiet. Other people might have been tempted to fill it with conversation—to try to steer Angie away from dwelling on what had happened to her and to her family. Instinctively Dan knew better than to try to talk her out of it. After all, the life she had known had been destroyed. Now she was trying to make sense of what was left. He knew that she'd be doing that for the rest of her life—just as he was.

"His arm was broken," Angie added eventually.

"Excuse me?"

"The bad man," she said. "His arm."

"What do you mean, it was broken? Was it in a cast?" Dan asked.

Angie shook her head. "I don't know about a cast. It was in one of those things around his neck."

"You mean it was in a sling?"

She nodded.

"And if you saw him again, would you know his face?"

She nodded again. "I would know him," she said.

"Can you tell me what he looked like?"

"Anglo," she said. "He didn't have much hair, and he was carrying a gun."

Daniel knew at once that he had just gained access to three important pieces of the puzzle, maybe three essential pieces. Solving the shooting wasn't part of Daniel Pardee's job description, but regardless of jurisdictional issues, Dan was now in possession of vital information that he intended to pass along to Detective Fellows. Immediately.

"I need to go make a phone call," he said. "Do you mind waiting here with Bozo?"

"Will you be back?" she asked.

"Yes," he said. "I'll be back."

"Okay then," she said. "We'll wait."

Sonoita, Arizona
Sunday, June 7, 2009, 9:30 A.M.
73° Fahrenheit

Leaving Diana and Damsel parked in the shade of a towering cottonwood, Brandon stepped up onto the front porch of June Holmes's Sonoita home and rang the bell. The silver-haired woman who opened the door was dressed in a church-worthy suit with a slim skirt and jacket, along with low heels and hose.

"Mr. Walker?" she asked.

"Yes," he said, fumbling for his identification, but she waved that aside.

"I'm sure that's not necessary. Please come in."

Brandon stepped into a darkened living room. The blinds were closed and the curtains drawn. A single lamp burned next to an easy chair. Just inside the door sat a small old-fashioned suitcase, one without rollers. Next to it was a cardboard cat container complete with a vocal and very unhappy cat who was yowling its heart out.

June went to the easy chair where she had evidently been sitting before the doorbell rang. She closed the book that was on a nearby end table. On his way to the sofa, Brandon found it easy to make out the gold-leaf letters on the worn black leather cover—*The Book of Mormon*.

"Please excuse Miss Kitty," June said, folding her hands in her lap. "Traveling anywhere makes her nervous."

In his years as an investigator, Brandon had seen enough body language to recognize that June Holmes was every bit as nervous as her unhappy cat.

"The two of you are going on a trip then?" Brandon asked. Hoping to put June at ease, he tried to keep his voice casual and conversational.

"I suppose so," June replied. "Miss Kitty isn't going far. My neighbor up the road has agreed to keep her while I'm gone, but she hates traveling so much that it's impossible to take her even that far if she isn't in a crate. Otherwise, she'd disappear the moment I open the door."

"If you're on a tight schedule, then," Brandon said, "perhaps we should get started. As you know, G. T. Farrell is in ill health at the moment and has been since before you sent him that note inviting him to stop by to see you. That's why I'm here. He's not in any condition to travel and probably won't be any time soon."

"I'm sorry he's ill," June said regretfully. "I know he's been involved in this case from the beginning. It must have been difficult having to pass it along to someone else."

"Yes," Brandon agreed. "I'm sure that's why he held on to it for so long. He thought eventually he'd be well enough to come see you himself. When it became apparent that wouldn't be possible, he called me."

"Let's get to it, then," June said. She picked up the book and slipped it into a large open purse that sat on the floor next to her chair. "There's no sense beating about the bush."

"This is about the murder of Ursula Brinker?" Brandon asked.

June nodded. "Yes," she said. "I called her Sully back then. That's what everyone called her."

"You were friends?"

June nodded again. "We were," she said. "Good friends. Best friends."

"Tell me about spring break of 1959," Brandon said.

June closed her eyes for a moment before she answered. "Five of us drove over to San Diego in Margo Mansfield's 1955 Chevrolet Bel Air."

"Who all went?" Brandon asked. He already knew the answer. The five names had been carefully listed in Geet's notebook.

"Margo, of course," June said. "She drove. Then there was Sully, Deanna Rogers, Kathy Wallace, and me. We drove over on Friday afternoon after the last classes let out."

"What did you do once you got there?"

"To San Diego? We checked into our hotel. We had a room that opened right on the beach."

"One room for all five of you?" Brandon asked.

"It was a big room with two double beds and a rollaway."

"What happened after you got there?"

"We'd stopped for dinner in Yuma on the way over, so we went for a walk on the beach."

"Who is 'we'?"

"All of us, all five. But on the beach Sully and I hung out together—that night and the next day, too. We were sort of . . . well, you know . . . acting up. My parents were strict Mormons. I wanted to sow some wild oats while I still had the chance, and I figured being out of town on spring break was the best time to do it. We smoked and we drank—we drank way too much. You know how wild kids can be when they set their minds to it."

Brandon nodded. He knew exactly how wild kids could be.

"What happened?" he asked.

June sighed, looking embarrassed and uncomfortable. "I thought Sully and I were just friends, but it turned out she wanted to be more than that, and right then so did I. This was the next afternoon, Saturday. We were in the room, changing into our bathing suits, when she came over and kissed me—on the lips. I was bombed out of my gourd on rum and Coke. At the time it didn't seem like such a bad idea. After all, considering the rum and Coke, going to bed with another girl was just another bit of forbidden fruit. We were on one of the beds, doing it, when one of the other girls walked in on us. I've always suspected it was Margo, but I'm not sure. It could have been any one of them."

"What happened then?"

"I was ready to die of embarrassment. I mean, I knew Sully was different, but I'd never put a name on it before. I don't think she had, either. I remember she just kept smiling at me, like what had happened between us was our perfect little secret. The thing is, as soon as I sobered up, I knew that wasn't for me—that it wasn't what I wanted. But Sully looked so happy—so over the moon— that I just couldn't bring myself to tell her."

"And then?" Brandon prompted.

"That evening we had a bonfire on the beach. We roasted hot dogs and marshmallows and drank lots more booze. At least I had more booze. I don't know about Sully. She was still out by the fire when I went to bed." She paused. "That's not true," she corrected. "The part about going to bed. First I was sick. Then I passed out."

"But Sully was still outside."

June nodded.

"By herself?"

"As far as I know. The last time I remember seeing her, she was sitting there in her bathing suit, looking at the moon on the water. The next thing I knew, it was morning. Someone was outside the room screaming and screaming. That's when I found out Sully was dead, that she'd been stabbed to death."

"The San Diego cops investigated?"

"Yes," June said. "We all had to go into the police station for questioning. It seemed like we were there for days on end, but none of us knew anything. One moment she was alive and on the beach with everybody else. The next moment she was dead. Finally the cops turned us loose, and we drove back to Tempe."

"What happened then?"

"First there was the funeral. Her parents were heart-broken. After that I really don't remember much. The rest of that semester was like living in a nightmare."

"Did you tell Sully's parents about what had happened between you and their daughter?"

June shook her head. "No," she answered. "Why would I? Finding out something like that about their dead daughter would have made things that much worse for them. Besides, I kept thinking that eventually we'd find out who had done it—that there would be some closure—but months went by and then years, and nothing happened. We all talked about it among ourselves. We figured her killer must have been someone—some stranger—who had found her alone on the beach. That's what I always believed, anyway."

Brandon heard that last throwaway sentence and immediately understood the implication.

"Now you know better?" he asked.

June nodded. First she smoothed her skirt, then she straightened her shoulders. "Yes, I do," she murmured, but her voice was barely audible.

By then Brandon's eyes had adjusted to the dim light. Every flat surface in the room and most of the wall spaces as well were covered with a collection of photos. He could tell from June's voice that they were venturing into dangerous waters, and he wanted to make it easier for her.

"Your kids?" he asked, nodding toward the nearest set of photos and breaking the tension.

June nodded. "Seven kids, fourteen grandkids, and two greats," she replied. "Fred died two months short of our fiftieth." She paused for a moment before continuing. "He died two months ago—about the time I sent that note to Mr. Farrell."

"And that was because . . ." Brandon prompted.

"Because Fred did it," June Holmes declared. Her lips trembled as she said the damning words. "He's the one who killed Sully."

"And how do you know this?" Brandon asked.

"Because he told me so himself—five years ago, when

he was first diagnosed with lung cancer. He wanted me to be grateful and to understand what he had done for me."

"For you?" Brandon asked.

June nodded. "I told you my parents were strict Mormons. So was Fred. The LDS Church doesn't countenance homosexuality now and it certainly didn't back then, either. The very fact that I'd had that one encounter with Sully—one other people knew about—made me damaged goods. When I came home from San Diego, I expected Fred to drop me like a hot potato if he heard any gossip about what had happened. So I told him myself. I thought he'd break our engagement, but he didn't. He said he could hate the sin and still love the sinner."

The imprisoned cat finally gave up and shut up. June seemed to be waiting for Brandon to say something more. When he said nothing, she continued. "Fred wasn't ever what you could call a forgiving kind of guy. I should have wondered about that, but I didn't. I was so incredibly grateful that he didn't turn his back on me and walk away. No one would have blamed him if he had."

"In other words, he got big points for standing by you?"

She nodded. "To say nothing of a proper marriage in the Temple—a marriage for time and all eternity, as they say. Then, five years ago, he got his cancer diagnosis and dropped his bomb."

"About Sully?"

June nodded again. "He told me one of his friends was in San Diego that spring break, too. He heard about what had happened, and he was the one who called Fred. Fred's father had just died. His mother was getting ready to sell their house and needed to have it painted. That's what Fred was doing over spring break—painting the house inside and out. Someone—this unnamed friend—called Fred that afternoon and told him what had happened. He drove over that night. After he did it, he walked into the ocean and rinsed off the blood. He left Phoenix after his mother went to bed and was back home before she woke up in the morning. As far as she was concerned, he never left. When he got back to his mother's house, he burned all the clothing he was wearing that night—even his shoes."

"Was he ever considered to be a suspect?" Brandon asked.

"Not as far as I know," June answered. "There may have been a few questions asked about him in the beginning, but his mother's word carried the day, especially since no one remembered seeing him in San Diego, no one who knew him, that is. He came and went without anyone being the wiser. Back in those days there were no credit cards. He paid cash for his gas and food."

"If he got away with it for that long, why did he bother telling you?" Brandon asked.

June shrugged. "I guess his conscience was bothering him," she said. "He thought he was dying. The doctors only gave him six months or so. That was before they let him into that first chemo protocol. He said he hoped that I could do the same thing for him that he had done for me."

"As in hate the sin and love the sinner?"

"I tried," June said. "But I couldn't do it. I had been in touch with Sully's parents from time to time. I went to both her father's funeral and, much later, her mother's. I knew how much it had hurt them to lose their precious daughter, and it hurt me to think it was my fault."

"You weren't the one wielding the knife," Brandon said. "It wasn't your fault."

"But if Sully and I hadn't had that encounter—if Fred hadn't found out about it . . ." June's voice dwindled to nothing.

"What happened after he told you?" Brandon asked.

"It was just a few months after Fred told me that I heard from Mr. Farrell again. I was surprised that he was still working on the case after all those years, but Sully's mother had won a bunch of money in one of the big lotteries, and she was using it to start a cold-case organization of some kind."

"Yes," Brandon said. "It's called TLC—The Last Chance."

"Mr. Farrell said he was going back through the case and interviewing everyone who had been connected to Sully. He wanted to talk to me, but I couldn't. I couldn't face telling him the truth and have my children's father go to prison. I was afraid they'd want me to testify against Fred, and I couldn't do that. Besides, to be honest, I guess I didn't want my children to know about what I had done, either. I've spent a lifetime trying to live down that one indiscretion, but it's always there with me. It never goes away. I also didn't want to lie to Mr. Farrell."

"Did your husband offer you any proof of what he'd done?"

"He didn't offer it to me, but I think I found it." June reached into her purse and pulled out a Ziploc bag, which she handed over to him. Inside it was an old hunting knife. Through the clear plastic, Brandon could see that the blade was dull and rusty, as though it had been left untouched for a very long time.

"One of my sons found this hidden in the back of one of Fred's toolboxes out in the garage. In all the years we were married, I never saw this one before. I know from watching TV that sometimes it's possible for investigators to get usable DNA evidence from items like this."

"You're giving it to me?" Brandon asked.

"Yes," she said. "I want you to take it and do whatever you need to do to find out for sure."

"All right," Brandon said, dropping the bag into his jacket pocket.

"So that's it," June said, using the arms of the chair to rise to her feet. "I'm ready to go whenever you are. I just have to drop the cat off on the way."

"On the way where?" Brandon asked.

"To jail," June answered. "Isn't that what this is all about? Aren't you here to arrest me? Doesn't all this make me some kind of accessory after the fact?"

Suddenly the suitcase and the crated Miss Kitty made sense. June Holmes had invited Brandon into her home with the expectation that he was there to take her into custody.

"No," Brandon said. "I came to find some answers, and you've provided those, but I'm not here to arrest you."

June seemed astonished. "Are you sure? I thought that since I knew about it and didn't tell . . ."

"No," Brandon said. "Knowing about it isn't the same as doing it."

Momentary relief flashed across June Holmes's face, then the doorbell rang.

"Now who can that be?" she asked. "I certainly wasn't expecting anyone. I'm usually at church at this time of day."

**Tucson, Arizona
Sunday, June 7, 2009, 9:40 A.M.
84° Fahrenheit**

Brian Fellows had gone back to his office, where he spent the better part of the early-morning hours on the telephone. Detective Mumford had gone to a hotel to interview Corrine Lapin, Jonathan Southard's dead wife's sister. Brian and Alex had agreed that he could participate in the interview by long distance. Brian knew that eventually some departmental bean counter would give him hell about racking up so many long-distance charges, but he would handle that when the time came. Right now, he and Alex Mumford were both on the trail of the same killer.

Corrine was able to provide a lot of information about what had been going on in Jonathan and Esther Southard's family in the previous several years—or at least what her murdered sister had told her about what was going on. Jonathan Southard had been let go by his bank and had been unable to find another job. He had been depressed and angry.

Corrine said she suspected there had been some instances of physical abuse, but she didn't know that for sure. She allowed as how she "thought" Esther might have been seeing someone, but she was coy about it. She either didn't know who the boyfriend was or wouldn't say. Brian was pretty sure the boyfriend's identity would become obvious once they gained access to Esther's telephone records.

"So Esther was planning on leaving Jonathan, but she was holding out for the arrival of Jonathan's 401(k) payout?" Alex asked.

"That's pretty much the size of it," Corrine admitted. "But Esther is the victim here. The way you're asking the questions, it sounds as though you're going to drag her name through the mud right along with her husband's."

"We're just trying to get the lay of the land," Alex assured her.

"About that 401(k). Do you have any idea about when those monies were due to arrive?"

Brian was the one who asked that question, and that was the real advantage of participating in a real-time interview. He was able to ask his own questions.

"The last time I spoke to Esther, she told me she expected the check to arrive anytime. As in the next few days."

And it probably did, Brian thought. *Rather than share it with his soon-to-be-ex-wife, Southard converted it into cash. That's what he's using for running money.*

"How much money was it?" Detective Mumford asked. The question let Brian know that she was following the same set of assumptions.

"Esther thought it was going to be close to half a million dollars. She expected them to split it fifty-fifty."

"The prospect of a quarter-of-a-million-dollar payoff makes it worthwhile for her to wait around," Alex Mumford said.

That comment had Brian Fellows's full agreement. *It's also enough to kill for,* he thought, but he didn't say that aloud.

Brian's cell phone rang. With the landline receiver still at his ear, he pulled his cell out of his pocket. He thought the caller might be Kath, letting him know that she and the girls were on their way to church. Not recognizing the caller ID number, Brian put the interview line on hold and answered.

"Detective Fellows? It's Dan Pardee."

"What can I do for you?"

"I was talking to Angie a couple of minutes ago. She told me the bad guy's arm was hurt. It may even be broken. I believe he was wearing a sling of some kind."

"So Major did get him," Brian murmured.

"Major?" Dan asked. "Who's Major?"

Detective Fellows paused for a moment before he answered. Dan Pardee was not an official part of the investigation into the Komelik shooting, but for some reason Brian Fellows didn't understand, the man seemed to have skin in this game. The Border Patrol agent was involved enough and cared enough that he was still at the hospital and still looking out for Angelina Enos long after most other officers would have gone home. And if Jonathan Southard was as screwed up as he appeared to be, Fellows reasoned that Angie might very well need to have someone looking out for her, preferably someone armed with a handgun and trained in the use of it.

"Major was Jonathan Southard's wife's dog," Brian said.

"Was?" Dan asked. "And who's Jonathan Southard?"

"Abby Tennant's son," Brian replied. "Her estranged son. Major was the son's wife's dog. We believe the dog died attempting to protect his owner, Esther Southard, Jonathan's wife. Major is dead and so is Esther, and so are their two kids. All three of them were shot to death. The bodies were found in Thousand Oaks, California, late last night or early this morning. I'm not sure which."

There was a period of stark silence before Dan Pardee spoke again. "He wiped out his whole family. When?" he asked. "How long ago did they die?"

"Long enough ago for Southard to get here from Southern California," Brian said. "Long enough for him to track down Jack and Abby Tennant and blow them away. His father and stepmother live in Ohio. We're concerned that he may try to target them next. That's my next call—to let them know what's happened but also to notify them that they, too, might be in danger."

"What about Angie?" Dan objected. "If what's-his-name, Southard, finds out he left a witness behind, what happens then? Who's to say he won't come back looking for her as well?"

"It's not a matter of *if* he finds out," Brian Fellows said. "Somebody already let that cat out of the bag. Mention of a surviving witness, an unidentified child, was on a TV news report earlier this morning. With a little motivated effort, the bad guy could probably find out who she is and where she is."

"Great," Dan muttered sarcastically. "That's just terrific."

"How long do you expect to hang around?" Brian asked.

"I told Angie I'd stay on until one of her family members shows up to take her home. I figured someone would have come for her by now."

"If and when someone does come by to pick her up, give me a call back on this same number," Brian said. "That way I can clue Law and Order in so they can keep an eye out, too."

"All right," Dan said. "Will do."

The interview line was still lit—still on hold—but now the desk phone was ringing again on the second line.

"Oops," Brian said. "Gotta go. There's another call."

This time when Brian picked up, the departmental operator was on the line. "A call from the big guy," she said.

Around the Pima County Sheriff's Department, "the big guy" was none other than Sheriff William Forsythe. It was not a term of endearment.

"You should have called me!" Forsythe said accusingly, once Brian came on the line. "The people who run Tohono Chul are constituents of mine—important constituents. Once you made that connection, you should have called."

Brian had pulled an all-nighter. The idea of being bitched out by the sheriff himself didn't go down very well right about then.

"It was five-thirty or six before we made the Tohono Chul connection," Brian said civilly. "So far we've got what looks like at least seven victims—three in California and four here."

"I don't give a rat's ass about the out-of-town victims," Sheriff Forsythe bellowed. "Those are none of my concern, and none of yours, either. Law and Order can run the reservation part of the investigation. I want some hands-on treatment for these local folks. That part of the investigation should be handled by one of our A-teams, not somebody working solo. I believe the Aces are next up. I've already called them, and they're on the way. Once they show up at the department, turn over whatever you've got to them, and go home."

Brian Fellows seethed with indignation. As long as Forsythe figured the victims were Indians or illegal aliens, he had no problem tapping Brian for the job. Once it was expedient to do so, the sheriff didn't hesitate for a moment about calling in the big dogs. Everyone in the department understood that the Aces, Detectives Abernathy and Adams, were Forsythe's go-to guys when it came to cases with the potential for any kind of political fallout.

"Right," Brian said through gritted teeth. "Will do."

When Sheriff Forsythe ended the call, Brian returned to the other phone. The interview with Corrine Lapin had ended, but Alex Mumford was still on the line, waiting for him. He might have mentioned to her that he'd just been sent to the locker room, but he didn't.

"How long do you think Southard had been planning this?" Brian asked.

"There's no way to tell. From what Corrine told us, I believe Esther intended to leave as soon as she had her share of the money."

"Did Jonathan know she was about to exit stage left?"

"Hard to tell," Alex said. "Some guys are so full of themselves that they can't imagine anyone would ever up and leave them. In other words, maybe he knew and maybe he didn't. Corrine indicated that regardless of whether charges were filed, there was some history of physical abuse."

Brian knew where she was going. In relationships where domestic violence is part of the equation, the moment one spouse tries to leave, things can get ugly.

"Wait a minute," Alex said. "The banking records I requested are just now coming in. Hang on."

Brian waited impatiently, drumming his fingers on the desk.

"Okay," Alex said after a long pause. "Okay. It looks like the 401(k) money landed in their joint account on Wednesday of last week, but it isn't there now. It was withdrawn on Friday, as soon as the check cleared."

"The whole amount?" Brian asked.

"Every bit of it," Alex answered. "I've also spoken to a neighbor who reported hearing two people, a man and a woman, involved in a screaming battle on Sunday night. She also said that by Monday morning things seemed to have settled down. Quiet, anyway."

"So Esther discovered that Jonathan had hidden the money from her, and the two of them went to war over it."

"Right," Alex agreed. "The only reason it was quiet on Monday is that Esther and the kids were already dead."

"The question is, was this his plan all along?" Brian asked. "Had he already gone to the trouble of setting himself up with another identity and made arrangements for fake IDs?"

Detective Mumford thought about that. "Those can always be had for a price, but you have to have some connection in that world. I have warrants for his phone and Internet records, and I'll know more once we have access. Banking records just showed up, but so far nothing else."

Brian was impressed. The investigation into the Thousand Oaks homicides was only a few hours old. Already Alex Mumford had managed to come up with court orders to cover banking and phone records. Considering it was 10:00 A.M. on a Sunday morning, that was pretty impressive.

"He obviously drove from California to Tucson in his minivan. If we put out an APB with information on his vehicle, we might find him. Then again, we may not. So far he must be paying cash for his gasoline purchases. There's no sign of any credit card activity. Since he evidently has plenty of cash, he may try to ditch his Dodge Caravan for something else in hopes of slipping by us. If he's trying to travel by air, my guess is that he'll still be using his own ID, or at least trying to."

"Have you released any information about finding the bodies on your end?" Brian asked.

"Not yet. We're still waiting on additional next-of-kin notifications."

"That won't last forever, but it's good for us. For right now Southard may not realize we've made the connection. If it hadn't been for that neighborhood block watch lady, we wouldn't have."

"Hang on," Alex said. "Here comes the phone record info."

Again, Brian was left twiddling his thumbs while Alex scanned the information that had been dumped into her computer.

"Okay," she said finally. "It looks like he stopped using his cell phone Monday night, so there's no chance of using that to pinpoint his location. He's probably got himself a new one by now."

"There were no phones at all found at the crime scene on the reservation," Brian told her.

"So he may be using a victim's cell phone? Can you get a court order for any of those?" Mumford asked.

Not likely, Brian thought, *especially since I've been thrown off the case.* "Sounds like you might have better luck with that than I would."

"All right," she said. "If you can get those numbers, send them over to me. Since we're handling this as a joint operation, I might be able to get court orders for those, too."

The Aces would not be pleased to hear that bit of news, and Brian guessed that Detectives Abernathy and Adams would have a hard time keeping up with Alex Mumford.

"Great," Brian said, smiling to himself. "I'll send you those numbers as soon as I have them."

"Can you dispatch deputies to the airport?" Alex asked. The Aces weren't there yet, so why the hell not?

"Will do," Brian replied. "The one here has only two concourses, so covering those shouldn't be too tough. I'll pull up his driver's license photo and hand out copies of that."

"Good," Alex said. "What about car rental agencies?"

"I'll check with those and also with the local FBOs. If that 401(k) cash is burning a hole in his pocket, he just might pop for a charter to get where he wants to go in a hurry. If he goes to Phoenix to fly out, however, Sky Harbor is a lot tougher to cover as far as concourses are concerned, and there are lots more FBOs there as well. It's also a hundred miles from here and out of my jurisdiction."

"Do you want me to contact someone there?"

"You can try. One other question," Brian added. "Did you find any brass at your scene?"

"Lots," she said. "All nine-millimeter. What about on your end?"

"Nobody found any last night, but some could have turned up now that it's daylight. The last I heard, CSI was still working the scene. Where'd Southard get a nine-millimeter?"

"He bought it," she said. "From a local gun shop here in Thousand Oaks. Even got himself a CWP. For defensive purposes only."

"Right," Brian said. "For protection only. I'm sure that's what the asshole told his dead wife and kids."

12

Sells, Tohono O'odham Nation, Arizona
Sunday, June 7, 2009, 10:30 A.M.
86° Fahrenheit

DAN HAD BEEN standing outside the hospital's front entrance to make his phone call to Detective Fellows. On the way back inside, he stopped off long enough to speak to the charge nurse. "Any word on when Angie Enos's relatives are going to show up?" he asked.

"Not so far," she said.

Dan started to go back to the room, then changed his mind and went back outside, dialing his cell phone as he went.

He'd managed a couple of hours of sleep in that dreadful chair, but he wasn't rested enough to stay awake through another ten-hour shift. It was already after ten in the morning. That didn't leave him sufficient time to drive home, grab some z's, and be back up and at 'em in time for his shift. Besides, what if Angie's relatives never appeared? What would happen to her then?

Dan Pardee already knew the answer to that question. Some unfailingly earnest CPS caseworker would ride up on her broom and whisk Angie off to foster care. Dan Pardee understood all too well about what was wrong with that scenario.

Marco Benevedez, the sergeant on duty, answered his call.

"Hey," Dan said, casting around for a plausible excuse, "I stopped by the feast house at Vamori last night. I think I picked up a trace of food poisoning."

"No shit!" Marco said, laughing aloud at his own joke.

"Just the opposite," Dan said. He hoped he sounded suitably unamused.

"Are you telling me you won't be in?" Marco asked.

"Not today." *And not Monday, Tuesday, or Wednesday, either,* Dan thought, since those were his regular days off.

"We need a full report on your involvement with that Komelik shooting."

"No problem," Dan said. "All I did was come across the victims after they'd been shot, but I'll be glad to type something up and send it."

One of the side benefits of working for a far-flung unit was that reports could be e-mailed in rather than delivered in person.

"Drugs, do you think?"

Dan knew that Marco's question was off the record.

Stopping the flow of drugs and people across the border was one of the Shadow Wolves' main areas of responsibility. Naturally Marco wanted to know if this shooting had anything to do with their mission. As far as Dan was concerned, the deaths of the people outside Komelik had nothing to do with smuggling. If what Brian Fellows had said was true, it was some nutcase from California going around killing people—starting with the people he should have loved above all others. That wasn't a Border Patrol problem. It was a humanity problem.

"I doubt it," Dan said. "Time will tell. Gotta go," he added.

"Right," Marco said, thinking Dan meant something else entirely. "So by all means, go!"

"Did you bring me another coloring book?" Angie asked when he came back into her room. "I've used up all the stickers for this one."

And you already have me pegged for a sucker, he thought. "Not right now," he said.

"When is lunch?" she asked. "I'm hungry."

"Soon," he said, and hoped like hell it was true.

Sonoita, Arizona
Sunday, June 7, 2009, 10:00 A.M.
73° Fahrenheit

When Brandon went inside to interview June Holmes, he left the convertible parked in the generous shade of a towering cottonwood. As Diana and Damsel settled in to wait, Diana wasn't surprised when Garrison Ladd was the next one of her unending collection of bad boys to show up. Why wouldn't he?

Even though she'd been expecting him, it was disturbing that he appeared right beside her in the driver's seat, sitting there with both hands on the wheel. At least Max Cooper had stayed in the backseat where he belonged. The good news about that was that the remains of the exit wound in his head were mostly invisible to her.

"No matter what you think, sometimes suicide is the best solution for all concerned," he said, taking up Max's line of attack.

"You of all people should know about that," Diana said derisively. "After all, that was your solution of choice. By my count you've been dead for more than thirty years."

"But don't bother selling the car," he went on as though he hadn't heard a word she said. "If you're gonna do it, you're gonna do it. It's as simple as that. Brandon has a gun. You know where he keeps it. Even someone as dim as you are should be able to figure out how to use it."

This was nothing new. Garrison Ladd had always maintained that Diana was pretty much too stupid to live.

"Don't even mention Brandon Walker's name," Diana snapped at him. "You're not in his league. Besides, I'd never use a gun for something like that. I wouldn't leave that kind of mess behind for someone else to clean up."

"You mean like Brandon or Davy or maybe even Lani?"

"Get out of the car," she ordered. "You're not here.

You're dead. I don't have to listen to you. I won't listen to you."

When he made no move to leave, Diana did. She got out, collected Damsel's leash, and walked up to the front door of the ranch house, where she rang the bell.

"I'm Brandon Walker's wife," she said to the silver-haired lady who answered the door. "Sorry to barge in like this, but it's too hot to sit in the car. Do you mind if we wait inside?"

"Of course not," June Holmes said, smiling hospitably. "Do come in. Let me get you something cool to drink and something for your puppy, too. What's the dog's name?"

"Damsel," Diana answered. "For Damsel in Distress."

Sells, Tohono O'odham Nation, Arizona
Sunday, June 7, 2009, 11:00 A.M.
87° Fahrenheit

When Lani jolted awake at eleven, Fat Crack's crystals were still in her hand and her mind was made up. The answer to Delia's question was yes—yes, she would take Angie. How could she not? Before she could turn that decision into action, however, there was something else she needed to do.

Once showered and dressed, Lani returned to the medicine basket she had woven for herself so long ago. As her fingers and awl had worked with the bear grass and yucca, she had sensed that she was communing with the spirits of those who had come before her, the people who had schooled her in the traditions and teachings of the Tohono O'odham—Understanding Woman, Looks at Nothing, Betraying Woman, and Nana *Dahd,* and, of course, Fat Crack himself. As the basket took shape strand by strand, it had seemed to Lani that bits of each of those wise old people were being woven into the pattern.

Once it was finished, it was only fitting that the basket should be stocked with all the treasured relics that had come to her from those folks as well.

Rita Antone's grandmother, Oks Amachuda, Understanding Woman, had been dead for decades before Lani was born, but two of the precious items came from her—a shard of red pottery with the form of a turtle etched into it and a hunk of geode covered with purple-shaded crystals. Understanding Woman had sent them with Rita, in a medicine basket very much like this one, when, as a young girl, Rita had been shipped off to boarding school at Phoenix Indian. That original basket still belonged to Lani's brother, Davy.

Nana *Dahd*'s *owij,* the awl she had used to make countless baskets, was there, as was the Purple Heart that was Rita Antone's sole remembrance of her only son, who had died during the Korean War. The other important men in Rita Antone's life were represented as well. Lani ran her fingers through the worn beads of Father John's *lasolo,* his rosary. Smiling, she examined Looks at Nothing's old Zippo cigarette lighter. The brass was smooth and fading to black in spots. It hadn't lit anything in years, but the lighter's connection to the past and to the old blind medicine man who had used it was almost palpable.

Now, returning the crystals to the basket, she pocketed the tobacco pouch. Each year she made a special trip out into the desert to replenish her supply of *wiw*, the Indian tobacco used in the traditional ceremony called the peace smoke. Today, in her meeting with Delia Ortiz, that pouch of tobacco was all Lani needed.

It was almost noon and scorching hot when Lani drove up to the Ortiz family compound behind the gas station. In the dusty open space inside the cluster of several mobile homes, two children—Gabe and Baby Rita—played a desultory game of kickball. The kids were evidently impervious to the heat while the adults of the several families hunkered down inside their air-conditioned houses and napped off the effects of being up all night at the Vamori dance.

"Hey, Lani," Gabe said. "Want to play kickball?"

"Not right now," she told him. "I need to talk to your mom."

"She's asleep. Want me to wake her up?"

"Please," Lani said. "Tell her it's about Angie and that I'll meet her at her office."

Lani was grateful when Gabe headed inside to awaken his mother without asking any of his usual questions.

Lani drove to the Tohono O'odham Nation's office complex and parked next to the spot reserved for the tribal chairman. Before Lani formally agreed to Delia's suggestion about Angie, she needed to be sure that she and the tribal chairman were on the same page.

Sitting for several moments in her parked car, Lani reflected on her long-term rivalry with Delia Ortiz. Fat

Crack had chosen both of them. Delia had been designated to be his political successor, and he had expected Lani to carry forward the traditional teachings that had been given to him by Looks at Nothing.

Both women had done all they could to live up to Fat Crack's expectations, with one major exception. He had thought they would become friends rather than enemies. Now, though, working together with the common purpose of salvaging Angie Enos, Lani glimpsed far enough into the future to see that perhaps Fat Crack had been right all along and that she and Delia would become friends.

Exiting the Passat's broiling interior, Lani walked over to the shaded picnic table where regular smokers of ordinary cigarettes could light up. Opening the pouch, Lani pulled out the paper and Indian tobacco and began rolling a smoke.

Sells, Tohono O'odham Nation, Arizona
Sunday, June 7, 2009, 11:30 A.M.
88° Fahrenheit

When Fat Crack first brought Delia Chavez Cachora back home to Sells to serve as tribal attorney, she had been away from the reservation for far more years than she had lived there. Her East Coast schooling and the years of living in D.C. made her seem far more Anglo than Indian. What made things happen in D.C. was thought to be pushy and abrupt on the reservation.

When Delia first returned to Sells, she would have walked up to Lani at the picnic table and immediately demanded to know what she wanted. But time had passed. Delia's Aunt Julia, along with Fat Crack and Leo Ortiz, had counseled her on ways of fitting in. She had learned, for example, that it was better to stop and wait to be acknowledged before speaking. The old Delia would have pressed for information as to why Lani had sent Gabe to awaken her. The new Delia stood silently waiting for an invitation to be seated and allowing Lani to speak at a pace of her choosing. An expertly rolled cigarette lay on the table along with a worn leather pouch Delia remembered had once belonged to Fat Crack.

Finally Lani motioned Delia to a spot at the table. "Do you know about Little Lion and Little Bear?" she asked.

"I guess," Delia said with a shrug. "I believe Gabe told me that story once. Aren't those the two boys who were raised by their grandmother, the ones who had beautifully colored birds?"

"Parrots," Lani said, nodding.

"People were jealous of the boys because they wanted the colored feathers. They killed the grandmother, but the boys managed to escape. Before they, too, were killed, they threw the birds off the mountains to the east, thus creating Sunrise and Sunset. Right?"

Lani smiled. "Yes," she said. "Do you know what happened then?"

Delia was dying to ask for Lani's decision about taking Angie, and the old Delia would have done so at once, but now she knew better. Posing that question directly would be rude. Instead she went back to what she remembered of the story.

"I thought the legend ended once the boys were dead."

"No," Lani said. "There's more. The spirit of the grandmother called for the dead boys to come home. She told them where to bury her body. Four days after they did that, a plant grew up there—wild tobacco, *wiw*. Little Bear and Little Lion harvested it the way Wise Old Grandmother told them.

"The people who had killed the two boys were worried when the boys came back. They called a council. They didn't invite Little Bear and Little Lion to join them, but the two dead boys came anyway, bringing the tobacco with them. When the people sat in the circle, the two boys sat there, too. Coyote was there and told them they should light the tobacco and pass it to the person next to them, saying '*Nawoj*,' which means 'friend' or 'friendly gift.' And that's the origin of the Tohono O'odham's peace smoke."

"As opposed to the peace pipe in all those cowboy movies."

Nodding, Lani held up Looks at Nothing's venerable old leather pouch in one hand and the hand-rolled cigarette in the other. "That's what I have here."

"Wild tobacco?" Delia asked warily. Her first husband had returned from his round of powwow travels with a penchant for smoking peyote, and the results of that had been nothing short of disastrous. "That's all it is— tobacco?"

Lani nodded. "Botanists will tell you it's really called

Nicotiana trigonophylla, and that's all it is, Indian tobacco. It was harvested and dried the same way Little Lion and Little Bear's grandmother told them to; the same way Fat Crack taught me; the same way Looks at Nothing taught him."

"But what's it doing here?" Delia asked.

"I'm proposing that you and I should have a council and smoke the peace smoke," Lani said.

Delia was mystified. "But why?"

Lani smiled to think how much Delia sounded like her son just then.

"On the day my brother Davy was baptized," Lani answered, "Looks at Nothing, Fat Crack, an old Catholic priest named Father John, and my father all smoked it together. Until that happened, Davy was a boy with two mothers and no fathers. From that moment on, he was a boy with two mothers and four fathers. The four men hadn't been friends before that, especially Looks at Nothing and Father John, but from then on they were. I'd like for us to do the same thing—smoke the peace smoke and become friends."

"Because of Angie?" Delia asked.

"Not just because of Angie," Lani said. "Fat Crack told my father once that someday he hoped the two of us would be friends. I'm beginning to think maybe he was right."

With that she lit the cigarette, using a match rather than the lighter. She took a long drag, and then passed the cigarette to Delia. *"Nawoj,"* she said.

For a time the two women sat in silence with the

desert heat shimmering around them and with the sweet-smelling smoke enveloping them as well.

"When I first came back here I was jealous of you," Delia admitted at last. "I didn't understand why Fat Crack spent so much time with you. I thought he should be teaching what he knew to Leo or Richard, to one of his own sons, instead of to someone else, especially to someone who was being raised by Anglos. Now, though, I understand why. Leo and Richard weren't interested in all those things— not the way you are. Not the way Gabe is."

Delia passed the cigarette back to Lani.

"And then, even though he was a Christian Scientist, Fat Crack insisted that we should invest tribal money in turning you into a doctor. I lobbied against that as well. I thought your Anglo parents should foot the bill for your education. Now, though, I understand that, too, because I see what you're doing. Yes, you're a medical doctor, but you understand the traditional ways and take those things into consideration."

There was another period of silence, punctuated by puffs of smoke. "Did you know my mother is gay?" Delia asked.

Lani shook her head. "No."

"My parents broke up when I was little," Delia said. "For a long time I assumed it was because my father was a drunk. It turns out that was one reason for the split, but it wasn't the only one. My mother was attracted to women. Ruth Waldron, the woman who eventually became my mother's partner—who still is my mother's partner—came from money, old East Coast money. Ruth saw to it that I had every educational advantage her money could buy."

"So you were a girl with two mothers, too," Lani murmured. "Just like I was with Diana Ladd and Nana *Dahd*."

Delia smiled and nodded. "With Fat Crack's encouragement, the tribe saw to it that you got your education. An Anglo paid for most of mine. I'm hoping that between the two of us we can do the same kind of thing for Angelina Enos—give her the same kind of advantages that were given to us. So have you made a decision?" Delia asked. "Are you willing to take her?"

"Yes," Lani said. "I am, and I'm willing to take her today. I think it's criminal that the Escalantes would turn her away just as they turned me away."

"Good," Delia said. "I'm glad to hear you say that."

"But how will all this work?" Lani asked. "I can't just walk into the hospital and insist that they hand her over."

"Yes, you can," Delia said. "Right after I spoke to you I called Judge Lawrence. He's drawing up a court order declaring you to be Angie's temporary guardian. All you have to do is go by his place and sign it."

Lani was taken aback to think that Delia had known in advance what her decision would be. "What about later?" she asked. "What if some other relative of Angie's comes forward and offers to take her?"

"They won't," Delia declared. "They didn't come for you, and they won't come for Angie."

Delia Ortiz took one last drag on the smoldering remnant of the cigarette. *"Nawoj,"* she said again as she passed it back.

Much to her surprise, Delia Ortiz realized that some-how the *wiw* had done its magic work. Through the haze of sweet-smelling smoke it seemed entirely possible that she and Lanita Dolores Walker could be friends after all, exactly as her father-in-law, Fat Crack, had intended.

Tucson, Arizona
Sunday, June 7, 2009, 12:00 P.M.
89° Fahrenheit

By the time the Aces showed up in person, Brian had typed up what he had, including the contact informa-tion for Detective Mumford in Thousand Oaks and a cell phone number for Dan Pardee. He would have been glad to hand off the paper and get the hell out, but things didn't work out that way.

"This is all you've got?" Jake Abernathy asked deroga-torily after scanning through the pages.

Detective Abernathy knew he was Sheriff Forsythe's "chosen one." He came complete with the requisite ego and attitude. He understood Brian had to be pissed about being taken off the case, and he couldn't help rubbing Brian's nose in it. At least he couldn't help trying to, but Brian refused to take the bait.

"Yup," he said. "That's all we have so far. You'll probably want to follow up with Detective Mumford over in Thou-sand Oaks. She's working on tracking phone records."

Making the suggestion was a deliberate ploy. Brian was reasonably sure that based on that, he could expect that the Aces wouldn't give Alex Mumford the time of day.

"I think Rick and I can track down phone records on our own," Jake told him. "Now what about this witness— the little girl who supposedly saw the killer. If we go out to the res to interview her, will we need to bring along a translator?"

Brian didn't call the Tohono O'odham Nation "the res" ever.

"No," he said. "Her name is Angelina Enos and she speaks English." *A lot better than you speak Tohono O'odham,* he thought.

"Where is she?"

"The last I heard she was in the hospital at Sells. But you have Dan Pardee's number. He can probably tell you where she ended up going."

Abernathy frowned. "According to this, he's the Border Patrol guy who found her along with the bodies. Why would this jerk know where she is? Is he a relative of some kind?"

No relation, Brian thought, *and no jerk, either.*

"I had my hands full, and he was willing to look after the kid," Brian said aloud.

"Okay, okay. We'll track him down and see what he has to say," Jake said. Then he turned to his partner. "We should probably check with Border Patrol and take a look at his statement, too."

He turned back to Brian. "You're pretty sure that Jonathan Southard is the guy?"

Brian nodded.

"Any leads on where he went?"

"Since he came here to take out his mother, there's some concern that his next stop might be Ohio. That's where his father lives. I spoke to Hank Southard a little while ago. He says there's some mistake. His son wouldn't hurt a fly."

"Right," Abernathy said. "That's what relatives always say."

Brian had made a stack of copies of Jonathan Southard's driver's license photo. Jake Abernathy noticed them for the first time. "What are those?" he asked.

"Copies of Southard's photo," Brian said. "I was going to have a deputy take them out to the airport. That way, if he tries to get on a plane, people there will know to keep an eye out for him."

"Good thinking," Abernathy said. "Why don't you do that?"

Why not indeed! Brian thought. He could have refused. He could have told Jake that he should send a deputy instead, but Brian didn't believe in confrontation for confrontation's sake. As far as Brian was concerned, a phone call to Homeland Security was probably also in order, just in case Southard was trying to head out of the country, but that was no longer his call to make.

"Sure thing," he said, tapping the stack of photos. "Glad to be of service. I'll drop these off on my way home."

Sonoita, Arizona
Sunday, June 7, 2009, 12:00 P.M.
79° Fahrenheit

It was close to noon when Diana and Brandon left June Holmes's house. With the summertime sun blazing down on them, Brandon overrode his wife's veto. He closed the convertible top and turned the AC to high for the ride back to Tucson.

"Did you get what you needed?" Diana asked.

Brandon sighed. "I'm not sure," he said. "I know what she told me, but I don't know how much of it to believe. What about you? When you came inside, you looked upset. Are you all right?"

Diana considered his question for some time before she answered it. "No," she said at last. "I don't think I'm all right at all."

Brandon looked at her nervously. "Why?" he asked. "What's wrong? Are you sick? Do you need to go to the doctor?"

"Because I'm seeing things," she replied. "I'm seeing people who aren't there—dead people. I talk to them. They talk to me. They tell me things."

"What people?"

"Garrison Ladd," she answered after another long pause. "Andrew Carlisle. My father. All those people from my past that I don't want to see keep showing up uninvited."

"How long has this been going on?" Brandon asked.

She noticed that he didn't try to talk her out of it. He

didn't tell her she was wrong or that she was making things up. Obviously he believed her.

"Several months," she said. "It started while I was trying to finish the book. It was like they ganged up on me. Is that what happens with Alzheimer's patients?" she asked. "Is that what happened to your father? Or is this some other kind of dementia? I suppose I should have gone to a doctor, but . . ."

Her voice trailed away. Even though that was what Brandon had been thinking—what he'd been worried about all along—it took his breath away to have the word spoken aloud like that between them, and he understood all too well why she hadn't wanted to discuss it with anyone, most especially not with her husband.

"I don't know," Brandon said. "I don't think anybody knows everything about those kinds of issues. They're complicated and not easily sorted out."

Diana nodded. "I know how much dealing with your father bothered you, and I don't want to put you through that kind of thing again. I had been thinking about going out in a blaze of glory—of taking this out for a drive and running it off a cliff somewhere. That's what my invisible friends all think I should do, but not you. Right?"

"You're right," he answered at once. "Not me." He thought about what she had said then asked, "Is that why you want to sell this?" He patted the Invicta's steering wheel.

Diana nodded again. "That's why. I knew you wouldn't want me to do it. I thought getting rid of the car would get rid of the temptation."

Brandon Walker took a deep breath. Diana's mental lapses were exactly what he had feared for days, weeks, and months, but now that they were talking about all this—now that it was out in the open—it didn't seem so bad. His father and mother had learned to cope. He and Diana would, too.

He reached across the seat and put his hand on Diana's shoulder. "If that turns out to be what this is, it's pretty damned grim," he said. "But I also remember the vow I made—for better or for worse, in sickness and in health. If Alzheimer's is what worse means, then I'm in for the whole ride and so is the Invicta. Even if I have to hide the keys."

Diana swallowed hard and nodded. By then nodding silently was all she could do. Her voice was stuck in her throat.

"Even toward the last, when my father barely knew up from down, he loved to go for rides, and that's what we're going to do—with the top down whenever possible. You, me, and Damsel—the three of us together. You took care of me when I had bypass surgery, and I'm prepared to do the same for you. Got it?"

"Yes," she managed.

"We'll need to talk to the kids," Brandon went on, taking charge and laying out a plan of action. "We'll need to let them know what's been going on and what we're worried about. Davy can help us deal with the legal ramifications. And now that we've got a doctor in the family, maybe Lani can give us some advice on what's happening these days as far as medications and care are concerned. All right?"

"All right," Diana agreed.

"In the meantime," Brandon said, "what are you doing this afternoon?"

"Nothing," she said. "Why?"

"Then I'd like to invite you and Damned Dog here to take a day trip to Casa Grande. I believe I finally have some answers for Geet Farrell, and I want to give them to him in person."

Diana turned and looked in the backseat. She was relieved to see that Damsel was there—the dog and no one else.

"They're gone," she said. "The people who were here earlier are gone."

"Good," Brandon said. "They may come back, but if they do, let me know. You're not in this alone any longer. They'll have to deal with me, too."

The idea of Max Cooper having to deal with Brandon Walker was something Diana had never considered before. For the first time in a long time she smiled and really meant it.

"Thank you," she said. "Next time I see any of them, I'll be sure to let you know."

Tucson, Arizona
Sunday, June 7, 2009, 12:15 P.M.
90° Fahrenheit

Frustrated by being shut out of the investigation but with the photocopied license photo in hand, Brian was just leaving his desk to head home when his phone rang.

Megan O'Rourke, Pima County's chief CSI investigator, was on the line.

"I thought you'd want to know that we did find some brass cartridges," she said.

"Great," he said, "but I've been moved off the case. You should probably pass that information along to Jake Abernathy."

"Believe me, God's gift to women has already let us know that he's taken charge of the case and also the universe," Megan said with a laugh. "When I asked him about a related investigation in California, he laughed it off and allowed as how he'd let me know about it if and when the connection was verified. That's why I'm calling you. Tell me about that other case."

"Last night three homicides and a dead dog turned up shot to death in Thousand Oaks, California," he said. "The victims had been dead for several days. We suspect it's the same shooter. Let me give you the lead detective's contact information."

Once Brian was off the phone, he took the copies of Jonathan Southard's head shot and set off for Tucson International Airport. When he arrived, two Pima County patrol cars were parked on the departing passenger driveway. That meant that the uniformed officers Brian had asked to be sent to the airport were still there and continuing to interface with the TSA officers at the passenger screening stations. Keeping a few copies of the photo for himself, he parked in the driveway and took the rest of the stack inside.

When he came out, working on a hunch, Brian drove

back around the circle and pulled up behind the queue of cabs that were parked near the far end of the terminal building, waiting for fares.

It was ungodly hot. The drivers, several of them smoking, stood in a knot outside their vehicles, looking bored and discouraged. Most of the time they would have been less than interested in talking to a cop, but in this instance they were happy for anything that would take their minds off their shared misery.

"We're looking for this guy," Brian said, holding up a copy of the photo. "He may be trying to fly out of town this morning. Have any of you seen him?"

Brian was astonished when one of the drivers raised his hand. "Let me take a closer look," he said. After examining the photo, he nodded. "Yes, that's him. I gave this guy a ride about an hour ago."

Brian's heart skipped a beat. "Did you bring him here? Did he say what airline?"

"That's just it. When I picked him up, he told me he was flying American, but when we came up the drive, he said he'd forgotten something back at the hotel and needed to go back."

"Were the patrol cars here then?" Brian asked.

The driver frowned. "I think so."

"What happened next?"

"I drove him back to his hotel. When he paid me, I offered to wait for him and bring him back, but he said it wasn't necessary."

"What happened then?" Brian asked.

The driver shrugged. "I watched him. He didn't go

back to his room or even into the office. He got in a car and drove away."

"What kind of car?"

"A silver minivan."

"What hotel?"

"Los Amigos downtown."

Los Amigos Motel was a name Brian recognized. It wasn't the kind of accommodations airport passengers generally preferred on their way in or out of town. It was a dodgy place with a reputation for renting rooms on an hourly basis.

After taking down the cabbie's name and contact information, Brian thanked him for his help and headed back to his own vehicle. If the driver was correct, Jonathan Southard had already checked out of the hotel, but accessing his registration records would let Brian know if he was still using his own ID or if he had managed to get his hands on a phony one.

The desk clerk at Los Amigos was not happy to see Brian Fellows's badge. Neither was the manager on duty, but they managed to give Brian what he needed. Jonathan Southard had checked in using his own name and his California driver's license. He had paid cash for his room, arriving late Saturday night and departing today. And yes, Mr. Southard's arm had been in a sling. He claimed that he'd been bitten by a neighbor's Doberman.

Probably thought that sounded better than being bitten by his wife's beagle, Brian thought.

He immediately relayed what he had learned back to the department to Jake Abernathy's voice mail. He also passed the same information along to Detective Mumford in Thousand Oaks.

"So he saw the cop cars at the airport and figured out that trying to fly wasn't going to work," Alex said. "His next move will be to ditch that car and pick up a new one. Can you cover used-car lots?"

The truth was, Brian Fellows was off the case. He couldn't "cover" anything, but he didn't want to admit that to Alex Mumford.

"I doubt he'd use one of those," Brian said. "If I were in his shoes and on the run, I'd be more likely to pick up a 'for sale by owner' vehicle from a street corner somewhere rather than going to a dealer. A private citizen would be only too happy to take a handful of cash. A dealer would be obliged to report it."

Alex Mumford sighed. "You're probably right," she said. "But even that will take time. He'll have to make contact with the seller. The cabdriver told you you're only an hour or so behind him. If that's the case, you may still be able to nail him before he can get out of town."

"Let's hope," Brian agreed. "But there is one piece of good news in all this. I was worried that the shooter might come back looking for our surviving witness, the little girl. But since he was trying to fly out of town, I don't think he's focused on her. I've had a Border Patrol officer keeping an eye on her. I just left him a message that he can probably stand down."

"Speaking of phones," Alex Mumford said, "have you made any progress on tracking the victims' phones?"

"Not on this end," Brian admitted.

"It sounds like my chief is a whole lot more motivated than your sheriff. I should be able to add them to my request for a warrant."

"I'm glad somebody is motivated," Brian said with a hollow chuckle. "Do what you can, and if you can make it work, call me on this number. Any time night or day."

"Will do," Alex said. "Night or day. But if the high-tech solution doesn't work, maybe the low-tech one will."

"What's that?" Brian asked.

"You know," she said. "That old standby. He gets pulled over for a broken taillight."

"One can always hope," Brian said.

Brian knew that buying a car from a dealer was a process that could take several hours, and purchasing one from a private individual wasn't a slam dunk, either. If Jonathan Southard was trying to replace his vehicle, there was still a window of opportunity to catch him. If anybody was paying attention, that is.

Brian had been dismissed from the case and he had passed on everything he knew to the new team of detectives. It would have been easy to forget about it—to go home for a much-needed nap and let Jonathan Southard be Jake Abernathy's problem—but there was a big difference between being removed from a case and being able to let it go.

Brian Fellows was a plugger. Yes, he believed there was such a thing as blind luck, but he knew luck came most often to the people who applied themselves and did the grunt work. Rather than heading home, Brian returned to the sheriff's department, where he settled in behind his desk and started working the phone, calling car-rental agencies and used-car lots.

The Aces wouldn't mind. Detectives Abernathy and Adams were long on flash and bang, but they weren't big on gutting it out.

Gutting it out was Brian Fellows's middle name. He picked up his phone and went to work.

Sells, Tohono O'odham Nation, Arizona
Sunday, June 7, 2009, 1:30 P.M.
91° Fahrenheit

Delia had made it sound as if the court order for Angie's temporary guardianship was already a done deal, but it took a lot longer for Judge Lawrence to issue the actual paperwork than Lani would have thought possible. As the two women sat side by side in the waiting room out-side the tribal judge's chambers, Lani wondered if this was the same place where her parents had come years earlier when they petitioned for her adoption.

But I was already their foster child by then, Lani thought. *They had clothes for me and furniture and all those other things little kids need. I've got nothing, and the bedroom that would be Angie's is full of unpacked boxes of books.*

When she voiced some of those concerns to Delia, the tribal chairman nodded. "When we go before the judge, we'll ask if he's able to permit you to go into Delphina's house to retrieve some of Angie's clothing and belong-ings."

Ultimately, that's just what the paperwork said. In addition to granting Lani temporary custody, Judge Lawrence issued an order stating that she, accompanied by an officer from Law and Order, was authorized to enter Delphina Enos's residence for the sole purpose of retrieving Angie's personal items.

That may have been what the judge ordered, but it wasn't what happened.

After leaving the judge's office, Lani and Delia went straight to Law and Order. Accompanied by a uniformed patrol officer, the two women caravanned to Delphina Enos's mobile home. They arrived there just as Carmen and Louis Escalante were preparing to drive away in a pickup truck that had been loaded down with their dead daughter's furniture and possessions.

Furious, Delia Ortiz signaled for them to stop. "What do you think you're doing?" she demanded.

"We came to get Delphina's things," Louis said with a shrug. "Everything she owned is stuff her mother and I gave her. It's only fair that we should get it all back."

Inside the mobile home, Lani and Delia were dismayed to discover that the place had been stripped of everything of value—clothing, furniture, dishes, pots and pans. If Angie had any special toys or remembrances, they were gone now, too, except for one—a single cheap stuffed toy, a bedraggled lion that had probably come from the stuffed-toy vending machine just inside the front door at Bashas'. Clearly the lion had been there in the dirt and debris under a couch for some time. Lani picked it up and gave it several hard whacks. The blows raised a cloud of dust.

"How could they do this to their own grandchild?" Lani wondered.

"Did you ever see the movie *Zorba the Greek*?" Delia asked in return.

Lani shook her head. "Never heard of it," she said.

"My mother and Ruth loved that movie, mostly because of Anthony Quinn," Delia said. "In it, some poor old woman dies. The townsfolk descend on her house like a pack of jackals and strip it of everything."

"Just like this?" Lani asked.

Delia nodded. "Just like," she said.

As Delia spoke, she opened her purse. Reaching inside, she pulled out two hundred-dollar bills. "This isn't much, but it's a start," she said, passing the money to Lani. "Take Angie into town and use this to get replacements."

"How can I take her anywhere?" Lani asked. "Legally I can't even drive her home from the hospital. I don't have a booster seat."

"Is that Border Patrol guy still anywhere around?"

"Dan Pardee?" Lani asked. "Yes. I believe he's still over at the hospital. Why?"

"He's the one who brought Angie into town from the crime scene last night," Delia said. "The officers there let him remove the booster seat from Donald Rios's Blazer in order to do that. I'm sure he still has it."

"I'm sure he does," Lani said.

Sells, Tohono O'odham Nation, Arizona
Sunday, June 7, 2009, 1:45 P.M.
91° Fahrenheit

By early afternoon, Dan Pardee was mad enough to chew nails. He had waited around all morning and well into the afternoon, but there was still no sign of Angie's missing relatives, and no sign of Dr. Walker, either. Angie was asleep again, and Dan was pacing up and down the hallway when he saw Dr. Walker's midnight-blue VW Passat pull into a parking space reserved for doctors. When Lani stepped out of the driver's seat, Dan strode out to meet her.

"Dr. Walker, where the hell have you been all this time?" he demanded. "Angie and I are still waiting. No one has come for her, not one person. Where are those people? What the hell's wrong with them?"

She handed him a piece of paper, an official-looking document. "What's this?" he asked, looking at Lani rather than the court order.

"It's what's taken me so long," she answered. "Nobody has come for Angie because no one is going to come for her. Her family doesn't want her."

"Why the hell not?"

"You and I both know that Angie's alive because the killer didn't know she was there. Her superstitious relatives have decided that since Angie wasn't slaughtered along with her mother, she is now regarded as a dangerous object—a Ghost Child. They won't come anywhere near her."

"And this?" he asked, nodding toward the document.

"It's a court order from the tribal judge declaring me to be Angie Enos's legal guardian."

"Why you?" he asked. "Did the judge just pull your name out of his hat?"

"Not exactly," Lani said. "It turns out Angie Enos is my second cousin." She collected the document, turned away, and started toward the hospital's main entrance.

"You and Angie are related?" Dan asked, falling in behind her. "Couldn't you at least have mentioned that to me earlier?"

Lani spun around and faced him. She seemed angry, and he didn't understand why. "I would have mentioned it earlier if I had known it earlier. It turns out I didn't find out about it until after I left the hospital."

"Wait a minute," Dan said. "How could you not know you were related?"

"I'm adopted," Lani said. "There's a lot about my birth family that I don't know. Now, if you'll excuse me . . ."

For the first time he noticed the bedraggled stuffed toy Lani held clutched in her other hand.

"What's that?" he asked.

Lani took a deep breath. "It's the only thing Angie Enos has left in this world," she said. "Some time this morning while you were here at the hospital, Delphina Enos's parents went to her house and emptied the place. They stripped it of everything—and I do mean everything. This worthless stuffed toy is the only thing they left behind. Angie Enos has nothing left," she added bitterly. "Nothing but this poor damned lion and me."

Sells, Tohono O'odham Nation, Arizona
Sunday, June 7, 2009, 1:45 P.M.
91° Fahrenheit

Lani's eyes filled with hot tears. The injustice of it was more than she could bear. It was bad enough that the Escalantes had turned away from their grandchild, but to take everything she owned and leave her with nothing . . .

Dan Pardee's hand went to his pocket. Initially Lani thought he was reaching for a hanky to offer her. Instead, he pulled out a wallet. Opening it, he shuffled through what he carried there. Then, unfolding a frayed envelope, he removed a single photo, which he handed over to Lani.

"Not quite nothing," he said. "She still has this. I found it at the crime scene last night. I probably shouldn't have taken it, but I did."

"Who is this?" Lani asked. "Angie and her mother?"

Dan Pardee nodded. "So you see there? Angie does have something after all—a lion, a photo, a pink-and-yellow pinwheel, a surprise cousin, a dog named Bozo, and me, the *ohb*. What else could a poor little kid like that possibly need?"

Lani looked up at him in amazement. Ever since hearing about Andrew Carlisle's appearance, Lani had been filled with dread that something bad was about to happen, that something Apache-like was about to enter her life. What she hadn't expected was to find herself faced with the real thing. She had also expected this Apache-like entity to be something evil.

"You really are Apache?" she asked.

Dan Pardee nodded. "I'm afraid so," he said.

Still holding the photo, Lani found herself smiling up at him through her tears. "You may be *ohb*," she said, "but right this minute, I believe, next to my dad, you're probably the nicest man I've ever met."

13

Tucson, Arizona
Sunday, June 7, 2009, 10:00 A.M.
76° Fahrenheit

JONATHAN SOUTHARD SLEPT in that Sunday morning. When he finally awakened, he felt rested, relaxed, and absolutely triumphant. Unbeatable. Part of that was due to having had a good night's sleep for the first time in days. The antibiotics seemed to be doing their work. The hand was still lame—the urgent-care doc had said something about a severed tendon—but at least the throbbing was gone and the infection seemed to be lessening.

But Jonathan was glorying in more than physical well-being. He also felt an overwhelming sense of accomplishment. Not guilt. Accomplishment. He supposed he should have felt like a monster, but he didn't. Timmy and Suzy had been collateral damage; the Indians, too. But everyone else deserved it.

There was only one thing he regretted, and that was the fact that one name was missing from Jonathan's deadly roster. Kathleen Bates had been Jonathan's old boss. She was also the one who had given him his "out-placement counseling session." Of course, the job she had should have been his. Had that been the case, she would have been the one getting the boot. And he knew that she had reveled in kicking him down the stairs.

For a moment he went so far as to consider going back to California and taking care of her before he left the States for good. He wasn't really worried about the cops. They'd never figure out what had happened. In Jonathan's experience, most police officers were too stupid to live, much less work in a bank. Besides, Jonathan's IQ clocked in at something north of 156. Not even his mother had ever so much as hinted that he wasn't smart.

Unfortunately, his sense of self-satisfaction lasted for only five minutes or so, until he picked up the remote control and turned on his television set. The hazy news broadcasters on his snowy, non-high-def set were busy reporting on the quadruple homicide that had occurred overnight out on the reservation. They didn't call it a reservation. They called it the Tohono O'odham Nation, but that was beside the point.

What mattered was the disturbing realization that the bodies had been found far sooner than Jonathan had expected. He had thought he'd have all morning to make his leisurely way to the airport and then catch his plane for south of the border. But the reporter on the screen was saying that police had yet to identify the victims, pending notification of next of kin.

Hearing those fateful words propelled Jonathan straight up in bed.

Once the authorities identified Jack and Abby Tennant—with their car right there at the crime scene, even a stupid street cop could probably manage that much—then someone was even now heading for Abby's son's home in Thousand Oaks, for Jonathan's home, to give him the bad news about his mother's death. When that happened—maybe it already had happened—the jig would be up. Once Esther and the kids were found dead, Jonathan, the missing husband, would move to the very top of the suspect list. Cops in two states would be looking for him—seriously looking.

Jonathan had made arrangements to meet up with new identification once he crossed into Mexico, but he had planned on crossing the border using his own ID. Now he spent some time second-guessing that decision, but since there was no alternative, he decided he would try going to the airport early. Maybe he'd be able to get his ticket and make it through security before anyone raised the alarm.

He called for a cab to come take him to the airport. Ignoring Los Amigos's paltry version of a breakfast buffet, he dragged his roll-aboard luggage out through the lobby. His minivan was parked in the far corner of the lot. Jonathan didn't dare glance in that direction for fear someone might notice and wonder why he was taking his luggage and leaving without taking his vehicle with him.

The cab arrived with amazing alacrity. On the ride to the airport, Jonathan couldn't help glancing over his shoulder once or twice, but when they drove up to the departure gates, Jonathan was appalled to see a collection of cop cars gathered there. Not city cops—county cops.

Jonathan understood at once why they were there—they were looking for him. They had to be. He also understood that if he stepped inside the airport, he might still be able to purchase a ticket, but he wouldn't make it through security screening and out to a gate. That's where the cops would be waiting and watching—at the security checkpoints.

Worried about airport security, he had left his Glock in the car when he left the motel. He had been afraid that if the weapon showed up in his checked luggage, it might arouse suspicion. Now, though, he wanted it back. Once the cabdriver returned him to Los Amigos and dropped him off, he went straight to the minivan and retrieved the weapon from under the front seat.

Is that how all this is going to end, he wondered, *in a hail of bullets?*

Jonathan still had that collection of pills he had brought along from California. That and some booze—well, enough booze—would probably do the trick if it came to that, but he had to believe that it was still possible for him to make a clean getaway. That would only be possible if he made his move soon—very soon.

He was hungry. He had planned on eating breakfast at the airport. Now he needed to find some food, but he didn't want to spend a lot of time driving around town in case someone had caught on and put out a bulletin of some kind on his minivan. When he left the hotel, he wound through downtown. A mile or so from Tucson's downtown area, he happened on a family-owned coffee shop called Chaffin's, the kind of place that was crowded with Sunday-brunch-style gatherings.

Seated at the long counter and relishing the anonymity, he ate his short stack and downed his coffee and orange juice. As he did so, he idly wondered if he'd even be able to find pancakes once he made it into Mexico. Years ago, in Tijuana, Esther had ordered French toast and had been disappointed when her order came with French bread toasted. Pancakes might suffer in translation the same way.

Finally the guy next to him got up and went to pay his bill, leaving an untidy stack of maple-syrup-spotted Sunday newspaper sitting on the counter. Jonathan appropriated it and opened it to the front page. The article about the shootings on the reservation didn't add much to what had already been reported on the local television news.

Using the newspaper as cover, he sat there for some time, reading it and drinking one cup of coffee after the other, but he wasn't really reading. Jonathan was thinking. When he finally put down the paper and went to pay his tab, he had analyzed his situation and come up with a plan of action. Leaving his waitress a respectable tip, he exited the restaurant and went looking for a grocery store. He was pretty sure that was where he'd find what he needed.

Tucson, Arizona
Sunday, June 7, 2009, 12:00 P.M.
81° Fahrenheit

By the time Brandon and Diana made it back to Tucson from Sonoita, it was early afternoon. They rode with the convertible's top closed. Even so, they could tell that the Invicta's aging air conditioner was losing ground in its war with the summer heat.

Rather than driving straight through to Casa Grande in that, they stopped by the house in Gates Pass long enough to trade Diana's vintage Buick for Brandon's CRV. As for Damsel? After her morning's adventure, she was more than happy to curl up in her favorite place on the couch and snooze the rest of the day away while her people went off to do whatever people do when they're out.

On their way north, Brandon and Diana talked. Yesterday Brandon had been trying to run away from his own worst fears. Today those fears were realized. Yesterday, isolated and dreading what the unknown future might hold, he had felt impotent and hopeless. Now he knew that there was a very real possibility that he would lose Diana—that she would drift away from him into that strange fog of unknowing. That was a terrible prospect—an appalling prospect, but if that truly was what was happening, if Diana's strange visitations were part of early-onset Alzheimer's, at least now they were dealing with a known opponent, a named opponent.

And, if nothing else, he and Diana were finally talking

about it. They were dealing with it together—would deal with it together. Somehow that made it less scary as far as Brandon was concerned. They had made it through tough times together before, and they would do so again.

One by one they tried to look the worst-case scenario in the eye, attempting to sort out strategies that would help them navigate whatever was coming and make the best of it. Now that they had decided the Invicta would remain in the family, they also determined that from now on, in case the fog descended again—or, rather, when the fog descended again—Brandon would take charge of all car keys, including locking them away in his gun safe if he deemed that course of action necessary.

Brandon had never tried his hand at golf. He just wasn't interested in chasing little white balls across grassy lawns and trying to herd them into holes, but he remembered reading somewhere that Alzheimer's patients who had once played golf were still able to do so long after their other mental faculties seemed to desert them.

For that very reason he was enthusiastic about Diana's sudden interest in trying her hand at making pottery. It was something that she had enjoyed once in the distant past. He hoped it would help hold her interest now. Since the Invicta would still be occupying its space in the garage, however, one of the bedrooms—most likely the one that had been Davy's—would be turned into Diana's pottery studio.

And if they needed more help around the house—both of them carefully avoided saying the word "attendant"—maybe Lani could help them find someone from the reservation who would be willing to come live in and be there to help out out as necessary.

As they talked, the miles seemed to melt away. Today, as Brandon drove into Geet and Sue Farrell's neighborhood, it didn't look quite as grim as it had appeared to him on the previous day. Yes, the trim on the house still needed scraping and painting and the thirsty palm trees were still wilting in the heat, but it wasn't as distressing as it had seemed yesterday.

The day before when he had noticed the wheelchair-accessible van parked in their driveway, he had taken that as a sign of defeat. Today, that same van with its handicapped-parking placard spoke to him in a different way. It was one of the tools Sue and Geet were using to get along—had used to get along. Brandon doubted Geet would be up to taking many more trips away from his living room hospital equipment and oxygen mask, but the van was part of how he and Sue had coped so far. It was how they had made it to here.

And we'll make it, too, Brandon thought.

He pulled into the driveway and parked next to the van. "Do you want me to wait in the car?" Diana asked.

"No," he said. "It's too hot. Come on in. You can talk to Sue while I visit with Geet. She needs company, too."

When the time comes, so will I, he thought.

He led Diana around the house to the back-door entrance and knocked. When Sue answered she looked marginally better than she had the day before. The haircut helped, but she also looked better rested.

"Back so soon?" she asked.

Brandon nodded. It seemed odd to him that he and Geet had been friends for years, but until this moment their wives had never met. Once the necessary introductions were out of the way, Brandon left Diana in the kitchen with Sue while he made his way back into the living room. This time he was better equipped to deal with the hospice equipment he saw there. Sue's tangle of sheets still covered the sofa, but now a kitchen chair had been drawn up close to the bed.

Geet himself lay propped up in his hospital bed with his closed eyes turned toward a muted television set where the Padres were playing the Diamondbacks. It seemed to Brandon that in those few intervening hours the man had wasted away that much more. The skin on the gaunt bones of his face was gray. His lips were almost white. Death was coming and it was coming soon. Brandon knew what this looked like. He had seen the same thing in the hospital room where they had taken his father.

Geet's eyes blinked open without warning. He studied Brandon for a moment as if unsure of who he was. Then he grinned—at least it looked like a grin.

"Hey," he said. "Weren't you just here, or do I have you mixed up with someone else?"

"I was here," Brandon said. "Yesterday. You handed over that case file."

"Ursula's," he said.

"Yes," Brandon agreed. "Ursula's."

Geet stirred. Cancer had robbed him of almost everything, but for a few moments the old intensity burned through. His eyes focused. He paid attention. "Did you talk to her—to the witness?"

"To June Holmes?" Brandon returned. "Yes, I did."

"Why wouldn't she talk to me before this?" Geet asked. "Why now?"

"Because her husband was still alive," Brandon explained. "She didn't send you that note until after Fred Holmes died."

"Why?" Geet asked. "What does that have to do with the price of peanuts?"

"She claims Fred was the one who did it—the one who murdered Ursula Brinker. She said she didn't know about it until five years ago. When Fred finally got around to telling her, he had just been diagnosed with cancer. She waited until after he was dead to send you that letter."

"But I checked Fred Holmes's alibi," Geet objected. "I had witnesses who placed him in Phoenix that whole weekend."

Brandon was struck by the fact that even after all these years and even in the throes of cancer, Geet still had a complete grasp of the details of that case. He had no difficulty recalling the names of the people involved.

For him it's like golf, Brandon thought. *Or throwing pots.*

"The alibi came from his mother?" Brandon asked.

"Yes."

"She may have thought he was there, but he wasn't. He drove to San Diego and back without his mother ever knowing he was gone."

"Why did it happen?" Geet asked.

"Ursula and June started out as friends. On that trip they evidently became closer than friends."

"As in a homosexual encounter?"

Brandon knew Geet had suspected as much. He

nodded. "Someone walked in on them and caught them in the act. Word about what had happened got back to Fred. According to June, it was just a onetime thing. Maybe it was; maybe it wasn't. At any rate, this was a long time before Don't Ask/Don't Tell. Fred and June had both been raised as devout Mormons where that kind of thing was then and still is a big no-no. When Fred heard about it, he went ape and drove straight to San Diego to put a stop to it. Ursula ended up dead."

"Who spilled the beans and told him about what was going on?"

"June said she thought maybe it was Margo."

"The girl who owned the car."

Brandon nodded.

Geet thought about that for a moment. "A couple of people hinted around that something like that might have happened between Ursula and June. I wondered about Fred from the beginning, but as far as I could tell, his alibi checked out. What if she's lying?"

"What if June Holmes is lying now?" Brandon asked.

Geet nodded. "What if June was the one who ran up the flag to Fred in the first place?" he asked. "Maybe she knew he was likely to overreact?"

"I don't think so," Brandon said. "I don't think she told Fred about what happened before Ursula died, but she did shortly after it happened. She thought that when she made her confession to him that he'd drop her like a hot potato. She's spent most of the last fifty years being grateful that he didn't. When he finally got around to telling her what had really happened, he was counting on her standing by him the same way he had stood by her. He figured those forty-five years of gratitude would keep her from spilling the beans. It was also a form of punishment."

"Sounds like it worked on both counts," Geet grumbled.

Brandon nodded. "She didn't say a word to anyone about it until after he was dead. By the time you reopened the case, Fred had already confessed to her. That's why she refused to talk to you. She didn't want her kids and grandkids to know what Fred had done. And she didn't want them to know about what she and Ursula had done, either."

Geet shook his head. "If you ask me, it seems a little suspect and way too convenient that she's blaming Fred now, after he's dead and unable to defend himself. Do you believe her?"

"Actually, I do," Brandon told him. "She had her suitcase packed and her cat crated. She fully expected that I was coming to pack her off to jail. She was under the impression that by knowing about it and not telling, that made her an accessory after the fact. I think she was on the level."

Reaching into his pocket, Brandon withdrew the Ziploc bag containing the hunting knife and handed it over to Geet.

"What's this?"

"That may be the murder weapon," Brandon told him. "After Fred died, one of their sons was going through his tools and found this hidden in the back of one of the drawers in his father's tool chest. In all the years June and Fred were married, she said she had never seen it before, didn't know it existed. I'll get it over to the crime lab and see if they can find any DNA evidence. There might be some, right there in the crack where the blade meets the handle."

Geet examined the knife through the clear plastic and then gave it back to Brandon. "What if there is?" he asked with an exasperated shrug. "What's the point? Ursula is still dead. So are her parents. So is Fred. What about justice? No one is ever going to pay for that crime."

"June is paying," Brandon said quietly. "She may not have murdered Ursula, but she knows now that what the two of them did together that day was the ultimate cause of her friend's death. I believe she'll regret it every day for the rest of her life."

Geet leaned back against his pillows, closed his eyes, and shook his head in obvious disgust. "So that's it, then," he said. "I've spent a lifetime chasing after this case and it's all for nothing."

"Not for nothing," Brandon told him. "We finally have a better idea about what happened. Regardless of whether it goes to trial, I believe we can both know that this case is finally closed."

"If Fred's the one who did it, I should have caught him sooner," Geet insisted. "There must have been something I missed, something that would have given the game away."

"What if you had solved it?" Brandon asked. "What then? Fred might have gotten sent up for a couple of years, but you and I wouldn't be here right now, Geet. It was because Ursula's murder wasn't solved that Hedda Brinker used her lotto millions to start The Last Chance. I personally know of at least fifteen separate families that TLC has helped over the years—families who now have answers about their murdered loved ones that they wouldn't have had otherwise."

Geet nodded. "I suppose that's true," he admitted, but the spark of focus that had briefly animated him seemed to have run its course. He closed his eyes briefly, then held out his hand. When Brandon took it, Geet's skin was hot and paper-thin, but the grip of his handshake was surprisingly firm.

"Thank you, Brandon," he said. "Following up on this last case of mine means more to me than you know."

"You're welcome," Brandon said, rising to his feet. "Glad to help out." He walked toward the door, then stopped. "Turns out it's probably my last TLC case, too."

Geet's eyes popped open. "Why's that?"

"Diana," Brandon said with a shrug. "I think we're facing some health issues, too. I'll probably let Ralph know that I'm going to have to stand down."

The fact that he'd made the admission surprised him. It was one thing to tell the kids. It was something else to mention the situation outside the immediate family.

"I'm sorry," Geet said. "I hope it works out."

"Thanks," Brandon said. "I hope so, too."

Tucson, Arizona
Sunday, June 7, 2009, 1:30 P.M.
87° Fahrenheit

When Brian's cell phone rang, he expected it to be Kath. He had told her he was still working—that he wouldn't be able to be there that afternoon to watch the girls while she went shopping.

The caller, however, turned out to be Alex Mumford. "Who the hell is Jake Abernathy?" she wanted to know.

"That would be one of Sheriff Forsythe's fair-haired boys. I take it he called you?"

"Why didn't you call me?" she returned pointedly.

"I got pulled from the case," he said. "Abernathy's lead."

"That may be, but he's also a jerk," Alex said. "He called me up and started throwing his weight around. Make that he was trying to throw his weight around."

"I take it that didn't work out for him all that well?"

"You think?" Alex replied with a laugh. "I'm all for interagency cooperation and all that crap, but not when someone pisses me off. So here's the deal. I did get those phone numbers added to the warrant, but I don't have any information back on that just yet. It is Sunday, after all, but when I do get some information, I'll be calling it in to you. I seem to have lost Detective Abernathy's number."

Brian laughed, too. "Thank you," he said. "I'll be glad to pass it along. When I do, Abernathy will go straight up and turn left. A ripple in the force and all that. He's not going to like it."

"Good," Alex Mumford said. "It couldn't happen to a nicer guy."

Tucson, Arizona
Sunday, June 7, 2009, 1:45 P.M.
88° Fahrenheit

Ginny Torres's heart was light as she wheeled her grocery-laden shopping cart through Safeway while her three-year-old son, Pepe, babbled happily if unintelligibly in the child's seat. It was close to naptime, but so far he hadn't hit the wall.

Ginny generally hated Sundays. There was always more than she could do in one day—laundry, household chores, grocery shopping. She worked five days a week at the AOL call center and one day a week at a hair-care kiosk at Park Place Mall. Not that she wasn't glad to have both jobs. She was.

They had been living in Safford and doing all right—up until Felix, her husband, had been laid off from his well-paying job with Phelps Dodge. That had come as a big shock to the system. In the end, they'd had no choice but to come limping back home to Tucson, where they were able to live not quite rent-free in one of Felix's parents' rentals.

In the process, Ginny had made the leap from stay-at-home mom to major breadwinner. Her call-center job didn't pay exceptionally high wages, but it did come with medical benefits. With a toddler to worry about, that was huge. Felix, on the other hand, found occasional construction and yard-work jobs. When he wasn't working one of those, he took care of Pepe. On those occasions when both he and Ginny had to work, Felix's mother looked after Pepe. That way, at least Ginny and Felix didn't have to worry about paying for child care.

In other words, things could have been a lot worse, but Ginny did find herself wishing sometimes that Felix didn't have such an aversion to doing housework—women's work, as he liked to call it. He could be home all day without seeing any need to pick up the vacuum cleaner, and he could step over or around the mounds of dirty clothes out in the garage without once taking it on himself to start a load of laundry. Felix never fussed when it was time to go to the store for beer, but going to the store for groceries? Never. Grocery shopping was something else that had to wait for Ginny's precious "day off."

Today, though, with the exception of two items, she was picking up staples only—laundry detergent, dog food, and canned goods—things that could sit in an overheated car for several hours without coming to grief, because today, after her shopping excursion, she and Pepe weren't going straight home.

Pepe's third birthday was on Monday, but they were celebrating it today with tamales and tacos at Felix's folks' place. All the cousins would be there for an afternoon of fun in the pool. All Ginny and Pepe had to do was to show up, bringing along the birthday cake and ice cream—those were the only perishables in the cart.

That cake was appropriately decorated with tiny plastic replicas of Wall-E and Eva and the ice cream was Pepe's favorite, all chocolate all the time.

Ginny was looking forward to the party. Her mother-in-law, Amelia, would be in her element, spoiling her husband, her sons, and her grandkids. The children would be busy splashing around in the pool, the men would be out on the patio drinking beer, and the sisters-in-law would sit around the kitchen table drinking iced tea and griping about their husbands, all of whom were cut from the same cloth. To a man, all five of Amelia Torres's sons were utterly incapable of lifting a finger around the house.

At the checkout stand, the cashier rang up the cake and then smiled at Pepe. "Whose birthday?" she asked.

"Mine!" he announced proudly, thumping his chest.

"And how old are you?" The cashier's name tag said "Helen."

It took some maneuvering on his part, but eventually Pepe managed to hold up three fingers.

"Three, really?" Helen asked.

Ginny and Pepe nodded in unison.

"Enjoy him," Helen said. "They grow up so quickly. Do you need any help out with these?"

On Sunday afternoons, the store wasn't normally that crowded, but today the open checkout stands all had lines, and the carryout clerks were totally occupied.

"No, thanks," Ginny said. "I can manage. Don't bag the cake, but double-bag the ice cream. Otherwise it might melt before we make it to Grandma's house."

A few minutes later, Ginny pushed the heavy cart out through the automatic sliding doors. The early-afternoon June heat was like a physical assault. It burned into her face and skin, and she was glad that the interior of her four-year-old and fully paid for Honda came with cloth seats instead of leather. The cloth might be harder to keep clean, especially when something sweet got spilled on it, but at least it didn't fry your bare skin when you climbed inside.

Pepe was still blabbing away as Ginny angled the shopping cart through the busy parking lot. She had hoped that she would manage to convince him to take a nap before the party, but it was beginning to look as though that wasn't in the cards.

As Ginny neared the Accord, she pressed the button on the remote. As close as she had to be before the doors unlocked, Ginny was pretty sure she needed to put in a new battery in her remote.

The parking lot was spacious. Even on this busy Sunday afternoon there were still plenty of open stalls, but a dust-covered minivan had parked close enough to her car that both tires were on her side of the designated parking lines. *Creep*, she thought.

With Pepe still in the cart, Ginny carefully loaded the groceries into the trunk, making sure the cake was properly wedged into a spot where it couldn't possibly come to grief. The ice cream she set aside to put in the front seat along with her purse in hopes the AC could maybe help keep it from melting before she made it to her in-laws' place on the far side of I-10. Pepe unfortunately took exception to her plan. He wanted to keep the cake with him, and he launched himself into a nap-deprived temper tantrum.

Once the groceries were loaded, Ginny lifted her son out of the car and then wrestled him, screeching at the top of his lungs, into his booster seat. With him screaming and kicking, Ginny was grateful that this car seat was a lot easier to operate than the backward-facing ones they had used when Pepe was younger. Then, with him properly belted but still howling, Ginny hurried to return the grocery cart to the cart collection point three cars away.

Even at the end of the aisle Ginny could still hear Pepe's full-fledged screeching. Returning to her vehicle, she edged between the poorly parked minivan and her Honda. She opened the door and prepared to put her purse and the ice cream on the front passenger seat. When she tried to do so, however, she was astonished to see a man, a stranger, sitting there in the passenger seat. Not only was he there, he was holding a gun.

"Don't make a sound," he growled at her. "If you do, your baby dies."

Ginny's breath caught in her throat. A charge that seemed like electricity shot through her body. Her fingertips tingled. The car keys dropped from her suddenly clumsy hands. The key fob fell to the floorboard inside the car. Her purse and the bagged ice cream landed with a splat on the pavement next to the car.

"Who are you?" she demanded when she was able to speak. "What do you want? What are you doing in my car?"

"Open the door of the car next to you," he said, pointing at the minivan. "There's a roll-aboard suitcase on the front seat. Put that in the backseat of this car. Then close that one and get in this one. Don't call to anyone. Don't make any fuss or your baby dies."

Ginny looked back over her shoulder at the grubby silver minivan. It looked innocuous enough—like a perfectly normal car. Surely this wasn't happening. It couldn't be happening.

"Did you hear me?" the man barked. "Do it now. Move."

Ginny looked at Pepe, who, still screaming in full meltdown mode, had yet to notice the stranger's presence. With her whole body quaking, Ginny backed away from the Honda and pulled open the passenger-side door of the minivan.

The car was filthy inside and out. The passenger-side floorboard was full of trash—empty fast food and drink containers. But the roll-aboard bag was there on the seat, just as the man had said it would be. It was heavier than Ginny expected, but she hefted it out and lugged it over to the back door of her Honda. As she shoved it inside, she looked around desperately, hoping someone was aware of what was happening, but she saw no one—no one at all. The minivan was tall enough that it obscured her movements from the view of anyone coming and going through the store's front entrance.

She started to reach down to retrieve her fallen purse and the ice cream. Then she stopped. If she left those items there, maybe whoever found them would be smart enough to figure out that something bad had happened. Then again, maybe whoever saw her purse sitting there on the ground might just steal it for themselves.

Trying to control her trembling body, Ginny got back into the car. The man sitting beside her was middle-aged, pudgy, and balding. There was a long scabby cut that ran from his eyebrow to his cheek, as though he had been in a fight of some kind. That was also when she noticed, for the first time, that the hand that held the gun was actually in a sling. One of his arms, the right one, was hurt and bandaged. Maybe that was why he had wanted help in moving that suitcase. Or maybe he thought that dragging luggage around a grocery-store parking lot might attract too much unwanted attention.

Ginny groped around on the floorboard and finally managed to find the keys she had dropped earlier. With her hand still trembling, she picked them up. It took several tries before she was able to insert the key in the ignition. When the Accord's engine turned over, the AC fans came on full-blast, spewing hot air into the vehicle. Without putting the car in gear, she looked back at Pepe.

"It's okay," she said to her hysterical son as soothingly as she could manage, but her voice felt brittle, as if it might shatter into a million pieces. "We'll be okay. Hush now."

But Pepe didn't listen and he didn't hush. He kept right on howling. He had no idea that they were in danger. All he wanted was his cake.

Ginny turned to the man. "Why are you doing this?" she asked. "What do you want?"

"Don't talk, drive," he ordered. "Get us out of here."

Ginny was an ordinary young woman—a young mother. This seemed impossible. Surely she and Pepe couldn't be kidnapped by an armed assailant in broad daylight right in the middle of Tucson! But clearly the unthinkable—the impossible—had happened, was happening. Ginny also knew that if called upon to do so, she would fight for Pepe's life with her last dying breath. That very real possibility forced her to try to calm herself. She held the burning steering wheel with both hands and used the pain on her palms to help bring her mind into focus. Her life depended on it; so did Pepe's.

She strapped her own seat belt in place. As she did so she remembered that weeks earlier someone had sent her an e-mail about this very thing. Usually, she discarded those Internet chain letters without even looking at them. For some reason, she had read that one all the way through, and the advice had stayed with her.

The message had said that if you were ever carjacked, you should smash your vehicle into something stationary and then get out and run like hell. The idea was that the deploying air bags would probably knock the weapon out of the assailant's hands, temporarily disarming him. Even if he ended up firing at you as you ran away, not that many people could shoot weapons well enough to hit a moving target.

But if I jump out and run away, she thought, *what about Pepe in the backseat?* He was strapped into his booster. That was something Ginny insisted on. In her vehicle, not wearing seat belts wasn't an option. And what if Pepe's belt didn't hold when she deliberately wrecked the car? What if it malfunctioned? What if he came loose and went smashing through the windshield? Or what if he was left alone in the car with an armed and dangerous criminal? All those ideas raced through her mind at once like waves of heat rising off the pavement.

Ginny took a deep breath and turned toward the man with the gun. "Where do you want to go?" she asked, straining to be heard over the noise of Pepe's over-wrought protestations.

"Mexico," he said.

"Where in Mexico?" she asked. "Nogales? Agua Prieta?"

"I don't care. Just get me across the border."

The car parked directly in front of Ginny's Honda, an SUV, pulled out of its spot. Relieved, Ginny followed it out. That way she didn't have to back up and show the killer that she had left her bag of ice cream and her purse sitting there on the ground in plain sight.

If the guy wanted to go to Mexico, Ginny knew she had another problem. Her driver's license was in the purse along with her cell phone. So was her passport, and Pepe's, too. She and Felix had gotten Pepe a passport when Grandpa and Grandma Torres had taken everyone—kids and grandkids included—with them on a Mexican cruise in honor of their fiftieth wedding anniversary. Since then, Ginny had discovered that racial profiling did happen. In southern Arizona, if you looked Hispanic, it was always a good idea to have plenty of government-issue ID available, especially if you happened to get stopped at a Border Patrol checkpoint.

But this time, when she reached the checkpoints, she wouldn't have ID of any kind. What would this man do then?

Suddenly she made the connection. It had been all over the news when she turned on her TV earlier that morning. Someone had killed four people out on the reservation last night. Was this the same man? If it was, this guy wasn't just desperate. He was a stone-cold killer who probably wouldn't think twice about taking another life—or two.

Ginny took a deep breath and glanced in the rearview mirror.

Behind her she saw a woman hustle up to one of the carryout boys. She was waving her arms and gesturing, pointing first in the direction of Ginny's Accord and then back to the place where Ginny's purse and her bag of melting ice cream sat abandoned on the burning pavement.

For one giddy moment, Ginny allowed herself to hope that help was on the way, but that moment of respite was short-lived. She knew it would take time for help to get there. She needed to stall long enough for that to happen.

"I need gas," she said.

That was true. She had less than half a tank, and there was a gas station right there in the corner of the parking lot. She also had no money and no credit card, but maybe she could get inside long enough to ask for help.

"We'll get gas later," the man said, waggling the gun in her direction. "Get us out of here now. Go that way." He pointed southbound on Campbell.

Ginny drove as far as the exit onto Campbell and signaled to turn left. Within a couple of blocks, Pepe finally finished crying himself out and fell quiet. It was his usual nap time. Tired from shopping and from crying, and still blissfully unaware of the danger they were in, he seemed to be falling asleep. Mentally Ginny uttered a prayer of thanksgiving. The sudden silence gave her a chance to concentrate on what she was doing and to get herself under control.

She tried desperately to remember everything she had ever heard or seen about hostage situations on television and in the movies. Wasn't she supposed to get the guy talking? Isn't that what hostage negotiators always did— try to establish a line of communication?

"Why are you doing this?" she asked.

The gunman shrugged and didn't answer.

"If you'll let Pepe and me out somewhere, you can have the car," she said. "We won't tell anybody. Just let us go. Please."

She knew even as she said the words that this was a futile hope. He would never let them go. She understood full well there was only one way this nightmare would end, and it would be with Ginny and Pepe dead. She would never see Felix again. Never have a chance to tell him good-bye. And she wouldn't live long enough to see Pepe go off to kindergarten, or graduate from high school, either. Her eyes filled with hot tears, but she blinked them back.

"Don't talk," he said. "Just drive."

Since there was nothing else to do, Ginny drove. She

forced herself not to look in the rearview mirror. If that woman in the parking lot had noticed something amiss and had summoned help—if by some miracle someone was following them—she didn't want to risk doing anything that might warn the guy that help was on the way. And if there wasn't anybody back there coming to help? Then it didn't matter anyway.

"What happened to your arm?" she asked.

He glanced down at his injured hand. Ginny looked, too.

"Dog bit me," he said.

That was all he said. He didn't explain which dog had bitten him or why, and Ginny decided not to ask for any further clarification on that score.

"Why did you choose me?" she asked finally.

"I drove around until I found a car with a car seat in it," he said. "I figured while you were dealing with the baby it would be easy for me to get in your car. And it was."

Crap, Ginny Torres thought. *They told you that you should always put your baby in a car seat. That was supposed to make it safer. Not this time.*

Tucson, Arizona
Sunday, June 7, 2009, 1:48 P.M.
88° Fahrenheit

Now that Annie and Amy were six, they were old enough that Kath Fellows was willing to risk leaving them alone for an hour or so at a time. On this particular Sunday afternoon she knew she'd be in and out of the neighborhood grocery store in far less time than that. So after giving the girls a pep talk and promising to bring them both Twinkies if they were very good, she left them in the living room with orders to stay there watching a video until she came back.

Kath was at the checkout line and just signing the credit-card authorization screen when one of the carryout boys came charging into the store yelling, "Call nine-one-one."

"Why?" the manager called back. "What's wrong?"

"There's an old lady outside who said she thinks a woman and her baby were just abducted at gunpoint, from right here in the parking lot."

As people hurried out the door, Kath followed, pushing her cart of groceries. A crowd was gathering around the supposedly "old" woman, someone who looked to be in her sixties, who was pacing back and forth, yelling excitedly, and pointing back toward the parking lot.

"He had a gun," she said. "I saw it. He got in the car while she was putting the grocery cart away. When she came back to her car, he made her get something out of this one."

The woman pointed toward a dust-covered silver Dodge Caravan. "She put whatever it was in the backseat of her little car and then they drove out of here in that. But her purse is still here—right there on the ground— and so are some of her groceries."

Kath listened to the chorus of excited voices as she

loaded groceries into the back of her own Odyssey on the far side of the parking aisle. By the time she finished, she knew that Tucson PD was responding to the manager's 911 call because she could hear the siren of an approaching patrol car wailing in the distance.

"What kind of vehicle were they in when they left here?" the store manager was asking the distressed woman. He was still holding his cell phone and still talking into it.

"Tan," she said. "Light tan. One of those foreign cars. A Honda, I think, but I don't know for sure."

"Which way did they go?"

"South on Campbell."

"And what about the guy? Did you see him? What did he look like?"

"Middle-aged, bald, and heavyset," the woman said. "One arm was in a sling."

That last comment hit Kath Fellows like a sledgehammer. She had spoken to Brian several times in the course of the day. She knew the man her husband was looking for—the killer he was looking for—was a middle-aged bald man with one arm in a sling. Slamming her car door shut, Kath raced across the aisle and pushed her way through the cluster of people until she was able to get a clear view of the tags on the back of the dusty silver minivan. California.

Long before the patrol car arrived, Kath Fellows was on the horn with her husband. Brian sounded groggy, as though he might have been caught napping at his desk when she called.

"Sorry," he mumbled. "I meant to call earlier. I'm tracking auto dealers, and I still don't know when I'll be home."

"It's about your killer," Kath told him. "Do you have a vehicle tag number for him?"

"Just a sec," Brian said, shuffling papers. "I have it right here. Why?"

"I'm looking at a very dusty silver minivan, a Dodge Caravan with California plates."

Brian read off the license information.

"That's the one," Kath said.

"What's going on?"

"I think your guy just carjacked a woman and her baby."

"Which way did they go?" Brian asked.

Kath heard the urgency in his voice. "South on Campbell in a tan sedan. Maybe a Honda. Is it possible they're headed for the airport?"

"No," Brian said at once. "Not that. Southard already tried the airport option this morning. It didn't work. Besides, we've got that covered. He's headed somewhere else. The smart money is on Mexico. Can you give me any more information on either the vehicle or on the victim, anything at all?"

Kath looked up in time to see that the arriving patrol car was still half a block away, wading through the intersection. The cops weren't on the scene yet, but the woman's purse was. It was still sitting where she had dropped it, on the ground next to the spot where her vehicle had been parked.

Before anyone could stop her, Kath had scooped up the abandoned purse. She had the wallet out and open by the time the cop car rolled to a stop in the midst of the milling crowd of excited onlookers.

"Stop her," someone shouted, pointing at Kath. "That woman is trying to steal her purse."

A burly young cop hurried up to Kath. "What's going on here?" he demanded. "Is that your property?"

"Her name is Torres," Kath said into the phone to her husband without answering the officer's question. "Virginia Torres. Her address is 231 South Fourth."

"Ma'am, I asked you once," the cop insisted. "You need to answer me. Is that your purse or not?"

"Hope this helps," Kath said. "I've gotta go."

She closed her phone, handed the purse to the police officer, and reached for her own ID. "No, it's not mine," she said. "My name is Kath Fellows. I'm with the Border Patrol. According to her ID, the purse belongs to a woman named Virginia Torres. I believe she and her baby have just been carjacked. I think the man who did it is the shooter who killed those four people out on the reservation last night."

14

Tucson, Arizona
Sunday, June 7, 2009, 1:50 P.M.
88° Fahrenheit

*B*RIAN FELLOWS WAS on the phone to Records as he raced out of the building. If the carjacked Honda was still on Campbell or Kino, it was probably headed for either I-10 or I-19. Depending on traffic and lights, the trip to the freeway from Broadway could take as little as seven minutes or as long as ten.

The sheriff's office was only half a mile or so from where Kino intersected I-10. Brian knew that if he hurried, he might well be there before the Honda. There was a chance a Tucson PD patrol vehicle might beat him to the punch, but that was strictly a matter of luck. Brian was afraid his quota of luck for the day had already been used up in spectacular fashion.

The fact that Kath had been grocery shopping in the same place where Southard had gone looking for a victim was beyond luck. It seemed to him that there was a higher power operating somewhere behind the scenes. There was also the disturbing realization that Kath could just as easily have been the carjacking victim. That, too, was strictly a matter of chance.

Brian was too low on the departmental totem pole to merit a shaded parking place. He piled into his stifling patrol car. The overheated steering wheel scorched his hands as he shot out of his parking place and across the lot. When he reached the exit, he was relieved to see there was no traffic at all on Old Benson Highway. He made a quick right-hand turn without bothering to stop and immediately moved into the far-left lane. He was tempted to turn on his lights and siren, but then he thought better of it. Until he was sure there was backup either from the city of Tucson or from Pima County, it was probably best to maintain a low profile.

Once on Kino, Brian drove as far as the intersection with I-10, where he hit a red light. Stopping for that gave him a chance to study access ramps going in either direction. There was no sign of the Honda on I-10, but while he was looking, Brian took a moment to radio back to Dispatch to let them know that they needed to contact Jake Abernathy and tell him that his homicide suspect was now a carjacking suspect as well.

It was nothing more or less than a CYA call. Jonathan Southard's case was now officially Jake Abernathy's problem. If someone from Tucson PD made the collar,

Jake would be pissed. If Brian made it, the man would be downright livid. In a perfect world, results should be the final judge and this would be all about *catching* the bad guy rather than *who* was catching the bad guy. But Brian Fellows had long ago realized that under Sheriff Bill Forsythe, the Pima County Sheriff's Department never had been and never would be a "perfect world."

His phone rang. "Okay," Kath said. "A Tucson PD unit is headed southbound on Campbell. Where are you?"

"At the freeway and Kino and headed north," Brian answered. "No sign of the Honda so far, but with any luck that unit from Tucson PD and I will catch it in a squeeze play."

"Be safe," Kathy said.

"I always am," he told her.

Tucson, Arizona
Sunday, June 7, 2009, 1:51 P.M.
88° Fahrenheit

Jonathan watched the woman as she drove. Fortunately she had finally stopped trying to talk to him. At first he had thought she was much younger, but now he realized she had to be somewhere in her thirties. And her baby—thank God the squalling kid had finally shut up and had evidently fallen asleep—had to be somewhere between three and four years old.

Jonathan didn't like thinking about what was going to happen to them. It was inevitable. The prospect of that finally forced him to think about what he had done to his own kids.

Esther had deserved whatever she got and more, but maybe he should have left the kids be. Someone would have looked after Timmy and Suzy, he supposed. Corrine, Esther's busybody sister, for one. If he had taken the time really to think about it before he shot them, he might not have done it. But he was having time to think about what would happen to this mother and her little boy now, and it bothered him, just like shooting the stupid Indians bothered him. In this case, however, the young woman and her son were already as good as dead. They just didn't know it. In fact, the woman was probably still hoping he'd give them a chance to get away.

As far as when he would finish them off and where that would happen? He knew that it would have to be somewhere between here and the border. He'd direct her to turn off the freeway onto a deserted road somewhere. Then, after he'd shot them both, he'd take the car. He'd park it somewhere close to the border and then walk across, using his passport to get him past the immigration people on both sides.

They had been driving south first on Campbell and then on Kino. He was glad she was sticking to the posted speed limit. So far they hadn't encountered any law enforcement vehicles, and once they merged onto the freeway system, Jonathan figured they'd be a lot more difficult to find.

They were nearing the intersection with I-10 where

Kino widened to lanes. The Honda was still in the middle lane.

"The freeway is coming up," he told her. "You need to get over."

"I was planning on getting on I-19 at Ajo Way," she said. "There's all kinds of construction on I-10 right now. That intersection might not even be open."

"I said get on the freeway," he insisted. "Do it now."

He saw her check in the rearview mirror for traffic. Even so, she didn't pull over right away, and the entrance ramp was coming up way too fast. The last thing he needed was for this dumb broad to wreck her car with him in it.

"Get over," he ordered again. "You're going the way I tell you. Understand?"

She nodded. At almost the last moment, she jammed on the brakes and slewed the Accord into the right-turn lane.

"You stupid bitch!" he yelled at her. "You almost took us out just then. What the hell were you thinking?"

Naturally the abrupt lane change woke up the kid, and he immediately started howling again.

Great, Jonathan thought. But at least they were entering the freeway now and could blend into traffic there. He breathed a sigh of relief. Things were finally starting to go in his favor.

It was about time.

Tucson, Arizona
Sunday, June 7, 2009, 1:52 P.M.
88° Fahrenheit

Ginny knew that each passing telephone pole and each passing bridge abutment were missed opportunities.

She understood that she needed to choose one and use it before they got on the freeway, but she just couldn't summon the nerve. All her instincts and all her experience were screaming at her: Do not wreck your car! But in these dire circumstances, wrecking the car was exactly what she needed to do. What she had to do.

Pepe was still asleep. If she did it while he was asleep, chances were he wouldn't be tensed up and frightened by the impending crash. In the mirror she caught a glimpse of his bare little neck with the tiny dark curls blooming around it. What would happen to that precious little neck, the one she kissed at night when Pepe was sleeping? Would it snap to pieces in the collision? Would she be dooming her child to death or, worse, to life as a quadriplegic? Pepe would never forgive her for doing that to him. Neither would Felix. Neither would her mother-in-law. In other words, Ginny needed a slow-speed crash, not a fast one.

Hoping to see a possible crash site—an appropriate crash site—Ginny wanted to stay on surface streets and at surface street speeds for as long as possible. She saw the street signs and knew the intersection with I-10 was coming up, but she didn't want to take it. She stayed in the middle lane.

"The freeway is coming up," he told her. "You need to get over."

If he was from out of town—his license plates had said California—he probably wasn't up on the latest news concerning highway construction projects around Tucson. At least she hoped he wasn't.

"I was planning on getting on I-19 at Ajo Way," she told him. "There's all kinds of construction on I-10 right now. That intersection might not even be open."

"I said get on the freeway," he insisted. "Do it now."

They were driving past the yard-shed sales lot. Reluctantly complying, Ginny glanced in the mirror. Just then she saw a car in the opposite lane, a vehicle that looked like a Pima County sheriff's car, jam on its brakes and jerk into a sudden U-turn. There were no flashing lights, no sirens, but as soon as Ginny caught sight of the brake lights, a spark of hope bloomed in her heart. Maybe someone was coming to help them after all.

While that was happening, though, she very nearly missed the merge onto the freeway.

"Get over," the gunman ordered again, shouting at her. "You're going the way I tell you. Understand?"

He sounded angry, but he was looking at her—staring at her. He wasn't looking in the mirror. Ginny swung the car into a hasty right-hand turn. They were going fast enough that the Accord almost didn't make it. Tires skidded on the pavement. The rear end of the car washed sickeningly from side to side. It was all Ginny could do to get it back under control and onto the entrance ramp.

"You stupid bitch!" he yelled at her. "You almost took us out just then. What the hell were you thinking?"

Jarred by the abrupt turn, Pepe awakened with a start and immediately began crying. Ginny ignored him and forced herself to look straight ahead. She wanted to know if the cop car was behind her, but she couldn't risk staring in the mirror. The guy might read a telltale expression on her face and would know that help was coming. The only thing Ginny could hope for now was that between the two of them—Ginny and this unknown police officer—they could find some way to surprise the gunman and take him down.

"Can't you go any faster than this?" he shouted now. "If you merge at twenty-five, some eighteen-wheeler doing eighty is going to run right over us."

Ginny didn't want to, but she stepped on the gas. He was right. Traffic on the interstate was moving right along. If she wasn't careful, they would be run down before they made the merge.

Ginny dared a quick glance in the rearview mirror. To her immense relief she saw what appeared to be an unmarked cop car turn onto the entrance ramp and come racing up behind them. The lights still didn't come on. He didn't signal her to pull over, but he stayed right there, a few feet off her rear bumper. Unfortunately, by then she had brought the Accord up to highway speed and made the merge. She had also passed the last of the light pole masts for the intersection. That meant that she had also driven past her last chance of making a partially controlled, low-speed crash.

"Mommy, Mommy," Pepe howled at her from the backseat. "Mommy, Mommy, Mommy!"

Every time he called to her it was like a stone through Ginny's heart. Her little boy needed her comforting presence and assurance, but she couldn't afford to look at him. She didn't dare. And she couldn't tell him she loved him, either. All she could do was hope she could find a place to wreck the car without killing both of them.

Moments later—at least it seemed like moments to her—she saw the first exit signs for southbound I-19. She knew as soon as she saw them that the exit ramp itself would be her last opportunity to do what had to be done. Once they started up and over the overpass and onto the other freeway, she would immediately resume highway speed. If she was going to do this, she had to do it now—before the overpass, not after it.

When she switched on her turn signal, she could see the gunman nodding in agreement.

"Good," he said aloud. "I guess you finally wised up."

Tucson, Arizona
Sunday, June 7, 2009, 1:54 P.M.
88° Fahrenheit

Brian was driving like hell and trying to get through to Dispatch at the same time. Before he made any kind of move, he wanted to have backup units in place. To do that and because they were still inside the city limits, he needed to coordinate with Tucson PD.

"And tell them no lights or sirens," he rasped into the radio as he charged up behind the fleeing Honda on the I-10 entrance ramp. "I'm pretty sure the driver knows I'm here, but the bad guy doesn't. I want to keep it that way."

"Do you know where they're headed?"

"All I know right now is they're westbound on I-10."

"Which means they won't be able to exit again until Prince Road," the Dispatch operator said. "Do you want us to have someone lay down tire strips?"

"Negative on that," Brian said. "Too risky. There's a baby in the backseat."

But then, as if to show the Dispatch operator how wrong she was, the Accord's turn signal came on again, blinking the notice that the vehicle was exiting after all, moving onto the exit ramp that led to I-19—the only exit ramp through the downtown area of Tucson that hadn't been shut down for construction.

"Suspect vehicle is exiting onto I-19," Brian shouted as he started for the exit ramp as well. "Tucson PD units are approaching."

He was relieved that someone had given the word about making a stealth approach. At least three marked patrol cars were coming up fast in the right-hand lane behind him. As he had requested, there were no lights and no sirens.

"Tell Tucson PD that we'll try to hem them in and bring the vehicle to a stop that way."

"Roger that," the operator said.

Then, just when Brian dared hope there might be a

good end to all this, the Honda suddenly careened off the road. It slammed into a guardrail partway up the exit ramp and then spun a full three-sixty before staggering through another guardrail and down the incline into westbound traffic.

All Brian could do was stand on his brake and try to avoid the flying wreckage that spun skyward in a whirlwind of chunks of metal and glass along with a storm of highway grit and dust. In the instant the car flew past him, he could see that the air bags had deployed, but that was all he could see.

From that moment on, things seemed to happen in slow motion. Before the Accord stopped moving, coming to rest halfway in the freeway's right-hand lane and facing the wrong way, Brian had stopped his Crown Victoria in the middle of the on-ramp, slammed it into park, yanked on the hazard lights, and erupted out of the vehicle. He vaulted over the remains of the shattered guardrail and slid down the steep shoulder, drawing his weapon as he went. Behind him he heard a cacophony of sirens as the Tucson PD units hit their lights and sirens.

He saw a woman scramble out of the driver's side of the Honda. "Get down," he shouted at her. "On the ground."

If she heard him, she ignored him. Rather than getting down, she stood there for several seconds, struggling to open the Accord's back door. When it wouldn't cooperate, she simply threw herself through what Brian realized must have been a broken rear window. And he knew, then, too, what she was doing: Virginia Torres was going after her baby.

Then, also in slow motion and moving as if in a daze, a man clambered out of the passenger side of the wrecked vehicle. Brian saw the figure first and then the telling details—the sling, the gun. Brian's first thought was that he would try to grab the woman or the baby and use them as human shields. That may have been what he had in mind, but for some reason the rear door wouldn't open and the window on that side hadn't shattered.

"On the ground!" Brian shouted again. "Drop your weapon."

Jonathan Southard looked up. Brian recognized the man's bloodied face from the driver's license photo. He seemed surprised to see Brian standing there, but he didn't get on the ground and he didn't drop his weapon. Just then the first Tucson PD officer arrived on the scene as well. He, too, had his weapon drawn.

"Drop your weapon." The arriving officer issued the same orders Brian had given. "Get on the ground."

Jonathan Southard did neither. He stood stock-still for a moment, as if assessing the situation and his opposition. Then, without checking for traffic, he turned and sprinted into the speeding freeway traffic.

Brian Fellows made as if to follow, but then he saw the woman again. She had managed to wrestle the child out of the vehicle. Now she stood there holding the baby and frozen in place, staring in horror back at the freeway.

Brian heard the bellowing horn of an approaching semi. He knew as soon as he heard it that it was coming too fast. He heard the thump of engaging air brakes and smelled the smoke from scorching tires. The woman was terrified and too dumbstruck to move. Brian wasn't. He leaped forward, grabbed the woman's arm and propelled her up the bank to safety. Then something smashed into him from behind. After that he knew nothing.

Tucson, Arizona
Sunday, June 7, 2009, 2:10 P.M.
89° Fahrenheit

Kath Fellows left the store parking lot and went home. She unloaded the car, put away her groceries, and waited for Brian to call. She didn't want to call him. If he was involved in some sort of emergency situation, the last thing he needed was the distraction of a ringing telephone. First ten minutes went by without any word. Then twenty. Then thirty. With each passing minute she grew more and more anxious. She was sure something was wrong—terribly wrong.

Finally, unable to wait any longer, she put in a call to Brian's office. She managed to bluff her way through to an emergency operator, but what she was told didn't help. "Sorry, Ms. Fellows. It's a chaotic scene right now. There are injuries. We don't know who or how bad."

As soon as Kath heard those words, she knew that she had to go see for herself. She didn't want Amy and Annie to know how worried she was, but she didn't want to take them with her, either. She called their elderly neighbor, Mrs. Harper, and asked for help.

"Of course," Estelle said. "Just let me turn off the ball game. I'll be right there."

Kath was standing by the front door with her purse in one hand and the car keys in the other when Estelle rang the doorbell.

"Okay," she announced as she let the woman into the house. "I'm going out for a while, girls," she called over her shoulder. "You listen to Mrs. Harper and do whatever she says."

"Where are you going?" Amy asked.

"Out," Kath answered.

"Why can't we come with you?"

"Because," she said, then she fled out the door and down the steps.

She drove toward the spot where she'd last heard from Brian—I-10 and Kino. She was half a mile from the intersection when she ran into stopped traffic. She still had a rooftop emergency bubble light in her glove box, one she'd never quite gotten around to taking out of the Odyssey. She retrieved the light, plugged it in, and slapped it on top of her vehicle. Then she threaded her way through the traffic jam until she reached a cop who was directing people away from the freeway.

"Freeway's closed, ma'am," the officer said when she reached him. "You'll have to go around."

She reached into her purse and pulled out her Border Patrol ID. "I'm off duty," she said. "They called in all available units."

The officer barely looked at her ID. He simply stepped aside, motioned Kath onto the on-ramp, and then stopped the car directly behind her.

As soon as she turned onto the ramp, she could see the jumble of traffic ahead of her. There were a good hundred cars or so, stopped here and there, parked at odd angles. Some of them had stopped so suddenly that they had rear-ended the vehicle ahead of them, which meant that there were several fender benders, but at the head of that field of broken and battered automobiles Kath could see a mass of wreckage. At first what she was seeing didn't make sense. As she inched her way closer, however, she realized that the debris field came from an overturned eighteen-wheeler that had spilled a massive load of construction materials in all directions.

All right, then, Kath thought. *Brian's up there, helping deal with this horrendous wreck. No wonder he couldn't call me.*

When Kath could drive no farther, she stowed the bubble light, left her car parked crookedly on the shoulder, and walked. She could see that the accident had started somewhere just after the I-19 exit ramp. And sure enough, there was Brian's car—the only one in the collection of cop cars that didn't have a red flashing lightbar. If Brian's car was here, that meant he was here somewhere, too.

Kath pulled her phone out of her purse and punched the green button that automatically called the last number dialed. Unfortunately, that turned out to be Mrs. Harper's number. She ended that call when Estelle Harper's answering machine came on. Then Kath scrolled through to the next number and dialed that.

The phone rang and rang. It rang six times. Just when Kath expected the call to switch over to voice mail, somebody answered—somebody who wasn't Brian.

"Hello?"

The voice belonged to a woman. It sounded tentative and uncertain. Kath tried to be all business.

"Who are you?" she demanded. "I'm looking for my husband. What are you doing with his phone?"

"I don't know," the woman said. "I heard the phone ringing. It was right here next to my car. I thought I should answer it."

"What car?"

"I'm in a Chevrolet Lumina," the woman said. "It's blue. We're stuck on this side of the truck. Thank God Bobby didn't hit it—the truck, I mean. It was so close I'm still shaking like a leaf."

By then Kath was shaking, too. She spotted the Lumina. Going up to the window, she flashed her ID and took possession of Brian's phone. The front of the phone was shattered. The battery cover was missing completely, although the battery was still in place. It was a miracle that the phone worked at all.

Determinedly Kath picked her way forward through the debris field. The broken semi had disgorged hundreds of rolls of roofing and hundreds of packets of shingles. Those were scattered in every direction. When Kath came around the front end of the disabled eighteen-wheeler, two more cops—DPS officers this time—barred her way.

"Sorry, lady," one of them said. "You'll have to go back."

"That's my husband's car over there," she said, pointing at the unmarked patrol car sitting undamaged on the shoulder of the road, with its hazard lights still blinking. "He's a Pima County homicide detective," she added. "He was chasing a killer with his arm in a sling."

"The guy with his arm in the sling jumped out of the wreckage and ran into traffic," one of the officers replied. "He got nailed by a car going eastbound. He's already been transported in an ambulance."

"Under guard?" Kath asked.

"Yes, under guard."

She peered around at the remaining slew of cop cars, fire trucks, and ambulances, and at a group of EMTs frantically working on somebody who had yet to be transported.

"Anybody else hurt?" she asked.

At first neither of the cops replied, but the look they exchanged spoke volumes. As Kath started forward again, one of them reached out to stop her.

"Really, ma'am," he said. "You probably shouldn't go there right now . . ." he began.

Kath shook off his hand. "Either arrest me or let me go," she told him.

He let her go. She reached the clutch of EMTs just in time to see a bloodied human form on a backboard being lifted onto a gurney and then into a waiting ambulance. There was nothing about the battered face or hands that she recognized, but she knew the shoes. Or rather, she knew the one shoe that had survived the impact and had stayed on Brian's right foot. Her husband was no clotheshorse, but shoes, more specifically ECCO, were his one personal extravagance.

As Kath approached, one of the ambulance attendants tried to muscle her aside. She pushed right back.

"That's my husband," she told him determinedly. "Wherever he's going, I'm going."

Nodding his reluctant assent, the EMT handed her up into the back of the ambulance. Then he stepped in himself, closed the door, and called, "We're in."

With a squawk of the siren and a lurch of tires, the ambulance sped off.

Tucson, Arizona
Sunday, June 7, 2009, 4:00 P.M.
93° Fahrenheit

By the time Brandon and Diana neared their home in Gates Pass, Brandon could see that his wife was running on empty. He had suggested they stop in Casa Grande and get something to eat. She had opted for coming straight home. The whole time they'd been in the car she'd been quiet again, quiet and brooding. Since she sure as hell wasn't talking with him, Brandon couldn't help wondering if one of those other haunting entities was once again communicating with her.

Pulling into the driveway, Brandon was startled to see a Border Patrol vehicle, a Ford Expedition, parked on the far side of the gate, blocking the way. He was sure the gate at the end of the driveway had been closed when they left the house. No one should have been able to drive inside and park.

"What the hell?" Brandon muttered under his breath. "What's all this? Wait here," he said to Diana. "I'll go check it out."

Leaving the engine and AC running, Brandon stepped

out of the CRV. What had once been a single backyard area had been carved into two separate yards in order to surround the lap pool with a kid-proof fence. Looking over the top of it, Brandon was dismayed to see a young man, a total stranger, splashing around in the pool. A little girl was with him. He would lift her out of the water and then splash her into it, while she alternately shrieked and giggled. Off under the gazebo lay two very wet dogs—Damsel and a huge German shepherd. The dog was a complete stranger, too, as far as Brandon was concerned, but Damsel seemed entirely at home with this arrangement.

The German shepherd caught sight of Brandon at the same moment Brandon saw the dog. He bounded up and came racing toward the gate, barking fiercely and sounding as though he was fully prepared to tear Brandon Walker limb from limb.

"Bozo!" the guy shouted. "No! Down!"

The dog immediately skidded to a stop and ducked down on his belly. He seemed to be under voice control, but Brandon Walker wasn't taking any chances. He stayed on his side of the gate and made no attempt to open it.

"Who the hell are you?" he demanded of the guy in the pool. "And what do you think you're doing in my backyard? This is private property. Now get the hell out."

"Sorry," the young man said, hefting the little girl onto his hip and making his way over to the steps. "You must be Mr. Walker. I'm Daniel Pardee. This is Angelina Enos. Your daughter is off doing some shopping. She thought she'd be back before you got home."

"Shopping?" Brandon shot back. "Sure she is. If there's one thing Lani hates, it's shopping. Now who the hell are you and what are you doing here?"

The dog—Bozo? Was his name really Bozo?—clearly took exception to Brandon's tone of voice. He leveled a withering look in Brandon's direction, a look accompanied by a low-throated growl and the baring of a set of very sharp teeth.

"Dr. Walker tried to call you to let you know that we were stopping by . . ." the man began.

"I was working," Brandon told him. "I forgot to turn my phone back on, but surely Lani understands we can't just have strangers dropping in and using our pool without any kind of supervision."

"She needed to do some power shopping," Daniel said. "She thought she'd be better off without having us along."

Diana walked up behind Brandon. "Who's that?" she asked. "What's going on?"

"Apparently our daughter invited some of her friends to stop by and go swimming in our absence," Brandon said sarcastically.

He was ripped, and he didn't mind sounding like it.

The little girl slithered off the young man's leg and went racing back toward the pool, scrambling over the dog in the process. The dog made no move to go after the child, but he still kept a wary eye on Brandon.

"I know your daughter wanted to explain all this to you," Daniel Pardee began. "I expected her back before now."

"Who's that adorable child?" Diana asked over Brandon's shoulder. "Where did she come from?"

Just then Lani's Passat came down the driveway. Glancing in the passenger-side window, Brandon could see that the entire vehicle was loaded with boxes. The guy with the kid had evidently been telling the truth about Lani being off on a shopping extravaganza.

"I tried to call," Lani began, rolling down her window. "I meant to be here by the time you got back."

Nonetheless, Brandon Walker was furious. It was one thing to have their own grandchildren splashing around in the pool, but to allow a total stranger to bring a child there when no one was home was just asking for trouble, to say nothing of a lawsuit.

Brandon walked over to his daughter's car. "What were you thinking? You have no business inviting people we don't know onto your mother's and my property. Family members are one thing—"

"Angie is family, Dad," Lani said quietly, stepping out of the car. "She's mine. Dan agreed to look after her while I went shopping."

Brandon stopped himself in mid-rant. Was it possible that Lani had had a baby her parents knew nothing about?

"What do you mean, she's yours?" he croaked.

"It happened this morning. Judge Lawrence issued a court order granting me temporary custody. The problem is, my apartment isn't exactly child-ready. That's what I was doing, buying what I'll need to furnish her room."

"I don't understand," Brandon said. "Why would you be given custody?"

"Her mother, Delphina Enos, was murdered last night," Lani explained. "Out on the reservation."

"But why—?"

"Delphina's maiden name was Escalante, Dad, from Nolic. I'm sure you remember them. She was my cousin. My birth cousin."

"But if her mother has been murdered, isn't there someone besides you who can take her?" Brandon asked. "Her grandparents, maybe, or else an aunt or uncle?"

"No," Lani said. "There's no one. No one wants to take her."

"Wait a minute," Brandon said as he finally managed to process what she'd been saying. "You mean those Escalantes? The same people who . . . ?"

Lani nodded. "Yes, the very same people who wouldn't take me back after the ant bites. This is evidently similar. Since Angie wasn't murdered along with her mother, her blood relatives have taken the position that she's now a dangerous object. They won't take her back. Angie's father is in jail. His parents don't want her, either."

For a long moment Brandon looked hard at his daughter and then at the little girl. Even now Angie was sitting on the edge of the pool, kicking happily with both feet and churning up a spray of water that splashed as far as Bozo who, Brandon noted, had not yet broken his master's down command.

Brandon glanced back at Dan Pardee. The interloper stood there still dripping and wearing a faded bathing suit, a Speedo Brandon was quite sure was one of Davy's cast-offs. The younger man was barefoot, but he stood poised on the balls of his feet. He seemed to be assessing the situation in the same way his dog was. He also looked more than capable of leaping to Lani's defense if that kind of protection seemed warranted.

Diana was the one who ended the uncomfortable stare-down between the two men. She walked past her husband as though he didn't exist. Opening the gate, she walked past Bozo as well, kicking off her sandals as she went. Rolling up her pant legs, she sank down on the pool edge next to the little girl, dropped her feet into the water, and began kicking, too.

"I'm sorry about not letting you know in advance," Lani continued, speaking to her father and motioning Dan to come join them. "This is Daniel Pardee, Dad. Dan. He's an officer with the Shadow Wolves unit of the Border Patrol. He's a friend of mine and of Angie's. Dan, this is my father, Brandon Walker."

Dan held out his hand. Brandon took it, mumbling a halfhearted "Glad to meet you" as he did so, but he wasn't really paying attention to the handshake. He was staring after his wife.

As she sat there, kicking her feet for all she was worth, there was an expression on her face that Brandon Walker hadn't seen in years. The smile he had once loved so much, the one that had gone dormant years ago, was back again. The ghosts were gone. Diana was vibrantly alive.

Between spasms of kicking, Diana beamed down at the little girl. "Hi," she said cheerfully. "My name's Diana. What's yours?"

"Angelina Enos," Angie said. "My mother calls me Angie."

"Good," Diana Ladd Walker said. "That's what I'll call you, too."

Brandon looked at his wife's shadowless face and then at his daughter's.

"Well," he said finally, shaking his head. "I guess I know when I'm licked. Come on, young man," he added, turning back to Dan. "How about if you and Lani and I go inside and rustle up some grub. You may not be starved, but I know I am."

Brandon led the way into the house. As he stepped inside, he handed Dan a beach towel from the stack of clean towels piled in a laundry basket parked just inside the patio door. He had no idea about who this half-naked young man was or what his relationship was to Angie or to Lani, but he was there. Lani evidently thought he was okay, so Brandon decided he could just as well follow suit.

"I'm glad you're here, Lani," he added, speaking to his daughter and glancing back outside at Diana, still sitting on the edge of the pool and splashing away. "Something's up with your mother. We need to talk."

**Tucson, Arizona
Sunday, June 7, 2009, 4:33 P.M.
94° Fahrenheit**

As far as first impressions go, Dan Pardee and Bozo were on the same page when it came to Brandon Walker. Dan could see that the man had a point—that he wouldn't be wild about having uninvited strangers making themselves at home on his property, but he could have been a little less confrontational about it.

Before stepping inside, Dan turned back to Bozo and

gave him the silent hand signal that released the dog from his earlier command. Without hesitating, Bozo made for the water, dived in, and swam from one end of the lap pool to the other. Bozo was entirely understandable. People? Not so much. Shaking his head and not sure what had just happened, Dan followed Dr. Walker and her father into the house.

Lani (she had told him to call her that, but Dan still thought of her as Dr. Walker) helped herself to sodas from the fridge, keeping one for herself and passing another on to Dan while her father set about taking a selection of foodstuffs out of the pantry and refrigerator and setting them on the counter.

"Enchiladas?" he asked.

Lani nodded. "That sounds wonderful," she said.

"Now tell me about all this," he said.

So Lani did. While she and her father bustled around the kitchen, she explained about the four people who had been murdered near Komelik. She told Brandon about how Dan had discovered the crime scene and how he had rescued the child from there—finding Angie, bringing her to the hospital, and then staying with her while they waited for Angie's relatives to come collect her, relatives who had no intention of doing so.

There was a lot about this conversation that didn't make much sense to Dan Pardee. Lani had told Dan and Angie earlier about being bitten by ants as a child, but he couldn't understand how that had made her unacceptable to her birth family. And he found it hard to believe that Delphina Enos could have been Lani's cousin without Lani's having any idea about her existence. It was also interesting to see that Brandon Walker was far more understanding about having Angie Enos air-dropped into his family than he was about coming home and finding unauthorized strangers in his swimming pool. That was as contradictory as it was interesting.

Dan also enjoyed watching what he later thought of as the enchilada dance. Lani and her father worked and talked together—chopping, dicing, grating, and stirring—without having to ask any questions and without ever stepping in each other's way. The batch of enchiladas had just gone into the oven and they had taken seats with Dan at the kitchen table when Brandon Walker glanced in Dan's direction and then abruptly changed the subject.

"I need to tell you about your mother," he said to Lani. "I know I should have talked to you and Davy about this before, but I couldn't bring myself to do it. She's been seeing people, Lani, and carrying on conversations with people who aren't there."

"Like Andrew Carlisle?" Lani asked.

Once again, Dan was listening to a conversation—a private but clearly important conversation, but one with big pieces missing. Who the hell was Andrew Carlisle?

"How do you know about that?" Brandon asked. "Did she tell you?"

Lani shook her head. "Gabe Ortiz did."

Once again Dan was left out of the loop. *Who's Gabe?* he wondered, while Brandon shook his head in apparent dismay.

"How did Gabe know?" Brandon asked.

Lani shrugged. "He's a spooky little kid," she replied.

"He sometimes knows things people don't expect him to know. But who all are we talking about here besides Andrew Carlisle?"

"Mitch Johnson, her father, her first husband," Brandon said. "All the bad guys who made Diana's life a living hell. She didn't mention any of this to me or to anyone else because she's scared to death that she's drifting into some kind of dementia—or maybe even Alzheimer's."

To Dan's surprise, Lani greeted that dire news with what appeared to be a relieved smile. "It's not Alzheimer's." She made the declaration with absolute confidence.

"It's not?" her father asked.

"Mom's hallucinating," Lani said. "For some people hallucinations come along in a much happier context—pink ponies, purple whales, whatever. Mom has lived through some pretty dark times, so it's not surprising that her hallucinations are darker, too."

"If it's not Alzheimer's or dementia, what's causing it?" Brandon asked.

"My first guess would be her medications. What is she taking?"

"I'm not sure. I know she's had trouble sleeping at times. She takes some over-the-counter meds and vitamin supplements. Why?"

"We need to gather up everything she takes, prescription and nonprescription, and get those bottles to a pharmacy. I'm guessing this is some kind of drug interaction."

"That's all it is?" Brandon asked.

"It could be all it is," Lani corrected. "We need to be sure, but if I were a betting woman, I'd be willing to put money on it."

The relief on Brandon Walker's face was apparent. "I'll do that," he said. "I'll gather up all the bottles and take them to the pharmacy first thing tomorrow morning."

The timer went off, announcing it was time to take the enchiladas out of the oven. Brandon had stood up and was reaching for an oven mitt when the phone rang. A moment or two after he answered, he nodded gravely.

"Thanks for calling, Kath. I'm so sorry to hear this. We'll be right there."

He took the baking tray of enchiladas out of the oven and set them on the counter, then turned to his daughter. "We've gotta go," he said.

"Why?" Lani asked. "What's wrong?"

"It's Brian," he said. "He's been in an accident. They've taken him to the trauma center at TMC."

And that's how Dan Pardee began to learn about the extent of the close connections between Detective Brian Fellows's family and Lani Walker's. That was also how it came to be that his day ended as it began, with him waiting patiently in hospitals sixty miles apart, worrying about people he barely knew and watching their looming tragedies unfold around him.

Dan went to the hospital because they asked him to go there with them. He helped out because he could help out—because that was the way his grandfather had raised him.

Ohb or not, that was who he was.

15

INITIALLY BRIAN WAS aware of living in a strange half-world that wasn't really waking and wasn't really sleeping. Sometimes he did sleep. Many of the people who appeared in his dreams were dead—Fat Crack Ortiz; his half brothers, Tommy and Quentin; his mother, Janie.

Kath was there, of course, sometimes in his dreams and sometimes standing next to him. Whenever he saw her, the expression on her face was strained. There were dark circles under her eyes, as if she hadn't slept well for a long time. He worried that she was doing too much and was too tired. Sometimes the girls were there. His girls. Amy and Annie. They looked sad, too. When they kissed him hello and good-bye, their lips barely touched his skin—as if they were afraid he might break. As if they were shy about being around the IV tree and the tubes.

He was aware that he was in casts. At least that's how it seemed. On his arms and both legs. The bed made funny noises and seemed to move under him, as if it were breathing or something. He wasn't sure what that was all about. And for some reason he couldn't ask. Couldn't talk. Other people did all the talking. And there were lots of them, although they generally showed up only one or two at a time, and they mostly talked to each other, not to him.

Initially he was aware of seeing people from work occasionally—his old partner Hector Segura came by several times. Brian and PeeWee had worked well together, but Sheriff Forsythe had seen fit to split them up. And, speaking of the devil, William Forsythe himself appeared at Brian's bedside a time or two. He never stayed long, but he'd be able to say he'd stopped by to check on his injured officer. That might be good for a few votes in the next election.

Oddly enough, some of Brian's visitors were total strangers. For example, who was that old Mexican woman who was there time and again, always with a black-beaded rosary in her pocket? She would tell him hello in Spanish and then sit there for hours on end, saying her Hail Marys. Sometimes a little boy came along with her. When he was there, the kid jabbered a blue streak and there was no time for "Holy Mary, Mother of God." Other times a young woman came with her and sometimes a young man, too. Brian gradually sorted out that the old woman was the little boy's grandmother. He couldn't tell if the woman was her daughter or if the man was her son.

The old Indian guy who came by from time to time was Thomas Rios from Komelik, but what about the guy who sometimes showed up in a Border Patrol uniform? He seemed familiar. Brian thought he might have seen him somewhere before, but he was there a lot of the time, too, although he didn't seem to have much to say one way or the other.

The Walkers came, Brandon and Diana. Diana seemed distracted, but she had always seemed distant to Brian. His connection had been with Brandon, who was there in the room more than anyone, including Kath. He sat there day after day, dozing or reading in a chair. Brian liked having him around. They didn't talk; they didn't have to. The older man's silent, watchful presence made Brian feel safe somehow—as though whatever was happening was going to be all right. Okay. That was the way it had been when Brian was little and the way it was now.

And Davy came, his good buddy Davy. He did talk. He talked about losing his son and his wife. Candace had divorced him and had moved back home to Chicago. Davy was angry and bitter about that. Of course, anyone who knew them had seen that coming a long time ago, almost from the very beginning. They were too different. Opposites may attract, and that might be good for dating, but not for marriage. In marriage, opposites can pull you apart. Brian wished he could say something to comfort his old friend, but he couldn't. All he could do was listen and give Davy a chance to talk—to vent. If nothing else, in his current condition Brian Fellows was an excellent listener.

Lani came by, too, sometimes accompanied by Fat Crack's grandson, Gabe, but always with a live-wire little girl named Angie. Brian couldn't imagine how that had happened or when. Had Lani—his little Lani, the girl he and Davy had loved to tease and torment—grown up and gotten married while he was lying here in this noisy bed? Or had he been to her wedding some time in the past and forgotten all about it? If so, whom had she married and when? It must have happened long enough ago for her to have a baby who was now this little girl. Clearly Angie resembled her mother.

Tucson, Arizona
June to November 2009

For Brandon Walker, that summer stretched into months of interchangeable days. With the exception of the one day off he took to go serve as a pallbearer at Geet Farrell's funeral, Brandon was at the hospital every single day. He got up early; he went to the hospital; he spent the day there; he came home late.

Kath was there every day, too, but not all day long. She couldn't. After a month or so, she'd had to go back to work. She had the girls to look after and a house to take care of, but Brandon knew enough about hospitals to know that Brian needed an advocate in the room not only to run interference with the medical people but also to let Kath know what was going on when she wasn't there.

After months of worrying about Diana, Brandon could spend his worrying capital on someone else. Lani had been right. What had ailed Diana all along had been drug interactions rather than something far more serious. Now that her meds had been adjusted, she was back to being her old self. Not quite her old self. She had handed the book rewrite over to a ghostwriter without so much as a backward glance. She would be going on one last book tour next spring, but after that she was retired.

Her pottery studio now took precedence over her computer. Between making pots and spoiling her new granddaughter—her accidental granddaughter, as she liked to call Angie—Diana Ladd Walker was busy and happy.

As the days moved into weeks and there was no visible change in Brian's condition, Brandon began to lose hope. He prayed about it. He meditated about it. All he knew for certain was that he didn't want to lose this man who had come to be so dear to him—his accidental son, he thought, mimicking Diana's term for Angie—but it was seeming more and more likely.

One day, when Lani came to visit, little Gabe Ortiz came along with her. He stood for a long time by Brian's bed. When he walked away, he stopped by Brandon's chair and touched him on the shoulder.

"Don't worry, Mr. Walker," the boy said gravely. "He's going to be okay."

"How do you know that?" Brandon asked.

Gabe shrugged. "I don't know," he said. "I just know."

Having heard the news from Fat Crack's grandson, the old medicine man's heir apparent, Brandon Walker began to believe it, too, maybe because he wanted to believe it.

Brian Fellows would be all right. I'itoi would see to it. It was just a matter of time.

Tucson, Arizona
Friday, November 27, 2009, 4:30 P.M.
82° Fahrenheit

Gradually the haze began to lift a little. There was less distance between Brian and what was going on around him. He was aware that he had been moved from what had been a hospital room to some other facility—to a rehab kind of place. He still had the same cast of regular visitors, but the focus here was different. There was a lot more emphasis on physical therapy.

And one day, late one afternoon, he simply woke up—as if from a long winter's nap. Why those words came to mind, Brian couldn't imagine.

From the way the sun was slanting in the window, he could tell it was late afternoon. Kath wasn't there. Brandon Walker was.

"Hey," Brian said. "How's it going?"

Brandon started so abruptly that he almost fell out of the chair. "Hello," he said as a slow grin crossed his face. "Another station heard from."

"Where's Kath?" Brian asked. Just saying that much made his throat hurt. His voice sounded odd—as if he hadn't used it for a very long time.

"She's at work," Brandon said, reaching for his phone. "I'll call her and let her know."

"So it must be Tuesday then," Brian said. "She usually has Mondays off."

"It's not Tuesday, Brian," Brandon said.

"What day is it then?" Brian asked. "How long have I been out of it?"

"Since the first week in June," Brandon Walker told him. "It's almost the end of November. Friday. The day after Thanksgiving."

"Thanksgiving? How can that be? How come it isn't June? What happened?"

"Don't you remember?"

Brian shook his head. "I don't remember anything. It's a blank."

"You were chasing a bad guy who took off on foot on I-10."

"Did I catch him?"

"Oncoming traffic is what caught him," Brandon said. "It turns out it caught you, too. There was a young woman there with her little boy. She had been taken hostage and you helped her escape. She had managed to get the kid out of the car, but a truck was coming. They both would have been killed if you hadn't shoved them out of the way. You saved them both."

While Brian tried to get his head around that difficult concept, Brandon was already punching numbers into his cell phone. "You're not going to believe it, Kath," he said. "You've got to get down here right away. Brian's awake! He's awake and talking."

On the table next to his bed sat a small vase, a reddish-brown clay vase with a high-gloss glaze finish. In it was a single apricot-colored rose. Brian pointed at it and asked, "Where did that come from?"

"The rose came from our backyard, but Diana made the vase," Brandon said. "She wanted you to have it."

Brian shook his head in wonder. "I didn't know she made pots."

"Neither did I," Brandon agreed. "I don't think anyone knew that about her, but she does now. And if you ask me, she's pretty damned good at it."

Tucson, Arizona
Saturday, December 5, 2009, 3:00 P.M.
68° Fahrenheit

Lani Walker and Dan Pardee got married the first Saturday in December in a small ceremony in her parents' house. The wedding was supposed to happen outside in the early afternoon. Naturally it rained—like crazy. The chill winter rainstorm would be good for flowers the following spring, but not so good for wedding guests.

Attending the wedding was Brian's first outing. They gave him a furlough from the rehab center, but only for a few hours.

There weren't that many people there. Still, Brian had a tough time sorting through them.

Most of the guests were family members and people Brian already knew, such as a family named Torres—including the young mother and son Brian had saved. There were several strangers as well, including Micah Duarte, the groom's grandfather. He was Indian—Apache—and uncomfortable in all the uproar. Brian's heart went out to the man. The only time he seemed at ease was when he was chatting with little Gabe Ortiz.

The other total stranger was an Anglo man who also seemed to have some connection to the groom.

During the reception, the man sat down on the couch near where Brian's wheelchair was parked. "I understand you're a real hero," he said by way of introduction, holding out his hand. "I'm David Blaine. Retired LAPD."

"You're related to the groom?" Brian asked.

Blaine shook his head and smiled. "Not really," he said. "At least I wasn't originally, but I guess I am now. When Lani and Dan used the Internet to track me down in Palm Desert and invited me to come to the wedding, you could have knocked me over with a feather."

Brian was struggling to connect the dots when Blaine explained. "I was the investigating officer years ago when Dan's mother was murdered. I didn't do that much, but I'm the one who carried him out of that terrible place. He couldn't have been more than four years old. I'm surprised he remembered."

Brian glanced wonderingly in Dan Pardee's direction. His mother had been murdered? Why was it Brian knew nothing about any of that, nothing at all?

"Who knows?" Blaine continued. "Maybe the same thing will happen to you someday. You'll get a call to come to the wedding of that little kid over there." He nodded in Pepe Torres's direction. "He may forget, but I can promise you his mother and his grandmother never will."

Tucson, Arizona
Saturday, December 5, 2009, 10:00 P.M.
61° Fahrenheit

Brandon shivered as he held the door open for Damsel to come back in one last time. The guests were gone. The caterer was gone. He and Diana and Damsel finally had the place to themselves.

He, for one, was glad the wedding was over. Brandon had been happy to see all those people, but he had been even happier to see them all go home. As far as he was concerned, the high point of the day had come about when Angie, the flower girl, had escaped Diana's clutches and raced to the bride and groom. She had grabbed on to Dan's tuxedo-clad leg and resisted all efforts to pry her away. Finally Dan had relented. He had picked her up and held her on his hip for the duration of the ceremony.

Before letting the dog out, Brandon had stripped off his father-of-the-bride jacket, dress shoes, and tie. *Thank God I don't have to wear those anymore,* he thought.

Damsel came in and shook, showering him with cold spatters of water. Outside it was still raining.

Going back through the house, Brandon was surprised to find Diana sitting on the couch in the living room.

The only light in the room was from a single lamp on an end table next to where she sat holding a basket. At first Brandon thought it was one of Rita Antone's, but when he came closer, he realized it was a burden basket he had never seen before.

"Hello," he said. "I thought you'd already gone to bed. And what's that? I thought you weren't going to collect any more baskets."

"I wasn't," she said. "It was a gift from Micah Duarte."

"I couldn't help liking that guy," Brandon said. "He reminded me of Fat Crack, only not nearly as wide."

Nodding, Diana passed the basket to her husband.

"Micah told me this originally belonged to his wife's grandmother," Diana explained. "He said he had heard about my basket collection from Lani and Dan. He thought it might be a good idea for me to look after it, either to pass along to Dan when he's finally able to appreciate it or else to give it to Angie."

Brandon examined the basket. It was old and frayed. In one spot some of the stitching had come undone.

"This doesn't look like it's made of bear grass," he said.

Diana nodded. "It isn't. The Apaches usually used willow and yucca. If you look closely you'll see there's even some yucca root."

"So it's valuable, then?" he asked.

Diana glanced around the room at all the other baskets—at Nana *Dahd*'s baskets. "They're all valuable," she said. "And that has nothing to do with money."

"She'd have a fit, you know." Brandon chuckled as he gave the burden basket back.

"Who would have a fit?"

"Rita Antone," he said. "The idea of having an *ohb* basket in here with all of hers."

"No," Diana said. After a moment's pause, she smiled. "I don't think Rita would mind one bit. Come on, old man. Let's go to bed."

Tucson, Arizona
January to June 2010

Lani and Dan had agreed from the outset that they'd live part of the time in her hospital-compound housing unit and part time at Dan's place in Tucson. Lani assured Dan that this was historically correct, since the Tohono O'odham had always been known as the people with two houses—one in the mountains to use in the hot summer months, and one in the low desert for the winter.

What staying in Tucson overnight on Lani's days off really meant was that she could spend more time with her folks without having to drive sixty miles one way. It also meant that Angie was able to spend more time with her new grandmother. Angie had taken to calling Lani's mother Nana. That was close enough to Nana *Dahd,* and it made Lani smile every time she heard it. Diana spent hours patiently teaching Angie about clay and how to form it. When Diana and Angie weren't closeted in Diana's studio, they were out on the patio carrying on long conversations they both seemed to find mutually delightful.

"Why does Nana call me Lani sometimes?" Angie asked her mother one day.

"I'm sure it's because you remind her of me when I was your age," Lani answered with a laugh. "You don't need to worry as long as she doesn't start calling you Damsel."

Lani had taken to calling her foster daughter—her soon-to-be-adopted daughter—Kskehegaj, Pretty One, because she was pretty. She was also spoiled rotten. Diana and Dan seemed to be in a contest to see who could spoil her more.

It was clear to Lani that when it came to getting her own way, Angelina Enos had Dan's number—in spades.

Tohono O'odham Nation, Arizona
Saturday, June 26, 2010, 5:00 P.M.
101° Fahrenheit

On the last Saturday in June, Dan and Lani packed a picnic supper and then, with both Bozo and Angie in the back of Lani's Passat, they set off to run a series of late-afternoon errands. First they stopped by the deserted village called Rattlesnake Skull, where they lit a candle for Rita Antone's granddaughter, Gina Antone. Over the months, Dan had heard all these stories and had finally learned how the Walkers' lives intersected with the Desert People. He had learned about Fat Crack and Nana *Dahd* and about how Lani had been abandoned by her family after almost dying of ant bites.

"Who's she?" Angie wanted to know when Lani mentioned Gina's name. She, too, had heard the stories time and again, but she loved having them repeated.

"A Tohono O'odham girl who died a long time ago," Lani explained. "We're lighting a candle for her today so she's not forgotten."

Months earlier, Lani had told Dan the story of Betraying Woman and her *ohb* lover. After she had told it to him for the first time, he noticed an odd expression on Lani's face.

"What's wrong?" he asked.

"I'm not sure," she replied with a frown. "Up until now I always believed what people said about Betraying Woman—that she had betrayed her people to the Apaches. But maybe that's not true. Maybe she really loved her young *ohb* warrior and maybe the Desert People were wrong to cast her out, shutting her away in a cave on Ioligam and leaving her to die."

"Stranger things than that have happened," Dan Pardee told her with a grin. "Look at the two of us."

After leaving the ruins of Rattlesnake Skull village in the hot late-afternoon sun, they went on to Ban Thak, Coyote Sitting. There, in the village's tumbledown cemetery, they lit another candle, this one for Rita Antone.

"Your godmother," Angie said.

"Yes," Lani agreed. "Nana *Dahd*. And now we'll light one for Fat Crack."

After that they drove to Komelik—to the place outside Komelik—the place where Angie's mother had died a year earlier. Dan and Lani had talked it over for days in advance. Lani had worried that bringing Angie there might be too traumatic for the little girl, but she didn't seem upset by it—more curious than upset.

"And now we're going to light the other candles for my mommy?" Angie asked.

Lani and Dan were always careful to maintain that Delphina Enos was Angie's biological mother, her real mother. The velvet-covered box containing the engagement ring Donald Rios had bought for Delphina had been in among the crime-scene wreckage along the freeway. That, along with the baptismal photo of Angie and her mother, were two treasures Dan and Lani Pardee were saving for their daughter.

"We have four candles left," Lani told Angie now. "We'll light one for your mother, one for Donald Rios, and one each for Mr. and Mrs. Tennant, the two Milghan people who died here."

"Can I light them?" Angie asked.

Lani nodded. "But only if you're very careful."

As Dan watched Lani and Angie set out candles and place rock barriers around them, he couldn't help thinking about how many lives had been impacted by what had happened here a year ago. *Was it only a year?*

When Dan had stumbled onto that nighttime crime scene, he'd had no way of knowing that Angie and Lani were about to walk into his life.

That was the good part of the equation. The bad part of tracking down the killer had to do with Brian Fellows. He had almost died as a result of a brain injury suffered in the course of the chase. He had spent months in a coma, and once he'd come out of that, he'd had to learn to walk again. Now he was learning to read again, too, right along with his daughters. He'd also been medically retired from the sheriff's department, letting him be a stay-at-home dad while Kath continued to work for the Border Patrol.

As for the killer? Jonathan Southard had been injured in that car chase, too, but not nearly as seriously as Brian Fellows. On the advice of his attorney, he had accepted a plea agreement—life in prison with no chance of parole. He had taken that rather than risk going back to California to face a trial in the deaths of his wife and children, where, had he been convicted, he might well have risked receiving the death penalty.

When Bozo walked off into the desert, Dan followed him. He found the dog lying in the shady sand beneath an ironwood tree—the same tree that had a tangle of deer-horn cactus snaking up its trunk and onto the branches. Dan was surprised to see that the cactus was still covered with fat buds that had not yet opened.

Calling Bozo to follow, Dan returned to his wife and daughter. "I thought the night-blooming cereus would have blossomed by now."

Lani shook her head. "The people at Tohono Chul told me last week that they're running exceptionally late this year. The Queen of the Night may not bloom until early July. The woman in charge of the party said that she'll let me know as soon as possible so I can go there that night to tell the story."

"I love stories," Angie said, clapping her hands with childish enthusiasm. "Can Dan and I come, too?"

That's what she called him, Dan, not Daddy, but that was fine.

"Probably," Lani answered. "You and Dan are Brought-Back Children, just like Old White-Haired Woman's grandson."

"Don't go laying that idea on my grandfather," Dan cautioned Lani with a smile. "He may have white hair now, but if you try telling that old black belt that he's really Queen of the Night, Micah Duarte's liable to take offense."

Lani smiled back. "He could do a lot worse," she said. "Now let's go find a place for our picnic."

Here's a sneak preview of
J. A. Jance's new novel

BETRAYAL OF TRUST

Coming soon in hardcover from
William Morrow
An Imprint of HarperCollins*Publishers*

I WAS SITTING ON the window seat of our penthouse unit in Belltown Terrace when Mel came back from her run. Dripping with sweat, she nodded briefly on her way to the shower and left me in peace with my coffee cup and the on-line version of the *NYTimes* Crossword. Since it was Monday, I finished it within minutes and turned my attention to the spectacular Olympic Mountains view to the west.

It was June. After months of mostly gray days, summer had come early to Western Washington. Often the hot weather holds off until after drowning out the Fourth of July fireworks. Not this year. It was only mid-June, and the on-line weather report said it might get all the way to the mid-eighties by late afternoon.

People in other parts of the country might laugh at the idea of mid-eighties temperatures clocking in as a heat wave, but in Seattle where the humidity is high and AC units are few, a long June afternoon of sun can be sweltering, especially since the sun doesn't disappear from the sky until close to ten PM.

I remember those long miserable hot summer nights when I was a kid, when my mother—a single mother—and I lived in a second story, one bedroom apartment in a blue-collar Seattle neighborhood called Ballard. We didn't have AC and there was a bakery on the floor below us. Having a bakery and all those ovens running was great in the winter, but in the summer not so much. I would lie there on the couch in the living room, sleepless and miserable, hoping for a tiny breath of breeze to waft in through our lace curtains. It wasn't until I was in high school and earning my own money by working as an usher in a local theater that I managed to give my mom a pair of fans for Mother's Day—one for her and one for me. (At least I didn't give her a baseball glove.)

I refilled my coffee cup and poured one for Mel. She grew up as an army brat. Evidently the base housing hot water heaters were often less than optimal. As a result she takes some of the fastest showers known to man. She collected her coffee from the kitchen and was back in the living room before the coffee came close to reaching drinking temperature. Wearing a silky robe that left nothing to the imagination and with a towel wrapped around her wet hair, she curled up at the opposite end of the window seat and joined me in examining the busy shipping traffic criss-crossing Elliott Bay.

A grain ship was slowly pulling away from the massive terminal at the bottom of Queen Anne Hill. Two ferries, one going and one coming, made their lumbering way to and from Bremerton or Bainbridge Island. They were large ships, but from our perch twenty-two stories up, they seemed like tiny toy boats. Over near West Seattle a collection of barges was being assembled in advance of heading off to Alaska. Nearer at hand, a many-decked cruise ship had docked overnight spilling a myriad of shopping intent cruise enthusiasts into our Denny Regrade neighborhood.

"How was your run?" I asked.

"Hot and crowded," Mel said. "Myrtle Edwards Park was teeming with runners off the cruise ships. I don't like running in crowds. That's why I don't do marathons."

I had another reason for not doing marathons—two of them, actually—my knees. Mel runs. I walk or, as she says, I "saunter." Really, it's more limping than anything else. I finally broke down and had surgery to remove my heel spurs, but then my knees went south. It's hell getting old. I talked to Doctor Bliss, my GP, about the situation with my knees.

"Yes," he said, "you'll need knee replacement surgery eventually, but we're not there yet."

Obviously he was using the royal "we," because if it was his knee situation instead of mine, I'm sure "we'd" have had it done by now.

I glanced at my watch. "We need to leave in about twenty, if we're going to make it across the water before traffic stops up."

Since we were sitting looking out at an expanse of water, it would be easy to think that's "the water" I meant when I spoke to Mel, but it wasn't. In Seattle, however, that refers to several different bodies of water, depending on where you are and where you're going. In this case we were looking at Elliott Bay, which happens to be our "water view," but we worked on the other side of Lake Washington, in this instance, the "traffic" water in question. People who live on Lake Washington or on Lake Sammamish would have an entirely different take on the matter when they used the same two words. Context is everything.

"Okie dokie," Mel said, hopping off the window seat. "Another refill?" she asked.

I gave her my coffee mug. She took it, went to the kitchen, filled it, and came back. She handed me the cup and gave me a quick kiss in the process. "I started a new pot for our travelers," she said then added, "Back in flash."

I had showered and dressed while she was out, not that I needed to. There are two full baths as well as a powder room in our unit. When I married Mel, rather than share mine, she took over the guest bath and made it her own, complete with all the mysterious vials of makeup and moisturizers she deems necessary to keep herself presentable. I happen to think Mel is more than presentable without any of that stuff, but I've gathered enough wisdom over the years to realize that my opinion on some subjects is neither requested nor appreciated.

So we split the bathrooms. As long as we share the bed in my room, I don't have a problem with that. Occasionally I find myself wondering about my first marriage to Karen who is now deceased. Most of the time we were married, we had two bathrooms—one for us and one for the kids. Would our lives have been smoother if Karen and I had been able to have separate bathrooms as well?

No, wait. Denial is a wonderful thing, and I'm going to call myself on it. Despite my pretense to the contrary, the warfare that occurred in Karen's and my bathroom usually had nothing to do with the bathroom. Karen was a drama queen and I was a jerk, for starters. Yes, we did battle over changing the toilet paper rolls and leaving the toilet seat up and hanging panty hose on the shower curtain rod and leaving clots of toothpaste in the single sink, but those were merely symptoms of what was really wrong with our marriage—namely my drinking and my working too much. All the squabbling in our bathroom— the only real private place in the house—was generally about those underlying issues rather than the ones we claimed we were fighting about.

For years, Karen and I never showed up at the kitchen table for breakfast without having spent the better part of an hour railing at one another first. I'm sure those constant verbal battles were very hard on our kids, and I regret them to this day. But I have to tell you that the pleasant calmness that prevails in my life with Mel Soames is nothing short of a dream come true.

And we are married, by the way. Mel is my third wife. She didn't take my name, and I didn't take hers. As for the single day Anne Corley's and my marriage lasted? She didn't take my name, either, so I'm two for one in the wives-keeping-their-own-names department. Karen evidently didn't mind changing names at all—she took mine, and later, when she married Dave Livingston, her second husband, she took his name as well. So much for the high and low points of J. P. Beaumont's checkered romantic past.

When the coffee pot—an engineering marvel straight out of Starbucks—beeped quietly to let me know it was done, I went out to the kitchen and poured most of the pot into our two hefty stainless traveling mugs. This is Seattle. We don't go anywhere or do anything without sufficient amounts of coffee plugged into the system.

I was just tightening the lid on the second one, when Mel appeared in the doorway looking blonde and wonderful. Maybe the makeup did make a tiny bit of difference, but I can tell you she's a whole lot better looking than any other homicide cop I ever met.

On our commute, she drives. Fast. It's best for all concerned if I settle back in the passenger seat of my Mercedes S–550, drink my coffee, and do my best to refrain from back seat driving. One of these days Mel is going to get a hefty speeding ticket that she won't be able to talk her way out of. When that happens, I expect it will finally slow her down. Until that time, however, I'm staying out of it.

And don't let all this talk about making coffee fool you. Mel is no wizard in the kitchen, and neither am I. We mostly survive on take-out or by going out to eat. We have several preferred restaurants on our list of morning dining establishments once we get through the potential bottleneck that is the I–90 Bridge.

The people who planned the bridges in Seattle—both

the 520 and the I–90—were betting that the traffic patterns of the fifties and sixties would prevail—that people would drive into the city from the suburbs in the mornings and back home at night. So the lanes that were built into the I–90 bridges have express lanes that are westbound in the morning and eastbound in the afternoon. Except there are almost as many people working in the 'burbs now as there are in the city, and "wrong-way" commuters like Mel and me, on our way to the east side of Lake Washington to the offices of the Attorney General's Special Homicide Investigation Team, pay the commuting price for those decisions every day.

If we make it through in good order, we can go to the Pancake Corral in Bellevue or to Li'l Jon's in Eastgate for a decent sit down breakfast. Otherwise we're stuck with Egg McMuffins at our desks. You don't have to guess which of those options I prefer. So we head out a good hour and fifteen minutes earlier than we would need to without stopping for breakfast. Getting across the lake early usually makes for lighter traffic—unless there's an accident. Then all bets are off. A successful outcome is also impacted by weather—too much rain or wind or even too much sun—can all prove hazardous to the morning commute.

That Monday morning we were golden—no accidents; no stop and go traffic. By the time the sun came peeking up over the Cascades in the distance, we were tucked into a cozy booth in Li'l Jon's ordering breakfast. And more coffee. Because our office is across the freeway and only about six blocks away from the restaurant, we were able to take our time. Mel had pancakes. She's a runner. She can afford the carbs. I had a single egg over easy with one slice of whole-wheat toast.

We arrived at the Special Homicide Investigation Team's east side office at five minutes to nine. We don't have to punch a time clock. When we're on a case, we sometimes work extraordinarily long hours. When we're not on a case, we work on the honor system.

For the record, I do know that the unfortunate acronym for Special Homicide Investigation Team is S.H.I.T., an oversight some bumbling bureaucrat didn't understand until it was too late to do anything about it. In the world of state government—and probably in the federal government as well—once the stationery is printed, no departmental name is going to get changed because the resulting acronym turns out to be bad news. S.L.U.T. (the South Lake Union Transit) is another local case in point.

But for all of us who actually work for Special Homicide, the jokes about S.H.I.T. are almost as tired as any little kid knock-knock joke that comes to mind, and they're equally unwelcome. Yes, we laugh courteously when people think they're really clever by mentioning that we "work for S.H.I.T.," but I can assure you, what we do here at Special Homicide is not a joke. And neither is our boss, Harry Ignatius Ball—Harry I. Ball as those of us who know and love him like to call him.

Special Homicide is actually divided into three units. Squad A works out of the state capitol down in Olympia. They handle everything from Olympia south to the Oregon border. Squad B, our unit, is in Bellevue, but we work everything from Tacoma north to the Canadian border while Squad C, based in Spokane, covers most things on the far side of the mountains. These divisions aren't chiseled in granite. We work for Ross Connors. As the Washington State Attorney General, he is the state's chief law enforcement officer. We work at his pleasure and direction. We work where Ross Connors says and when Ross Connors says. He's a tough boss but a good one. When things go haywire as they sometimes do, he isn't the kind of guy who leaves his people blowing in the wind. That sort of loyalty inspires loyalty, and Ross gives as good as he gets.

That morning Mel and I both managed to survive the terminal boredom of the weekly staff meeting ritual. After that, we returned to our separate cubicle-sized offices where we were continuing work on cross referencing the state's many missing persons reports with un-identified homicides in all other jurisdictions. It was cold case work, long on frustration, short on triumphs and even more boring most of the time than the staff meetings.

When Squad B's secretary/office manager, Barbara Galvin, poked her head into our tiny offices and announced that Mel and I had been summoned to Harry's office, it was a real footrace to see who got there first.

Harry is a Luddite. He has a computer on his desk. He does not use it. Ross Connors has made sure that all his people have the latest and greatest in electronic communications gear, but he doesn't use that, either. It's only in the last few months that he's finally accepted the necessity of carrying a cell phone and actually turning it on. He and Ross Connors are really birds of a feather in that regard—they're both anti-geeks at heart. Occasionally we'll receive e-mail with Harry's name on it, but that's because he has dictated his message to Barbara who dutifully types it at the approximate speed of sound and then presses the send button. The same goes for electronic messages that come our way from Ross Connor's e-mail account. His secretary, Katie Dunn, sends out those missives.

In our unit, Barbara Galvin and Harry I. Ball are the ultimate odd couple in terms of working together. Harry is now, and always has been, an exceptional cop who was kicked out of the Bellingham police department due to a terminal lack of political correctness that survived several employer-mandated courses in sensitivity training. He would have been stranded without a job if Ross Connors, no P.C. guy himself, hadn't taken pity on him and hired him as Squad B's supervisor.

Barbara Galvin is easily young enough to be Harry's daughter. Her body shows evidence of plenty of piercings, but she comes to work with a single diamond stud in her left nostril. I suspect that her clothing conceals any number of tattoos, but none of those show at work. She's a blazingly fast typist who keeps only a single photo of her now ten-year-old son on an otherwise fastidiously clean desk. She manages the office with a cheerful efficiency that is nothing short of astonishing. She prods at Harry when he needs prodding and laughs both with him and at him. When I've had occasion to visit other

S.H.I.T. offices, I've also seen how Squads A and C live. With Harry and Barbara in charge, those of us in Squad B have a way better deal.

When Mel and I walked into Harry's office he was studying an e-mail that Barbara had no doubt retrieved from his account, printed, and brought to him.

"Have a chair," he said, stripping off a pair of drugstore reading glasses.

Since there was only one visitor's chair in the room, I let Mel have that one. When Harry looked up and saw I was still standing, he bellowed, "Hey, Barbara. Can you round up another chair? Who the hell keeps stealing mine?"

Without a word, Barbara brought another office chair to the doorway and then rolled it expertly across the room so it came to a stop directly in front of me.

"Sit," Harry ordered, glaring at me.

I sat.

Harry picked up the piece of paper again and returned the reading glasses to the bridge of his nose.

"I don't like this much, you know," he said.

Mel and I exchanged looks. Her single raised eyebrow spoke volumes, as in "What's he talking about?"

"I'm not sure why it is that you're always Ross's go-to-guy, but you are," Harry grumbled, sending another glower in my direction. "This time the Attorney General wants both of you in Olympia for the next while. It's all very hush-hush. He didn't say what he wants you to do while you're there, or how long he wants you to stay. He says you should 'pack to stay for several days,' and you should 'each bring a vehicle' which leads me to believe that you won't necessarily be working together. You're booked into the Red Lion there in Olympia."

"I'm assuming from that we probably won't be staying in the honeymoon suite?" I asked.

"I would assume not," Harry agreed glumly. "Now get the hell out of here. Time's a wastin'."